CAN WE
START
AGAIN?

T

Also by Shirley Benton

Looking for Leon

Published by Poolbeg

Shirley Benton

CAN WE START AGAIN?

POOLBEG

Published 2012
by Poolbeg Press Ltd.
123 Grange Hill, Baldoyle,
Dublin 13, Ireland
Email: poolbeg@poolbeg.com

A catalogue record for this book is available from the British Library.

ISBN 978-1-84223-510-2

Typeset by Patricia Hope in Sabon 10.5/14

Printed and bound by CPI Group (UK) Ltd, Croydon, CR0 4YY

www.poolbeg.com

About the Author

Shirley Benton lives in Dublin with her husband and their two children. Her debut novel *Looking for Leon* was also published by Poolbeg.

Acknowledgements

Sometimes, you only realise how appropriate a book title is after you've come up with it. You see, I had written my entire second book before my second child was born, ten weeks before the book was due to my publisher, and thought I was great for being so organised. But at the back of my head, I felt something wasn't right with it. I put the notion down to pregnancy hormones and morning sickness driving me to distraction. But then I read it after my baby was born and realised that the morning sickness hadn't made me take leave of my senses after all – the book just *wasn't* right and I just *wasn't* putting it out there. So a week after my son was born, with two months left before the deadline and two months to the release of my first book, I started to write a completely different book (with the sound of my husband saying "Oh dear God, Shirley, *no*" in the background). There was no talking to me, and I'm glad about that because I am so happy with what I wrote instead, i.e. this book. I chose the book title because I thought it was a perfect reflection of the book's story, but now I realise that it actually works on a whole other level too.

As a result of my stubbornness, though, there are several people I have to thank. Aforementioned husband Michael for understanding me well enough to know that

vii

this was something I had to do (after his understandable initial shock!), my mother Bernie for all her help with minding the children and for practically moving to Dublin to accommodate my writing, and Paula Campbell for being flexible with the deadline to allow for a second second book. Oh, and to Fionn for being a dream baby and sleeping through the night from a very early age – and to Aoibheann for teaching him everything he knows about it, as I hoped she would.

Moral of the story – never write a book while suffering from nine-month-long morning sickness. Or at least, not if you're me.

Sincere and heartfelt thanks also go to:

All at Poolbeg for giving me such a great opportunity, and for all the support you gave to *Looking for Leon*. I really appreciated your faith in me and my book.

My agents, Prizeman and Kinsella, for your help and for generally being lovely. The booksellers and all the media who helped me spread the word about my debut novel. Thanks in particular to Mairtín Tom Sheanín on Raidio na Gaeltachta for facilitating my very first live radio interview – as Gaeilge! It was a baptism by fire and I have never been nervous about speaking Irish in public ever since (which is handy when you are trying to raise two children bilingually), or about radio or TV interviews in English now for that matter. And thanks to Pat Kelly for organising the interview.

Gaye Shortland for being so wonderful to work with. I really hope we get to meet up face-to-face some day to chat about personal pronouns (!) over a pint – preferably in Kinsale or Dingle. We might even invite Fungi along!

All of my friends and family, who were a wonderful help in promoting *Looking for Leon*. I was blown away at how many people contacted me, came to my launch or showed their support in other ways, such as Aideen Lowe setting up my Facebook advertising campaign. I am very grateful for it all. Two special words of thanks must go to Diarmuid McNamara for getting me into Tindersticks all those years ago (we won't mention how many) and inadvertently giving me the title for this book, and to Lisa O'Meara for never getting bored of book talk (or if you do, you hide it well!).

The Galway gang for baby-sitting favours.

The writeon girls for their continuing support – Oonagh Considine, Megan Wynne, Claire Prins and Susan Flood to name but a few. Thanks also to Claire Allan for being supportive and always having a wise word to impart.

The readers who contacted me from all over the world with their feedback on *Leon*. I'm so glad that it seemed to strike a chord with so many people, and I appreciate you taking the time out to give me your thoughts on it.

And a big *go raibh maith agat* to you for choosing this book. I hope you enjoy it and would love to hear from you through my website. **www.shirleybenton.ie**. Thank you for your support.

To Mam,
for going above and beyond the level of regular
grandmotherly duties – and motherly duties, for that
matter! Thank you so much.

1

It was the best and worst thing that could possibly have happened to me on New Year's Eve.

I answered the door expecting my delayed takeaway, but there he was instead. My ex best friend. My former lover. The man I was supposed to have married that very day.

I froze on the doorstep, completely at a loss as to what to do. I think I was expected to say something. After everything that had happened, there was no shortage of subject matter. Where to begin could well prove to be an issue, though . . .

The fireworks saved me. We both jumped as they suddenly began to pop and sizzle in the night sky over Dublin Bay. A rousing cheer brought a neighbouring house to life. A drunken version of 'Auld Lang Syne' began to drift towards us from another. It was exactly midnight.

He smiled. "Happy New Year, Tammy."

Happy New Year indeed. It would have been if all had gone according to plan. But the plan was out the window, and all I was left with was a man on my doorstep looking as if he expected something of me.

I said the only thing I could say. "I suppose you'd better come in, Alvin . . ."

It had been a year and a half since I'd last seen him. Well, a year, seven months and three days, but a year and a half sounded better. Like something that someone who was in recovery would say. I led him into the sitting room, praying feverishly for something to happen immediately that would prevent this encounter from taking place. Why ever had I walked around that grate on the street on my way home earlier instead of stepping on it? Maybe it would have fallen in and I'd still be trapped underground now . . .

My housemates Jess and Simone weren't due home to interrupt us. There was no escape. The conversation that had been on ice for nineteen months was going to happen.

We looked awkwardly at each other for a few seconds before I folded my arms across my chest and stared at the floor. There was no question of me offering him a cup of tea or any other such niceties after how we'd left things on the night that he'd walked out of my house for good. When I looked up a few seconds later, he'd focused in on the prints on my wall. He stared at them in tourist-in-an-art-gallery fashion, his brow frowning in forced concentration.

"New?" He pointed to a painting of a sultan's palace.

I nodded.

"It's . . . different." He looked around the room. "Everything is now."

That was for sure. "Yes, it is."

He looked sad. "It's nice."

"Yes."

"So how've you been?"

I shrugged. "Okay." There was a pause. "And you?"

He shrugged. "Okay." Another pause. "Keeping busy."

2

He looked back at the prints.

I tried not to stare at his profile. He was even more attractive than he'd been when I'd last seen him. His curly hair was slightly longer and a glow of health enveloped him – his skin was tanned and smooth, and his body was outdoorsy and looked fitter than ever. I felt an urge to go for a ten-mile run the second I laid eyes on him – although maybe that was down to the nerves that were shouting at me to run away. How had someone like him ever been mine?

He looked away from the print and smiled at me. I smiled back tightly. It was all very civilised. And awkward.

"When did you get back from Australia?"

"Christmas Eve."

"Ah. Always nice to come home for Christmas."

"Yeah. Mum was really disappointed when I didn't come back last year."

I smiled. I missed Claire. "How is she?"

"She's good."

"Oh. That's nice." There was that word yet again.

Silence.

"And Adrienne?"

"She's okay."

I didn't miss Adrienne Harrison. Alvin's sister and I had never got on.

More silence.

I couldn't stand the tension any longer. "Alvin, *what* are you doing here?"

"If a man can't visit his ex on the day he was supposed to marry her, when can he?"

His attempt at a smile turned to a grimace when I said nothing. "I'm sorry. It's hard to find the right words after a year and a half of not speaking."

3

"Is that why you're here? The day that's in it?"

"Amongst other reasons. I really needed to see you, Tammy."

I caught sight of myself in the mirror in my best slob-around-the-house attire – cotton pyjamas, cosy socks, hairband – and tried not to flinch. "You could have warned me you were going to call!"

"I wasn't sure if I was going to come at all. I didn't think I'd get past the front door, to be honest. But as it got closer to midnight, I knew I had to . . ."

"How did you even know I'd be here? It's New Year's Eve!"

"I know you. You despise New Year's Eve."

"That doesn't necessarily mean I might not be out tonight!"

He shrugged. "I was going on something you said a few years ago. Something like 'I'm never going out on New Year's Eve again. Ever!'"

Oh. That.

"In fact, the reason why we chose New Year's Eve as our wedding date was because you wanted to always have a reason to enjoy New Year's Eve for the rest of your life . . ."

Stop talking, Alvin. Stop talking right now!

". . . and one thing I know from the last few years is that once you've made your mind up about something, there's no going back. Knowing you'd be in was a safe bet if you didn't know I was calling over. If you'd known, I'm sure you would have made up an excuse not to be here."

"So, you're here now," I eventually said. "You needed to see me, and now you have. Have you got what you wanted from it?"

He smiled. "You were never one for small talk."

"This is hard, Alvin. All that time without contact, and

now this . . . why exactly are you here? What good can come of it?"

Alvin stared at the ground and looked shifty for a good ten seconds. Eventually, he delved a hand into one of the back pockets of his jeans and pulled out a folded paper.

"Remember this?" He handed it to me.

I took it, realising what it was before I even unfolded it. And right there and then, the progress I'd thought I'd made in moving on with my life disintegrated.

2

It had been Blu-Tacked over our bed right up until the day Alvin moved out, a tatty piece of A3 paper that had been totally out of keeping with the décor of my room but had once meant more than all of the other house-trimmings put together.

"Our pre-parental plan," I said in a voice that was little more than a whisper as I stared at the words on the page. "I knew you'd taken it – I just didn't think you'd have kept it . . ."

"I tried not to, but I couldn't bring myself to throw it away either."

I smiled wryly. Our attic had once been full of things like old *Beano* annuals from the eighties and every edition of *Hot Press* published throughout the nineties because Alvin had never been one to part with things easily. And now it seemed that, even though he'd moved to Australia and started a new life, he'd kept the list we'd written together of everything we'd planned to do as a couple before we had children.

I was confused. "Okay, but why are we looking at it now?"

Alvin crossed the space between us and moved to my side. He gently took the sheet of paper from me.

"I've never stopped thinking about where it all went wrong between us," he said, looking at the plan as he spoke. "We never got a chance even to start to do this list because of how things fell apart. We shouldn't have let that happen, you know. We should have fought harder to sort things out."

I stepped away from his proximity. "What's the point in raking this up now? It's too late . . ."

"Is it, Tammy?" He gave me a searching look. "I'm going to be very honest with you here – after all, this might be the only chance I get to talk to you properly as you've refused to communicate with me since we broke up. I've spent the past year and a half building a completely different life, and yet in my mind, I'm still back here. With you."

There was a horribly long pause. I hoped Alvin would say something else, but he seemed to be waiting for a reaction before he moved on.

"But your life is in Australia now. This is just a holiday, isn't it?"

"Forget about that for a moment. I'll be here for the next few weeks, and I'd like for us to have a chance to get to know each other again and see if there's any possibility of us getting things back to how they used to be . . . and that's where this list comes in. I've often thought about how doing everything on this list could only have brought us closer together. Actually, I feel pretty cheated by this thing. As soon as we wrote it, things started to go wrong between us."

"I don't think what we went through was down to a piece of paper," I said, trying not to shudder as I remembered the misery of it all.

"No, but I feel it owes us all the same. This is

7

something that we should have had a chance to do. Don't you remember how much it meant to us at the time we wrote it? It represented everything that we were as a couple who were planning to have children together."

Confusion engulfed me again. "Yes, Alvin, '*were*'. We're no longer that couple –"

"We could be that couple again," he said in a low voice. "How would you feel about that?"

I lifted one shoulder in a pathetic half-shrug. I hadn't dared to hope that he might want to get back with me, but was there any point in trying? If we hadn't been able to make it work first time around, why would it work now?

"I know I can't just walk back into your life and think we're going to pick up where we left off," he said.

"We wouldn't want to. Where we left off was bad," I reminded him.

"Yes, but where we were before things got bad was just about as good as it got. You haven't forgotten that, surely?"

I looked away. Forgotten it? I'd tried to, but I'd never succeeded. But I just didn't get this.

"Alvin, we've just gone from having no contact to talking about starting all over again and you presumably leaving your life in Australia! How can we do that?"

He raised an eyebrow. "We both know why there's been no contact, but there's no point in recriminations. I just want to move forward, if you're willing to give it a chance."

He stood in front of me and put his hands on my shoulders, trying desperately to make eye contact.

"We'll work the details out, I promise you. The main thing is to see if we can get this back."

I shook him off and moved away. "You make it sound so simple, but it's not. It's taken me forever to get over us. What if we try this and it doesn't work?"

"And what if we don't try this? I've spent all this time trying too. It hasn't done much good. Honestly, Tammy, the last thing I want is to mess you around."

"I don't know about the list, though – maybe we should just meet up and see how things go . . ."

"Look at us today. This couldn't be any more awkward, could it? The list will give us things to do while we get over the initial strangeness of being around each other, and ease us into a place where we might actually be able to talk to each other again. Everything that's on the list is stuff we can do together without it being too uncomfortable. It's not as if we had a Kama Sutra night on it, although I seem to remember I suggested that and you said no."

I seemed to remember that most nights with Alvin were Kama Sutra nights anyway when we'd written the list and hence there was no point in including it, but it was probably best not to mention that now.

I walked over to the window. "This is crazy, Alvin. We can't just start doing everything on our pre-parental plan when we're not even a couple now!"

"I know it sounds crazy. But I also know that you and me should still be together. Can you tell me that you've never thought that too over the past few years?"

I didn't answer him, but I knew my face was doing the talking for me. He stared at me before slowly walking over, clearly seeing the answer he'd been looking for. I had no idea what he'd do when he reached me, or what I'd do. I put both of my hands behind my back and gripped the windowsill to make sure they were occupied when he reached me.

"You've never left my mind, Tammy. I need to know if we still have something. Do you think you can do this?"

I could barely breathe.

"I . . . really don't know."

9

He moved closer. "Are you willing to try, at least?"

I gulped, audibly.

For a crazy second, I thought he was going to kiss me. The gap between us was dissolving and I was sure that something else was crackling in the space that remained. In that second, I knew I never wanted anything so badly in my life as for him to kiss me.

Then I remembered the last time I'd seen him. The scene had been replayed in my head so many times that remembering was effortless, involuntary. I remembered, and suddenly realised how foolish I was to think Alvin would kiss me right then. Not after how things had ended.

I pulled away from him and walked to the door.

"I need some time to think about this, Alvin."

He exhaled slowly. "Okay."

I went into the hall and opened the front door. I stared out as his footsteps slowly approached me. The fireworks in the bay were still popping.

"I'll ring your landline tomorrow afternoon. Say, two o'clock?"

I nodded. Fourteen hours. Was that enough time? Probably not, but fourteen days mightn't have been enough either in the confused state my mind was in.

His lips flitted against my cheek hesitantly before he left. I fought down the golf ball in my throat as I watched him walk down my driveway and get into a car I recognised as Claire's.

He was right – we should have tried harder to save what we had. And if there was any possibility of getting it back, surely it was worth the potential pain involved?

It was a question I didn't have a clear answer to, but I had a feeling I was about to find out.

3

"Jesus, I'm dying!"

Jess slumped forward onto the table. Rogue clumps of her long chestnut hair landed in a mound of leftover ketchup and chips on the plate beside her head. I pulled the plate forward, grimacing as Jess's hair plopped off and formed gooey ketchup trails across my freshly polished table. It may have been New Year's Day, a time of new beginnings, but some things never changed – Jess was no stranger to either hangovers or creating kitchen mess, and it was going to take more than a new year for that to stop.

"I would feel sorry for you if you hadn't been so thoroughly spoiled by Ciarán last night in the fanciest hotel in town," I said, taking a napkin and removing the ketchup from Jess's hair as best I could before it coagulated, as any good cousin would do. She didn't even notice. "Three bottles of the most expensive champagne on the market will have that dying effect on you, but at least you're going down in style."

11

Simone, another of my cousins, lifted her head up. As she was in the middle of a very painful-looking handstand, this was no mean feat. "Tammy Taylor! How am I supposed to achieve a Zen-like state with you creating that type of mental image? Jess's intimate life is her own business."

I grinned, more at the carry-on of Simone than her words. She'd declared before going out last night that her new year's resolution was to be more positive (being the possessor of a somewhat downbeat disposition by nature) and to embrace a lifestyle that would nurture said positivity. Yoga was going to be a pivotal component of her new venture, but until she could attend a class and learn some moves, handstands picked up in teenage gymnastic-training days were as far as her capabilities went. I wasn't complaining, though. Simone had taken philosophising on the senselessness of life rather too seriously over the past while, constantly burying herself in some existential tome about the futility of man's being and quoting lines back to us about the absurdity of the human condition. If you were having a bad day, it didn't help to be told that you were essentially fucked anyway.

"So when are we going to meet this great man, anyway? You've been knocking around with him for a good few weeks now," Simone said, tottering along the kitchen floor on her hands with her legs swinging precariously in the air. Six foot one in her socks, you didn't want one of Simone's legs to accidentally swing your way.

"I'll sort something out as soon as I get over this hangover. Give me about two weeks." Jess took a sip of water and scowled. "*Ugh*. What do they put in that stuff?"

I looked from Jess to Simone and realised I wasn't exactly going to have a captive audience for what I wanted to say.

"Girls . . . any chance we could go into the sitting room? There's something I really want to talk to you about."

"Oh, please, no! Not the 'you didn't clean the grouting in the shower' talk again!" Jess groaned.

"No, no," I assured her. Jess's grouting-cleaning did leave a lot to be desired, but it was very far down my list of things to worry about right then.

"Wow! What could possibly be more serious than that in your world?" Jess dragged her tiny frame up slowly and smiled at me before stumbling into the sitting room, grabbing a Crunchie from her hangover stash en route.

She never tired of slagging me off about what a neat-freak I was, but I never minded. Seven years my junior, she was more like a cheeky younger sister to me than a cousin and could get away with saying pretty much whatever she wanted.

I tried not to wince as she pulled my expensive handira Moroccan wedding blanket off the back of the couch and wrapped it around her neck, shoulders and ketchup-streaked hair. I redecorated whenever I was bothered about something, introducing a whole new theme to brighten up the place, and the current one was all things Moroccan. It had been looking good up to a few seconds ago.

I ushered Simone in too when I had Jess inside. She was panting by the time she'd walked in on her hands and got herself upright again.

"God, this positivity lark is hard work."

The girls looked at me expectantly. I took a deep breath.

"Something's happened, girls. Alvin called to the house last night."

"*Jaysis*!" Simone yelled. "Ah *fuck* – I'd given up cursing as part of my positivity buzz too. Fuck Alvin Harrison anyway!"

13

"No *way*!" Jess shrieked, then shook from the effort it had taken. "He's home? What did he have to say?"

"Quite a bit, actually . . ."

"So what are you going to do?" Simone liked to cut to the chase.

"I'm still trying to decide. My only plan was to thrash the pros and cons out with you guys and hopefully come to a decision at the end of it."

"You know me – I'm more than happy to thrash things," Jess said.

"Yes, I've seen your bedroom, thank you. But right now, all thrashing is accepted – he's ringing me at two o'clock today and he'll want an answer."

"Jesus – Hutch – back," Jess said through a mouthful of honeycomb. She had always called Alvin 'Hutch' because she'd thought he was the spit of Michael Hutchence from INXS when she first met him, something she'd said to him every single time she was drunk as if she'd never mentioned it before.

Now, she looked at me with a concerned expression. "We're not going to have to go through a phase of being woken up by Radiohead in the middle of the night again, are we?" Then her face softened. "Oh God, I just remembered. Yesterday was the date you'd set for your wedding, wasn't it? I'm such a tit, I totally forgot."

"It's fine, you're grand," I assured her.

"I just thought you were staying in last night because you hate New Year's Eve in general."

I did another round of 'you're fine' and 'it's grand', but it was no use.

"I'm sorry, Tammy – I'm so wrapped up in my own world with Ciarán at the moment . . ."

14

"I'm more worried about you being wrapped up in my very expensive throw and getting chocolate crumbs on it, but I'll let you off for being good enough to listen to my moaning. And don't apologise for having your own life and being happy, Jess. But what do you guys think I should do?"

Jess sat up, looking more confident now. "It's a no-brainer – do the things on this list of yours and take your opportunity to see if what you had with him is still there. Simple as that."

I wasn't expecting that. "But don't you think it'll be weird for us to do the things we'd planned to do before we had kids when we're so far from that point now?"

"No."

She didn't elaborate. The certainty in her "No" seemed to imply that no elaboration was required.

"Simone?"

"It'll be as weird or not weird as you guys make it. But either way, Tammy, I think you need to do this."

Even though they genuinely seemed shocked to hear about Alvin's arrival home, they immediately both seemed to think his suggestion was a good thing. Surely they were going to question it more than this?

It seemed not. Silence reigned.

"I don't get it, girls."

Jess sighed. "I'm sorry to bring this up and confuse things even further, but let me refer to another list of yours that is turning out to be far weirder by the day." She got up and wearily made her way to the bookshelf, where she pulled out a laminated piece of paper from where it lived within *Wuthering Heights*.

"'*Fifty ways to meet a man*'" she read, slowly and deliberately. I was blushing before she even got to number

15

one. "If you want to talk about weird, let's discuss some of the crazy things you've done over the last year in a bid to bag a man." She scanned the list. "Tag rugby, salsa classes, Irish lessons" – she snorted at that one – "golfing, hanging out in hardware stores until you were practically accused of shoplifting, dog walking, dog kidnapping as a result of us not owning a dog to walk in the first place – amongst many, *many* other insane activities – and you're not even done yet – there's still three more to do: clay-modelling lessons, gardening classes and hanging out at the erotic museum." Jess shook her head. "You weren't even drunk when you wrote this list, Tammy!"

"Hang on a second! I spent months wallowing over Alvin and you two chastised me over it. You told me to pick myself up and rediscover my life, remember? And I have. I'm out all of the time meeting new people, doing new things –"

"And you're never happy with any of them," Jess interjected. "You've met plenty of men over the last while that had nothing at all wrong with them but you wouldn't give them a chance. Remember the florist who you dumped for smelling too nice? Who dumps a man – any man, but we're talking about a fucking *florist* here – for smelling too nice?"

"I can't help it if I haven't met anyone I'm really into!" I said quickly.

"You'll never be into anyone while you're comparing them to the great love of your life," Jess said.

I turned my attention to the other armchair occupant. "What do you think I should do, Simone?"

She grimaced. "Old Simone or the New and Improved Simone – well, the 'needs a few tweaks and is still cursing but I'm doing my best' Simone, rather?"

"Just tell me what you really think."

"Are you sure?"

"Yes."

Her face brightened momentarily. "Okay. Old Simone then." She sat up straight.

I knew I was in for one of her philosophical speeches, delivered in the manner of a preacher addressing a congregation.

"Each and every one of us on this planet is just going from one day to the next trying to find happiness to divert ourselves from the fact that life is essentially meaningless. If you're offered any sort of a chance at happiness, you should take it even if you're scared of where it may lead you. At best, that chance could give you exactly what you want and at worst, it'll occupy your mind for a while and pass a bit more of your life while you're sitting around waiting to die."

I was stunned into silence for several seconds after Simone finished speaking. "Jesus, Old Simone, you've outdone yourself."

She sat back, wearing a self-satisfied smile. "Thanks. The bottom line is that you haven't been happy since Alvin left. Even if you do the plan and things go wrong, what you have lost? Not your happiness, that's for sure."

"There are different levels of unhappiness, you know," I protested. "What am I saying? Of course you know – you're the one who always says that! What if I end up feeling worse afterwards?"

"And what about if you feel *better*? See, New Simone is in the house too."

"She's right," Jess said.

"Who? New or Old?" I asked.

"I'm not sure – I'm too hungover – but she's right. That's all I know."

"But if this doesn't work out, it might bring me right

17

back to square one . . ." I looked from Jess to Simone, willing them to understand.

Jess threw her eyes up to heaven. Simone fiddled with the buttons of her dungarees and looked at me with a dubious expression.

Jess turned to Simone. "You tell her. I'm in a blunt mood today and she won't like it if I say it."

"Just today?" Simone said doubtfully. She adopted her best counsellor's pose and leaned forward. "Tammy, this *is* square one. You haven't moved on anywhere to *be* brought right back."

"Therefore, you have nothing to lose," said Jess. "And even if this doesn't work out, it might still give you the closure you need. The only sensible option is to go for it."

I almost managed a smile. Jess knew I liked sensible. I *was* sensible. "Going for the jugular there, Jess."

"Needs must."

"And can I just remind you that it's a new year, and therefore an opportunity to break away from the things that have been dragging you down," Simone said.

"Good woman, Simone. I like that," Jess added.

"I'm just getting that in now in case I change my mind about this positivity thing," Simone said, ruining the effect of her words somewhat. "It's wearing me out already."

"And what if I mess Alvin up all over again?" I said in a tiny voice, despite my concern being a big one.

"Alvin's a big boy. He wouldn't have come back into your life if he wasn't able to deal with the consequences."

"You have to do this," one of the Simones said.

When my cousins eventually fell silent, I got up and picked up the cordless landline phone. "I'm going upstairs to try to work out what I'm going to do. Thanks for your advice, girls."

"We'll call up in a while to see how you are," Simone said.

"Ah no, I'll be fine. Don't get me wrong – I really appreciate your help, but I have to think this over by myself now."

"Hmm. Something tells me the Moroccan theme's days are numbered," Jess muttered as I left the room.

4

I'd thought about the plan several times over the last two years. It was hard not to when there were still faint marks on what had been a perfectly painted wall from the Blu-Tack Alvin had used to affix it over our bed – marks that irritated the bejaysus out of me but that I'd never done anything about either, despite my manic redecorating of the rest of the house (I'd even wallpapered the other three walls and left that one as it was, deeming it to be my mood wall). Blu-Tack was on my list of banned substances, but Alvin had somehow snuck his contraband in.

The night we'd written the list of items in the plan, I came out of the en suite after brushing my teeth to find Alvin squashing the Blu-Tack onto the back of the A3 sheet and looking ominously like he was going to deface my wall with it.

"*No!*" I screeched, but it was too late.

In one fluid movement, he pressed the page up against the wall. "There. We've no excuse now for forgetting to do anything on this list."

It hadn't taken us long to take the plan from a high-level concept in Alvin's brain to a complete set of ten items that were now going to be watching over us as we slept, but that was a good reflection of how we once did everything. My relationship with Alvin had something of the Shanghai Maglev Train about it from day one. Our first date happened two hours after we'd met at a team-building activities day that my team at work and I were attending, run by the adventure centre Alvin was an activities instructor for. By the end of that date, Alvin was joking about how he'd have moved in with me before the month was out. As someone who'd lived on their own for years and had never been all that interested in long-term relationships, focusing my entire life around my career instead, I was hugely surprised to find myself laughing along and hoping he was serious. I tried to act cool at the beginning in case the whole thing fell apart, but after he'd brought me around to meet Claire and Adrienne two weeks after we met, I allowed myself to believe that he was actually really into me. Men didn't put themselves through The Girlfriend Meeting the Other Women if they weren't truly interested in someone. (I'm sure he would have had me meet his father too, but his father had died when Alvin was fourteen.)

On the last day of that month, by mutual consent, he gathered up his belongings to transfer them to my place. Nobody was more surprised by this unexpected turn of events than me. We were completely different in every way, but it just worked. He was a free spirit who lived for the moment and just went with whatever felt right at the time. When I was eighteen, I'd made up a business-card-sized list of what I wanted to achieve in my life and when I wanted to achieve it by, laminated it and carried it around in my wallet so that I could look at it every day and keep myself focused on my life plans. I still took it out first thing every morning. I was what Jess dubbed a corporate whore, working in the Human Resources department of one of the biggest global multinationals, Branda, in a permanent and pensionable role. My work was intense and my work-life balance always tipped towards work, with me taking work home with me most nights. Alvin's job in the adventure centre involved instructing and leading groups in a range of activities that he absolutely adored – abseiling, hill walking and archery, to name but a few – and he didn't even seem to view it as work. Unless another staff member called in sick and he was needed for a few extra hours, he was free to leave work on the dot of whatever hour his shift finished on. I was a senior personnel manager, a position I'd spent years trying to achieve and had fought hard for. Alvin's job didn't have a specific career-progression path, something he was fine with as long as he was happy with it on a day-to-day basis. I seemed to worry about something or other every second of every day. He never let anything worry him, and always took the attitude that things would work themselves out. Although it wasn't a great match on paper, when we were together it was amazing.

As soon as he'd moved in, it wasn't long before the talk turned to marriage and babies. The most astounding thing of all was that Alvin was the one that initiated most of the talk, even though I was considered by both of us – and everyone else – to be the intense one in the relationship.

"He'd been dropping hints about moving to Australia for the surf, and now all I hear is how handy a drive it'll be from your place in Donnybrook over here to me in Stillorgan when the kids come along," Claire would say, her voice a mixture of happiness, relief and sheer disbelief. "He talks about nothing but kids these days – he can't wait to get you in the club! He's a changed man."

My life became a weird mixture of unadulterated joy and inner panic. Joy, because I couldn't believe I'd bagged a guy like Alvin – he was beyond gorgeous and made me feel more alive than anyone I'd ever met before – but panic because, even though I knew I wanted the whole package with Alvin, all of this moving-fast business was way outside of the boundaries of my safe world.

When I'd brought the subject of my growing panic up with Alvin early one morning two months after he'd moved in, the conversation had gone along these lines:

Me: "Em, Alvin . . . do you think there's any chance that we might be moving a bit too fast with all of this?"

Alvin: "Uh-oh. This is the whole obsessive-worrier thing you warned me about coming out, isn't it?"

Me: "It's just that this isn't usually how I do things. I spend five minutes trying to decide between two bags of peppers in the supermarket, you know?"

Alvin (sighing): "Yes, I've been shopping with you, remember?"

Me: "Although not recently, now that I think about it . . ."

Alvin: "That's a conversation for another day. If you think anything about this is wrong, you only have to say the word and we'll slow things down – but for me, it's a case of why wait when you know what you want?"

Me: "I'm not used to knowing what I want as fast as I have done with this. I keep thinking about stuff like what if having kids brings out things in us that we've never seen in each other before and may not like?"

Alvin: "Have you been watching *Supernanny* again?"

Me: "Don't be daft! Well yes, I have, but that's not the point. Having kids pushes people outside their comfort zones. What if it pushes us and we don't like what we see?"

Alvin (after a long pause): "Well, maybe we should make sure we do see each other outside of our comfort zones as much as possible before we have children so . . ."

Me: "What do you mean?"

Alvin: "Leave it with me. I'll think of something . . ."

"Tammy!" Alvin roared down the stairs that night after dinner. "Come up to the bedroom!"

I placed a dish into the dishwasher before I walked out to the hall. "Why? Will it take long?" I looked back at the mess in the kitchen and tried not to wince.

"Oh, it'll take the rest of the night." Alvin winked as his head appeared over the top of the banister.

I couldn't but smile. The mess in the kitchen drifted away. "Promises, promises!" I ran upstairs and followed Alvin as he made his way into the bedroom.

"Remember what you said about comfort zones and having sprogs and so on?"

I mumbled a "Uh-huh" in what I hoped was a suitably

nonchalant manner. Naturally, I hadn't been able to get the latter topic out of my mind since we'd talked about it earlier. I tended to obsess when I got my teeth into a question that interested me, and this had turned out to be a juicy mental subject.

"Well, I've thought of something that'll make sure we get to do all the random things we ever wanted to do together before we have children and that'll also let us see each other in ways we might not otherwise have a chance to." He flipped back the cover of an A3 notebook and handed the notebook to me.

I stared at it. "Alvin, this is a blank page. Where's this something?"

"We're about to create it together, of course. Okay, here are the rules. You take a turn, then I do, at thinking of things that we want to do before we get to the point where we have kids, things that'll move us outside our comfort zones and ultimately lead to us finding out more about each other's characters. We keep going until we reach ten things. Whatever either of us chooses, the other person can't quibble about it. What you pick doesn't have to be mindblowing or dramatic – just relevant to moving us outside our comfort zones, as we will be if we have children. It shouldn't be overly expensive either, which means that we can get started on the list as soon as possible without money being an excuse for not doing each and every thing we come up with. All very simple."

I wasn't exactly sold. "Alvin, I know we're moving fast but do you know me at all? I make out colour-coded charts of what I'll have for breakfast, lunch and dinner on a monthly basis . . . if there's anything we need to do as a couple, do you not think I'll be anal enough to make damn sure we do it?"

"I'm not questioning your ability to be anal for one second, darling. The thing is, this is something we need to create *together*, you know? That's the whole point. If we have children, we'll be creating them and bringing them up together. Start as we mean to go on, eh?"

It was a fair point, and one that even a control freak like me couldn't really argue with. I knew Alvin was going to come up with things that would probably terrify me though. But fair was fair, and it couldn't get much fairer than a fifty-fifty list. It took us a few hours to finish it, and although as expected the thoughts of some of his activities frightened me, I couldn't help but feel excited about the end result. The truth was that I didn't really care what I did over the next while as long as it was done with Alvin – and that was why I managed to stop myself from pulling the Blu-Tack and the list off the wall even though it made the room look untidy. I had a different set of rules when it came to Alvin.

The list hung over the bed for over two years, watching over us in admonishment as we failed to do everything on it. I hated the sight of it by the end of our relationship. I'd been glad when Alvin had taken it the day he'd moved all of his belongings out while I was at work. What I hadn't banked on was him actually keeping it, despite his hoarding proclivity. I'd assumed its days were numbered and Alvin had only taken it for the sheer pleasure of tearing it into tiny bits in the same way that our hopes for the future lay in shreds around us.

But now we had a second chance to take it seriously, a chance that I'd never thought we'd get.

The problem was that I wasn't sure that something as broken as Alvin and I were could ever be whole again.

5

Just when my head was about to burst, there was a knock on my door. "Tammy, it's us!" roared Jess. "Ready to talk yet?"

One of the biggest issues about living with family is that they don't bother with the niceties of listening to you if you say you don't want to talk about something. It's even worse when you've grown up with your cousins as if they were sisters. My mother and Jess and Simone's mothers were the last three children in a family of twelve, dubbed 'the triplets' by the rest of the family. They were so close that they built houses right beside each other on their parents' land in Lucan. They lived in each other's pockets, which consequently meant that the three of us had to as well. In fact, my family were like a pack of ex-pats in some far-flung land, rarely mixing with the locals because they preferred to stick to their own. It wasn't down to snobbishness on their part, more the fact that being from such a large family they had everything they needed in a social network already. Plus it was easier to fight with your own family, and there was nothing my family liked better than a good quarrel. Simone and Jess could be relied upon to carry on the family tradition on occasion if a contentious issue raised its head.

They were all delighted that there was only a month in age between Simone and me, and even though Jess didn't come along until seven years later because my aunt had problems conceiving, the age gap was almost irrelevant. All that mattered to our mothers was throwing us together at every feasible opportunity, which meant that as a seven-year-old I changed more than my fair share of Jess's shitty nappies under the guise of making me bond with my new cousin. Even when Simone and I went to college and Jess was way too young and uncool for us to want to hang out with her at the weekends, we never had any choice in the matter as our mothers plonked themselves, and us, in each other's houses every evening anyway.

From Monday to Saturday every week, each of our mothers would cook for all the other mothers, children and husbands for two evenings each, gathering in each other's houses Italian-style. The routine was military. Assembly in the house of choice would commence in time for everyone who wasn't involved in the cooking to watch *A Country Practice*. None of our fathers could stand the show, but that didn't seem to matter to our mothers. Simone would have her head buried in a book for the entire show while Jess talked incessantly, especially whenever there was a good bit that the mothers really wanted to watch. Then we'd be dragged into the kitchen to feast on whatever slop our mothers took the notion to dish up that day. Whether it was genetic or a coincidence, not one of our three mothers could cook. We had the constitutions of oxes from all the food-abuse our systems had been put through over the years – undercooked meat, meat that was just plain raw, cremated mince and fish that looked like they'd just come out of the ocean, eyes and all still intact.

We all had our roles. When I was a child, I always seemed to be the clown in the family – not because I was particularly funny but because I was awkward. Jess was the daring, outspoken one they all despaired of, Simone was the introverted one they all worried about, and I was the one they all laughed at because I always seemed to be in some scrape or another. If someone was going to get an apple-seed stuck under their eyelid, wee in their underpants in a public place or fall head-first into the bin and be stuck there with their legs sticking out until parental help arrived, it would have been me. Mum would then go into 'Oh, isn't she a devil?' mode so that she wouldn't look like she had the worst-behaved child in the family, but the thing was, I was such a *good* child. I was just clumsy, and the more conscious I became of it, the worse my clumsiness was. I'd envisage things like calling around to our elderly neighbour with Mum and breaking the old woman's best china – *and it would actually happen.* One minute I'd be standing at the other side of the room away from her best cabinet of china, the next thing I'd be hitting off the side of it by accident and causing her best plates to come tumbling down – and I was overweight too, so even a slight brush of my backside against something had seismic repercussions. My awkwardness got to the stage where I was afraid to go outside the door in case I somehow caused a natural catastrophe that would kill off our entire parish.

Things didn't get any better when I grew up to be a gangly teenager with limbs and big feet everywhere, all the better to trip people up with (although it did sort out my weight problem to some extent). Simone was even taller, of course, but she was so busy being sad about other things as a teenager that her height was something she had no room left to be concerned about. Besides, she didn't have my ridiculous levels of gracelessness to worry about. It left its mark, and it wasn't long before I started trying to excel at absolutely everything I did in an attempt to be tagged for something other than being awkward. The only thing that made the whole sorry situation better was that my cousins were always around to laugh it off with me. Between the shared trauma of our mothers' cooking and the sheer frequency of our interaction, the girls and I knew pretty much everything about each other and there were no holds barred between us. The flipside was that there wasn't much in the line of privacy either.

So, ready or not, Jess and Simone were beating at the door.

"Come in," I eventually said. God knows, they wouldn't go away even if I said no.

They trundled in. Thankfully, Simone was using her legs to walk with on this occasion. The inside of my head was enough of a circus in itself without any further instances of her handstands to contend with.

"We could hear you thinking through the ceiling and thought you might need to be forced to take a break," Jess said.

Maybe they were right. "You know me too well," I said with a grimace.

"Come to a decision yet? It's five to two . . ."

"Other than the fact that I can't make decisions when it comes to my love life, no. Put me in a room with ten candidates for a job and I'll pick the right one every time, but ask me to sort out my personal life and I'm lost."

30

My clock radio blinked: *one fifty-six.*

I didn't know if it was even possible to say no to all of this any more. It had already gone too far. Just seeing Alvin on the doorstep had started something that needed to be finished – or resumed.

One fifty-seven.

"What's a bit more mental turmoil at this stage?" Jess said, as if reading my thoughts. "If you let him go this time, Tammy, that's it. He'll go back to Australia, eventually meet some woman with a sexier accent than yours and that's the end of it. *Then* you'll know all about mental turmoil."

One fifty-eight.

"You and he should never have broken up," Simone said softly. "You know that, don't you?"

I took so long to answer that even I wasn't sure if I was going to say something or not, but eventually, I did. "Yes. I know."

One fifty-nine.

"Then you know what you need to do." Jess got up and hugged me before she left. Simone gave me an uncomfortable pat on the shoulder, the closest she came to affection, and followed Jess out of the room. And then, exactly on cue, my phone rang and Alvin's name appeared on the screen.

"This is nuts," I said into the phone as soon as I'd hit the answer key. "This kind of impromptu thing is just not me."

"I know it's not. But is that a yes?"

I sighed. "I think it is. But Al, I have no idea where we're going with this, and I can't promise you anything . . ."

"No promises. Just a chance. Okay?"

"Okay."

I hung up after we'd made a decision to start the plan in two days' time, torn between being grateful that the decision was made and being suffocated by indecision as to whether I was doing the right thing. We might never get to the point where we would have children, but the pre-parental plan was soon to be underway nonetheless. And God only knew where it would all end up . . .

6

Pre-parental plan activity 1: The Irish Road Trip to Anywhere

Tammy, your comfort zone is planning. Several trees have been sacrificed from the printouts of research you've done on everywhere we've ever been together all over the country (and I can only imagine how many forests would have been wiped out if you weren't afraid of flying - it's a good thing we never get to go abroad!). It's cute but very (VERY) time-consuming, and while I love you enough to let you away with it, the sprogs won't. If we ever have the time or money to go somewhere when we have a house full of our progeny, you'll be too busy finding time to get dressed to investigate the history of our destination. Take a deep breath - this won't be easy - but I want you to close your eyes and drop your finger on a map of Ireland, and wherever it lands, we're going there. No research, no agenda for when we're there - we just drive and arrive. Comfort zones are so overrated anyway!

Two days later, I was sitting in Alvin's mum's car at half eight in the morning prodding in the general direction of Alvin's lap.

"Kinsale!" I said when I opened my eyes and looked at where my finger was resting in the South of Ireland.

"Kinsale it is." Alvin folded the road map, handed it to me and started the car.

I'd been hoping I might land just down the road on Celbridge. Even though we'd be travelling on the motorway from Dublin and the journey would go fast, Kinsale in Cork looked as far away as Antarctica to one as nervous as I was. My knees were knocking against each other so badly that I was sure I'd have to have Alvin detour to a hospital in Cork city to get me treated for fractures. I tried spreading my legs as far apart as possible to save my knees but noticed Alvin giving me a funny look, so I contented myself with bunching up my scarf and stuffing it between my knees. For the first time, I realised why some people carried hip flasks on a daily basis and wondered where would be the best place to leave the motorway to buy one.

I still couldn't quite believe that I'd agreed to this. Although we'd had a phone conversation the previous day about the organisation of the ten activities, I hadn't fully internalised or accepted that organising them meant that I was actually going to have to go through with them. And with Simone and Jess involved – particularly Jess – there hadn't been much chance of backing out of it either. They'd done their best soccer-mom impressions that morning, getting up with me and cheering me on from the sidelines as I painstakingly chose and discarded outfit after outfit amid bouts of fretting and worrying.

"I must be insane," I said as I stepped out of the

fifteenth outfit and hung it up neatly, making a mental note to iron every outfit again later. "Maybe I should ring him and cancel."

"Maybe you haven't noticed that your phone is missing. That's because I've taken it and I'm not giving it back until Alvin lands at the doorstep to collect you." Jess handed me another outfit.

"I can't believe I'm doing something like this . . ."

"It's not really up there with prostitution in terms of shocking behaviour, Tammy."

"But I haven't thought it through properly! He only gave me fourteen lousy hours to make a decision, most of those being sleeping hours – I mean, who can make a rational decision in that kind of a timeframe?"

"That would be most people." Jess sighed. "Just go with it, okay? Accept that it doesn't fully make sense, but do it anyway if that's what your heart is telling you to do."

I harrumphed.

"*Just go and give him a chance*! If you find it all unbearable, just get the bus or train back from wherever you are and tell him you've developed the runs from a dodgy curry last night or something. That should turn him off enough if you really want to see the back of him! But at least try."

"Interesting advice, Jess – very appealing – but I can't say it's convinced me."

"Simone, say something positive!" Jess said – she'd clearly run out of steam herself.

Simone shrugged. "Maybe you might look at him today and wonder what the hell you were ever doing with him. You've probably built him up as some sort of god in your head over the last year and a half, but I bet all of the things that used to annoy you about him will resurface again once you spend time in his company."

Jess rolled her eyes. "Alright, thanks anyway. Forget I asked!"

I raised a hand in Jess's direction. "No, no, that's good. Keep talking, Simone."

She suddenly looked a bit out of her depth. "That was just a best-case scenario for you not getting hurt again. I don't really believe that you're actually over him – I was just trying to be positive . . ."

"Try harder," Jess said, "because that *really* didn't work."

"But it's a fair point all the same," I said. "Maybe I've made more of the relationship in my head than what it was. If that's the case, I might actually be able to risk spending time with him and not be screwed if it doesn't work out. You're a genius, Simone."

Both Simone and Jess looked equally uncertain about that, but I ignored them and clung to Simone's theory to give me the strength to go ahead with meeting Alvin.

And so off I went half an hour later wearing the first thing I'd tried on, the dread of what lay ahead of me interspersed with faint hope that maybe I was over Alvin and just didn't know it. That hope was now growing fainter by the second.

I'd managed to get three weeks' last-minute annual-leave holidays from Branda, and we were going to do the plan over that timeframe, before Alvin was due to fly back to Australia. It was going to require careful planning to fit all ten items into three weeks, but we'd mapped out the days we would plan things for on the phone yesterday and would organise them as soon as we could. I don't know what my boss, Malcolm, had been more shocked about when I'd rung him – that I was requesting three weeks off the day before I was due back to work, or that I was requesting holidays without having to be forced to take them. While he loved my workaholic nature on a professional level, the human in him reminded me on a regular basis that we did actually have a holiday entitlement if I ever wished to avail of it. Every year, my holidays would run over and he'd be forced to have "the chat" with me. It was becoming more and more embarrassing every year. Malcolm was a company man through and through, but even he failed to see how an employee wouldn't want to take their holidays – and although my unexpected departure from the office would cause him a good deal of reassigning, I think he was so relieved to be able to tick my accumulated annual leave off the calendar that he really didn't care.

"Fancy a bit of old-school music?" Alvin said. I shrugged, which he took as a yes. He pressed a button on the steering wheel to switch from the radio to the CD player and Blur boomed out of the car's speakers. Alvin had always been into nineties' indie music, and the CD had the effect of a Tardis. A part of me loved the familiarity, but it belonged to a time when we'd been happy. Hearing it now made me feel a fresh rush of sadness for how we'd mucked everything up.

I felt Alvin's eyes on me as we stopped at a red light on the Naas Road. "Something tells me you're thinking yourself into a tizzy there," he said with a smile on his face.

I adjusted the scarf between my knees. "No, no. Just admiring the scenery." I nodded in the direction of a nondescript hotel on our right.

Maybe I find him attractive because I've been telling myself that I would. By the end of today, I might not see him as anything more than a friend. I repeated my new mantra to myself as Oasis replaced Blur on the CD.

We passed most of the trip with safe chit-chat – my job, his activity instructor's job in Australia, and the inevitable discussion on the state of the global economy and how it had impacted us. When an hour had passed and neither of us had mentioned his family yet, I asked if Claire had enquired about why he needed the car for the day.

"Yeah, and she was delighted when I told her."

"Really?"

"Of course. She always liked you and was sorry when we broke up."

There was a slight emphasis in his tone on 'she'. I knew what that implied.

"Adrienne wasn't quite so happy about it, I'd imagine."

"Adrienne is never happy in general so I wouldn't worry," he said, confirming my suspicions. He changed the subject and that was probably a good thing.

When we ran out of safe topics, we drove in reasonably comfortable silence for about fifteen minutes before Alvin decided to address the elephant in the car.

"So, how were things for you after we split up?"

My heart pounded and my cheeks flamed. Despite rehearsing what I would say to him about our break-up a million times in my head over the past two days, I had no idea what to say.

"They were . . . you know. Break-ups are never easy."

"Ours certainly wasn't."

I think he was expecting me to come back with something – not an unreasonable expectation – but either my brain or my mouth, or perhaps both, was frozen.

"I know this is difficult, Tammy, but we will need to talk about how things went wrong between us and why, if we have any hope of moving on, and what's gone on in our lives since . . ."

38

I shook my head fervently. "One thing at a time. Let's just see how we get on together first. I don't want to get bogged down in analysis and breaking open old wounds if this isn't going to work out anyway."

He didn't look convinced. "We have to have the conversation sometime though, Tam –"

"Sometime, but not straight away. Let's just see how things go. I'm sorry, but this is the most I can give you for the moment. This has come out of nowhere for me –" My voice broke, much to my mortification.

"Okay, let's leave it for now. I didn't mean to upset you. Let's see how we get on today and maybe then it'll be a better time to talk."

He changed the subject to movies and TV shows. The transition was awkward and it was a good five minutes before the fire in my cheeks died down, but we somehow got back to talking as if everything was perfectly normal.

When he stopped in Cork city to get petrol, I whipped out my phone to text Jess: I am actually considering the dodgy curry line ...

We arrived in Kinsale shortly before midday. As we approached, I was struck by how picturesque it was. The town itself, famous for its annual gourmet festival or so Alvin's dog-eared *Guide to Ireland* told me, was situated on the wide estuary of the Bandon River and was neatly snuggled between hills and shoreline. With its large yachting marina near the town centre and obvious potential for leisure activities such as sea angling and fishing, it was easy to see why it was such a popular vacation and tourist destination. From my point of view though, it bristled with opportunities to do Alvin-style activities and filled me with trepidation.

We spotted a car park to our left and Alvin swung into it, then we walked to the tourist office, me in a state of nerves and Alvin in high spirits. We left shortly afterwards with a handful of brochures, deciding to retire somewhere to review our options over lunch. We wound our way through narrow streets until we stumbled upon a bar called Jim Edwards and, happy with the options on the menu, went inside.

As soon as we'd placed our order, Alvin thrust a brochure in front of me. "There's a beach near here where you can go horse-riding – what do you reckon?"

I frowned. "I like my beaches with sun and garden-sized towels. Sorry."

"How about this instead?" He handed me a water-sports leaflet, the glee in his eyes unmistakeable. "There's a number here to ring – I can check out what activities they're running. I'm sure we can rent out all the gear we need."

"You know something, I think the walking tour to Charles Fort sounds great," I said quickly. I fumbled through the brochures until I found the one about walking tours. "Look, I'm even wearing flat heels, so I'm good to go."

Alvin shrugged. He looked disappointed. "Okay. Walking it is."

"Is that okay?"

"Yeah, I just thought . . . no, it's fine, forget it."

"What?"

"Nothing, nothing."

"Alvin!"

His face reddened. "It's just . . . this was supposed to be about stepping outside our comfort zones, right? And I was just remembering a time when you were all for trying new things, even if they scared you. Sorry, it's not fair to even bring that up. I shouldn't have said anything."

I blushed too. I'd been a total scaredy cat when I first met Alvin – I still was one and always would be by nature – but he was right. There'd been a time after I first met him when I was up for anything, purely because it was with him. But then everything had gone wrong, and the fear had returned.

Mercifully our food arrived, breaking the awkward moment.

As soon as Alvin had cleaned his plate of hake and I'd covered the remains of my picked-at chicken with a napkin, he moved into up-and-at-'em mode. "The brochure said the next tour leaves from the tourist office in thirty minutes," he said before calling for the bill.

A small group of four people and a woman tour guide had already assembled for the walk to Charles Fort when we arrived at the tourist office.

"I'll go and pay for the tour," I said to Alvin and ran off quickly before he could argue with me about it.

When I returned, Alvin was deep in conversation with a couple who looked to be in their late twenties – and hugely loved-up.

"Tammy, this is Brett and Angie from the States."

Brett and Angie smiled blinding and almost identical smiles that instantly made me want to buy a teeth-bleaching kit.

"They're on their honeymoon in Europe, starting here in Ireland."

"Lovely!" I said. *Shit*, I thought. Hanging around with a couple could only serve to show how separated we now were.

Alvin seemed to have no such doubts, though, as he

chatted to them about their honeymoon plans. As soon as I heard Brett exclaim "You're into surfing too?" in response to something Alvin had said, I knew we were stuck with this happy-clappy couple for the next few hours.

We set off, leaving the village and making our way to an area of Kinsale called Scilly where we would begin the Scilly Walk on our way to Charles Fort. Our route took us along a precipitous hill right beside the sea, and as soon as we reached the top, the sun came out of absolutely nowhere and made the vista of the marina look picturesque and undeniably romantic. I peeked at Alvin to find that he had glanced at me at exactly the same time. I yanked my head in the opposite direction, catching him doing exactly the same thing in my peripheral vision. I was relieved when the tour guide gave us the nod to walk onwards.

We emerged into a wooded area. Between the tour guide's stories and pearls of wisdom from our guidebooks, the time it took us to walk through the woodland flew in a haze of information about the local area. We were at Charles Fort before we knew it.

When we arrived, the guide told us that the fort, overlooking the harbour, was built in the late 17th century to defend the town from possible French invaders. It was built on the site of an old castle, destroyed during the 1601 Battle of Kinsale which was a turning point in Irish history with its final defeat of the old Gaelic aristocracy. The tour guide pointed out another fort called James Fort across the estuary, Charles Fort's partner in crime in their role of protection. Underwater chains used to be positioned across the harbour from one fort to another, with the purpose of scuttling enemy ships in times of attack.

We followed the tour guide around the ruins of the

impressive fort and, as we walked, the sun went into hiding again and a distinct nip crept into the air. I saw Angie snuggling into Brett and had to hold myself back from rolling my eyes – although it was hardly her fault that my love life was pear-shaped while hers was an obvious success – but then I noticed her burrowing into the inside pocket of Brett's coat and producing something that looked distinctly like a hip flask. Given my thoughts in the car earlier, I couldn't help wondering if I was hallucinating.

"Whiskey, guys?" She offered the hip flask to Alvin and me first before taking a slug herself.

I wasn't sure if I was more impressed by her manners or her unexpected behaviour. Alvin took a quick sip, declining any further offers due to the fact that he'd be driving later. I took a generous mouthful, noticing as I did that Angie's name was engraved on the flask.

Meanwhile, Brett produced a matching personalised one and joined in the drinking. "Best wedding present of the lot," he said between slugs. "Our friends know us well."

We were walking past the Bulman Bar in Summercove when Brett announced that he needed to use the bathroom urgently. It appeared Angie did too when she ran after him without any explanation. They emerged two minutes later, red-faced and panting with ridiculous matching smiles on their faces. The tour guide rolled her eyes and ordered everyone to get moving again.

"They do a great slice of lemon with your tequila in there," Brett said with a wink when he stepped into line with us – although it wasn't quite a straight one. "The sambuca isn't bad either." Then he pulled out his hip flask again and glugged from it. He and Angie held hands and wandered sideways down the hill until Brett hit his hip off a wall.

"Jesus. They're going to be shitfaced if they keep this up!" I hissed to Alvin.

"I know! They'll fall into the sea before the tour is over at this rate."

I managed to talk Brett and Angie into linking arms with Alvin and me and skipping along the return path as a way to keep warm – a thinly disguised bid to sober them up.

"Let's sing Irish rebel songs!" Brett said, skipping with a crazed energy while the tour guide threw him evil looks. "We learned loads of them as part of our honeymoon research, didn't we, sweetheart?"

Angie responded by blasting into an out-of-tune version of 'A Nation Once Again'. Brett instantly joined in, only stopping to admonish Alvin and me for not singing along. I couldn't help but smile at their sheer wild abandon. The thought of being that out of control scared me, but it seemed to be working for them – and what harm would come of it? (Unless they did actually fall into the sea – that would probably count.)

By the time we got back to the tourist office, Brett and Angie had sobered up somewhat but were making noises about being thirsty again. The tour guide said a grateful goodbye to us and told us that the 1601 pub on Pearse Street served a great hot whiskey if we were in the mood for more. Brett threw his arms around the tour guide and hugged her as if she'd just saved his life, then jumped up and down excitedly and clapped like a seal.

"Come on, guys – what are we waiting for? Let's hit the 1601!" They ran off, beckoning us to follow.

"You on for it, Tammy?" Alvin asked. "Maybe we

should go and keep an eye on those two. They're great *craic*, aren't they? Mad as hatters!"

Something about Alvin's hopeful expression melted me and in the spirit of going along with unplanned things, I nodded. It had probably looked like a reluctant one, but a nod was a nod and soon we were in the 1601.

"So, hot whiskeys all round?" Brett asked.

"I can't – as I said earlier, I'm driving today," Alvin said, regret etched all over his face. Impromptu piss-ups with new faces were right up his street.

"You know what, you have the whiskey and I'll drive," I said.

"Ah no, that's not fair . . ."

I waved away his objections. "What else is open insurance for?" I was a lightweight drinker anyway.

"Well, okay then." He leaned forward and kissed me on the cheek. "Thanks, Tam."

We looked at each other for a bit too long before turning our attention back to our new buddies.

"How long are you guys staying in Kinsale?" I asked Brett and Angie as soon as we'd settled ourselves in hugely inviting seats beside an open fire in a cosy back room.

"We'll be here until tomorrow morning and then we're going to get a bus to Dingle for a few days," Brett said. "You know Dingle? It's in County Kerry – a fishing town on the Atlantic. Sounds amazing."

"Oh, it is! I love Dingle," I said wistfully, thinking back on happy summers spent there at Irish college – the Dingle peninsula is a Gaeltacht area. "You'll have a great time."

Alvin and Brett commenced a lengthy conversation about water sports in Dingle. Angie skipped off to the bathroom during the course of it, and I pretended to listen to the guys but really turned my thoughts to assessing how this first list-item was going. As I watched Alvin talk animatedly and passionately about a particular type of wave, I wondered how he thought things were going so far. I prayed he wasn't thinking that he'd made a big mistake. Didn't look like it.

Even if he isn't, how can we possibly move on from how we left things?

I fought back the doubts that instantly flooded my brain. After only a few hours in Alvin's company, I realised that I had no choice but to do this if I was ever again to have a minute's peace inside my head. Nothing in the world had made me feel as vibrant as being with Alvin had, back in the day. He had the ability to make a suggestion like jumping from one rooftop to another the most sensible thing in the world to do – the *only* thing in the world to do. He'd always been able to work magic on me without even trying, and as the discussion continued without me taking in a word of it, I realised that I wanted in on that magic again. I wanted to feel alive, the way I used to whenever I was with him. I was sorry now that I'd wimped out earlier by choosing a walking tour.

"I hear you guys are going to Dingle tomorrow and planning on swimming with Fungi," Alvin said somewhat enviously to Angie when she returned.

Fungi was Dingle's famous in situ dolphin.

"We are," she said. "And you guys are driving back to Dublin this evening?"

"Yeah. We just took a day trip down here," said Alvin.

I cleared my throat, not quite believing what I was about to say.

"Maybe we should stay the night and join you guys in Dingle tomorrow? Only if you don't mind, of course . . ."

"Oh wow, that would be awesome!" Angie said immediately.

"Yeah!" Brett held his hand up to Alvin for a high five. Alvin just looked at it as if he'd never seen anyone trying to high-five before, so profound was his confusion at what he'd just heard me say. He eventually high-fived Brett back half-heartedly, too busy staring at me as if he'd never seen me before to put much into it.

"Angie and I have planned an amazing pub crawl of the most historic pubs of Kinsale tonight," Brett said. "It would be awesome to share it with real Irish people."

I bit my lip to stop myself from laughing. Were the other Irish people they'd met in Kinsale waxworks or something?

"A pub crawl before swimming in the sea?" I said, ever the sensible one.

"Yeah, isn't it an awesome idea? Are you in?"

Saints preserve us. "Erm – absolutely. Kinsale isn't going to know what's hit it."

From the shocked look on Alvin's face, he clearly didn't know what had hit him either.

And so it came to pass that I booked two single rooms for Alvin and me in the Blue Haven hotel and we joined Brett and Angie's pub crawl that night, with me drinking prudently because I would be driving everyone to Dingle the next day. Drinking, and silently marvelling at what had just come over me.

After a three-hour drive to Dingle the following day, during which Brett and Angie insisted on singing Michael Jackson songs back-to-back and repeatedly lamenting his untimely passing, we finally arrived just after one o'clock. The sun made an appearance from behind the clouds to greet us, and we all oohed and aahed at the vista of the briefly illuminated harbour with its backdrop of rugged mountains.

As I pulled into the car park of the B&B we'd booked over the phone, Brett asked us what we thought of the controversy over Dingle's name several years ago. Silence greeted his question. When he realised we hadn't a clue what he was talking about, he told us that the Irish government announced that the English names for Gaeltacht towns and villages would no longer be put on official signposts, but the move caused great controversy in Dingle because of fears that tourists might not understand the Irish name, Daingean (meaning 'fortress'), on signposts and bypass the town. Because of this, some people spray-painted "Dingle" on road signs that only had the Irish version of the town's name. He also told us that we needed to learn a bit more about our own country, but we decided to park that issue as well as the car.

It turned out that Brett had been pulling my leg about going swimming after an epic pub crawl. The swimming trips with Fungi could be done only between eight and ten in the morning, so it was scheduled in for the following day. There was to be no downtime in the interim, though. Brett announced over lunch that he was going to hire a car and drive a route around the Dingle Peninsula called the Slea Head Drive. I tried not to let my horror show on my face – Brett was still half pissed – but I must have failed because I caught Alvin giving me a weird look.

"Tell you what, how about we take my car instead?" Alvin immediately offered. "I'll be fine to drive now and it'll save you guys a few quid."

"Wow! You'd *do* that?" Angie suffocated Alvin in a heartfelt embrace while Brett banged Alvin's back repeatedly and told him how awesome he was.

Alvin told them to feck off, sure it was nothing, and told us all to get moving because the drive would take several hours. I made a mental note to thank him later for probably saving all of our lives.

Brett and Angie were slightly out of steam on the drinking front after Kinsale, but they had a list of four pubs that they absolutely *had* to go to when we got back to Dingle (or Daingean), so after dinner we spent our evening flitting from one to the other. We started in Dick Mack's, a pub and a cobbler's shop all on one premises, where a traditional music session was taking place. Foxy John's was next up, a pub that was once a hardware store and still displayed some of its old stock. It had its very own Walk of Fame outside, in the form of names in the pavement of Hollywood stars that had visited the pub over the years. Then it was on to James Flahive, a former tailor's shop, and finally the Lord Baker, reputedly the oldest pub in Dingle.

The volume of activities we packed in meant that I didn't have too much time to analyse how it felt to be with Alvin again, and having the buffer zone of Angie and Brett between us made things a lot less awkward than they would otherwise have been. And if Angie and Brett were wondering if Alvin and I were just friends or something more, they didn't voice it. Judging by the amount of pawing each other that they were doing, they were too wrapped up in each other to really care what was going on with anyone else's love life. They just saw us as good fun to hang out with, and thankfully that was enough for them.

Keep up the good work, guys.

I rounded everyone up at seven for breakfast the following morning in advance of our swimming trip with Fungi. I would have been just as happy to let them sleep in, though. Swimming in the sea in January . . . were we absolutely crazy? The three amigos had no such concerns, of course. Words like 'invigorating' and 'rejuvenating' were thrown around over breakfast as they anticipated what was ahead of us that morning. 'Certifiable' was the one I'd been thinking of.

At eight o'clock, we departed on the boat that would bring us to Fungi. Although the boat accommodated twenty swimmers, the group was small due to the off-peak season. Our instructor started telling us about the dolphin, but I was so horrified at the thought of going into seawater in January that I only barely listened.

"Fungi the dolphin moved to Dingle in the early eighties. Where from, we don't know – he just appeared, and started escorting the fishing boats to and from port. After a while, it became obvious that Fungi was going to make his move to Dingle a permanent one. Following a long stretch of extensive interaction with aquatic mammal experts, Fungi grew even more communicative with humans – and that's why he'll be looking forward to swimming with you today."

Brett gave us a huge thumbs-up that ended somewhere way beyond the top of his head. Meanwhile, I thought I was going to throw up all over my unflattering wetsuit. I'd been praying we'd be told that Fungi was having a sulky day and didn't want to see anyone, like Chris the sheep in *Father Ted*. Surely dolphins had those days too?

"We're nearly there now, guys," the instructor said after an unidentifiable period of time in which I chewed a nail obsessively and wondered if I was going to die. Although I could swim, I really didn't enjoy it – particularly in the open sea where a multitude of bad things could happen.

In fact, I hated water. I didn't even like dolphins much. What was I doing here?

"Ah, here he is now! Look, everyone!" The instructor beckoned us all over to the side of the boat.

And sure enough, Fungi was right ahead, doing somersaults and tail flips and even something that must have been the mammal equivalent of a bum wiggle, leaving a torrent of water in his wake each time he disappeared into the depths of the ocean again.

"Oh my *God*!" Angie covered her mouth with her hand and danced a gleeful jig. Brett pumped his arm in the air and screamed "Yeah!" repeatedly every time Fungi reappeared. The pair of them couldn't have been more excited if Michael Jackson had risen from the dead and appeared in our boat.

Alvin was a bit more sedate, but looking pretty pleased with life all the same. Then he looked at me and frowned.

"You okay?"

I fiddled with my snorkelling gear. "Ah, yeah."

"What do you think of Fungi?"

"I think a picture of him would have sufficed for me. But look, I'm not complaining, honestly. This was my idea."

"This is going to go great, Tammy. It'll be fun."

"Yeah, of course it will. I'm just worried. I wouldn't be me if I wasn't."

"Worried about what?"

"Well, this is a much bigger swimming pool than the ones I'm used to, for starters."

"You're in good hands on this tour. Besides, *I'm* here. Taking care of people in the water is part of my job, remember?"

"I know, but . . . what if Fungi attacks us? Dogs always

try to attack me, you know. I might draw him on us and we'll all end up dead in the water."

"He's not Jaws, Tam! Anyway, I don't think we'll be allowed to get close enough to him for that to happen."

I crossed my arms across my freezing chest. "You're going to have an answer for everything I say, aren't you?"

"Yep. Anything else?"

I grimaced. "That water will be cold. It'll be bloody *freezing*, Alvin!"

He laughed. "I think we're getting to the heart of the issue now. Don't worry – I'm sure we'll find a way to heat you up afterwards. Maybe a . . . hot whiskey or something."

"Yeah. Maybe that."

Alvin suddenly looked a bit embarrassed, as if he was sorry he'd said anything. I looked into the sea, purely because I didn't know where else to look.

Our boat pulled up just off a beach close to where Fungi was flipping around, and one of the team working on the boat tried to draw Fungi closer to us by whizzing around nearby in a smaller boat with a loud engine. As Fungi approached and the crew declared themselves happy with his position, they told us it was time to get into the water.

"Now guys, he may come closer and he may not," the instructor warned us. "We'll do our best to draw him to us even more, but we can't promise anything. And no going *too* close and definitely no touching him, okay?"

Fine by me.

I bit my arm through the sleeve of my wetsuit as I lowered myself in. By the time the water reached my knees, I felt like I'd just plunged myself into a barrel of ice cubes totally naked. Why was everyone else looking perfectly at home and smiling inanely, as if they were having afternoon tea somewhere? How come they all still had their teeth while mine were sure to pop out of my gums any second from all the chattering they were doing?

"Hey, are you okay there?" Brett was suddenly beside me. He seemed to have glided through the water in a split second. "Here, let me help you down." And with that, he reached up and pulled me down into the water before I could object.

I *screamed* on my way down. Screamed like a room full of babies on vaccination day. With microphones.

"Oh, well done! You've scared Fungi away now!" someone in the group yelled at me when I came back up for air. Sure enough, there was no sign of him when I looked over to where he'd been before I'd been pulled into the water. Everyone except Alvin seemed to be tutting and throwing their eyes to heaven. Suddenly, my cheeks weren't so cold any more.

Then Fungi resurfaced – almost right beside us. Everyone gasped, even the instructor.

"He rarely comes this close!" the instructor said. But no sooner had he said it than Fungi started to flip away in the opposite direction again.

Oh well, it was nice while it lasted. Can we go home now?

Brett asked the instructor if we could start swimming out in Fungi's direction, but the instructor just frowned.

"Let's try something first. Could you swim out a little bit with me and do that screaming thing again?"

I suddenly realised he was talking to me. My heart lurched.

"There must have been something in your voice he liked. He's gone out much further now than he was when you screamed, so how about the pair of us swim out and try to entice him back in to the rest of the group?"

53

"But . . ." Oh no. God, no. "There's nothing special about my screaming, I'm sure. Can't someone else do it?"

I looked around frantically for Alvin before the instructor could answer me. "Al, help me out here . . ."

"You can do this, Tammy. Getting into the water was the hard bit. You're a great swimmer, you have the equipment and the instructor will be beside you all the time. What's there to be afraid of?"

I noticed Brett giving me a look of complete incomprehension. He almost looked jealous.

I clutched Alvin's arm like a little girl. "There's a lot of water out there. And I bet it's even colder the further you go in. I can't feel my legs, Alvin. I don't think I'll ever walk again, never mind swim."

He gently removed my arm, squeezing my hand as he did so.

"Just try it, and you can turn back if you want to. I'll be watching and I'll come and help you if you need it.".

The instructor coughed. "We need to get moving. Fungi will be dead, as will the rest of us, if we wait much longer."

I looked from the instructor to Alvin frantically for a few seconds. And then, something inside me made the decision.

A few minutes later, I was screaming at the top of my voice about thirty metres away from the rest of the group, no longer even feeling the cold.

The instructor grabbed my arm after the fifth scream. "Look! He heard you!" And sure enough, Fungi was swimming over to us again.

We swam back towards the group, with me swimming faster than I thought I could because Fungi's proximity was freaking me out, and screaming intermittently to keep him interested. After what felt like half an hour but was only a few minutes, we reached the rest of the group with Fungi following us.

"Tammy, you were awesome!" Brett did his back-thumping thing before swimming off. Everyone else told me that I was variations of awesome too before they made their way towards Fungi.

"You see?" Alvin said, a big goofy smile on his face.

"I must be the only person in Ireland who's a bit scared of that dolphin. I really didn't think I could do it."

"What changed your mind?"

The same thing that made me want to come to Dingle to begin with. "Do you know, I can't quite put my finger on it. Maybe I just wanted to go from zero to hero, I don't know."

"Well, it worked. Good job, Tammy." He gave me a quick, wet hug before pulling back quickly.

I couldn't think of anything clever to say, or indeed anything to say at all, so I just smiled – idiotically no doubt, but it was better than doing nothing. I couldn't think straight when he was that close to me.

"Right. Better go and see this dolphin after all of your hard work." He swam off, somewhat reluctantly it seemed.

After we bade our goodbyes to Brett and Angie later that day amidst many promises of keeping in touch via email, Alvin spent the entire journey back to Dublin reliving the events of the past three days and declaring the first item on our list to be the best *craic* ever. And you know what? I couldn't but agree with him.

Simone and Jess looked up expectantly when I walked into the sitting room.

"Sorry – Positive Simone, but I'm screwed."

Both Simone and Jess nodded knowingly in unison.

If you'd told me a week before that all the work I'd put into getting over Alvin was about to be undone, I would have been devastated – but now, I just felt strangely excited and worried in equal measure. If this all went wrong I would probably be broken beyond repair this time and maybe even Simone and Jess would give up on me, but it was already too late to turn back. And even a broken heart had to be more fun than clay-modelling lessons.

7

I sat out on the patio at the back of my house the morning after the Road Trip to Anywhere so that I could mull over the Alvin situation in peace. There was a nip in the January air, but it was nothing that a hat, coat and scarf couldn't take care of. Just staring down the expanse of my one-hundred-foot garden made me feel calmer. Even though nothing was in bloom at present, the promise of how the garden would look in a few months made me smile.

I had to hand it to my dad – he'd known what he was doing when he bought this place, even though I hadn't thought it at the time. When I started college, Dad insisted on buying a house as an investment property with the possibility that I might buy it off him further down the line. At the time, houses were going for a song for anyone who had the money and the foresight to buy them before the property boom kicked in. Mum and Dad had presumed I'd live at home and commute to college, but I'd been adamant about moving out so that I could reinvent myself as someone less awkward in peace. As soon as I'd filled up my CAO form, I told them I wanted to move out and the rows started – but Dad didn't put up as much of a fight about this particular issue as he usually did, and it was soon agreed that I'd be moving out if I got my college place. I was delighted, if a little surprised at how easily I'd got off the hook (and vaguely insulted that he was so happy to be getting rid of me), but it became apparent that he was too excited about the prospect of looking for a suitable house to worry too much about me moving out. After a few weeks of searching, he found a dilapidated four-bedroom semi in upmarket Donnybrook that you wouldn't let a rat sleep in (although I was pretty sure a few already were) and fell madly in love with it. It had two elements that made him react as if he'd won the Lotto – location and potential. The house had belonged to an elderly lady who'd recently died and bequeathed it to her sister, who was living in Galway and had no use for it. She wanted a quick executor sale, but the house was in such bad condition that nobody would even consider buying it despite its location, and it had been on the market for over a year.

The front and back gardens were like something you'd find Tarzan and Jane hanging around in. As for the interior, you didn't dare touch off anything for fear of raising a cloud of dust and suffocating yourself. Painting and decorating hadn't been high on the list of the owner's priorities as unfortunately she'd battled illness for years before her death, so the house sported a set of yellowed and peeling wallpaper, threadbare carpets and a smell of dog wee that even turpentine wouldn't shift (the dog had also been bequeathed to her sister, in case you were wondering).

"Nothing a good decorator and gardener can't sort out," Dad had said after he'd first viewed the house.

"And a plumber, and someone to do the wiring, and

probably loads of other tradesman who do jobs that I don't even know exist. Even the A-Team couldn't sort out that mess of a place." I hadn't seen it, but I hadn't relished the prospect of living in a place that would permeate my clothes in the smell of dog piss. I'd never make any friends at college.

"Nonsense. That house is the safest bet on the market. You'll be begging me to sell it to you in years to come."

"So why hasn't someone else snapped it up, then?"

"Because they're all too lazy to put the groundwork into making it an amazing place. Me, I have vision, Tammy. Vision."

"We'll see how much vision you have out of the two black eyes Mum'll give you if this doesn't work out."

"I don't know what you're complaining about. This place is a ten-minute walk from the college you've applied to. And if we can get the sale completed quickly, we have months to get the renovations done before the college year begins."

"And what if I don't get my college place in UCD?"

"Then we'll rent your room out. We'll be renting three of them out anyway. In fact, it'd probably be easier to rent the whole house out to a group of friends or something – you being in the equation is messing things up a bit, now that I think of it."

"Even though the entire reason you're buying this house centres around me?"

"Don't be arguing with me for the sake of it, Tammy. Right, it's time to ring the estate agent and put in an offer."

Dad's idea of an offer was most people's idea of an insult – he offered half of the asking price. But, miraculously, the lady in Galway accepted it. Dad immediately set to work on renovating it, ringing every tradesman in town to haggle with them on prices. He'd drawn up a set of plans for what the house would look like when he'd finished – his *vision*, I should say – even having the foresight to make the two double rooms en suites. "Those bedrooms are massive, so we don't need to worry about losing a bit of space," he explained, "and it'll make it much easier to rent out the second double." Every last piece of wilting wallpaper was to be torn off and replaced with neutral shades of beige, accompanied by a chestnut-feature wall in the sitting room ("It'll hide the drink stains well," Dad, who was nothing if not a realist, said). Coffee-coloured carpets would replace the mess of 70s flowery creations that currently stuck to our shoes, and new furniture would ensure that neither the students nor I would be suing Dad in the future for irreversible damage to our bodies. But no internal change could have made a difference that was as dramatic as the garden's metamorphosis was. After the long grass had been razed to the ground, I realised that the rear of the house was less garden and more football pitch – a football pitch with apple and pear trees at the very end of it, no less. For the first time, I got the potential that Dad had seen in the place.

When the renovations were complete and I had secured my place in UCD, I knew I was the luckiest student in Dublin to be living in a house that was as nice as this one had turned out to be, and because it was my dad's place, the other students we rented out the spare rooms to kept the place in good shape too. As soon as I finished my degree in Arts and my postgrad in HR and started working in Branda, I got a mortgage and bought Dad out.

I was lucky enough to have a low mortgage and therefore to be in a position to live on my own if I so wished, which is exactly what I did right up until Alvin moved in. After he left, I hadn't envisaged living with anyone ever again – but a few days later there were two extra place settings at the dinner table.

They'd landed on my doorstep two nights after Alvin moved out, Jess with more suitcases than could even be counted and Simone with only one, which was probably full of books. Jess was dressed up to the nines even though it looked suspiciously like her only plan for the night was to move all of her many things into my house, and Simone looked like a condemned woman but that probably had nothing to do with her standing outside my front door – just life in general. I suddenly saw a glimpse of my future, but felt I had no choice but to let them in to unpack.

The pair of them practically accompanied me to the toilet over the next few months. "If we leave you on your own, you'll start wallowing," Jess said any time I encouraged either of them to do something that didn't involve me.

And so commenced a time of ludicrously random activities such as going to a seminar on Beckett's impact on literature and life with horrendous acrylic nails (applied on Jess's request to keep me out of trouble while she was getting a waxing job done) that someone in the room pronounced as a reflection of life's vulgarity. That period of my life didn't end until I began dating again, although in truth it was replaced by a time of even more random activities that I'd enjoyed a lot less than hanging out with my cousins.

The thought of all those dreadful dates brought me back to Alvin again. The Kinsale/Dingle experience had left me with a huge feel-good factor. I suppose Alvin was right – the plan gave us something concrete to do, instead of us just gawking at each other over the top of a pint glass and wondering what we'd say next to make the whole experience less awkward. But had he felt something for me during the trip? I replayed every conversation we'd had, while I stared into the depths of the garden, but half an hour later I was still none the wiser. Alvin was a friendly guy in general. Any signs I may have thought I'd seen mightn't have been signs at all.

I sighed and got up to go inside. I'd already been to the shops to buy provisions for the week ahead, cooked my lunch and dinner to be reheated later, tidied the house and done an hour of practice on my piano (my latest activity in the continual pursuit of bettering myself) – not to mention the fact that I'd organised the first of my choices of activities in the plan. It looked like I would have to pass the time until my next interaction with Alvin with a bit of telly. Thankfully it was Jess's TV day, so the chances of having to watch a documentary about controversial snubs in the history of the Nobel Prize for Literature were slim. I was just glad that the latest series of *America's Next Top Model* was over. Jess had turned into a Tyra Banks wannabe over the past few weeks while the series had been airing, and if super-rich Tyra was going to live in my house, she really should have been paying more rent than Jess did.

8

When I walked into the sitting room, Jess was on her knees in front of the DVD player. It looked like her plans for the day were similar to mine.

"Were you out in the garden dreaming about Hutch?" she said as she pushed a DVD into the player.

"Just thinking about how the road trip went," I said, sitting down.

"Any conclusions?"

I shrugged. "It went well and was lots of fun, but I couldn't really tell if he was feeling something for me or not."

"Oh, come on! You know he feels something pretty bloody strong when he came all this way back to see if you two still have something worth fighting for!"

"But what if he's built me up in his head over the last few years, just like how Simone suggested I might have done for him, and now that he's spending time with me he'll realise that I'm not that great after all?"

"Bullshit! It's like when kids bring home a picture from school with nothing but two squiggles on it and their parents act like they've outdone every Renaissance artist in history. Every single thing related to you was always great in his eyes."

"I don't know about that. But as for how I feel about him . . ." I closed my eyes and shuddered a little bit (and it wasn't entirely put on) to get my message across.

"Spare me – I can tell you have it bad already. You're probably acting all cool around him though, are you? I remember when you first started going out with him and you'd pretend you weren't half as interested in him as you were. I used to feel so sorry for the poor guy, with you playing hard to get while he made it obvious that he was crazy about you."

"Ah, that was only at the start. You know I just couldn't believe my luck that someone like him was interested in me. I soon thawed out when I realised that he was actually into me."

"Yes, I remember – and that was nearly worse! You two should have been given an x-rating once you got past your phase of playing games." She faked her own shudder (or at least I hope she faked it, and it wasn't that we had genuinely been that bad). "I just hope for all our sakes that it works out. Tell that auld bitch Adrienne I said not to be causing trouble this time around or I'll call around and sort her out."

"I have a feeling you could be making a house call very soon. Alvin hinted that Adrienne isn't too happy about us doing the plan."

"She's just jealous because you have everything she wants – a good job, a brand new car, a house in the best part of town with the best housemates imaginable — and you used to have a relationship while she always seems to be on her own. I've seen her in action at parties you've had and she always tries to imply that you're a snob because you have a bit of spare cash to spend on branded stuff and the like. Ha – as if anyone from our family could be a snob! Our mothers would have no truck with that type of thing and would bring us down to earth fairly fast!"

"But it's nonsense! I only have this house because Dad had the sense to buy it cheap and then sell it to me, I have my car because I don't have to fork out a fortune on my mortgage – so again, because of Dad really – and my job might pay well but I have to work damn hard for the money. She hates me for no good reason."

"Unhappy people always find someone to pour their misery on. Ever seen *Cougar Town*?"

"Nope."

"Neither have I, but let's sort that out." She jumped up on the couch, tucking her bird's legs beneath her, and pressed *play* on the DVD remote.

I decided to see if I could get into it. It was bound to be better than thinking about the possibility of Adrienne causing trouble in the future.

Two hours later, I was hooked. I was enjoying it so much that I barely noticed the gloom that descended on the room when Simone walked in with a few blankets and a battered copy of *Samuel Beckett: The Complete Dramatic Works*. Oh God, Old Simone was coming back. I loved Beckett when I was in college, but prior to her positivity drive, Simone *lived* Beckett. I always thought about moving out whenever she was in a Beckett mood. Even though I owned the house.

In her defence, I should mention that Simone had been made redundant from her job as an auditor six months previously. Despite fervent efforts and ten years' experience, she hadn't secured another job so far and consequently had nothing else to do but sit around and think all day. It had been fine at first. When she wasn't polishing up her CV and applying for jobs on the Internet, Simone had occupied herself by creating a book of money-saving strategies to see her through her post-redundancy period until she got another job, a task that had taken care of a good two months of her time. But as soon as her guide to how to financially survive her new circumstances was completed, it wasn't long before her long-time love of philosophy became something more than a pastime. Her introspective nature lent itself well to long bouts of musing on the ways of the world and human nature, but Simone didn't always like the results of her musings. I think I can speak for both Jess and me when I say that we didn't either. We'd been delighted to hear about her new positivity drive, albeit dubious about how long it would last.

"You're slipping," Jess said to Simone as she pointed to the book.

"I didn't know what I was getting myself into. Being positive in today's world is almost impossible. I just need a little pick-me-up, okay?"

Jess smirked. "Beckett, a pick-me-up. The irony." She turned to me and raised her voice. "Unintentional, I'd imagine – Simone takes herself so seriously that she's irony deficient. I'm sure there are tablets she could get for that though."

Jess was a great woman for teasing and Simone was usually her subject, an arrangement that seemed to suit them both as it brought Simone out of herself in a safe, familial environment. Even as a teenager she knew that handling being slagged off in any way wasn't her strong point, and that having Jess around to harass her was good practice for the real world. Jess, of course, never meant any of it maliciously, and this was just the dynamic between them and always would be.

Simone didn't reply.

"Wow." Jess tilted her head to one side. "Things are bad when you're not even up for a bit of banter, Simone. Is everything okay?"

"Yeah, yeah. You guys just watch your show. Thanks for asking though."

Simone flicked open her book while Jess and I settled back into *Cougar Town*.

"I wonder if Jules and Grayson will get together," Jess mumbled as the credits rolled on the episode we'd just been watching.

"From what we've seen so far, I'd say so," I muttered back.

Simone swooped at the DVD remote on the table and pressed *stop*.

"Of course June and the guy with the stupid name will get together!" she said. "Do you think this show would have been commissioned if the scriptwriters wanted your woman to lust after your man for the entire series and never get him in the end? God forbid that these cock-eyed shows might actually portray a realistic depiction of most people's love lives!"

Jess gave me a knowing look. "I saw this coming when she walked in with that book."

"Sorry, maybe that was a bit much – but can you please stop talking about me as if I'm not here? Better still, could you just stop talking altogether for a few minutes and let me speak? There's something I want to run by you both." She cleared her throat. "The thing is . . . I made a list on New Year's Eve of the things I wanted from life this year, and one of them was . . . well, I kind of wouldn't mind meeting someone this year." She blushed furiously. "Or at least try to. That was kind of where the positivity buzz came from. Maybe if I believe it's possible to actually meet someone at my age even though it's years since I've been with anyone, then it might actually happen." She picked up her book and fiddled with it, her face purple. "But I don't have a clue how to even go about it. Real life isn't like that show you were just watching – or at least, it's not if you're me. I know I said I wasn't going to bother with relationships any more after Simon, but maybe I was wrong."

Ah. Simon. It had been a while since his name had last come up in conversation, which wasn't surprising when you considered that Simone had vetoed any mentions of him since they'd broken up three years ago. While the whole name thing sounds a bit unfortunate to an outsider, it actually seemed perfect when you saw Simone and Simon together. Everything about them was in sync, so why wouldn't their names be? They dressed alike. They sounded alike. They were each as dark and gloomy as the other. Although for the three months that they were going out, Simone was a different person. There were days where you'd go so far as to say she was contented. She even bought a few new tops and a pair of green combats (all of which she still possessed and wore frequently – even before she'd been made redundant, Simone and spending money were uneasy bedfellows). From the day she started going out with Simon, Jess and I never saw Simone without her other half in tow. As Simon was so like Simone in every way, we got used to having him around pretty fast. We felt like we already knew him. Jess and I had actually been speculating, over a drink in Kehoe's, on when Simon and Simone would move in together at the very moment that Simone rang us to tell us Simon had ended it with her. He never gave her a tangible reason beyond the fact that things ending and feelings changing was part of the horrible reality of living. And Simone had never been quite the same since.

"So I thought that maybe you two might have some ideas about what I can do to meet someone, especially after all of the things you got up to last year, Tammy. I know none of them worked out for you, but we all know your heart wasn't in them because of Alvin."

"Don't mind Tammy," Jess interjected. "We all know I'm the only one around here who's good with men. And you know what, Simone? I'm delighted you've finally come around after Simon. Don't think I haven't noticed that stash of girlie romance books on the bookshelf in your bedroom! Can you recommend *Mario's Menage*, actually? That was a well-thumbed one."

Simone reading something other than existentialism? Surely not! "Simone, is this true?"

"I . . . just bought loads of that type of books at a second-hand book fair at work, that's all. I haven't even read them."

"Sure you haven't." Jess smirked. "You know, I'd usually pick you up on this because of how you always give me dirty looks whenever I'm reading what you call chick-lit books instead of one of those so-called classics you're always trying to palm off on me, but I'll let it go this time. I have too much other important work to do for you right now." She got up and made for the door.

Simone just stared at the door after she left. "Why am I suddenly feeling nervous? Maybe I should have just asked for your help, Tammy – Jess is a loose cannon sometimes. She's probably calling some escort line and sending them round to me now." She buried her <u>head</u> in her pile of blankets.

She was probably right. "Don't be daft. She wouldn't do that." I hoped.

Simone's head didn't resurface.

Jess came back downstairs a few minutes later wearing a self-satisfied smile. "Right, that's that sorted."

Simone sighed deeply and emerged from the cocoon of her blanket. "What have you done?"

"I filled your mother in on how you're feeling and she's on her way around."

The escort was suddenly looking like a get-out-of-jail-free card. I covered my ears.

"What the *hell* are you playing at?" Simone disentangled herself from her blankets and leapt to her feet. "Why did you have to make a miserable situation a million times worse?"

"I thought that's how you liked things to be! The deeper the misery, the closer you are to your heroes – a tortured soul and all that."

"I've no problem with misery, but bringing my mother into this is just too low, even for you. Tammy, I need to borrow your car keys and get out of here before she arrives."

"Not a hope. Sorry." It wasn't that I didn't want to entrust the Lexus that I'd saved for years to buy to Simone – the fact was that if Simone wasn't here when my Aunt Patty arrived because I provided the escape vehicle, I'd be the one who'd end up miserable. Patty was a force of nature and not one to be trifled with.

"Patty won't rest now until you find a man," said Jess. "I wouldn't be surprised if you have a new partner before the end of the month, actually. Oh, and Patty says you're to go straight to the shops and buy some fashion magazines before she gets here – she wants to help you revamp your image. No need to thank me -- what are families for? Although if you fancy making hot chocolate before you go for those magazines, I wouldn't say no to one."

"I hate my family," Simone said as she shuffled out of the room.

Honestly, it was like being a teenager all over again. The only question was if we'd ever grown up between those days and now.

9

Pre-parental plan activity 2: A literary pub crawl

Alvin, although our kitchen table constantly has your newspapers doubling as tablecloths and your music magazines as coasters, I know you're not into reading books. Fine by me, but my obsessive-compulsive worrying gene had a word in my ear and warned me that I'll be the one that'll end up reading books to the kids every night while you watch the soccer. If the kids pick up on us not being on the same page (no pun intended) about this, it might discourage them from discovering the sheer unadulterated joy of reading. So maybe it's time to awaken that joy in you.

"Ah, the literary pub crawl. I've been looking forward to this one." Alvin's wry laughter crackled down the phone when I rang to tell him I'd booked the first of my activities. "I'm sure I can dredge up a few Oscar Wilde quotes as I'm falling from one pub to the other. The one about '*We're all in the gutter*' would be fairly appropriate for that, wouldn't it?"

"You won't even need to – our tour guides on the event

will do the science bit. This tour has actors that perform some of the works of James Joyce, Samuel Beckett, Brendan Behan –"

"Maybe you should have invited Simone on this trip instead of me."

"She was actually the one who told me about it." She hadn't recommended it though – one of the actors had mistakenly said that Beckett's middle name was Frank. When Simone pointed out that Beckett's middle name was actually Barclay and that it was his father and his brother who were named Frank, the actor fobbed her off with a nervous laugh and tried to move on as swiftly as possible. But he had no idea who he was dealing with. Simone loudly demanded her money back and declared the actor incompetent and unfit for his position, not to mention disrespectful to the most amazing writer Ireland had ever produced. He'd given it to her too, just to get rid of her. I hadn't even told Simone I was going on this trip, as she'd tried so hard to blacken the tour's name ever since and would have killed me for handing over money to a lost cause like it – I just told her we were going to take books from the library and bring them on a pub crawl, reading sections from the books in each pub. But if this tour got Alvin into reading, then I didn't care if the actors thought Beckett's middle name was Sputnik.

"Well, I was sold as soon as the word 'pub' was mentioned, so let's do it."

I had a fizzy feeling inside this time around when I met Alvin at the Heineken building in the city the next day, twenty minutes before the tour started. I was still nervous, but excited nervous. He seemed enthusiastic about our day's upcoming activities and I had no problem getting him to the tour's starting point, the Palace Bar in the heart of the city. The problem was stopping him going inside and missing the start of the tour completely.

"My mate Josh works in here," he said when we arrived ten minutes before the tour was due to start. "Haven't seen him since I came back – I'll just go in and say hello."

"No, Alvin. Leave it until the end of the tour. You'll be in there talking until closing time otherwise."

"But the tour ends somewhere else, and we won't be walking by here on our way home again. I'll just head in for a second –"

"You will not!" Some things never changed . . . I grabbed his arms and forced him to look at me. "Okay, look into my eyes, Alvin. Focus, focus – that's it. Now, what are we here to do, can you tell me?"

"Ah, you're no fun."

"And you're only noticing that now?"

He laughed and shrugged me off. "Alright, I get it. No pub."

"That's a good boy."

He swatted me on the arm. It felt nice. Or as nice as being swatted can feel.

Focus had always been a big sticking point in our relationship: Alvin's lack of it, my overabundance of it. Alvin tended to drift from one day to the next, never worrying too much as long as the day that had just passed had been an enjoyable one. I just had no capacity to relax into a lazy day and enjoy it like Alvin had. My day felt worthless unless I'd achieved something – a work to-do list with nothing outstanding on it at the end of the day, a better workout than the one I'd done the previous day, a house-cleaning session where the skirting boards were not only dusted and washed, but polished and buffed too. (I never said that what I wanted to achieve wasn't *sad* on occasion.) I always tried to apply myself to get what I wanted. With Alvin, he was so wide open on what he wanted from life that focus was something he didn't feel the need to apply too often. And that was where I'd always come in, when needed. Like now. It felt strange to be back in this role again, and yet it was one we'd both always been very comfortable with.

"Maybe we can talk instead, so, until the tour starts," he said. "You know, catch up on what's gone on over the last two years, people we met . . ."

My heart sank. It had all been going so well, and now I would have to inevitably hear about who Alvin had been with in Australia. I knew that he was bound to have had partners since me, but that wasn't going to make hearing about them any easier.

"Well, I met a door-to-door salesman specialising in pillows, which was handy when I needed one at the end of our one and only date, a mortgage broker who did a sideline as a clown for kids' parties and insisted on wearing his red nose out to dinner for laughs, and an estate agent who tried to buy my house off me," I said with a laugh, even though everything I'd said was true and nothing about it was even remotely funny at the time. "I'm sure you met a lot of people too but, honestly, you don't need to tell me about them. A year and a half is a long time and you were a free agent. Let's leave it at that, okay?"

Two men in top hats approached us and the other people who were standing outside the pub. *Impeccable timing.* "Here for the literary tour?" they asked in perfect unison, receiving a series of yeses. My yes was one of the loudest.

"*'The bright stick trapped, the breeze adding a third party to the couple kissing on an old seat'* – name that poem!" The smaller of the men took off his top hat and pointed it at me. "You look knowledgeable, you'll know this." And I did, I knew I did, but I couldn't for the life of me place the line at that moment.

"Isn't that from the depressed fella from Monaghan who sits down by the Grand Canal near the Baggot Street Bridge?" Alvin whispered.

"Oh yes! It's Patrick Kavanagh's 'Canal Bank Walk'!" I said as quickly as I could before someone else did. My cheeks burned furiously. Alvin mightn't read much, but he had the memory of an elephant for facts and figures and clearly hadn't forgotten the English school curriculum like I had – not to mention forgetting the contents of my English degree. How mortifying. I'd sat on the Patrick Kavanagh seat down by the canal near the Baggot Street Bridge only a few weeks ago when I'd been out on a walk.

"We'll never mention that again," I said through gritted teeth as the tour guides rounded us up and led us away. Alvin just smiled. But he never would – that was the type of guy he was.

The next two and a half hours encompassed a mélange of information about Ireland's most famous writers, street performances of those writers' work and refreshments at their most frequented, historic watering holes. Our tour guides, James and Joyce (both male), doubled as actors and, as we walked from pub to pub, they performed scenes from some of the writers' most famous plays, recited poetry or started up their literary quiz again, firing lines from a play or a poem at us when we least expected it.

Once we were snugly ensconced inside each of the four pubs we visited, James and Joyce spoke about how the famous Irish writers would meet journalists and editors from the big newspapers of the day in the pubs we were drinking in to try to organise publication of their work. However, the literary scene was small and writers often fell out with those around them, and would then choose to drink in another pub and spurn their former haunts. Luckily for the organisers of this tour, that meant there was a vast choice of literary pubs to bring us to. By the time we hit the fourth and final pub, we'd heard about Beckett, Joyce, Shaw, Yeats, Kavanagh, Wilde, and some of the more recent greats like Heaney.

"And that brings us to the end of our tour," Joyce said. "Almost. Before we go, we need a victim."

"I knew Joyce was the one to watch," Alvin muttered.

He was right – Joyce had the head of someone who was out for mischief every hour of every day.

Joyce held out a book. "We like to finish our tour with a reading from this book – any reading of your choosing, as long as it's from one of the great writers we discussed today. Oh, and that *you* do the reading, not us. Now, I know that might sound intimidating in a place like this" – he swept his arm around the crowded pub – "but I'm sure we are among friends. So who'd like to be the lucky one who gets the gig?"

I grabbed Alvin's arm and stuck it up in the air. I knew public speaking held no fear for him, but doing a poetry reading definitely wasn't something he'd usually do – which made him the perfect man for the job.

Alvin tried to pull his arm back down. "Ah, Tammy!"

"Two words: comfort zone," I whispered. "Go on."

"We have a volunteer! A very willing and enthusiastic one, it seems! Come on up – I won't bite. James might, but he's had his shots so you'll be fine."

Alvin shrugged, then walked up to Joyce with the look of someone who wasn't wholly comfortable but was willing to give it a go.

Alvin flicked through the book to choose a reading while a couple on the tour quizzed James and Joyce on where the best place was to find traditional Irish food. It didn't take Alvin long to choose something. He gave Joyce the nod that he was ready to start and Joyce shushed the crowd – not just our group, but everyone in the pub. He even got the barman to turn off the telly, which didn't cause any huge upheaval because nobody seemed to be watching it anyway. I felt the way I imagined a parent would at their child's school play as Alvin started his reading.

"I've picked a poem from Oscar Wilde called 'Her Voice'," Alvin said.

I was surprised. I don't know exactly what I was expecting him to pick, but an Oscar Wilde poem definitely wasn't it. And for the second time that day, I was embarrassed. I didn't know this poem at all.

It started innocuously enough, with talk of a wild bee reeling from bough to bough, but suddenly grew darker as Alvin read about the poet making a vow that two lives should be like one, then declaring that those days were over. A shiver enveloped my body as the words spilled out of his mouth. He raised his eyes from the page to make eye contact with our group after each pause. Was it my imagination, or was he giving me a particularly searching look?

> *I made that vow,*
> *Swore that two lives should be like one*
> *As long as the sea-gull loved the sea,*
> *As long as the sunflower sought the sun,*
> *It shall be, I said, for eternity*
> *'Twixt you and me!*
> *Dear friend, those times are over and done;*
> *Love's web is spun.*

Heat crept up my neck. I listened intently to the rest of the poem, picking out lines about how there was nothing left to say except that love is never lost and that there was nothing to rue. Why did he pick this poem if it didn't mean something? What type of message was he trying to give me – that we'd messed up, but there was still something between us? Or was he even trying to give me a message at all?

> *One world was not enough for two*
> *Like me and you.*

Alvin closed the book and looked up. This time, I was in no doubt that his look was for me, and me only.

"Fantastic choice," James said as Alvin returned to my side.

"And a most uncommon one," Joyce added.

"And we're very glad to have had such a great choice, aren't we, Joyce?"

"Oh yes, James. Yes, indeed."

"Because today's tour isn't just any tour. Today's tour, my friends, is our five thousandth tour!"

James and Joyce clapped furiously, and our group responded with a ripple of the requisite 'Yay!'s and 'Good job!'s from the overseas contingent.

"And that means we have an opportunity for someone. A lucky member of this group is going to get the chance to be a guest reviewer on the breakfast show on Éire TV! The person we pick will get to review any classic novel of their choice as part of a panel on the Breakfast Show tomorrow."

"I think Alvin should get the opportunity for doing such a, like, *heartfelt* reading," a twenty-something woman in the group said loudly. She looked at me and winked. She was backed up by a few other people muttering 'Yeah's.

"What do you think, Alvin? Are you up for it?" Joyce winked suggestively at Alvin.

I was sorry now I'd volunteered him for the reading. Things were getting a bit out of control. "Don't do it if you don't want to," I said to him.

Alvin pulled a face. I recognised it as his 'I'm about to say no to this' expression. Then he looked at me, and the cloud on his features lifted.

"Sure, why not?" he said with a smile as he turned to face Joyce.

"That's the spirit!" Joyce raised his hands high in the air and started to clap, encouraging the rest of the group to join in. "Well, folks, that's the end of our tour. We hope you enjoyed it, and thanks for choosing us. Alvin, stick around and we'll fill you in on what will happen with the review."

I sat at a table and watched Alvin as he got the details of his upcoming TV slot. I envied his ability to go with the flow. I could always think of a million reasons not to go for a new opportunity whenever one came up.

"Looks like I'll need to borrow your copy of *Little Women* as soon as possible,' Alvin said after he'd taken his leave of James and Joyce and had come over to my table.

I laughed. "So what book *are* you going to pick for this?"

He frowned. "The one I just asked you for. That's why I asked for it. That's how asking for something works, isn't it?"

"You can't be serious!"

"Why not? They never said it had to be an Irish classic book, just a classic book in general –"

"It's not that – it's just that I know you'll hate *Little Women*! It's not your type of book at all!"

"Tammy, am I missing something here – or are you? Isn't that the point of all of this?" he laughed. "Come on, let's go back to your place to get it."

Little Women was my favourite book. Alvin knew it. And the fact that he'd picked my favourite book to read had filled me with a warm feeling and a little fluttery-heart thing that I hadn't experienced in a long time. A year, seven months and six days, to be precise.

10

"*Little Women* was, to my mind, a very *visceral* work . . ."

I covered my face with my hands to block out the breakfast show on TV. *Visceral? Oh, Alvin.*

On one of our first dates, we'd gone to an art house movie and I'd been very impressed when Alvin had described it as – you've guessed it – visceral. I'd thought he was spot on at the time. A few months into our relationship he revealed that he hadn't a clue what it had all been about, but he had a battalion of words and phrases stored up to describe pretty much anything when he got stuck. A great plan, unless someone decided to delve a little further into his reasoning.

When you were being interviewed on live TV, chances were that delving would be done. And that car-crash TV would be impending.

". . . a very skilfully conceived plot . . . evokes innate but perhaps forgotten emotions . . ."

What? I peered at the TV through my fingers, feeling guilty beyond measure for volunteering him for the review. I held my breath as I waited for the presenter to ask Alvin to clarify his thoughts. But instead, the presenter nodded sagely. And then I realised – she wasn't even listening to anything he was saying. She was too busy staring at him in barely disguised lust.

"There's a – a *universality* about the characters . . ."

More nodding. Much, much nodding. *Alvin and his charm strikes again.*

You see, Alvin was one of those men who just seemed to ooze sex without even trying. It didn't matter what he wore, where he was, who he was with (i.e. me) – women just flocked to him all of the time. He walked into a room and heads, male and female, would turn. He didn't get second glances so much as incessant ones. I never even got a first glance when I was with him (I didn't get many of them when I wasn't with him either) except the odd one where you could tell people were trying to work out if he was with me and then surmising that, nah, he surely wasn't. A guy like him could have anyone, after all.

While I hadn't forgotten just how potent his appeal was to people in general, its impact had faded somewhat since we'd parted company. But now, watching him as he confidently spoke what amounted to gibberish about *Little Women* and getting away with it, I remembered all over again how hard it had been sometimes to be the unlikely girlfriend of someone like him.

Pub and club nights out were the worst. The weekend after we'd moved in together, we decided to go to a pub in Donnybrook. It was a place with a strange mix of clientele – an old style pub, the type that'd never do table service, but it had somehow become trendy and attracted a young crowd while holding on to its old faithfuls. There were old men sitting up at the bar drinking pints of Guinness while groups of funkily dressed movers and shakers crowded around tables. A very noisy hen party was finishing shorts at the back end of the pub and making moves towards leaving.

Alvin was coming down from the bar when he was accosted by the hen party on their way out. *Here we go again*, I thought. We mightn't have been together all that long, but it hadn't escaped my attention that uninvited groping of my boyfriend by members of the public seemed to happen on a regular basis. This time, it started with one girl at the front of the group grabbing his torso as he tried to cross her path with our drinks and, within seconds, the entire hen party had descended on him like a pack of wolves. I could almost smell the pheromones oozing collectively from them as they tried to engage him in hen dares, all thoughts of leaving gone until they snared their prey. I sat back, pretended I couldn't see what was going on in front of me and wondered when someone would write a really good self-help book about this type of thing. Knowing the seven habits of the woman with the boyfriend that other women just couldn't seem to help blatantly throwing themselves at would be useful right now.

Alvin managed to extricate himself from the pack, half of our drinks dripping from his sleeves. I seethed silently inside as the girl at the back of the group pinched his bum just before leaving. Apart from a slight upward jump combined with an almost imperceptible butt-clench, you'd swear it had never happened as Alvin just completely ignored it. It annoyed me. It was one thing me pretending that this type of thing didn't happen but Alvin did too, and I wished to God sometimes that he'd just turn around and tell these women to bugger off with themselves. He never would though. It wasn't just the fact that he was a gentleman by nature, but also that he was too self-deprecating to ever say anything that would hint at an admission that he was gorgeous. The whole being-gorgeous thing was almost wasted on him and, in truth, he just wasn't really all that bothered about it.

"I hope those girls remember to leave paracetamol by their bedside lockers tonight," Alvin said as he sat back down with our half-drinks.

"I hope they don't," I muttered.

"Ah, they're just having a laugh. They seemed like good fun."

I stared at Alvin. "Would you like it if I was falling all over the place like that on a night out?"

"God, yes. You'd buy all the booze, maybe even buy the chips on the way home and then want to ravage me as soon as we got in the door – what's not to like?" When I pulled a face, he put an arm around me and smiled. "Of course I wouldn't like it if you were falling around langers all of the time, but I doubt those girls are either. Hen and stag nights are different – people just go all out for them."

"Not all people."

"True. I haven't forgotten the story you told me about coming from your cousin's hen night stone cold sober and writing an essay for the night course you were studying for at the time. And all credit to you – you're the most disciplined person I've ever met." He paused. I knew there was a 'but' coming. "But, you know, you might actually enjoy it if you went wild on a night out for once."

"And do what?"

"I dunno. Maybe get up on a bar and dance like that virginal girl in *Coyote Ugly*?"

"I am not virginal!"

"Oh, I know you're not." He smiled so wickedly that

I just had to smile back. "But you wouldn't get up and dance on a bar, I know that too."

"Who says I wouldn't?"

He pointed to the bar. "No pressure, but if you want to back that statement up . . ."

"Not now, obviously." I threw my eyes up to heaven, as if Alvin was a complete idiot. "Someone could – get injured. It's busy in here tonight. But someday."

"Sure." Alvin sat back, satisfaction that I'd just proved his point written all over his face. "But even if you don't, I won't be complaining. You're perfect just as you are."

He hadn't thought I was quite so perfect once upon a time. And yet here he was, not only back in my life again but going on television talking about something he really had no interest in just because it was something that interested me. Surely that meant something? Or was this just another element of his continuous bid to cram as much of life in all its forms as he could into every single day?

And to complicate matters even further, he'd made another attempt to get me to talk about everything that had happened before and after he left as we'd walked back to my place to get *Little Women*. I'd fobbed him off again, the familiar feeling of panic rising every time I thought about dissecting where it had all gone wrong. But he was right – it was a conversation that would have to take place sometime. But if I wasn't ready now, when would I be? I really didn't know.

All I could conclude as the interview ended was that I was looking forward to the next day, when we'd be doing the third item on the list. In the meantime, I pressed rewind on live TV and sat back to watch the most gibberishy interview in TV history all over again.

11

Simone and I stared at each other in alarm when Jess walked in later that day. She had no make-up on and it was obvious that she'd been crying. Both situations were unheard of for her.

"What is it? Is it Granddad?" I said, grabbing my phone and checking to make sure I hadn't had a missed call from Mum as I spoke. Granddad wasn't sick, but he was ninety-nine and we all knew he'd have to go some day. Somewhere in the back of my ever-worrying mind I was expecting the news – and whenever there was news in our family, Jess was always the first one to know about it.

"What? No."

"Is it one of our aunts in Wales?" Simone said. Nobody ever heard from those three unless there was bad news.

"No! They're fine. Everyone in our family is alive and well – last I heard, anyway. No, it's Ciarán."

"Ciarán has died?" Simone said in a low tone. "Oh, Jess, I'm so sorry!"

"Ciarán's not dead, you big eejit! He's hale and hearty, the bastard."

"Oh, you've just broken up or something, is that all? *Phew!* I thought we had a new reason for your relationships not lasting long there."

Jess threw Simone a look that made her cower.

"It was a joke," Simone said weakly. "What happened?"

"A wife," Jess said as she too sat down. "He's married. I don't believe it, girls! How did I not cop this sooner? Me, of all people!"

How indeed? If there was anyone out there that you would trust to suss out a married man on the prowl for a bit on the side, it would be Jess. The three of us settled down to chew the cud over Jess's tale. It transpired that she initially had her doubts about Ciarán when he continually refused to come around to meet us. "Why wouldn't you want to meet the important people in someone's life if you were crazy about them, like he said he was about me? And it was nothing too heavy either – it's not as if I was asking him around to meet my parents, just you guys."

"Which could have turned out to be much harder than meeting your parents any day," I said, looking at Simone.

Simone always put Jess's boyfriends through the ringer in an attempt to suss them out and see if they were good enough for her younger cousin. She'd test their nerve by refusing to talk to them at all for the first few encounters, staring blankly at them whenever they asked her a question, then she'd interrogate them military-style about their previous girlfriends to ascertain if they were still hung-up on their exes and therefore likely to mess Jess around, rebound-style. If they got past this, she would then treat them like a member of the family – it was questionable whether or not that was a good way to be treated, in a family like ours, but that's another story. But many of them fell by the wayside before that, not because of Simone but because of Jess's exacting standards in men. Surprisingly, Jess never minded Simone's treatment of her boyfriends, seeing it as a stamina check for them.

"Well, he didn't know that. And once I started to think about things, I realised that our meet-up schedule had been very dodgy. Like, remember that time I met him on Sunday in the airport hotel, where he was staying before he flew out to his company's German office the next morning? No companies pay for overnights in airport hotels now – they just get their employees to fly out the morning of travel to save money. Then there was the fact that he'd always choose to eat in northside suburbs even though we both live southside, then pass it off as being down to them having the best chef in such and such a place – that kind of thing. And he's quite a bit older than me, but was still apparently single until he met me – call me ageist, but most men his age have a story behind them. Once I started thinking, I couldn't stop."

"And there he was on New Year's Eve, pouring champagne down your neck," Simone said. "God only knows what kind of lies he told his wife to get out that night!"

"Yeah, New Year's Eve was the tipping point. I didn't say anything to you two on New Year's Day because we were busy analysing the Alvin situation, but I had my suspicions. He kept getting calls the previous night and it was as if he was trying to get me drunk to knock me out so that he could sort something out."

"So what sort of espionage did you have to get up to find out the truth?" I asked.

"Oh, none. I asked him straight out and he admitted it."

"Oh."

"Don't sound so disappointed! I have enough on my plate without driving myself crazy hiding in bushes spying on my lover!"

"Ex-lover," Simone pointed out.

"Well, that's something, I suppose," I said. "At least he didn't string you along and you'd find this out in three months' time or something. I'm sure he probably had enough sense to realise that the option of lying wasn't an option at all when it came to you." I sat back and waited for her to agree with me.

It's a good job I wasn't in a hurry.

"He said he has too much respect for me to lie to me, and he still wants to be with me – he loves me," she eventually said in a quiet voice that I wasn't sure I'd ever heard before from her. I wasn't even sure if it was *her* voice that had said it. Her mouth had been moving, but the words sounded so unlike something she'd say.

"Of course, he wasn't lying to you before – he just wasn't telling you the truth. Lying by omission doesn't count, I suppose." Simone shrugged. "I know it hurts, Jess, but we'll have him on the list of 'People we laugh about when we're drunk and can't believe we ever went near' in no time."

Jess dropped her head and looked at her lap.

"What's going on here?" Simone's voice was sharp. "You have finished with him, haven't you?"

Jess shrugged. "I told him I needed time to think about it . . ."

"What's there to think about?" Simone stood up. She looked even taller when she was angry and, right then, her head was pretty much skimming the ceiling.

Other than people getting their facts wrong about

Beckett or otherwise disrespecting Beckett in any way, the one thing in life that was guaranteed to raise Simone's heckles was affairs. This, of course, wasn't a random adverse reaction. When Simone was eleven, her father Jacksie had a year-long affair with a neighbour's wife, something that shook her family to its core. It barely survived the impact and it took months of negotiation and counselling to move forward from the crisis. When I say 'counselling', it was nothing official – this happened in the days when you didn't 'do' counselling in Ireland – the counsellors in question were my mother and Jess's mother Gobnait, or Gobby as the entire family called her, but between them all and with the passage of time, Patty and Jacksie somehow kept it together. The impact on Simone lasted a lot longer, though. Being somewhat of a reserved, moping child, she was always destined for bouts of teenage angst but her dad's affair sent her disposition into orbit, heralding the arrival of moods that swung from one negative emotion to another. Aunt Patty had tried to diminish Simone's anger by forcing her to partake in various sports activities – gymnastics being among the medley – but Simone would usually bunk off after the first few weeks and read a bleak book under a tree somewhere.

Jess had been on shaky ground before she'd even opened her mouth, and she didn't stand a chance with Simone on this.

"I know it's all very black and white from the outside – he's married, so I exit stage left – but you have no idea how he makes me feel, girls. I've never experienced anything like this before. I didn't think it could be like this."

"What? Adultery?" said Simone.

"*Love*, you wagon!" Jess stood up and pulled herself

up to her full five foot two, throwing her neck backwards. "You might know more about it if you pulled your head out of your books for a while and got a real life!"

"Okay, let's calm down here," I said. "And sit down while you're at it, the pair of you." *At opposite sides of the room, preferably.*

"I don't expect you two to understand," Jess said as she reluctantly sat down. "I'm not asking for anything from either of you, not even that you listen. I've only told you this much because you asked."

"Yes, because you came into the room with a cried-out head on you," Simone said. "Of course we were going to ask!"

"Look, I know it's wrong." Jess spread her hands apart. "There's no denying that continuing to sleep with another woman's husband is one hundred per cent wrong. I already feel bad about it and I didn't even know I was doing it – and you know me, girls. This is not the kind of thing I would ever do."

It wasn't, to be fair. Although Jess's sharpness could sometimes make her come across as abrupt and she definitely wasn't someone you would mess with lightly – unless you were Ciarán, by the sounds of it – she was one of the kindest people I knew. But I felt a 'but' coming along.

"But this is different. I've never felt anything like this before. All the way home I've been thinking to myself that I've never intentionally done anyone any harm in life, ever. If I stay with Ciarán, this will be the first really bad thing I do. But wouldn't I just be bad to myself if I didn't go for what I wanted? Shouldn't I put myself and my own interests before that of someone else that I've never even met? And if she was in my situation, do you think she'd do it for me?"

"Are you trying to convince us or yourself?" Simone was bringing out all her best parent-lines.

"But where do you think this can ever go?" I asked. "You're only together a short while, Jess. You must know he's not going to leave his wife for you. Don't you think you're worth more than a fumble in a hotel every now and again?"

"Of course I do!" Jess flipped her hair back and raised her head. Lack of confidence in herself had never been an issue for her. "But I can't go from everything I thought we had to just . . . nothing."

I had to ask. "Does he have children?"

Jess hesitated for a few seconds before nodding, then bowed her head. "Two girls."

"This has to stop now, Jess," Simone hissed. *"You're. Having. An. Affair.* You're destroying two children's lives!"

"I'm not having an affair! I didn't know he was married!"

"But you're thinking about having an affair," I said quietly.

"I suppose that would be more accurate, yes. Oh girls, don't judge me. I can't help how I feel about him."

"How can you still have feelings for him after what you've discovered?" Simone demanded. "Do you not despise him now? He's not the person you thought he was at all!"

"You can't just switch feelings on and off," Jess said softly.

"Don't do this, Jess," I said. "I know it's a big shock, but Simone is right – your feelings have no basis in reality.

You were in love with an illusion. You don't know Ciarán at all, just the front that he's presented to you."

"And that's supposed to make it easier, is it?" Jess didn't wait for a reply. She just got up and stormed out, leaving a fug of perfume and angry vibes in her wake.

12

Pre-parental plan activity 3: Live without money for a whole day

When we have children, we'll have no money, I am Fact. Might as well get used to it now!

Alvin bounded along the street like a puppy that had just been unleashed after being locked in the boot of a car on an overnight journey. "Come on, walk faster. This is your free gym for today."

For the first time that day, I was glad Alvin had ordered me to put on my big ugly runners when he'd arrived at my front door that morning. They were so white that they gave me snow blindness every time I looked down but were also as comfy as a down blanket on my feet. Which was handy, as from the little Alvin had told me about what was ahead of us that day, it sounded like we'd have clocked up a marathon amount of miles before the day was out. There'd be no buses, trains or taxis anyway, that was for sure.

'*When we have children, we'll have no money.*' Wise words in a hypothesis format, but even so – in the parallel universe where this was supposed to happen – we'd surely have money for the odd loaf of bread to keep us going. According to the rules of this list item we weren't allowed to spend any money at all – not so much as two cent on a penny sweet. I liked money, and it liked me. It made me feel comfortable and safe and secure, things I very much wanted to feel. The thought of being out there in the world without it scared me, even if it was only for a day. One good thing though was that it made me realise how lucky I was to have any at all – there were millions of people in the world for whom this was a concern every day of their lives.

We walked down Grafton Street, which was heaving with buskers and street performers, and turned left down a lane towards the Powerscourt Centre.

"Before I forget, my mother told me to invite you over for lunch tomorrow," Alvin said as we reached the end of the lane. "Are you on for it?"

"Oh . . ." Was I on for it? I wasn't sure.

Claire and I had always rubbed along together exceptionally well, but things were bound to be awkward when we met. She'd made several attempts to contact me after I'd broken up with Alvin, even calling to the house on three occasions (I'd been out every time, thanks be to Jesus), but I'd had to tell her by text that, much as I liked her, I just couldn't talk to her at that time. The only way I'd been able to deal with the break-up was to shut out everything and everyone related to my life with Alvin. I couldn't imagine she'd been too pleased at how I'd handled things, and I couldn't blame her. But if she was inviting me to lunch, she must be over all of that. Claire was a good ally to have if this crazy thing I was doing with Alvin somehow came to something – and, besides anything else, it would be good to see her again. I'd always had a lot of time for her.

"If you're wondering if Adrienne will be there, then I'm sorry to say that she will – but don't mind her," Alvin said as he led us behind the centre and walked down a street I wasn't familiar with. "She's not working at the moment, so she's around the house a lot."

"She hadn't even crossed my mind," I said truthfully. But now that he'd mentioned her – *ugh*! Now that was a reunion I wasn't looking forward to.

Alvin stopped outside a rather dingy-looking hair salon.

"We'll need to look our best for where we're going tonight. And don't even ask where that is or why – just go with this." He held the door open for me.

I peered into the salon. It was full of brightly dressed young people with impossible hairstyles and Pete Burns from Dead or Alive style make-up. "We're in the wrong place, then . . ."

Alvin approached the front desk. "I rang yesterday and was talking to someone called Dawn about the free trainee haircuts and styles here today . . ."

"Oh yes, I'm Dawn. I remember your voice," a minxy-looking young woman with a face full of piercings purred at Alvin. "You said you'd be coming in with a Sammy." She looked me up and down. Her disapproval at my sensible white shirt and plain sky-blue jeans was evident.

"Tammy," Alvin said, placing his hand on my back for a few seconds before drawing it away again. It was something he'd always done if anyone ever slighted me in any way – he'd move in physically, as if trying to protect me against someone else's snub. I wasn't sure if it was appropriate any more, but it wasn't as if he'd just snapped the hook of my bra either – and I couldn't help but like it.

Most of the trainees in the salon were female. A solitary male was washing the long grey hair of a man who was loudly proclaiming he'd only come into the salon to get a free cup of tea. The women swooped around Alvin as soon as we sat down, each of them fingering his long locks and staring at him like he was a supernatural being. I was completely ignored.

"Nice. Very nice. You wouldn't want to take too much off," a girl with pristine copper ringlets and a lime fringe said to Alvin. "I'll take this fella," she declared loudly, flicking a hand at the others in an attempt to scatter them away from her prize. "One of you lot look after her."

All of the others walked away towards the coffee area and ignored me completely. I was sure I heard a whisper of "What's he doing with her?" as two of them flicked through a magazine, but I wasn't sure if they were talking about Alvin or someone in the magazine. Eventually, a girl with predominantly blonde hair, punctuated by intermittent black stripes that were crimped 80s style, came over. I told her I wanted a chignon-type upstyle – how wrong could someone go with an upstyle? Meanwhile, Missy Ringlets – who'd announced herself to Alvin as Kerrie – had led Alvin over to a basin, where she was currently whipping his head into a frenzy of suds and looking like she was enjoying it far too much.

I probably should have spent more time looking at what was going on with my own barnet instead of watching the interaction between Alvin and Kerrie at the other side of the room in the mirror. If I had, I might have noticed that my hair was going less in the way of a sleek chignon and more towards the clip-covered bubbles look. And if such a look didn't exist, it did now.

"It looks like tennis balls are tangled up in my hair!" I shrieked at Alvin as we walked down the street and I looked at my reflection in every shop window. The hairstyle – if you could call it that – had added about three inches to my height. My head looked like a cone. I'd tried to rip the whole thing out before we'd left the salon, but Alvin had held my hands down and reminded me of the whole going-outside-the-comfort-zone thing. It was all right for him to say that. Kerrie had treated Alvin's hair as if it was spun gold, and had taken off only the barest shavings in a bid to preserve his curls. Somehow though, it had taken her a full hour to do, an hour that was full of high-pitched giggles.

"It's . . . creative," he offered.

"That's one word for it." I decided to try to forget it. "So how are we going to eat? Should I be on the lookout for bins to rummage through?"

"You can if you want, but I have something far more sophisticated in mind."

We traversed the river via the Ha'penny bridge and headed down the quays before turning right towards the Jervis Street area, then crossed Henry Street and walked until Alvin stopped outside a hotel.

He looked at his watch. "Perfect timing."

He marched into the lobby as if he owned the hotel. A hum of activity drifted towards us that seemed to be coming from an area to the right of the lobby. I followed Alvin as he moved towards the noise, hoping I looked like I knew where I was going. We swung a right into a wide corridor lined on one side with a table bearing canapés, sandwiches, biscuits and refreshments. People were spilling out of a conference room to our left.

"So what's the deal – have we gatecrashed some company's team-building event or something?" I whispered to Alvin before stuffing a canapé into my mouth.

"Something like that. Do you remember my friend Jack?"

I nodded.

"He works for the multinational Corpora now. He mentioned that the whole company had an offsite event on here today, so I asked him for the agenda to find out what time lunch would be served."

I probably should have had some ethical concerns about what could be interpreted as stealing, but I knew from attending these kinds of events at Branda that loads of food would be left over and chucked out anyway. And it beat eating out of a bin. I grabbed a plate and loaded it up before Alvin had chosen his first canapé. I abandoned him and joined a queue to get a glass of water, munching my prized food as I shuffled along. I glanced around to locate Alvin and saw he was deep in conversation with a man I'd no idea if he knew or not. As soon as I'd sloshed sparkling water into two glasses, balancing them on my now almost empty plate, I made my way back to him.

I handed him his glass.

"Can I have a word when you're ready?" I said, trying to rescue him.

"Sure – I'll be with you in a second." He smiled at me then returned to where he'd left off mid-sentence, talking about emerging challenges in the present-day workplace (and sounding like he knew what he was talking about too).

I finished my food, gulped down my water and went to refill my glass just for something to do. When I'd finished, a man was waiting to take my place in front of the drinks.

"Hello there," he said with a smile.

I wasn't sure if I was meant to know him or not. He was looking at me in an almost expectant fashion. Amazingly, he didn't seem to be looking at my hair in horror.

"Hello," I said, returning the smile uneasily. I glanced over at Alvin in the hope he'd come over. He was still talking, even more animatedly. He had the look of someone who wasn't going anywhere fast. God, you really couldn't bring him anywhere.

"I'm trying to get around and meet as many people as possible today, as I said in my talk earlier," he said.

Oh Lord. He was obviously one of Corpora's bigwigs. "Ah, yes. Wonderful." I put my glass up to my mouth and slurped my water.

"And you are?"

"I'm – em – Mary."

"Mary. And what department do you work in, Mary?"

"Operations," I said quickly, throwing a smile in there too. Operations was always a good one – the departments were usually big and the title was vague.

"Operations."

I was finding his habit of repeating what I said discomfiting.

"Remind me who's the head of Operations?"

This man sounded ominously like someone who knew that I was a canapé thief. I gulped at my water – and whatever way it went down, it wasn't the right one. I choked furiously and spluttered water all over the bigwig's tie, shirt, trousers and shoes, completely at a loss to understand how one mouthful of water could seem like so much when someone else was wearing it.

"I'm sorr–" I began in an attempt at an apology, but I

couldn't stop coughing. I coughed so much and so loudly that I was aware of the chatter around the room easing off.

And then Alvin was by my side. "Come on, let's get you some fresh air."

I croaked another attempted apology at the bigwig as Alvin led me away, but he was too busy patting himself dry with paper napkins to notice.

"Well, I don't think the CEO of Corpora will want to talk to you again in a hurry," Alvin said after he'd thumped me on the back a bit and I eventually stopped coughing. "It's his first week in the job, and look at how the Irish office treats him."

I shook my head. "The CEO. Of all people . . ."

"Yeah, the guy I was talking to said the CEO had gone on about how much he was looking forward to doing a meet and greet with his new team over the course of lunchtime. I have a feeling he didn't see that one coming though."

"Did you know that guy?"

"Of course not. Just making conversation. Sorry, I tried to get away from him but he was one of those people who just likes to talk."

"There's a few of them about all right."

He smirked. "Point taken. Right, let's move on to our next activity."

We walked to Temple Bar, stopping when we reached the Irish Film Institute.

"I have my name down for free tickets for two movies they're screening today – we just have to collect them in the box office. The second one begins fifteen minutes after the first one ends, so that's the whole afternoon taken care of."

I'd been to the IFI with Alvin several times in the past. It had been one of 'our' haunts. Sadness swept over me when we went inside and it hit me that we were now just a platonic pair of friends watching movies together, but then Alvin caught my eye and smiled, and I copped myself on and resolved to enjoy the movies as best I could. After a year of strange dates, this was the most normal dating type of thing I'd done in a long time.

13

When we left the IFI four hours later, I was hungry again. "I hope you have a free pass for a five-star restaurant up your sleeve next."

"I can sort you out with a five-star sandwich. This way."

We walked to Stephen's Green.

"When was the last time you were at a book launch?" Alvin asked.

"Last never. And you?"

"Last month, actually. Mate of mine in Oz wrote one." He pointed to a lane up ahead. "It's just down here."

I looked in the window as we walked to the door. It all looked very civilised. Groups of people were standing around drinking wine and there were a number of individuals sitting down leafing through paperbacks. A woman in her thirties was sitting at a table signing copies of what presumably was her book.

"Alvin, I can't go in here. My hair looks ridiculous – and I'm wearing runners!"

"Relax. People will probably think you're trying to

make an artistic ironic statement or something. Nobody goes out with hair like that unless there's a good reason for it – no offence. Besides, it's comfort-zone-free and that's what we want, ultimately. That wasn't the intention with the hair, but let's take what we can from it."

"How did you hear about this?"

"I know the author."

Had Alvin always known every single person in Dublin, and it had somehow escaped my attention? "How?"

"She went to my school. Our whole family were invited because her mother is friends with mine, but Mum and Adrienne can't make it and you're my guest."

"Your empty-handed guest. We're at a book launch where we can't afford to buy even one copy of the book between us."

"We don't need to. I called into the bookshop last night and bought two copies, and left them in the shop to get them signed tonight. That means you have a guilt-free pass to sandwich-cramming and wine-slamming."

"Cramming and slamming it is."

We queued up, got our copies of the book signed by the rather lovely author, then laid into the copious and diverse array of sandwiches.

"It's half seven and we still haven't spent a cent," Alvin pointed out over a glass of launch wine after the author had given a speech thanking everyone for coming.

"You better hope it stops raining or we'll be forced to pay for a taxi," I said, pointing out the window at the teeming rain that had come out of nowhere. "In fact, we're going to have to pay for a bus or a taxi anyway. We can't walk all the way to Donnybrook and Stillorgan in the dark."

"And we can't fall at the last hurdle either. There'll be

105

no taxis and no buses. We'll use our imaginations to bring us home."

Next thing he'd be suggesting we clicked our heels to get us there.

"I'll say nothing," I said, thinking it instead. If Alvin was in one of his fanciful moods, God alone knew what he'd come up with.

As soon as the rain eased off, we bid the author goodbye and walked towards Leeson Street.

"Right, you're the good-looking one in this relationship," he lied. "Stick out your thumb there."

"What? I'm not sticking anything out there!"

"Well, we won't get far with thumbing a lift home without a thumb."

"You want to go hitch-hiking in the middle of the city? We haven't a chance of getting someone to stop for us!"

"Stick your thumb out there, so, and prove that we haven't." He grabbed my hand, wrestled my thumb into a sticking-out position and thrust it out in the road, holding it with one of his hands. My hand felt like it was on fire, but just like last time, Alvin acted as if this was all completely normal.

The first ten minutes of our attempt to thumb a lift proved me right, and people seemed to drive faster when they saw us instead of slowing down. Thumbing a lift just wasn't something people did any more. And never in city traffic. This was not going to work.

And then a van pulled up right beside us. I was so shocked that I wasn't sure what to do next. Getting into it would have been what was expected of me, but I did nothing.

"Are you going out the Stillorgan way?" Alvin asked the driver.

"You tell me. I'm looking for the Donnybrook theatre. Is this the right road?"

"It is, but it's a bit tricky to get to the Donnybrook theatre from here," Alvin fibbed. The Donnybrook theatre was a straight run out with just one left turn to take – but it was only a five-minute walk from my house. "If you give us a lift out we'll make sure you get there safely."

The driver hesitated for a second. "Alright so, get in. I've a bunch of fellas in the back there that need to be on stage in forty-five minutes."

As soon as they were mentioned, the bunch of fellas appeared. The back door of the van slid open and four heads appeared in the manner of the Queen 'Bohemian Rhapsody' video. Four drunken heads at that.

"Ah, it's the Mad Dogs!" Alvin said to me. "They're the band from down the country that won that Irish talent show a few months ago. Lads, how's it going?"

This was getting beyond a joke. Alvin had been out of the country for a year and a half, but still seemed to know everything that was going on in it on top of knowing everyone who was ever born here! I'd never heard of the Mad Dogs.

"Slowly, that's how it's going. Are ye gettin' in or not?" one of them said.

"We are," Alvin said without a second's hesitation.

"Get in to fuck so," another head said.

They shuffled back from the door on their knees to give us room to enter.

I wasn't sure about this. "I'll sit in the front."

"You will in your arse. Get in here and have a can." One of the bunch pulled a can of cider out of a crate and shook it at me.

"Go on, I'll mind you," Alvin said.

107

I stepped in gingerly.

"Clean off that seat there and let herself sit down," the guy with the can in his hand said to one of the others, who promptly pulled down his sleeve over his hand and ran it along the crisp crumbs on the bench-style seat on the right-hand side of the van.

The driver pulled out onto the road fast, sending the bodies in the back flying all around the back of the van like a pack of Skittles that'd just been hit by a bowling ball.

"Straight on out this road," Alvin yelled out the grid to the driver.

I wondered if he'd had to get one fitted or if it had come with the van. Was Alvin mad? These people could be anyone!

"I'm Redser," a not surprisingly ginger-haired guy said. "These three are Johno, Spud and Mars."

"Alvin and Tammy," Alvin said.

"They sound like they should be in *Home and Away*," Redser said to the others.

"Here, take your can," your man with the can said to me.

"Could I get one that hasn't been shaken up? That one will explode all over me if I open it now."

"Well, yes, of course it will. Isn't that the fun of it?"

"Yeah, you have to see how much you can drink through your nose when that happens."

I wasn't sure if I was seeing things. It looked like there was a pack of grown men in their twenties sitting around me, but all I could hear were teenagers, so I might have been wrong. This was loopy!

"So what in the name of Jeesis are ye doing thumbin' a lift on the streets of Dublin? Have ye no buses up here?"

"We're trying to see if it's possible to live without money for a day," I said. *Now who sounds loopy?*

If you'd said that to anyone else, the first thing they'd ask you is why you were doing something like that. But the Mad Dogs collectively nodded, the timing of their head-bobbing so uniform that you'd swear they'd rehearsed it.

"Sure, of course it's possible. We haven't spent anything between the lot of us since we got up this afternoon."

"What about the cost of your cider? And you must've eaten somewhere along the way too?"

"The brother gave us the cider. 'Twas left over from his young fella's christening."

"And Mattie Malone from the local corner shop gave us free packed sandwiches for the road. Only condition was that we have to throw the plastic sandwich packaging into the crowd during the gig to get him free advertising."

"Lots of people from up here come down our way during the summer, you see," another one of them explained. "Now they'll remember Mattie Malone's when they want to buy a sandwich."

"We'll fire them out during 'Burn the Nearest Supermarket' – that's our biggest hit. Do you know it?"

They burst into a version of it without waiting for us to answer, all four of them roaring at the tops of their voices about the scourge of corporate globalisation.

I reached over and grabbed a non-shaken can. I needed it. This lot were, as their names warned, quite insane.

By the time we got to the Donnybrook theatre Alvin had four new best friends. I'd ended up giving the driver the few directions he needed because Alvin was too busy discussing the Mad Dogs' rivals in the final of the talent show they'd won (it transpired that Alvin had watched the show on the Internet).

"Thanks very much for the lift," I said in a shaky voice as I got out of the van. The driver had swerved through lanes as if he'd been driving in India, and I wasn't the better of it. "I'd love to hear your music sometime now that I've met you, so I'll keep an eye out for you on TV." A slight lie – what I'd heard of them singing had been more than enough – but there was no harm in being polite after they'd been good enough to drop us home.

"But, sure, why would you need to do that when you're about to hear us live and dangerous?"

They loaded our pockets up with cans and brought us into the theatre with them.

"You all right with this?" Alvin said as we made our way backstage.

"Sure," I said. "The guys are good fun."

And they were. I pulled the ring open on my can, sloshed it back and realised I was quite enjoying myself as I watched them from the side of the stage, with Alvin standing right beside me. The whole day had been typically Alvin – unpredictable, and one that I'd never experience if I was left to my own devices.

We fell out of the theatre a few hours later, leaving the Mad Dogs to a post-gig drinking session that we'd been invited to but had declined due to lunch at Claire's tomorrow.

It started to rain again as Alvin walked me home. We huddled in a doorway and waited for the worst of it to pass. Alvin whipped off his coat, threw it over my head and huddled under it beside me. There it was again – familiarity. What exactly did it mean? Was it just Alvin being his usual tactile self, or was it something more? And suddenly, the situation annoyed me. Were there vibes between us or was I only imagining it? Why could nothing ever be simple?

"Keep it," I said, pushing it off my head. "I like the rain. Actually, let's walk again."

I instantly regretted walking right back out into rain that pelted against my face like sheets of glass, but there wasn't much I could do once I'd started, only stay going. I was almost afraid to look behind me in case Alvin hadn't followed me, but when I eventually got up the courage to turn around, there he was. I couldn't see him under his coat, but unless someone had stolen it and had some reason to impersonate him, he was there.

"You can't walk to Stillorgan in this rain," I said when we reached my front door after the coldest five minutes of my life.

"I'll be fine."

"As fine as someone with pneumonia would be. At least come inside until the rain eases off a bit."

He lifted up his coat and stared at me, then moved towards me and tucked my wet hair behind my ears with one hand. We were now in blurry territory. I had no idea what he was about to do and even less idea what I wanted him to. Everything in me was mentally screaming at him to kiss me, and yet so much had been left unresolved when we broke up that every ounce of sense I possessed was telling me not to do this just yet . . .

Alvin dropped his hand and backed away from me. "I have to go," he said, already halfway down the driveway. "See you tomorrow for lunch."

And suddenly, the words Alvin had said about me being the good-looking one in our relationship came to mind. Was that how he was seeing this again now? As a relationship?

111

14

I was sitting at the kitchen table drinking a glass of hot water and lemon in advance of lunch at Claire's when Jess arrived home. Guilt was written all over her face when she walked into the kitchen. I'd heard her leaving the house at eight that morning and thought she might have gone to the gym, but one look at her tousled demeanour revealed she'd been up to activity of a different kind.

"Is Simone here?" she asked, confirming my suspicions.

"No, she's out running." I dropped my chopping knife. "You're still seeing him, aren't you?"

"Ah Jesus, Tammy, couldn't you at least work up to it?" She sighed, suddenly looking very tired.

"I'm just worried about you, Jess. Why are you doing this to yourself when you know it can only end badly?"

"It's not that simple. Relationships never are. I was leaving work yesterday when there he was, parked outside the building, and I tried to walk away – I swear, I did. I walked past the car to get to mine, but he drove after me and blocked my car in until I agreed to speak to him."

"*What*? What sort of a bully does something like that?"

"Oh no, it wasn't like that! He was desperate to speak to me. You should have seen him – he looked wretched."

Not as wretched as he would have looked if I'd been there to sort him out.

"He says he adores me and that he's been waiting his whole life for someone like me."

All there was left for her to say was that his wife didn't understand him.

"When he lost his job back in the 90s, his wife – her name is Audrey, by the way – hadn't given him the opportunity to find another job himself – she'd set him up with a job that he hadn't wanted in her parents' company. She's browbeaten him into living a life full of decisions that weren't of his choosing, and eventually he accepted that things were this way just to have a quiet life. He says that when he's with me, I give him the space to be his own person for the first time in twenty years."

And there it was. Not in so many words, admittedly, but it wasn't far off.

"And you accept that from him?"

"Well, of course. Why wouldn't I?"

"Maybe she was just looking after her husband by setting him up with a job, and he's just using that as an excuse to fob you off with –"

"If she really loved him and cared about him, she'd have given him the space to do what he wanted to do with his life."

Where had my sassy cousin gone to?

"I told him that for my own sake, I had to walk away. So I did, but I felt so hollow afterwards. He rang me non-stop yesterday and last night, and when he rang this

113

morning I just couldn't hold out any more. I had to see him."

How did he get away with making all of these calls without his wife noticing? And more to the point, how could Jess even consider being with someone so deceptive?

"Jess, bad relationships are insidious. This will never have a good outcome for you – you can only get hurt from it. You can take the pain now or later, but the longer you let this go on, the more it's going to hurt."

"I can't not be with him. Surely you understand what that's like?" Her eyes searched my face.

"It's a different situation, Jess."

"But the feelings are the same. I know what I'm doing is wrong, but he's like a drug to me, Tammy. It's as if I have no choice in the matter."

The sound of a key in the front door travelled up the hall into the kitchen.

"Say nothing," Jess whispered. "Please?"

"She'll find out eventually –"

"I'll tell her myself after lunch. Just leave it for now, please? I really need to have a shower before I can tackle Simone and her ire."

I quivered at the thought of why she needed that shower. "It's your life, Jess. I just don't want you to fuck it up – and I'm speaking as someone who's been to the fucked-up zone."

She nodded before leaving, but it was the kind of nod you apply when you want someone to think you're listening to them but you really aren't.

"Hi, Tammy. What's up with Jess?" Simone asked as she walked into the kitchen with a scarlet face from her running exertions. "She just brushed past me in the hall there without even slagging me about how I look like I've fallen asleep on a sunbed after I run." She held the back of a chair and panted. "Janey Mac, I need to get fit. These legs might be long, but they're useless at running."

I avoided Simone's eyes as I got up. "She's fine, as far as I know. Fancy some hot water and lemon?"

"Who wouldn't? That's a no, by the way. One step at a time with this new me thing. When are you going to Claire's anyway?"

"I'll leave in a few minutes. How do I look?"

Simone looked me up and down, taking in my coral forties-style tea dress and beige peep-toe wedge court shoes.

"Like you've tried very hard, but you look great so don't even think about changing. Alvin will want to eat you up."

"I don't know about that."

"Oh, come on. From what you told me this morning, it's a no-brainer that he does. The hair-tucking in the rain – very *Four Weddings and a Funeral*."

"Hmm."

"And you still fancy him, obviously. You wouldn't get dressed up like that for a Sunday lunch if you didn't. So what's holding you back?"

"It's not that simple. We haven't even spoken about the issues behind us breaking up yet."

"Then maybe it's time to start."

"I can't. I have too much to lose. Think about it – we have one hell of a postponed row on our hands. We break up, we have no contact for a year and a half and then we're hanging out together again as friends while ignoring the eight-hundred-pound gorilla that could destroy everything. If that row starts, it could be the end of us spending time together, and . . . I couldn't bear that,

Simone. Now that he's back in my life, I have to keep him here for as long as possible."

"You're only postponing the inevitable, Tammy," she pointed out, her words eerily similar to the advice I'd given Jess only a few minutes ago. "There's only so long you and Alvin can circle around each other like cats in heat. I know how much you fear failure and how hard it was for you to accept it when things didn't work out last time, but you have to deal with what happened."

"And I will, but not today."

"Huh. This is what you get for always being pupil of the year when we were at secondary school. All that being-good-at-everything business for all of your life meant that when you thought you did eventually mess something up, you didn't know how to accept the situation. Well, it hasn't gone away, you know."

"Maybe you're right, but I don't want to argue with you about it now, Simone. Just leave it."

Simone held her hands up in surrender. "I was trying to help in my own way, not to argue. You'll have enough of that on your plate with the barbs you're bound to get from that wagon Adrienne today."

"Don't remind me."

I didn't even like to think too much about all the attempts Adrienne had made to split Alvin and me up in the past – friends of her friends claiming to have seen me out with other men when I'd been at home with a hot-water bottle, me being presented with a copy of an Irish celebrity magazine containing a photo shoot of one of Alvin's gorgeous exes, that kind of thing. According to Alvin, Adrienne had felt threatened when she'd seen that things were serious between us. She constantly told him he was moving too fast with me and was ultimately making a mistake, but I often felt there was more to the story than that – it felt like she really disliked me as a person too.

"I want a full report when you get back, not only because I'm interested but because you'll also take the heat off me. Mum is coming over yet again this evening for another make-up experimentation session. I'm thirty-fucking-five, Tammy, but try telling her that. This is all bloody Jess's fault."

I left before I somehow let it slip that Simone had another much more serious reason to be mad at Jess now, if only she knew it.

15

All the way to Alvin's place, I imagined how the scene of my reunion with his family would unfold. I hoped things would go well with Claire. She was a really lovely woman once you got past her eccentricities, if a somewhat hard person to work out. With her sprawling belly, her short mousy greying hair and an array of trousers that did absolutely nothing for her rear end, her whole look screamed conventional Irish Mammy, yet she seemed to pride herself on being as unconventional for her age as she could possibly be. She refused ever to attend Mass, preferring instead to talk to the spirits. ("They're everywhere, you know. I don't get a minute's peace from their chatter, even when I'm trying to do a poo in the so-called privacy of my own bathroom," she informed me one day as I was eating a subsequently abandoned dinner.) She'd been doing tarot-card readings in a shed at the side of the house for several decades, but had branched out into a tarot-card premium hotline a few years ago and was apparently making a mint from it. She was generally just not of this planet at all, but I suppose there were worse things in the world than that.

I remember being surprised when I first met Claire that she wasn't stunningly beautiful. She was – everyday, I suppose, a face in a crowd, if that's not too harsh. When I first started going out with Alvin I'd always throw covert glances at pictures of his dad on the mantelpiece to see if he was some sort of Adonis, but he was pretty unremarkable too in the looks department. I realised that when it came to Alvin and his sister, it was a case of the children being lucky enough to get every good gene going, and the combination of the good stuff resulted in inordinately attractive people. They had their mother's olive skin and brown eye-colour, but not her big nose, the googliness factor of her eyes or her lank mousy-brown fine hair. Their dad's hair looked bushy in pictures, but on his children it looked thick, lustrous and healthy. Adrienne's looks were more subtle than Alvin's, but she got her fair share of attention all the same despite the fact that she never really played up on them, to give her her due. It was just a pity that her aggressive attitude usually sent people in the opposite direction once they got to know her.

As I pulled up outside Alvin's mother's semi-detached on the Kilmacud Road, the familiarity of what I was doing was overwhelming. How many times had I parked my car in this very spot when I was with him? If I turned my head to the left, I would probably see Claire peeping out the front window to see who'd deposited their car outside her house. I could almost hear her launch into a 'Holy Mother of God, would you look who it is' spiel, even though she was expecting me, as I turned off the engine. I tried not to smile in case I looked a bit crazy. She'd be pleased to see me, I knew she would. Why else would she have invited me?

I rang the doorbell, arranging my features into my brightest smile while I waited for Claire to open the door.

And waited.

I rang the doorbell again. When nobody answered, I peered in the front window. There was nobody in the sitting room. I could hear vague noises that seemed to be drifting towards me from the back of the house. I moved towards the gate that I knew Claire always transported her wheelie bins through and listened intently. Through the trees and shrubs that encased Claire's large garden and were liberally dotted here and there throughout her lawn, I could just about make out a male voice which I judged to be Alvin's and a cacophony of female tones.

When calling over the gate got me nowhere, I went back to the front door and tried a few more long rings of the doorbell. I was just about to give up when Claire appeared at the door.

"Tammy! What the hell are you – I mean, why are you here so early?"

Hmm. Not quite the reaction I was hoping for . . .

"You said half one – it's two minutes past one now, so – I just thought I could give you a hand with lunch, maybe." I could feel a furious blush creeping up my cheeks.

"Oh yes, I forgot that you always show up far too early for things."

I gave a half-smile. There wasn't much else I could do after that statement.

A few seconds passed. Claire seemed to be guarding the access into her hall.

"So, will I . . .?" I pointed into the hall to try to move things along.

Claire looked over her shoulder, then at me, then behind her again. She looked completely at a loss as to what to do next.

"Claire, is everything all right?"

"Oh yes, yes indeed. Never better! It's just that . . . well . . ." She looked over her shoulder one last time before turning around and leaning forward. "*Clarry* is here," she hissed.

She paused in what might well have been a meaningful fashion, as if her words were meant to awaken something in me. Then I realised – Clarry must be one of her fecking spirits. Of all the times to start going on about this *craic*! I knew from experience that I'd have to humour her until she got out of whatever funk she was in, so I plastered a smile on my face.

"Ah, good old Clarry. I'd love to see her," I said. It felt like I was talking to a toddler about an imaginary friend.

"Really?" She lowered her voice. "You know you can tell me if you hate her guts. It might be a while since we last met, Tammy, but you were almost like one of my own before you and Alvin broke up and you fucked up my son for a long time afterwards. We can be honest with each other, can't we?"

"Em, yes." I swallowed, wondering if Claire's talk of honesty was about to spill into a barrage of recriminations.

But instead, she focused on Clarry again.

"I'm so angry that Clarry's here, upsetting the apple-cart just when I thought things were going to settle down! I've a good mind to put the run on her right now this minute!"

Bloody hell. Claire sometimes took against some of her spirits, and it was never easy to talk her down when she did.

"We won't let her upset anyone. Trust me, Claire, we'll keep her in line between the pair of us, okay?"

She looked at me with something approaching admiration in her eyes. "It sounds like you've toughened up since we last met, Tammy. That's no bad thing and was well needed, if you don't mind me saying so – you always let Adrienne get to you far too much years ago. Mind you, it sounds like you were pretty tough on my Alvin when you two split, refusing to have any contact – but lookit, there's no point in going down that road now, is there?"

"No," I said as firmly as I could.

"Right, you better come in so." Claire stepped back to let me in.

I walked into the hall, inhaling the familiar smell of old wallpaper and the marijuana-scented incense sticks that Claire burned all day, every day, which apparently inspired her tarot readings. As we walked through to the kitchen, I wondered how the hell this situation was about to play out. Was I supposed to start talking to this non-existent Clarry person? Was she meant to be standing in front of me right now or something? For a few seconds, I even wondered if it was possible that Claire was pulling my leg to see how I'd react – perhaps it was some sort of punishment for having ended things with Alvin, a kind of 'You needn't think you're going to just walk back in here again without dealing with me first' sort of thing – but that just didn't seem like something that would be Claire's style.

The unmistakeable smell of a barbeque filled the kitchen through the open door to the garden. I glanced out the window and didn't spot Alvin or anyone else, but I knew that was because Claire's decking area and outdoor seating was to the side of the house. For feng shui reasons, she liked to look out her window and see nothing but greenery. Whenever Alvin or Adrienne had a bone to pick with her or really wanted to piss her off, all they'd have to do was randomly dump one of the outdoor chairs between two of the trees to induce a full-scale hissy fit. It usually backfired when Claire had to burn several handfuls of lavender incense to calm herself down and they ended up choking like people who'd been caught in a house fire but, according to Alvin, it always seemed worth the pain at the time.

Adrienne's head bobbed past the window. I sighed and waited for the inevitable onslaught of thinly veiled abuse. She'd been named after Adrian in the *Rocky* movies. Her parents had had the decency to give her a more feminine spelling to her name, but the fighting association was bang on for her as she'd start an argument with the Dalai Lama. She'd been damn lucky she was a she – they'd been planning on calling her Apollo after Apollo Creed in *Rocky 1* if she had been a he. If it had been anyone else but Claire, they probably wouldn't have gone through with that plan once the baby was born – but, with Claire, you just knew anything was possible. As for Alvin's name, they'd just taken a fancy to calling him that because Claire had always loved the name.

"Tammy!" Adrienne burst into the kitchen with a huge smile on her face. "I was delighted when Mum told me you'd be calling around today!"

Oh, okay. This was new, this heavy-sarcasm effort.

"Adrienne. I've missed you." Two could play that game.

"You probably have too. It's always great to live vicariously through more exciting people, isn't it? Shall we pop the lid on a bottle of sparkling water and I can tell you about all the travelling I've done over the last few years?"

Cow. Adrienne always managed to get a dig in about my relatively clean-living lifestyle. She smoked forty fags a day, drank at least a two-litre bottle of Diet Coke daily and rarely went a day without getting at least one glass of wine in there somewhere. And she still looked better than me for it. Bloody genetics. As for her travelling, I was so terrified of flying that I wasn't one bit envious of it. I didn't even bother replying.

"Did you buy that new mop you were talking about, Mum?" Adrienne said to Claire as she crossed the room and sat down at the kitchen table. "I have a feeling you're going to have plenty of shit to clean up in approximately . . ." – she looked out at the two heads that were currently passing by the window – "five seconds."

Alvin immediately looked shifty when he walked into the kitchen and took in my presence. His eyes flicked to a glass zodiac clock on the wall. "Tammy, you're here . . . I lost track of time, sorry."

"She's early! Stop apologising to her!" Adrienne snapped.

It looked like things were going back to normal with Adrienne then. I suppose I would have been sucked into engaging in our usual rounds of insult flip-flopping if I wasn't so mesmerised by the presence of the striking woman who followed Alvin into the kitchen. She was one of those lustrous-hair types that you couldn't miss, purely because her hair was vomit-inducingly amazing. It was long, chestnut, thick and glossy, with a set of perfect waves that you usually saw only in a L'Oréal ad, and complemented her tanned skin perfectly. The rest of her was pretty okay too but, with that hair, her other bits didn't need to be anything above average for her to be someone who turned heads. And boy, did I know from experience all about her turning heads.

Clarry. It was bloody Clarissa! What the hell was *she* doing standing in Alvin's mother's kitchen as if she owned the place?

16

Clarissa and I had a long and uneasy history. My initial encounter with her was in my first year in college when we were both studying English. She used to deliberately wait until everyone else had walked into the lecture room and had taken a seat before she'd waltz in, determined to make an entrance. She'd glance around to see who was looking at her before eventually plonking down beside some poor sod who'd have to endure having Clarissa's waist-length chestnut mane flicked into his face for the duration of the lecture. The lecturer wouldn't have taken a breath to utter his first sentence before Clarissa would be in there asking questions, challenging the lecturer on everything from how poetry was going to help us all find jobs at the end of the course to whether Chaucer was really all that good at all when it came down to it. She got away with this because she had the confidence of a queen. Men loved her, girls hated her – but in a jealous, I wish-I-could-get-away-with-that type of way rather than a disdainful one, a type of hatred Clarissa seemed to relish. Nobody on my course – or rather, no female – was too sorry when we heard that Clarissa had dropped out. I welcomed the opportunity to erase her from my brain, and I never thought of her again until many years later when Alvin mentioned a new colleague of his at work.

"Just letting you know that I won't be around next Tuesday night – we've a work night out," he'd said the previous Wednesday over our dinner of potatoes. We weren't just eating potatoes – there was some veg and a bit of chicken on our plates too, but really they were just there for show and for us to convince ourselves that we were eating a healthy and balanced diet. Alvin loved potatoes more than any other man ever born, and refused to eat any dinner for which potatoes weren't a component. As a result, we had a seven-day menu with potatoes cooked in a different way as the main feature every night. Tonight's ones were baked, with lashings of butter for Alvin and just a teaspoon's worth for me.

"No bother. Bit of a dead night to be planning a work night out though, isn't it? There'll be nobody out on a Tuesday!"

"Oh, it's the brainchild of this new girl at work. She's only in the door and she's trying to revolutionise everything. This is her self-arranged 'welcome to the company' drinks night out, and it's harmless compared to the other changes she's been trying to impose."

"You never mentioned that they took on a new manager! What happened to Jamie?"

"Oh, they didn't. Jamie's still our manager. This girl is an instructor like the rest of us, but she's hell bent on making her presence felt."

"Sounds like a bit of a dose."

"And you sound like all of the other women I work with. They all hate her. I think it's because they're slightly

126

threatened by her though – she's a power to be reckoned with, this Clarissa."

Clarissa? No. Surely not . . .

"What does she look like?"

Alvin smiled benignly. "Ah, is this you being jealous? Should I be flattered?"

"No, you frigging well should not. I think I might know this girl. Is she about five foot eight and slim?"

"She's fairly tall, yeah, and it would be no harm for her to have a good feed of baked potatoes."

"Does she have Rapunzel-style hair that could whip the eye out of someone's head if she flicked it?" I couldn't imagine she'd cut it all that much – it seemed to be her trademark and, besides, it was just too gorgeous to cut.

Alvin shrugged. "Dunno. It's long. Very long."

"That'd be her all right." *Shit.*

It was ridiculous that I suddenly felt uneasy, but I did. Even though I knew by then that Alvin was devoted to me, I also knew Clarissa was the predatory type. Alvin was the best-looking guy in his company by a country mile – I might have been biased, but I knew I was right about that. In fairness, though, the number of staff working in the adventure company was very small and the competition was limited. You had Elliott, a skinny twenty-something who was physically very fit but somehow looked chronically emaciated. He had an unfortunate penchant for wearing tutus and always whipped one out of his bumbag towards the end of a night out. The first time I witnessed it on one of Alvin's team nights out, I wasn't sure if I found the tutu or the whole non-tourist-man-wearing-a-bumbag thing more shocking, but either way I was mentally scarred for days afterwards. He also had a proclivity for giving four cheek-kisses every single time he bumped into someone, despite the fact that Ireland wasn't France and, to the best of Alvin's knowledge, Elliott had never even been to France. Then there was Desmond. Originally from a rich family in London, he looked and sounded like he should have been rambling around some country manor shooting game instead of getting his boots dirty trekking through puddles on a peninsula, but a lifelong obsession with archery had led to a qualification in outdoor instruction. He was a confirmed bachelor and of no interest to a red-blooded female. And finally, we had Les, the oldest adventure-centre instructor in the world. He said he was fifty-two, but unconfirmed reports put him in his early sixties. It didn't matter, because he was the fittest man ever born. He did Croagh Patrick climbs for breakfast and only considered his yearly Mount Kilimanjaro climb worthy of the title of dinner. The man was a machine, but definitely not a sex god. And then you had my young, fit, gorgeous and trendy boyfriend. Call me paranoid, but . . .

Okay. Calm. The good news from my perspective was that she was a total in-your-face pain in the ass. This made me feel a little better for a few seconds, until bad news insisted on creeping into my head to even up the balance. One person's in-your-face pain in the ass was another person's strong, self-assured woman. And Alvin always saw the positives in people . . .

From that night onwards, it seemed like it was always Clarissa this and Clarissa that as we dissected our days over dinner. Like, I'd never guess what great idea Clarissa had come up with to make the challenge course even more challenging, or I'd have to see Clarissa's agility on the low-ropes course to believe it – that kind of thing. I somehow swallowed down any feelings of jealousy that could potentially overwhelm me and suffocate my relationship with Alvin if I let them, and thought I was great for managing that. But then the inevitable happened – I came face to face with Clarissa on one of Alvin's team nights out, and instantly became convinced that they were having the world's most torrid affair.

It was a Thursday evening and I'd gone into Dicey Reilly's in the city centre to meet Alvin, who was having a few drinks with his colleagues after they'd gone for dinner together. It was after nine when I got in. There'd been a five o'clock drama at work that had necessitated a call to the States to brainstorm a solution in time for the next day. The call had gone on for an hour and a half, and was followed by a post-call analysis meeting for the Dublin team in which we all tried to work out what the hell we'd just discussed. Nobody had a single brain cell left after a full day of manic work, which was somewhat of a problem. Eventually, we had a plan of sorts in place for the next day, and I managed to get to Dicey Reilly's only three hours later than expected. I was looking forward to seeing Alvin, even more so than usual after such a crazy day, but little did I know it would be hard to find him – and not because the pub was busy. I spotted Clarissa and her hair first. It was around then that I was sure my heart stopped.

I couldn't say Clarissa had been all over Alvin when I walked into the pub – that wouldn't have been fair. No, she was *on top* of him. On his lap. All that was visible of the Alvin I knew and loved was a pair of green combats protruding from underneath her shapely body. It was every one of my worst nightmares encapsulated in one horrible second of time, and I was sure I had just witnessed the start of the end of my relationship. Then I realised that she was only sidling across him in a bid to get back to her place on the couch and she was actually shuffling from one person's lap to the next on her way there. I say only, because it was far better than what I'd thought was going on – but still, surely they could have pushed the table out a bit?

Alvin spotted me, smiled and beckoned me over. My stomach flipped as I walked to the table, my eyes never leaving Alvin's face. Sometimes, I still found it hard to believe that he was actually mine. I said a general hello to everyone and squashed my way in. It was tight, but I managed to do it without giving everyone a brush of my rear end Clarissa-style. She gave me a disdainful look as I sat down between Alvin and Les.

"We meet again, Clarissa," I said to save Alvin going through the motions of the obligatory introduction.

"Do we?" She pulled a face. "Which of you own this one, then?" She looked from Alvin to Les.

Alvin took my hand. "Tammy's my girlfriend," he said with a welcome look of annoyance on his face at Clarissa's rude choice of words. I squeezed his hand gratefully.

"As if you really needed to clarify that," Les said with a laugh.

"We haven't met on one of these nights out," Clarissa said to me. "I didn't even know Alvin had a girlfriend."

I ignored the barb. "We know each other from English class in college. We had to do a Franz Kafka group project together, remember?"

She frowned. "No, not really."

"That'd be because you only showed up to one of our meetings and left the rest of us to do the whole thing."

She shrugged. "I vaguely remember having a project to do, but I left that awful course shortly afterwards so it wasn't an issue."

"It was for the three of us left to do four people's work." I was getting sucked in and I knew I shouldn't, but I didn't believe for one second that she didn't remember me. She was just trying to be a bitch and doing a very good job of it too.

"A drink, Tammy!" Desmond said, his voice several octaves higher than usual – and that was saying something. "You're gasping for a drink, I'm sure."

"You had to fecking ruin it," Elliott hissed as Desmond got up to get me a drink. Elliott was renowned for his love of a good row.

Clarissa spent the rest of that evening bringing up work stories with the gang. From where I was sitting, it was a blatant attempt to exclude me. I had her pegged as someone to keep an eye on from the second I heard her name mentioned, but from that night onwards, her cards were well and truly marked.

Alvin was having none of it though.

"Do you know that Clarissa fancies you?" I dropped into the conversation one night over thinly sliced fried potatoes.

"Oh yeah, of course I do," he said without looking up, seemingly engrossed in the important task of spearing his food.

"Really?" I'd expected him to be all self-deprecating about it! "And does that bother you?" I chose my words carefully.

"Of course not. Why, does it bother you?"

"Well . . . maybe . . ."

He kept a straight face for a few more seconds before bursting out laughing. "Relax. I'm only teasing. Of course she doesn't fancy me!"

I wasn't placated. "You didn't sound too surprised

131

when I asked you if she did though. Is it something you've wondered about before? That she might fancy you?"

"No, but I was warned by the lads that we might have this conversation. All of their partners met Clarissa before you did because they all went out last weekend when we were at my cousin's engagement party, and they all said exactly the same thing as you – that she fancied them. Even Desmond's boyfriend thought it. That's just Clarissa's way, Tammy – she likes to look like she's everyone's best buddy."

"Jesus, what is she trying to prove? Talk about childish!"

"Don't pay a bit of notice to her. I don't think she means any harm. Maybe she was neglected when she was a child or something."

"She looks pretty good for someone who might have been neglected in their formative years." I threw the subject of Clarissa's looks out there to see what Alvin's reaction would be, and watched him closely as I said the words.

"I suppose. She doesn't look like she has lifelong scurvy or rickets anyway," he said through his last mouthful of potato. "Any more fried spuds left in the pan?"

I knew a fob-off when I heard one, but I let the matter drop and decided to just keep my eyes and ears open. And although Alvin knew I wasn't a Clarissa convert after how rude she'd been to me in the pub, it didn't stop him from thinking she was a decent enough skin behind her brazen exterior and he continued to drop her name into the conversation over our evening spuds. I filed every single mention away for analysis, not wanting to seem like a paranoid android by saying too much to Alvin but determined that I wouldn't miss the signs if there were some there.

Nine months later, Alvin told me that Clarissa was leaving the adventure centre to go travelling. She was going backpacking around South East Asia and had no definite return date in mind – that was, if she decided to return at all. But now, here she was in Alvin's mother's kitchen, looking better than ever with a healthy sun-kissed glow in tow. It was the third time she'd been an unwanted visitor in my life, only this time I wasn't sure if she was going to be a visitor or a long-term resident – something told me that her presence was about to cause big trouble. And if she was a long-term resident, was that going to make me the visitor in Alvin's life?

17

Questions raced through my head, but I said nothing. I was already feeling at enough of a disadvantage without flapping my mouth around the place like a demented goldfish, firing out questions I shouldn't have had to ask. What the hell was Alvin playing at?

"Clarissa just arrived earlier. Unexpectedly." He gave her a look that I couldn't quite read.

"Just in the area, were you?" I said when she didn't follow up Alvin's statement with any words of her own.

"I'm home from Australia for a few weeks and wanted to catch up with this man." She threw an arm around Alvin's shoulders. "After living with him for the past year and a half, I kinda miss him when he's not around."

The significance of her words thudded against my brain. He'd told me he lived with two other Irish people in Australia, but he'd omitted to mention that one of them was Clarissa! What exactly did this mean? Surely they weren't together? No . . . Alvin wasn't the type of guy who'd chase after his ex if he was seeing someone. But that didn't mean nothing had ever happened between them . . . A surge of nervous adrenaline made my stomach jolt at the thought of it.

Alvin looked uncomfortable. "Clarissa moved to Australia after her travels, and she sorted me out with a place to stay when I landed."

Clarissa smiled. "And he liked it so much that he's still there over a year and a half later."

"It's time for tea!" Claire muscled in on the conversation. "I have green, white, black, ginseng, cinnamon, Oolong, chamomile, jasmine –"

"Any Barry's or Lyons?" Clarissa said rather curtly.

Claire looked confused. "No, sorry."

"I'll stick to water," Clarissa said.

"No wonder you've got such great skin," Adrienne said to Clarissa.

I was somewhat taken aback – Adrienne wasn't one for either compliments or for being overly friendly with other women. From what Alvin had told me, she didn't really have many friends and didn't have much interest in having them either.

But then she said "Don't you think her skin is amazing, Tammy?" and I realised she was just trying to goad me into a frenzy of jealousy. She could have saved herself the hassle, because I was doing a great job of that all by myself.

I muttered a "Mmm" and looked at the floor.

"Any tea for you, Tammy? I have a new brand of Pu-Erh tea that you'll love."

"That shite? I knew you never liked Tammy," Adrienne said.

"That Pu-Erh costs a fortune! I only share it with people I hold in very high regard!"

"She bought it years ago when Posh Spice was on it,

but she hated the taste of it and has been trying to foist it off on anyone she thinks is daft enough to drink it ever since," Adrienne drawled. "She can't bring herself to throw it out because it cost twenty quid. There's one born every minute –"

"Adrienne, leave it," Alvin said, frowning at his sister.

"Don't mind her, love," said his mother. "Will you have a cup, Tammy?"

"I'm fine, thanks, Claire."

I wasn't, though. My stomach was starting to churn, as it always did when I felt really upset about something. Clarissa's appearance now reminded me of her presence when things between Alvin and me were at their absolute worst. That, coupled with the doubt as to whether or not they'd been together in Australia – or were together now – was taking my stomach to places I didn't want it to go to.

"Oh no, sure you'll have one cup anyway!" Claire fussed around the kettle as if that would make it boil quicker. "It makes you lose weight, you know!"

"Only because it gives you a dose of the shits," said guess who. "Or worms. Or both."

"Not that you need to lose weight, of course," Claire said, far too late. Clarissa was already grinning her head off.

A menacing gurgle emanated from somewhere in my stomach region. It wasn't a hungry gurgle.

"Claire, I'm really sorry but I'm going to have to go. I'm not feeling well at all."

Claire's eyes instantly flicked to Clarissa. I knew what she was thinking – that Clarissa's presence had intimidated me into leaving. Maybe if she consulted her tarot cards later they might be able to tell her the truth, but there was no way I was going to announce that I had a nervous stomach upset while Adrienne and Clarissa were in the room.

"Are you okay, Tammy? Do you want me to drive you home?" Alvin said.

"No."

He tried to approach me, but I put a hand up to ward him off. I was glad I hadn't so much as taken off my coat because it was time for me to make a swift exit. "Thanks for the invite, Claire, and sorry about this," I said as I scuttled out into the hall in the most undignified manner imaginable and ran out the front door.

I felt better as soon as the fresh air hit me and made it to my car without vomiting. I put the windows down and breathed deeply, praying that concentrating on driving would divert my stomach from the sickening fact that it looked like all my hopes of a reunion with Alvin were about to come to nothing.

18

After I'd driven away from Claire's house, my stomach had begun to settle as I put some distance between myself and the scene of my distress. I knew Statler and Waldorf would be waiting in their usual balcony seats to boo me at home and, as I felt like a Muppet already, I didn't need their heckling (plus Simone would blame it all on the hot water and lemon and say it was good enough for me, for trying to be healthy), so when I reached Donnybrook, I just kept driving.

I headed northside, with no particular destination in mind. As I drove through Clontarf, I saw Bull Island ahead and decided on a whim to take a right onto the narrow wooden road bridge to access the island. I'd always loved the rose garden in nearby St Anne's Park and had frequently dragged Alvin for walks there followed by a trip to Bull Island, so it was familiar territory and one that I knew I loved. It was said to be five kilometres long and one kilometre wide, and had a beautiful sandy beach that ran the entire length of the island.

I parked up and made my way to the beach. As it was a cold day, it wasn't overly busy. There were a few power-walkers, joggers and dog-walkers, but most people who were interested in conducting those activities today were walking the nearby Clontarf prom instead. There were days for the beach and this wasn't one of them, which made it perfect for the quiet musing I fully intended to do. That, or obsessing. I wasn't sure yet which way this was going to go.

I sat on a large rock facing the sea and stared absently at a ferry making its way into Dublin port, trying to look at the situation I'd just experienced at Claire's as logically as I could. If I was truthful, I had to admit that I'd always been jealous of Clarissa. She was attractive, a brilliant flirt and worst of all Alvin had always seemed to really enjoy her company. She'd been heavily involved in his life right around the make-or-break time in our relationship, and I'd been convinced she was interested in him and would try to capitalise on the growing crevices in our underpinning. Initially, I'd had enough faith in Alvin, and in us, to believe that even if Clarissa did make a move, he'd never respond to her advances. As time went on and things got worse and worse between us, I couldn't help but worry that our problems were driving him into her arms. But then she'd moved away, and I was too taken up with dealing with our issues to give her another thought. I believed that that was the end of her in my life.

I suppose it was safe to assume that going to Australia after South East Asia had been a natural progression. I'd never done the South East Asia/Australia travelling myself because of my woeful and all-consuming fear of flying, but it was a rite of passage for a lot of young people in the early noughties. I trawled through the cobwebs of my memories of the time when Alvin and I had been struggling, and remembered that Clarissa had moved away a few months before we'd broken up and he'd gone to Australia, which meant that she mustn't have stayed in South East Asia for long before moving to Australia herself.

And then another horrible thought hit me. Had Alvin moved to Australia specifically to be with her? Had he been in contact with her and she'd invited him over to live with her as a way to escape his problems here, ostensibly offering him a shoulder to cry on but really just using his situation as an excuse to get her claws into him? Or worse still, had I been right all along and had something been going on between them? Maybe he'd been hugely relieved when we'd broken up, as it would have given him a chance to be with her . . .

I wasn't sure if this was logical or hysterical thinking, but either way I was starting to feel sick again. My thoughts turned to what Alvin had said about us needing to talk about what had gone on for us over the last year and a half. Was that what he'd meant? That something had happened with Clarissa? But if so and it hadn't worked out, why were they still living together? It would be extremely difficult to live platonically with someone you'd been seeing. There was, of course, always the possibility that they really were just good friends and he'd moved in with her in Australia just because he'd known her – but in my experience, the best-case scenario was rarely true.

But then common sense came to join the party. If they were together, why had he come back to me when Clarissa was very obviously in Ireland too? Alvin had never been a bastard, and I knew in my heart that he'd never do something blatantly disrespectful to any woman. Anyway, we had arrangements for the entire duration of his holiday – if he was with Clarissa, she'd be questioning where he was for all of that time. But even if she was just coming to lunch as a friend, why hadn't he warned me she would be at his house today? He knew I didn't like her, and yet he let me walk into a rabbit-in-the-headlights scenario that his sister clearly enjoyed witnessing . . .

My phone chimed and vibrated. When I looked at the screen, I saw that the only person who could answer all of the questions that were rolling around my head was ringing. I hesitated; I wasn't sure if speaking to him right now was such a good idea. I was bound to blurt out everything that was going through my mind and then wish I hadn't afterwards. I knew myself well enough to realise that I needed time to talk myself down before asking any questions that I'd live to regret.

I set my phone to silent and got up to pace up and down the beach. I walked for hours until the day started to draw in and the darkness of dusk caused me to be the only remaining guest on the sparsely populated island. As I drove home I surmised that although I'd worked very little out, I'd realised that my only course of action now was to stay calm and see what explanation Alvin could offer. He was no longer my boyfriend for me to be staking claims on him, and regardless of the uncertainty surrounding the status of our relationship, I knew he wasn't someone who treated people's feelings lightly. I would wait and see what he had to say before panicking further. And then, if I found out that something had gone on or was going on with Clarissa – then, and only then, would I have a meltdown.

I found a tinfoil-covered plate on my doorstep when I got home. I lifted the tinfoil and saw a plate of lamb, cabbage, mung beans and quinoa on the Capricorn plate from Claire's set of delph.

It still wasn't the right time to call Alvin, but I walked into my house feeling slightly warmer inside than before.

19

Looking back, it was easy to pinpoint the moment that would mark the beginning of the end for Alvin and me. We'd been living together for three months when it occurred and things had never been better between us, and I'd gone into work the previous day full of the joys of life. That was just as well, because if ever there was a day to be a workaholic, this was it. Work was absolute madness. Our contingent of colleagues from the States had arrived in our offices that morning, all five of them super-psyched to be in Dublin and waxing lyrical about how much they were looking forward to that day's set of presentations and brainstorming meetings. I say that day's because there was another set of them lined up for the next day, most of which I had organised and co-ordinated at Malcolm's request – just like today's set.

Not only did I have two jam-packed days of activities to organise, but evening entertainment had to be provided too. As soon as we finished our day's work sometime around six that evening, our HR team and our visitors were going en masse to a Michelin-starred restaurant *downtown. Although I was all for work and was buzzing from all that I had to organise, the heavy schedule would make the coming weekend even more sweet, when Alvin and I would be carrying out the first item on our list – the Irish road trip, Destination Anywhere.*

I was at my desk in the office at six that morning. I completed three glorious hours of uninterrupted work before the office started to go mad. We had three meetings back-to-back from nine to twelve before a reprieve of a half an hour, ostensibly to eat but really for everyone to check their emails in case the world had fallen apart while we weren't at our desks. Thankfully, I wasn't too interested in eating anyway. My period was due the next day, and judging by the cramps that were working their way around my stomach region, it was working its magic slightly early.

My mobile phone vibrated frantically in my handbag as I replied to an email, carried out an instant-messaging conversation and spoke to an IT colleague on my desk phone about an application that I needed for my presentation that afternoon that was no longer working. Ten seconds after my mobile rang off, the vibrations started again. The calls went on and on for the ten-minute duration of my attempt to explain to IT why my computer wouldn't open the application I needed. Of course, the minute IT had taken control of it, it had worked perfectly.

When I eventually hung up and started work again – upon which the application froze and gave me a 'Not responding' message – my desk phone rang again. The number was reception. Reception never rang me. I sighed before picking it up, wondering how fast I could get off the phone and get back to work. My to-do list had expanded from thirty to fifty over the course of the morning.

"*I have a call from a man called Dessie to transfer to you,*" *Helga in reception said.*

"*Dessie?*" *I said. The only Dessie I knew was my father.*

I whipped my phone out of my bag. Ten missed calls. The home landline.

"*Thanks, Helga.*" *Oh God. Something was wrong. Something really big. Dad never rang me at all, never mind at work.*

"*Dad? What is it?*" *I said as soon as Helga transferred him.*

"*Well, that's a lovely hello. 'How are you, father dear? How is the man that gave me life?'*"

I relaxed a bit – he sounded okay. "*I thought there was a problem when I heard it was you.*"

"*That's nice. You get a call from your father and assume there's a problem? What if I just wanted to say hello? Although as it happens, we do have a problem. It's your mother.*"

"*What? She's not sick, is she?*"

"*Oh God no. Healthy as an ox. No, it's much worse than that. It's about her age.*"

"*What about it?*"

"*It has increased.*"

I was flummoxed. "*Dad, we're all getting older every day.*"

"*It's increased a lot. Try a year.*"

Things still weren't any clearer. "*But everyone gets a year older on their birthday . . .*"

"*Her birthday isn't until tomorrow, Tammy! Don't tell me you thought it was today? Holy Jaysis, you can't even remember the birthday of the woman who brought you into the world!*"

I thought he was taking credit for that one. "I know when her birthday is."

"Well you should have told me then, because I didn't. No, that's not true – I knew her birthday, but not her age. She's a year older than I thought she was!"

"What?"

"Did you know about this, Tammy? Tell me the truth if you did. I'm not angry – I'm quite amused at it all, truth be told."

"No! I have no idea what you're talking about!"

"Let me tell you so."

I heard shuffling in the background.

"Wait a second now. I'm just moving in to the armchair in front of the fire."

"Dad, no – you can tell me another time, I'm in a bit of a rush here . . ."

"Nobody is ever too busy for their family." There were two clunks as his shoes hit the carpet. "Now. Actually, no, wait a second. Where did I leave my cup of tea?"

I covered the phone while I exhaled deeply. "I'm sure it's on the coffee table in the hall, Dad. Where you usually leave it."

"Hang on there now and I'll tell you. Well, will you look at that – there it is!"

"Dad . . ."

"Yes, yes. Give me a second. I want to have a sup of this."

I held the phone out from my ear as he took a long slurp of his tea.

"Ah, that's lovely. Nothing like a cuppa. Right, let's get on with this – I haven't got all day. Yes, I fell asleep in front of the fire last night and when I woke up, your

mother wasn't in the sitting room. I could hear her beavering away at the dishes in the kitchen so I got up to see if there was any chance of getting a cup of tea. I heard her yapping as I walked through the sitting room towards the dining room and for a second I thought she was talking to herself, then I heard Patty. I decided I wouldn't bother going out for the tea then – I'm not talking to Patty, remember?"

"Em, no. . ."

"Did I not tell you about this? She fell out with me last month when I asked her if she'd put dog food in a shepherd's pie she served up when we were around to visit. She won't wear her glasses, you see – too vain – and she gives half of the tin to the dog at a time and keeps the other half in the fridge, and sure didn't she take a plate of raw mince out of the fridge just after she served up our dinner and put it on the floor for the dog – anyone with any sense would ask the same thing . . ."

I tried to open my presentation on the PC while Dad rambled on, only to be informed that the application I wanted to use needed to be re-installed.

"So I stopped in my tracks at the dining room door and was about to sit down again when I heard Patty say to your mother: 'So, sixty tomorrow!' She burst her arse laughing – you know that evil laugh Patty has when she has one up on someone?"

"Mmmm," I said vaguely. It wouldn't do to agree. Agreement could mutate into 'Tammy thinks your laugh is pure evil too' the next time Dad and Patty had one of their puerile arguments. It was ironic that we were talking about growing older when it was this lot who were involved.

"And sure you and I know that your mother is meant

146

to be fifty-nine tomorrow. Then Patty said 'If only Dessie knew. Hoodwinked for forty-one years!' and was off with the cackling again. The guts of what they were saying amounted to this – your mother was nineteen when she met me, but she convinced me she was eighteen! And there's no point in saying that I must have got it wrong, because I confronted her last night and she admitted everything."

"Why would she do that?"

"Sure hadn't she been caught red-handed when I'd overheard everything and was able to repeat the conversation word for word?"

"Why would she lie, Dad? About her age?"

My colleague Samantha gestured frantically over the desk partition to my left and pointed to a printout of meeting minutes I'd typed up earlier that day and sent around by email. We all had to take a turn at doing them, even the senior personnel.

"Sorry, Dad, can you hold on there for a minute?" I covered the mouthpiece. "Yes?" I said as haughtily as I could. Surely whatever it was could wait?

"Just letting you know that although you typed up my point about needing to get the suggestions for the new HR project management mini-team name back by Friday – at least five suggestions per person – you forgot to write that we want something more imaginative than alliteration. No 'Tiger Team' or boring names like that, you know?"

I hadn't forgotten. I just hadn't deemed it important enough to bother including. "Not now, Samantha," I said, then waved her away. "In fact, not ever. It's not significant enough."

She shrank back into her seat, looking a bit wounded. I'd usually feel bad about that, but today wasn't a usual day at the office. Besides, I never took personal calls even though everyone else in the office did, including Samantha, and I wasn't going to be intimidated by a colleague on the one occasion that I did.

"Sorry, Dad, I was rudely interrupted there," I said, loud enough for the whole floor to hear. "You were saying?"

"You need to get an office, Tammy. Are you sure you weren't lying about that promotion a few years ago?"

"Open plan policy."

"Too cheap to pay for private office spaces, more like."

"Mum lying about her age!" I prompted. "Why?"

"Ah, it's kind of nice. Remember we told you we met at my local dancehall in Kildare when we were eighteen? Well, your mother was so tall that she looked a good bit older than eighteen – about twenty-six, if I'm honest – and she said she didn't think I'd be interested in her if I thought she was a year older than me. Bit paranoid about looking so old before her time, you see. But it's stood her in great stead over the years – she's aged mighty well. Very classy, very elegant, isn't she?"

"She is."

"She needn't have worried, of course – sure I thought she was the bee's knees from the minute I clapped eyes on her – but she warned all of her brothers and sisters to say nothing to me about her age, ever. Sure there's so many of them in that family that half of them wouldn't even know her real age anyway. Take her brother Mossie, for example. Sure if it doesn't score a goal, he's not interested in it, whatever it is – poor Mossie never took much notice of what was going on around him except the football . . ."

"Dad –"

"*Your poor mother was mortified when she had to tell me all of this last night, but I think it's a howl. She's a gas woman.*"

"*It's a great story, Dad, but could we possibly continue talking about it later? I'm so busy here.*"

"*Sure I haven't even got to the good bit yet. The party.*"

"*What party?*"

"*The one you're going to arrange. You'll have to get your skids on though . . . tomorrow night isn't all that far away, and you know how fussy your mother is . . . she'll want the best of everything for her 60th celebrations.*"

He had to be bloody joking! "*What?*"

"*Well, you hardly think we can leave an occasion like this unmarked, do you? It's her 60th, for heaven's sake!*"

"*But there's no way I'll be able to organise everything by tomorrow night! That's madness! We'll have a party for her next weekend – that'll give everyone a bit of notice, and –*"

"*Sure what use to anyone is a party the week after their birthday? It's like giving someone pancakes on Ash Wednesday. Her birthday is tomorrow, so the party is tomorrow. Simple as that.*"

"*But Dad –*"

"*'But Dad' nothing. Did your mother ever give you a birthday party a week after your birthday?*"

"*That's not fair. If I'd known it was her 60th, then I'd obviously have organised a party –*"

"*You have all day to organise it. Look, I have every faith in you – no bother to you. Sure don't you spend all day troubleshooting and innovating and all the rest?*"

There was no way out of this, not if I wanted to get a scrap of work done for the rest of the day anyway.

"I'll see what I can do," I said wearily.

"Ah, good girl. Make sure now you get a nice venue with decent catering, all right? Oh, and Baked Alaska for dessert for everyone."

"Baked Alaska! This isn't a wedding!"

"Your mother loves Baked Alaska. It's her 60th. She'll have Baked Alaska. Now, off with you and get started on the phone calls."

I hung up quickly before I said something I'd live to regret.

Dad was right. There was no point in moaning about this – it was time to take action and start the phone calls. I picked up my mobile and left the office.

"Hello?"

"Alvin? I need you to do me a teeny-weeny favour . . ."

20

"Oh, my goodness!"

Mum seemed genuinely taken aback when Dad led her into the hotel conference room and she was greeted with a sea of faces shouting "Surprise!" with drink-fuelled volume. Of course, everyone else had been when they'd heard they were unexpectedly attending her 60th party, so why should she be left out on the surprised score?

"I dare you to let me do the food shopping this week." Alvin had said a few nights previously. "I don't have a thing to do in this house. Doesn't the feminist in you object to that? I mean, what would Simone say?"

"Simone understands that I'm a militant control freak when it comes to running the house," I replied. "Doesn't the chauvinist in you enjoy having the woman running the house?"

"Seriously, Tam, I know I'm not an organised person by nature like you but you can still pass over stuff to me whenever you need to, okay? I might actually shock you."

He had. Alvin had performed miracles. In an eight-hour organisational extravaganza, he'd whipped out my contacts book and rung a list that I'd emailed to him of Mum's friends and relatives to see who was available the following evening. He'd then contacted ten local hotels and haggled with each and every one of them to get a good price for a function room and food for the thirty-four people who'd said they were free to attend. When he'd chosen a hotel, he spent a half an hour arguing with the restaurant manager about getting Baked Alaska on the menu – apparently nobody eats it any more, and he wasn't sure if his chef even knew how to make something so completely passé. He'd eventually succeeded, but he had no time to celebrate his success – he was too busy ringing back each of the guests to inform them of the location.

He'd also pulled a band out of some great big hat, a three-piece sibling effort consisting of Larry, Gary and Harry. The Harry in question was a Harriet, who according to Alvin looked like she was stuck in an eighties country-music time warp in her picture on the band's website, and even spoke with a Nashville twang in her County Meath accent when he rang her to suss the band out. She said they would belt out traditional numbers in the style of Christy Moore meets Tricia Yearwood – which sounded like my worst nightmare, and therefore the perfect choice. Mum and I had never liked the same music.

Three further calls from Dad had been routed through to my landline at work informing me of things that absolutely had to be put in place. Six bunches of roses, one for each decade Mum had been alive. Red roses only, mind – no yellow or pink. Oh, and could he stick them on my credit card, and he'd fix me up sometime? Then there was the call about the music. I'd have to make some compilation CDs up, naturally. The first one would have to be classical music, to be used to greet the guests as they arrived. The second was to be jazz, to be played as the guests ate their dinner and Baked Alaska. And the musical pièce de résistance was to be the dancing music after the band finished – traditional Siege of Ennis type of stuff mixed with country classics. The fact that I didn't possess any of that type of music meant that a busy period of downloading and burning lay ahead.

The third call was the biggest challenge. Mum didn't have a sweet tooth so much as an entire mouthful of them, and Dad was insisting that we bring out plates of chocolate bars after the Baked Alaska for all of the guests. But not just any chocolate bars, oh no. He wanted those little bars that you used to be able to buy for ten pence back in the eighties that now cost about fifty cent and were next to impossible to get.

"Honeybee bars, Time bars, Mint Crisps, Giggle bars, Macaroons," Dad had listed off.

When I was young, Mum used to bring me down to the sweet shop every evening after dinner to choose "something nice". The whole reason we made these trips was to satisfy Mum's sweet tooth under the guise of "bringing the child down for a treat". I didn't care about the whys and wherefores, though – all that mattered was coming out with a pawful of yummy stuff. To this day, I still remember the sense of anticipation as I ran through the door, savouring the dilemma that was ahead of me as my eyes devoured the rows of goodies. Drumsticks. Black Jacks. Fruit Salads. Giant chewing gums. Rolls of collectible stickers, some of which contained a coveted rare one that everyone was looking for to complete a collection. That shop would have been my perfect port of call if it hadn't been knocked to the ground years ago and replaced by anonymous-looking apartments. I wondered if anyone would mind if I called around and had a root through the basement apartment to see if there were still any old boxes of stock lying around from two decades ago (that stuff had a best-before end date of sometime around the year 3000), because that was about the only hope I had of getting the goodies he wanted – I hadn't seen that kind of stuff in years. I added the demand on to the list nonetheless, then promptly passed the three new things to do on to Alvin via text. I couldn't help but think that this was going to be the first "Fail" on his list.

It wasn't. There were no fails whatsoever. The entire night was the Carlsberg experience of surprise parties. The turnout was big enough to make Mum feel she was loved, but not so big that you'd be queuing all night at the bar for a pint. The dinner was delicious and plentiful, but the portions weren't so big that nobody had room for dessert. The band turned out to be around the same age as Mum and Dad (the picture on their website having been taken several decades ago, it came to light), so they were totally in tune with Mum's friends' choice of requests. The younger people, of which I suppose I was one, were kept so entertained by Harry's incessant wig-changing at the side of the stage that the awfulness of the music from our perspective became entirely irrelevant. Assembled family members actually spoke to each other. A first for a family gathering for us, no doubt about it. And, best of all from Mum's point of view, everyone was talking about how great the Baked Alaska was. There were whispered conversations about it in adjoining toilet cubicles by two of Mum's best frienemies who vowed to get the recipe before the night was out.

Alvin was really going to be flavour of the month after all of this. He wanted me to say that I'd organised everything, but I'd explained to Dad earlier about how *busy I'd been at work and that it was Alvin who pulled the night together. I was far too proud of him to take the credit for all of his hard work.*

I walked up behind Alvin and put my arms around his waist. "You've played a blinder with this," I whispered in his ear.

He twisted his body around and kissed my forehead. "If I have, it's because I've learned from the best."

"Maybe we should jack in our jobs and set up an events-management company?"

"God, no! All of this was fine as a once-off, and I enjoyed being able to organise something for you for once, but –"

"But you'd rather rip off toenails for a living than do something like this again?"

"Exactly. Thanks – you saved me having to spin the hell out of that there. It was – sort of enjoyable, I suppose, but this is your arena. You could organise ten of these a day by lunchtime. I'd be in the Irish Priory getting treated for nervous exhaustion tonight except I was curious about how this would all pan out."

"Well, I'll personally pay for you to get a taxi there first thing tomorrow morning after all the hard work you've done."

"No, you won't, because I have plans for you first thing tomorrow morning." He kissed my neck, leaving me in no doubt about what these plans of his were.

"Hmm, I'm not sure about that. I think my period will be here by the morning."

"Better make it an early night then . . ."

"If you think there's any hope of getting out of here early, you're mad. You organised a bar extension, remember? This lot will stay going until dawn, and there isn't a hope of us sneaking away unnoticed."

"Damn my efficiency. I always said it was a mug's game."

"Well, look, we have lots of fun ahead of us getting stuck into the list. I'm sure the Irish road trip might involve us staying overnight in a swanky hotel somewhere."

"Or better still, one of those old-fashioned B&Bs where you'd get the disapproving looks when you go down for the fry in the morning. There's no fry like a B&B fry."

I shook my head. "I owe you one after all of this, but I have some shame about having breakfast with a room full of people who have heard things they shouldn't have. It's a swanky hotel or the side of the road."

"Swanky hotel it is then. It's a tough life."

I saw my mother wobbling over our way, already the worse for wear. "And it's about to get tougher. I'd tell you to run and hide but I know she'd only hunt you down."

"Alvin! I must dance with the man who's behind this extravaganza of a night! Dessie filled me in earlier. Tammy, go get yourself drunk or something – you look far too sober, as always."

All I could do was smile as she dragged Alvin away and led him onto the dance floor. But the smile left my face fast as a sharp pain overtook my abdomen. This damn period was going to be a painful one by the looks of things. I went to the bathroom, and just as I entered a cubicle, another pain overtook me and caused me to double over.

And that's how the nightmare started.

21

When Alvin rang again shortly after I'd eaten his mother's dinner, I relented on my stance of not speaking to him until the following day and answered the phone. The more I'd thought about it since I came home, the more I believed there was a rational explanation behind all of this. If there was one thing I knew about Alvin, it was that he was fundamentally a good person. That fact didn't make me any less peeved with him, but he deserved a chance to explain all the same.

"Before you say anything, this is not what you think," Alvin said when I answered the phone.

"You're ringing to sell me insurance instead of explaining what today was all about?"

"Does an attempted joke mean you're not as mad or upset as I thought you were?"

"Do the words 'attempted joke' indicate that you didn't find my joke funny?"

"The hole that is today is just getting bigger and bigger, isn't it?"

"Go on. Hit me with your best explanation." I was

very proud of myself for managing to sound so breezy over something that I'd had a mental freak-out about earlier.

"Well, the only reason I didn't mention that I'm living with Clarissa in Australia when we were driving to Kinsale was because things were a bit tense and I really didn't want to say anything that would ruin things or give you the wrong idea. It's just never come up since and, really, it's of absolutely no consequence anyway. It's just like me living with some random woman except it's someone you happen to know."

"Did you go to Australia to be with her?" I said bluntly. My breeziness mask was slipping somewhat.

"No! She just happened to be there. I always wanted to go to Australia. You know that."

"Okay, fair enough." *Bit of a coincidence all the same.* "So what's the deal with her being over at yours today?" I tried to inject an appropriate degree of nonchalance into my question.

"Where do I begin . . . okay, here's the short version. Two months ago, Adrienne came over for a visit. She and Clarissa got on like a house on fire and have been Facebook friends since. Clarissa is only just home for her Christmas hols – she had something important on where she works and couldn't come home any sooner than a few days ago. When Adrienne found out she was back, she invited her over to ours for lunch today to catch up. Of course she didn't bother telling Mum or me. She arrived only about five minutes before you did, so I didn't get a chance to ring you and warn you."

"But surely Adrienne and Clarissa couldn't have struck up all that much of a friendship in the time she was over on holidays?"

"Well, apparently they have."

Something didn't add up. Did that mean Adrienne knew that Alvin was going to contact me when he came home? She must have – otherwise, why bother maintaining a friendship with Clarissa, a woman she'd only just met who lived in Australia? She would know very well that bringing Clarissa into the picture would cause trouble, and Clarissa had probably mentioned to her that she'd be home around Christmas. We'd been out on the town for her birthday shortly before we split up when she'd overheard us having a row about Clarissa, and she could barely conceal her delight. I imagined she'd been thrilled to meet the object of my jealousy in the flesh, and had probably shaken Clarissa's hand when Alvin wasn't looking. I couldn't really imagine Alvin telling her about trying to meet up with me though when he'd know that she'd have a negative opinion about it. It still didn't add up, but I was fairly sure that whatever her reasons were, they were related to causing trouble.

It was one thing thinking that but another articulating it. I was going to have to tread carefully.

"You and Clarissa seem to follow each other around," I said in what I hoped was a suitably jocular tone. "Australia, Stillorgan – where to next?"

"Tammy, you do know that there's nothing between us other than friendship, don't you? Between Clarissa and me, I mean."

I was glad he clarified his words. "Sure. I just got a surprise when I saw her, that's all."

"I would of course have warned you if I'd known she was going to be at our place. I'm sorry if you felt you had to leave because she was there –"

"No, it was just bad timing that I didn't feel well. I would have had to leave anyway."

Alvin said nothing for a while. "Okay. Well, I hope the

dinner helped – or that it didn't make you feel a hundred times worse. I don't even know what that thing that looked like slug-pellets was."

I laughed. "It was lovely, thanks. Tell Claire I'll make sure to give her plate back to you to give to her."

"I'll take it home with me after the next item – assuming you still want to do the next one? Are you okay about me living with Clarissa?"

Was I? Well, I'd prefer if he wasn't, of course, but he was and nothing was going to change that, me biting off my nose to spite my face included. And having spoken to him, I felt a lot better – but that being said, I was going to watch Clarissa. And Adrienne too. If there was any hope of Alvin and me working things out between us, the last thing we needed was two other women interfering.

"I'm on for the next one if you are, and yes, I'm fine about Clarissa." It was one of those situations where a white lie was called for.

We made arrangements for the next list item. But before I hung up, there was something I had to ask Alvin about, something that had been rattling around the back of my mind.

"Alvin . . . did you ever tell Adrienne about the stuff we went through?"

"Of course not. I promised you I wouldn't, remember?"

I did, and he had. "Sorry for asking."

After a long pause, Alvin sighed. "It still feels shit, doesn't it?"

I croaked out a "Yes", barely able to speak. It felt worse than shit. It was a form of torture to even remember it all, and yet no matter how much I'd tried to block it out each and every day over the last few years, it would creep into my daily thoughts somehow or other.

"I have to go," I said to Alvin. I'd held up well over the course of the conversation, and I wasn't going to ruin it all now by ending it with a bawling fit.

I hung up, feeling rude but somehow knowing he'd understand. And suddenly, him living with Clarissa didn't seem like such of an issue any more. All that mattered was us taking our chance to try to make things work out again and putting the past to rest.

Suddenly, I couldn't wait for our next list activity the next day.

22

Pre-parental plan activity 4: Spend a day watching
our favourite Christmas movies back-to-back

*You know me, Alvin. I'm going to be one of those parents who
don't want their kids to watch TV at all because I'll think there
are a million more educational things they could be doing. As
for you, you'll probably have them outside even if it's monsoon
weather teaching them how to swim in extra large puddles. But
if you cut out TV, you also deny your kids the delight of TV
movies – something that's always a huge treat at Christmas. I
know it will be a challenge for you to sit still for this, but let's
spend an entire day doing nothing but watching our favourite
Christmas movies, and let's try to remember what it was like to
feel young and innocent again. Eating a tin of Roses until you're
sick is optional.*

Hmm. A good choice on my part for a few years ago, but
I couldn't help thinking that it was a bit too cosy – and
hence awkward – for our present situation. It had, of
course, been an activity that we would have done at

Christmas time if things had gone to plan, but there was no law against watching Christmas movies in January either. My place had been designated the home cinema because we could hardly take over Claire's house for a twelve-hour period (avoiding Adrienne hadn't been a consideration, but it was definitely a bonus), but Alvin had never been to my house for a long period of time in the capacity of a friend and I imagined it was going to be very weird. I wasn't sure if we could even be classed as friends now or if there was a word to accurately describe this – thing – that was going on between us, but it wasn't going to end up in the bedroom as it always had before anyway. More's the pity.

At least I had the logistics sorted out. As always with that kind of thing, it made me feel much calmer to think about how everything was in place for the day ahead. We'd chosen three movies each, and Alvin's choices were *It's A Wonderful Life*, *National Lampoon's Christmas Vacation* and *Bad Santa*. I'd picked *The Holiday*, *Miracle on 34th Street* and *ET*. Although it wasn't the most seasonal movie in the world, Christmas was never Christmas for me unless I watched *ET* at least three times. I'd downloaded all the movies from a paid site on the Internet and uploaded them to the external storage drive that I'd just need to connect to my TV.

Jess and Simone had kindly agreed to stay with their parents for the night to give us some space. I was glad of the opportunity to have some breathing space from them both too, because Simone had found out that Jess was still seeing Ciarán and had hit the roof over it. She'd overheard Jess on the phone to Ciarán before Jess had had a chance to tell her, and had grabbed Jess's handset and screamed every obscenity imaginable down the phone at Ciarán.

The girls hadn't stopped arguing since. Although I didn't approve of Jess's choice, I'd decided to stay out of it. I'd told her that I believed she was going to get hurt from this and that she should walk away but, aside from that, I didn't think there was much else I could do or say to help. My plan was just to be there for Jess when the house of cards inevitably fell. Simone was annoyed with me for not getting more involved in saving Jess, but I in turn was annoyed with her for not seeing that her sticking her oar in wasn't helping Jess one bit either. We could talk to Jess all we liked, but she wasn't listening. This was one conclusion she was going to have to come to on her own.

The doorbell rang at ten. My stomach lurched in the best possible way when I opened the door to a smiling Alvin, holding a tin of Roses. His smile was irresistible. How was I meant to stay away from him when he was looking like that?

But there was just one little thing . . .

"Em, Al, did you forget to get dressed?"

"Nope. I never used to get dressed on Christmas Day when I was a kid because we always stayed at home, so I'm trying to get in the spirit of things."

He was wearing a grey granddad top and grey striped pyjama bottoms. And he looked . . . amazing. His brilliant physique and strong face somehow managed to make his loungewear look trendy. I always looked like a frumpy old maid in pyjamas. Bad luck had really whipped my ass by making me be caught in them when I opened the door to Alvin on New Year's Eve.

"You can join me if you like?"

"Ah, I'll pass, thanks. Come on in."

"I noticed the last time I was here that you got rid of the denim cushions," Alvin said as he walked into the sitting room. "And, Christ, the denim rug has gone too . . . what's become of this place?"

We both laughed. One year I went through an unfortunate denim phase that made my sitting room look like it had members of Bon Jovi embedded in my couch and wooden floors. It had seemed like a good idea at the time to look for something completely different and non-trend driven, but it had started to look naff very quickly.

"Well, you should see what I've done to the bedroom!" I said without thinking. I instantly turned bright red. Bringing Alvin up to my bedroom – the one that used to be our bedroom – would be just about the most stupid thing I could possibly do. "I mean . . . the kitchen!" I walked into the kitchen as fast as I could, hoping the colour in my cheeks would have faded by the time Alvin caught up with me.

"It looks . . . exactly the same, actually," he said when he came into the kitchen. He was right – the kitchen was one place in the house that never changed when I redecorated because it was just too damn expensive to do so.

"Right. Yes. Let's get stuck into the movies, shall we?"

"Just a second. Do you still store your Christmas decorations in the attic?"

A half an hour later, the Christmas decorations that had only recently been put away were up again in honour of us watching movies at Christmas as kids. My yearly artificial tree twinkled with icicle fairy lights that hung between the zigzags of tinsel that Alvin had hastily thrown on the tree while I'd affixed dangling glitter snowflakes to the ceiling. When we were finished I pulled the curtains and put National Lampoon's Christmas Vacation on. I tucked my legs under me in one of the armchairs, leaving Alvin the option of the couch, but he ignored it and sat in the armchair beside mine instead.

After the first movie, I brought in two plates of sandwiches before putting on *The Holiday*. We sat on the rug beside the coffee table as we ate. Most of the rest of the day flew by in a haze of James Stewart, Richard Attenborough, a cursing Santa and lots of shared smiles between Alvin and me that I couldn't quite interpret. He wasn't as restless as I'd thought he would be at being stuck indoors either. One chicken-and-chilli pasta dinner later, we were ready to watch *ET*.

I'd hummed and hawed about this one. I'd deliberately avoided anything too schmaltzy, because I didn't want to spend a day suffering through weepies as a single person with her ex in the room. The only reason I'd selected it was because there was no way I'd get away with not including it, as Alvin had been around for enough Christmases to know about the three-time rule. I'd forced him to watch it with me so many times in the past that it was going to be bittersweet to watch it together now.

"You okay?" I said when the movie ended.

Alvin looked quite upset, and I suspected it wasn't anything to do with *ET* going home.

He nodded, but not very convincingly.

"What is it?"

"Well . . . I've enjoyed today and watching the rest of the movies, but that one just brought me back."

"To good times or bad ones?"

"To good, of course. It wasn't all bad between us, you know." He sounded annoyed.

"The end was bad . . ."

"That's the second time you've said that, but what about what came before the end? Do you think I'd have started all of this if the rest wasn't worth it?"

"Okay, I'm sorry. Let's just drop it."

166

"I've a better idea. Let's talk about the end."

"Can't we just leave it? Today has been lovely and I don't want to ruin it . . ."

"Today is just a means for us to get to the point where we might be able to save this! How can we do that if we don't even talk?"

His phone rang. And he picked it up.

Well, you said you wanted to talk . . .

He frowned when he looked at it. "I'll just let that go to voicemail," he said. "I'm sure it's nothing too urgent."

The phone immediately rang again.

"Take it if you want," I said.

"It's just Clarissa – I can ring her back later."

Clarissa? What did she want? The phone stopped ringing. Alvin put it on the table. Within seconds, it was off again.

Don't take it, don't take it.

Alvin sighed. "I'll answer it just in case it's anything to do with Adrienne." He picked up the phone and pressed the answer key on the screen.

"Hi, Clarissa. Everything okay?"

I strained to hear Clarissa's words, but couldn't catch anything other than the tone of her voice. It sounded quite frantic.

"All right, calm down. I'll come and get you, okay? Yes, stay there . . . I'll meet you there." He hung up and turned to me. "Clarissa was waiting for a Nitelink home when a few fellas started giving her hassle. They asked her for money and, when she told them to get stuffed, they made a grab at her handbag."

"Is she okay? Where is she now?"

"She ran into a nearby pub and got away from them, but she's too afraid to come back out now and get a taxi in case

167

they're waiting for her. She asked me to go in to collect her and drop her home. Sorry to ruin the night, but . . ."

"No, you don't need to explain. As long as she's safe, that's the main thing."

"Yeah." He stood up and looked down at himself in his pyjamas. "I think I might be more harm than good to her going into town like this. I've got 'Beat me up' written all over me. You don't happen to have any spare clothes of mine here from before, do you?"

"No," I said more sharply than I'd intended to. "Sorry," I added. "I gave whatever you accidentally left behind to charity after you went to Australia. I hope you don't mind, but –"

"No, no, it's fine . . ."

"I would have posted them over, but . . . well, I didn't have your address, and I was going to drop them at Claire's, but –"

"Seriously, it's not a problem. You were never a hoarder anyway. It was a stupid question."

And so there we were again, trying to out-polite each other, all fluency between us gone astray.

"Okay, well . . . I'll call you," he said when I walked him to the front door.

"Yes. Let me know how Clarissa is later."

"Sure. I'll text you or something."

"Yeah. Okay."

"Bye then."

"Bye."

You knew this wasn't going to end up in the bedroom . . .

Things had suddenly grown so awkward that I should have been relieved when he walked out the front door, but a bad part of me was desperately willing him to stay as I watched him walk to Claire's car. Of course I didn't want

Clarissa to be in any danger, but that didn't make seeing him walk out the front door any easier. And then the bad part of me reared up again. Why was Alvin the first person she thought of when she was in trouble? Did she have nobody else to help her? What about the friends she'd been out with earlier – surely they hadn't just left her at a Nitelink on her own and, even if they had, they probably wouldn't have got very far on their journey home – surely they were closer to town than Alvin would have been?

"Tam?" Alvin looked up just as he was getting into his car.

"Yeah?"

"Sorry about leaving you so abruptly after the Mad Dogs' gig."

"Oh, that's okay." I hadn't expected that. Clarissa's appearance at Claire's house had knocked that discussion off the radar completely, and neither of us had raised it since.

"It's just . . . difficult, you know. Today has been too. I'm not used to being around you when you're not mine."

He didn't wait for a response from me, but got in the car and drove off immediately. I went inside to take down the Christmas decorations for the second time that year, my concern about competition from Rapunzel and my delight at what he'd just said taking the confusion of my relationship with Alvin to a whole new level.

23

"*Pregnant? I couldn't have been twelve weeks pregnant! I'm on the pill! I haven't missed any periods!*"

Nothing was making sense. One minute I was at Mum's party trying not to cringe as she led Alvin into an embarrassing hokey-cokey-style dance, and the next I was being told that I'd had a miscarriage. With some terrifying moments in between.

"*I understand this has come as a shock to you, Tammy,*" *the doctor said gently,* "*but I'm afraid there's no doubt about the fact that you were pregnant. Do you remember missing any pills, having any vomiting or diarrhoea, or did you take antibiotics that might have impacted the effectiveness of your pill?*"

"*I had to take antibiotics a few months ago for a kidney infection, but we took other precautions at that time,*" *I said, looking at Alvin. He nodded. I'd been militant about insisting on condoms, and he'd duly produced them whenever they'd been required.*

"*No method of contraception is foolproof,*" *the doctor said in what I imagined was his best diplomatic manner.*

"As for your periods, I suspect they were probably breakthrough bleeding. Did you notice any difference in your flow?"

"Well, yes." I explained to the doctor that when I'd gone on the pill shortly after meeting Alvin, I'd experienced bad nausea from it and I'd changed to the mini-pill after the first month. I'd experienced a lot of irregular bleeding since then, but I'd been warned by my GP that irregular bleeding was a possible side-effect. I hadn't considered that it might be anything other than that because we had practised safe sex at all times. Or so I'd thought.

I remembered thinking to myself that the periods were lighter than usual, and told the doctor as much. He nodded and scribbled some notes.

"Doctor . . . why did this happen? The miscarriage, I mean? Is it because I was still taking the pill because I didn't know I was pregnant?"

"There's no conclusive evidence to suggest that taking the pill while pregnant will harm a foetus. You must understand, Tammy, as many as one in four pregnancies end in miscarriage," he said softly.

And that was that. A life we hadn't known existed was over before it had begun. I was transported to a hospital bed in the middle of the night and Alvin was asked to leave. I fell into an exhausted sleep, too tired and dazed from the night's events to really think about what had just happened. But I knew that the thinking time would come.

When I woke up the next morning, Alvin was by my side.

"So, all of that really happened then," I said as I sat up in the hospital bed. "Jesus, Mum will never forgive me for ending her party before midnight. We'd barely wiped the

Baked Alaska meringue-moustaches off our faces before everything kicked off."

Alvin smiled, a rather sad smile that didn't suit his usually animated face at all. "I was talking to her a few minutes ago. She said to tell you she'll come in to visit you later today if they keep you in."

I nodded. "This is all a bit surreal, isn't it?"

"That's one word for it. Thank God you're all right though, apart from . . . well, you know."

Poor Alvin. By the looks of it, he still wasn't the better of the state he'd found me in when the haemorrhaging started after I went to the bathroom. I'd screamed at someone in the adjoining toilet to find him and tell him to come in immediately. He'd taken one look at me and called an ambulance.

"Twelve weeks. That means I've been – I was – pregnant for most of the time we've been living together," I eventually said after a long silence in which neither of us could find any words. "But I just don't understand how this could have happened in the first place. We used condoms every single time anything happened while I was on the antibiotics."

Alvin said nothing.

"What?" I eventually said. I knew by the look on his face that he was thinking something but wasn't sure if he should say it or not.

"Remember the night you had the hot whiskeys because you caught a head-cold on top of your kidney infection?"

"The medicinal hot whiskeys – yes, I remember them . . ."

"Do you remember much else from that night? Those medicinal hot whiskeys turned into a bit of a session, with me drinking them as well, as a preventative measure . . ."

"*Except yours were doubles,*" I said. "*Of course I remember what happened at the end of the night . . . but we were careful! I know we were!*"

Alvin paused for a long time. "*We were as careful as two drunk people usually are, which probably doesn't amount to being very careful at all.*"

"*We used protection, Alvin! I might have been drunk, but I didn't have a personality transplant! I'd never forget to use extra protection while I was on antibiotics!*"

"*We did use a condom, but . . . oh God, this is all my fault . . .*"

"*What?*"

"*Well, drunken sex can be messy sex, you know? I remember vaguely thinking at the time that – well, the condom didn't look one hundred per cent on when we finished . . .*"

"*So the condom was half off. I see. And you never thought to mention that at the time?*" *My voice was so deep and ominous that I barely recognised it.*

"*You wanted cuddles!*" *he practically screamed. In contrast to my voice, his was so high-pitched that it would have made me laugh if doing such a thing wasn't hugely inappropriate when you'd just been told what we'd been told.*

"*I could have got the morning-after pill if you'd told me! How could you not think it was something you should have mentioned?*"

"*I didn't really think for one second that anything had . . . escaped. It's only now that I know about the pregnancy that I'm thinking that maybe that's when it happened.*"

"*It must have been. That's the only time I was drunk, and I put on the condoms every single other time. I know they were on correctly." I bit my tongue to stop myself from uttering another thing. Saying what was on my mind would only make the situation worse, considering that it involved the words 'irresponsible' and 'eejit' – in that order. It was all very well for Alvin to go through life in a happy little 'Ah, it'll be grand' bubble but, as we'd just found out, things didn't always work like that. This was as far from grand as it got.*

"I'm sorry, Tam. We were drunk and I wasn't thinking straight . . ."

He suddenly looked so stricken that I was glad I hadn't laid into him. "We were both drunk, so we're both to blame," I conceded. "Granted, my drunkenness was therapeutic so I'm less to blame than you are, but I'm still in the mix all the same. Jesus though, Alvin, this is serious shit. We've lost a baby that we didn't even know was there."

He just nodded. He looked like how I felt – completely conflicted as to what I was actually feeling about all of this. A part of me thought I should be experiencing immense grief for the loss of a child, but I hadn't known it had been there to feel anything for it until it was gone. This line of thinking then made me feel immensely guilty for not being more upset. Something I knew I did feel, though, was a gnawing sense of fear for our future plans to have children. Why had I miscarried? Was something wrong with me?

My breathing grew slightly ragged. I took a few deep breaths and tried to rouse myself from my mental slump. It was amazing how every single occasion of feeling out of control dragged me down so much mentally, but this wasn't just any old occasion. An unplanned pregnancy was something I'd never visualised happening to me. Not in a million years.

I was let out of the hospital the next day. I had no idea what to do next except to go back to work on Monday and get on with my life. But I had a horrible feeling that it wasn't going to be that easy.

24

"Tammy, you have to read it!" Jess shrieked in our local wine bar, The Vine (we always referred to it as The Whine Bar though because of what we usually did there). One glass of wine was all it ever took for her volume to increase considerably.

"Do you not think I have enough problems at the moment without Simone catching me reading her money-saving strategies book?"

"All your problems will melt away as soon as you read Simone's penny-pinching ideas. They're just too funny!"

Jess was just getting into her stride of regaling me with tips from the book when Simone walked in. I shushed Jess just in time.

"What the hell are you doing here? Why aren't you off shagging Derek somewhere?" Jess yelled into Simone's face, loud enough for everyone in the bar to hear.

"Oh, God," was all Simone could say before she burst out crying.

The evening had started off so promisingly. When Jess baldly told Aunt Patty that Simone wanted a man, Simone had been terrified that Patty would come up with some diamond-jumpered type of fifty-something bachelor. Instead, she'd arranged a date for Simone with Derek, a young accountant at the firm Simone had worked for pre-redundancy that Simone had fancied the pin-striped pants off. In typical Dublin everyone-knows-everyone fashion, Patty was pally with Derek's mother Jemima. Derek's mother had been only too keen to talk her son into going on a date with her friend's daughter. Simone had always been far too reserved to ever do anything about her crush on Derek, and it turned out that he knew who she was even though they had never spoken – the company they worked for was a big one, just like Branda was – and he was willing to give the blind date a go as he was actively looking for a girlfriend, apparently. "Did you hear that bit?" Patty had said to Simone after she'd called around and filled the three of us in on all her hard work. "He's 'actively looking', Jemima said. That means you could have the ring on your finger after a few months!"

Simone threw her eyes up to heaven, but she looked excited. My heart twinged a little bit. I was in no position to feel sorry for anyone over the state of their love life, but poor Simone had had even less luck than me over the years. I recognised that look of hope on her face and prayed it wouldn't be dashed.

The rift between Simone and Jess thawed a little as the three of us had a chat together for the first time since Simone had found out about Jess still seeing Ciarán. Jess and I had rifled through Simone's wardrobe until we'd found something suitable for her date. Simone hadn't minded, admitting that she hadn't a clue what to wear. Patty had bought her loads of clothes over the last week or so, but Simone had deemed them too girly and had taken them all back. We hadn't exactly had a long rifle with the lack of variety on offer, but we managed to cobble together an ensemble that really suited her colouring and height – a slate-grey blouse under a silver cardigan, grey pinstripe trousers and peep-toe silver sandals. Admittedly, it was all a bit . . . grey, but it was the best we could do with limited resources. We should really have taken her shopping, but I'd been so busy with work and Jess had been away on a business trip earlier that week so we hadn't had time to cajole her into it. Hopefully things would go well on this date and we'd be able to do a tour of the shops at a later stage – and if she was in love, she might be more likely to spend some of her redundancy money on some much-needed clothes. None of her coats matched the outfit, but Jess talked her into risking pneumonia for the sake of looking good. And she had looked amazing earlier when she popped into the sitting room for an inspection prior to leaving the house. She was nervous as hell, but excited and glowing at the prospect of a good night ahead. Now, she just looked dreadfully broken.

"It can't be that bad," Jess said. "What would Samuel Beckett do in this situation, whatever it is?"

"He'd probably move to Paris and start drinking heavily," Simone blubbered.

"Don't let her up to the bar," I hissed at Jess. Simone hated Paris – it had too many hollow romantic connotations for her liking – so we were probably okay with that one. "What happened, sweetie? Take a deep breath and tell us."

She took a deep breath, as instructed. "Okay, but don't you ever call me 'sweetie' again. If you do, I swear to you that I will move out of our house. I'm not someone you call a sweetie and you should damn well know that by now."

Oh Jesus. I should have known that I'd somehow come out of this as the scapegoat for her anger. She wouldn't dare try this with Jess.

"Right."

Simone took another deep breath, closed her eyes and dove into her tale of woe.

"Well, the first thing you should know about Derek is that he was always very conventional-looking in work. He always had the perfectly ironed shirt and suit on, the hair was always perfect – not my type at all really, but there was just something about him. He was all dark hair, dark eyes, dark skin – very . . . brooding, very Heathcliff. Anyway, I was waiting to meet him in front of the Phil Lynott statue in the city when a strangely dressed guy approached me. It was his footwear I noticed first – black boots covered in chains, with a heel that must have been around two inches. When I looked up, I saw a pair of skinny legs nestled in these horrible circulation stopping leather trousers. Further up, there was a flash of flesh followed by a denim waistcoat tied up with a shoelace. But the pièce de résistance was what lay above all of that. Derek's head."

Jess snorted wine out of her nose and onto the wooden floor.

"This is no snorting manner," Simone assured her.

"What did you say to him?" I said, for once ignoring the urge to tell Jess to clean up her mess immediately. It wasn't my pub.

"I just said hi. What else could I say? 'What the fuck happened to you? What the hell are you dressed like Sasha Baron Cohen in *Bruno* for?'"

This time, I was the one who had to try not to snort.

"He leaned down and kissed my cheek, and he almost won me over again because you know how hard it is for me to find a man who's taller than me. He said 'I know. I look pretty different outside of work, right?', then smiled, and for a second he almost looked like himself again. A version of himself with two inches of eyeliner. Once we started to walk down the street, I noticed that his torso was sticking out so far that his back was bent – he had no coat on either so it was really obvious. I'm there watching him waltzing down the street with his chest puffed out, wondering what's going on. Then I had a private Oh – My – God moment as it hit me what was going on with him – he was trying – it's almost too funny to even say it – to get people to look at his chest! There he was, puffing himself out like a peacock, gawking at everyone who passed him to see if they were gawking at him."

"What are you trying to say? The man had tits?"

"Moobs," I offered.

"No, he had what I'd thought up to that point was a pretty impressive set of pecs. He'd never strutted around like this in work – he'd be laughed out of the engineering team if he had – but, Jesus, the state of him pushing them out as we walked down the street . . . I was mortified."

"I'm surprised you didn't turn around and come home at that point."

"I was operating under the belief that things could only get better, Tammy. I asked him where he wanted to go. He was too busy smiling obliviously at the people smirking at him as they walked by to answer me at first. *Smirking at us,* girls! We must have looked absolutely ridiculous together – the sensible parent-in-training accompanying the Emo teenager on a night out. It was insane. This was my dream date, for heaven's sake!

"He suggested that we went to a new pub called Adventurers. We're walking there anyway and he just starts *chatting*. He's a consummate babbler, so not my type – I was hoping we'd have long periods of saying nothing as we stared off into space – but no, not so much as one uncomfortable silence. And when he smiled, he had the whitest teeth – all perfectly straight too. It was awful. He had identikit teeth, not a bloody flaw in them."

I could tell Jess's sympathy was disintegrating rapidly. "Why am I getting that déjà vu feeling of when Tammy dumped the florist?"

"A bit of respect for Simone's story, please," I said to Jess as harshly as I could. "Go on, pet . . . I mean, just go on. No 'pet'. No nothing."

Simone tutted, but continued. "It gets worse. So much worse. I was expecting somewhere dark, grimy and shady when Derek led me through a side door off a side street, and I wasn't disappointed. Dark – check. Musty smell – check. People cavorting and gyrating into each other to sleazy music on an excuse for a dance floor even though it wasn't yet even eight o'clock – check. But people turning away from their partners and immediately getting off with someone else . . . !"

Jess suddenly looked a bit more interested in the story.

"'Impressed, huh?' he said to me. Can you believe it? Impressed! I told him I was blown away. How could I not be? I was in a swingers club on my romantic night out. A fucking swingers club! Then he goes 'Well, I hope you aren't getting any ideas, young lady. I want you all to myself tonight.'"

Jess looked confused. I wasn't far behind her.

"I know. 'So why are we here?' I had to ask. He said, 'The atmosphere, of course! You won't experience

181

anything like this in any other bar in town at this time of evening.' No, you wouldn't – which is precisely why I don't go to them, girls! We'd just got settled at a table when I spotted something that made me duck under it. He flung himself down beside me on his hunkers. 'Are you all right?' he said. 'Em . . . one of my earrings fell out,' I had to say. Derek looked at my earlobes and frowned. 'You're not wearing earrings.' So I'm like, 'Oh damnit, don't tell me I've lost both of them now!' I had to scurry around the ground on my hands and knees, peering under the table to see if the source of my worry was still around."

"Doggy style. Sounds like the right place for it too," said Guess Who.

"I'll ignore that. Anyway, Derek just sat back and folded his arms over those pecs. 'Funny how they went AWOL just when you spotted that newspaper photographer coming our way,' he said. 'Is the prospect of being photographed with me in a place like this that terrifying?' I just shrugged and said, 'It's not the 'you' part' – adding to myself 'If you were wearing normal clothes'. I suddenly felt a bit bad – he looked as crushed as a kid who'd just discovered he didn't get any presents from Santa. I suggested that we get pissed, so we drank loads and went out to the dance floor. Once the alcohol kicked in and I thought I might actually be able to enjoy this night in some shape or form, it happened. Right in front of my eyes, Derek pinched the butt of some guy that passed us on the dance floor."

Jess's eyes grew as wide as saucers. "Patty really needs to reassess her matchmaking skills."

"Yes. I had to tap Derek on the shoulder and say, 'Erm . . . why are we here?' He goes, 'Babes!' He called me *babes* – can you *believe* it? 'Don't get all philosophical on me! We live, we die, we have fun in between. You don't need to be Plato to –' I had to stop him and say, 'No. Why did you agree to go on this date with me?' He shrugged and said he always thought I looked interesting. I'm there with a face wrinkled up in confusion, going 'Derek, you're clearly . . . not into women. So what's this all about? What do you want from me?' Oh, girls, his face when I said it . . . it scared the life out of me. He went off on a rant then. 'I don't know what it was about you that made me think you'd be different . . . you passed judgement on my sexuality the second you laid eyes on me today based on what I was wearing, just like the way you made a completely different judgement on me when I was all suited and booted at work . . . yadda yadda yah . . . you put me into a box, then when the box didn't turn out to be the one you expected, you immediately lost interest' . . . all of this kind of stuff. So I pointed out that there's no point in me being interested if he's interested in pinching the arses off men! 'That was just for a laugh!' he said. 'That's the kind of place this is – a place where people who are suits all week, robots for a company, come to let their hair down and get their arses pinched. There's no harm in it.'

"I swung my handbag onto my arm. 'Sorry, Derek, but this is not my scene,' I said to him. He just shook his head. 'I'm disappointed in you,' he goes. 'I thought you weren't part of the world of couples' dinner parties, scented candles and pretentious wine. I thought you'd be able to understand other people's worlds.' He got me there, of course. I have to say, girls, I was suddenly so ashamed of myself for being so intolerant. We all know that my world isn't quite like regular people's, after all. When I told him as much, he said he found that hard to believe and that I looked about as sensible as it got. I told him I'd never done a sensible thing in my life. I even filled him in on how I'm living with my crazy cousins in my mid-thirties, which most people seem to think is rather weird, but he wasn't convinced. So of course, I had to do something to convince him that I could do weird."

"Oh no."

"Yes. And this is where the story gets worse."

"Gets good, you mean," Jess said.

"I said 'I'm a very weird person at heart, actually. Look!' And with that, I raced across the room and dragged the photographer away mid-photo over to our table. 'I'd love to be in your publication,' I said. 'I've admired your work for years.' He gave me a funny look and said 'We're a new newspaper.' 'Weeks. I meant weeks,' I said. I threw myself onto Derek's lap and wrapped my arm around his neck. 'We'd love to have our picture taken if you're looking for beautiful people. Look at this guy.' I grabbed Derek's chin. 'How could you refuse?' The photographer looked distinctly unimpressed by Derek's beauty, but shrugged and lifted his camera up anyway. Then a tall transvestite smothered in feathers walked past us, so I beckoned him over. 'Join us! Join our happy family!' I roared, and he took me up on the offer. I jumped down off Derek's lap and pulled Mr Feathers to the right of what had been my chair before I went lap-dancing on Derek. Then I shoved Derek off his and pulled it beside mine, hauled two other ones over and plonked them beside the existing two. 'Right. Mr Feathers, this'll be your chair,' I told him, pointing to the one on the right. 'Derek, this is yours.' I prodded a finger to the one on the left. As soon as Mr Feathers and a bemused-looking Derek had taken their seats, I popped up onto the seat beside Derek, threw my head into his lap and swung my legs up into Mr Feather's, balancing the rest of my body on the other two stools. 'Simone!' Derek roared at me. 'What are you doing? Your head is sticking into my . . .' 'We're ready for our pic!' I shouted at the photographer. He didn't need to be told twice – he suddenly seemed to have a renewed interest in taking our picture. And took it he did."

Jess had an enormous grin across her face and I knew my eyes were out on stalks.

Simone covered her face with her hands. "That was all well and good while I was drunk, but I'm getting more and more sober by the minute and I'm starting to freak out."

"So what's the problem?" Jess said. She looked genuinely confused. "You got your picture taken and you're freaking out?"

"Today's reading is tomorrow's chip paper," I said confidently.

"Not now with the Internet," Simone pointed out. "I was stupid enough to give my real name because I didn't want to lie in front of Derek! That paper is online. If a prospective employer Googles me, it'll probably be the first result they get for me. How will I ever get a job now?"

"I wonder are there any flights still going out to Paris tonight?" Jess said.

"Bring on the other option," Simone said. "And if you dare to deny me access to that bar, Tammy, I'll go home and drink my emergency absinthe stash and that will probably make me get sick later all over the lovely carpet you put down in my room."

Simone went to the bar, and after another few visits,

the whole thing got funnier and funnier. Still though, her swingers story had made me appreciate being out of the dating world – for the time being, at least. I had nothing against swinging but it wasn't my scene, and if I'd kept up my dating carry-on it was only a matter of time before I'd somehow end up in a similar scenario. Alvin and I were doing our next activity item the next day and after what I'd just heard, I felt luckier than ever that he'd come back into my life.

Now, if only I could work out how I'd get over the past and keep him there.

25

"Al, what is it?"

"Hmm?"

"You seem really distracted today. Is everything okay?"

It's such a stupid question really, isn't it? You ask someone if everything is okay only when all the indications are that things are far from all right.

"Yeah," he said in a most unconvincing tone.

Of course, people usually answered that question with a yes even if things were pants. It was just a vocal game everyone played in life so that we wouldn't sound like Moaning Minnies before following up with "It's just that . . ." I couldn't help thinking that this was a new development for us though. Alvin usually told me if something was on his mind. He rarely worried about things anyway, so this must be something big. And I could easily guess what it was.

"Okay. Well, just remember that you can always tell me anything – even if it's something like you think I look like a prostitute in that red lipstick I bought yesterday." I left it at that, hoping he'd elaborate.

"The red lipstick is great," he said with a smile. "It's not the lipstick. It's just that . . ."

Aha. Breakthrough.

". . . it's the whole thing with the baby." He paused and looked at me as if he wanted to gauge my reaction.

"I know what you mean." And I did, without him having to say another word, but I nodded at him to continue anyway.

"It's been seven months now and the baby would have been due next week if we hadn't lost it. You rarely mention it, so I haven't wanted to bring it up because that seems to be your way of coping with it – you might have noticed that I haven't even brought up that pre-parental plan we wrote in case doing things from it upsets you, even though it's still hanging over our bed – but I just can't get it out of my mind, Tammy. I know lots of people go through miscarriages, but that doesn't make what happened any less . . . shit."

"Shit is the word for it all right," I said with a huge sigh. "I haven't been talking about it because I haven't wanted to wallow, but not talking about it hasn't made it go away either."

"No, it hasn't."

Alvin tapped his hands against his knees in a repetitive pattern, something he did only when he was very agitated.

"All of this has really upset you, hasn't it?" I said quietly.

"How could it not? I love kids – you know that. And even if I didn't, who wouldn't be upset by something like this happening to them?"

Who indeed? I suddenly felt horribly selfish. I'd been so immersed in how I felt about all of this and worrying that I might miscarry again at some stage in the future that I hadn't truly considered how Alvin was coping. As I hugged him, I tried to put my fears of not being able to carry another baby full term to the back of my mind. Trouble was, I had a feeling that even if I succeeded, they wouldn't stay there for long. But for now, it was time to let Alvin talk.

"What do you fancy for dinner tonight?" I said as I rifled through the drawers of the freezer a few nights later. "We have frozen lamb curry, or I have fresh chicken breasts there if you want me to make something up from that . . ."

"Let's have a baby."

I retracted my head from the freezer very slowly. "For dinner?"

"Very funny." He walked over to me and closed the freezer door. "What do you think? Isn't now as good a time as any?"

"I had no idea you were thinking this way."

"It's like this, Tammy. I'm with the person I want to spend the rest of my life with, and I just keep asking myself, why wait? And obviously after what happened to us, it'd be lovely to have another child – not in a replacement sense, of course . . ."

"No, I know what you mean."

"And I'd like to be a father while I'm still young enough to enjoy it. I'm ready to move on to the next chapter, you know? I'm done with going out and having hangovers that last a week. But if all of this is coming too soon for you, then I'm completely fine with waiting until you feel ready . . ."

"No, no, it's not. In fact . . . I was actually thinking about the same thing and wondering if I should bring it up with you!"

"Why didn't you tell me? You know you can say anything to me . . ."

I shrugged. "I suppose I didn't want to scare you off."

I'd been sitting around since the miscarriage thinking about a garden full of dark-haired Shirley Temple lookalike babies. The possibility of scaring him off was a pretty valid concern. I also wasn't sure if wanting to have a baby was an emotional reaction to the miscarriage – after all, it hadn't been what I'd wanted before, so why now? I'd waited every month to see if the urge to get pregnant again would dissipate, but it hadn't. For someone who liked to plan and control their life as much as I did, this unexpected turn of events was hard to get my head around – but my feelings were getting stronger every day. I hadn't said anything to Alvin though because the fear that I would miscarry again was balancing my desire to try for another baby, and I didn't want to say anything to him unless I was sure. My head was all over the place.

"Come here, you goose!" He pulled me into his chest, where I nestled comfortably. "We're way beyond the point of you scaring me off now, so don't be daft."

"What about getting married first?"

"That's up to you really. You know I want to marry you – I won't embarrass myself by mentioning how many times I've asked you in the past, but you've always said it's too soon –"

"Maybe it's not too soon any more."

Alvin looked stunned. I was stunned. I hadn't even realised I was going to say that. But as soon as I'd said it, I knew I meant it.

"Is that a request for a proposal?"

"I think you've done enough of that. It's a yes to your previous proposals, if you'll still have me . . ."

Alvin slid his hands around my neck and pulled me to him. "If I'll still have you? What do you think?"

I didn't get a chance to answer. His lips searched out mine and I responded instantly.

"Consider yourself engaged, Tammy Taylor," he said, before carrying me upstairs.

Hours later, our conversation returned to marriage and babies.

"I suppose you'll want the big Irish wedding with loads of fiddly bits to organise?" Alvin said.

"Absolutely. It will be an organisational dream." I sighed contentedly. "Oh, and marrying you will also be wonderful, of course."

"I know my place in the pecking order. We'll have to think about setting a date – I suppose sooner rather than later if we want to try for a baby . . ."

I couldn't but smile. "You really want a baby as soon as possible, don't you?"

"Of course I want our baby. Only when you're ready though, of course."

"Well then, who says we have to get married before we have a child? Despite how much I love to organise, it'll still take a long time to pull our dream day together – not to mention the fact that we don't have the money lying around to pay for a wedding outright and we'll need some time to save for it. I'm good with money, but I don't have a spare thirty grand in the mattress either."

"Would you be happy with that?"

"Yes, but there is one problem . . . I'm really worried that I might miscarry again, Alvin. What if there's something wrong with me and that's why this happened?"

"I doubt it very much. The doctor told us that one in

191

four pregnancies end in miscarriage, but that most couples go on to conceive without any problems next time around. We have no concrete reason to believe that you'll miscarry again."

I sighed. "I know. I'm just incapable of not worrying, though."

"You're addicted to worrying, but enjoy it while you can. You won't have time to worry when we have a houseful of children."

"Hey! We said a baby!"

"That's what they all say."

"I'm going to ignore that. Look, how about this – I'll do an Excel spreadsheet up of how long it'll take us to save up for the wedding, factoring in all the set-up costs for a baby, and we'll set a date based on that?"

Alvin laughed. "You make it all sound so romantic, but if that's what works for you, then I'm easy. I'm getting a baby and a wife out of today's decisions, so you won't hear me complaining."

"It'll realistically be a few years before we'll be able to get married though. You won't go anywhere in the meantime?" I joked.

"I'll never go anywhere."

And he looked like he really, really meant that.

26

Pre-parental plan activity 5: Being extras
on a TV show

There are so many people out there who want to be
on TV for one reason or another. You're not one of
them, Tom. Thing is, there's a difference between not
wanting to be on TV and being afraid of being on it.
Unfortunately, we both know the latter case is
yours - and even worse, you have a complex about
being filmed in general. You've often said things like
you won't allow a videographer at our wedding and
that you'll never let a camcorder past our front
door. But here's the thing. When we have kids, I'll
want to capture every important moment of their
lives on film - and as you'll be jointly behind all their
milestone moments like teaching them how to walk,
I want you to be in our home movies too. (Relax -
not those types of ones!) Let's break this complex
once and for all by going on TV. Everything after that
can only be easier!

When the doorbell rang at five in the morning, I stumbled down the stairs with crusty eyes running through all the possibilities for who had died. Surely nothing other than a death could necessitate someone coming to my door at that hour? It looked like the activity Alvin had organised for us today would have to be rescheduled then.

I opened the letterbox. "Who is it?" I yelled out the gap.

"It's Alvin," the man himself said, bending down to the letterbox and waving in. *Shit*. He wasn't supposed to be here until nine o'clock! I ran a hand through my mangled hair, as if that was going to do anything for it, and rubbed the sleep out of my eyes. All thoughts of why exactly he was here at this time were shoved to one side in my worry about my presentability, or lack thereof.

"One sec," I said before slamming the letterbox shut.

I ran to the downstairs bathroom and rifled through an old cupboard that I knew contained a little tube of toothpaste and an old comb. The tiny comb looked like something that came with a head-lice kit, but it managed to tame the mass of hair at the front of my head after a good few minutes of yanking violently at it. I squeezed some toothpaste on the tip of my index finger, rubbed it onto my teeth and into my gums, rinsed and hoped for the best as I left the bathroom and opened the front door. I'd left the bathroom light on – as long as I didn't turn on the hall light, things mightn't be too bad.

"You know what I'm going to say, don't you?" I said as Alvin walked into the hall. "*Don't turn on that light!*" I hissed as he put his hand up to the light switch.

"You caught me out there," he said as he dropped his hand. "I'd been expecting your best rant about being woken up."

"You might get that from Jess and Simone the next

time they see you. But as you've brought it up, why exactly are you here at this time?" From his tone it didn't sound like anyone was dead anyway.

"Waking you up in time for our big roles today."

"But I could throw a stone from here and hit the TV studios!" The national broadcaster was less than a half a mile away from my house.

"Who says we're going there? Aren't you forgetting somewhere else?"

I thought about it for a moment, and then it hit me. "Gaeilge TV? We're going to Galway?" Gaeilge TV was an Irish language broadcaster.

He nodded, a big grin spreading across his face. "We're going to be extras on *Iarthair*." *Iarthair* was the nation's only Irish language soap.

"Crikey. What time do we need to be there?"

"Ten. We'll need to leave here at six." He pulled two cereal bars out of his coat pocket and handed one to me. "You have fifty-five minutes to eat and get ready."

I came downstairs at ten to six looking and feeling a lot more human, and found Alvin fast asleep on the couch. Something inside me jolted as I looked at his sleeping face. I stood over him and gazed at him for a long time. Why had I been stupid enough to ruin everything?

I leaned towards him to wake him up and shook his shoulder more roughly than I'd intended to. "It's six," I said, then snapped my hand away.

He opened his eyes, smiled for a second when he saw me, then sat up abruptly.

"Let's go then."

Alvin drove, as he'd taken Claire's car to come over to my place that morning. As soon as he'd put some indie compilation or other on the CD player, I fell asleep. I hadn't thought I would be able to with Alvin beside me, but I was already falling back into comfortable patterns with him. When I awoke, we were approaching Galway city. The sun was rising over Galway Bay, bathing the city in a warm glow, as we drove down the docks. It wasn't long before we were on the coast road to Connemara, watching all of the morning's traffic edge past us in the opposite direction while we cruised along.

My thoughts turned to what was ahead and I started to feel nervous. When I was eleven, the Government's Minister for Education came to the school I'd attended to open a huge extension, and I was chosen as the student who would give the minister a tour of our school after an initial meet-and-greet by the principal. The official opening of the extension was due to be covered on the national broadcaster's evening news show. I hadn't been one bit fazed by the filming and had hugely enjoyed bringing the minister around our school, but I nearly died of embarrassment when I saw the footage on TV. I looked an absolute state. I was three times the width of everyone else that was shown, adults and pupils alike. I'd always been given a hard time by my schoolmates about my weight, but the insults reached meteoric levels after the recording of my lardy arse thundering and wobbling along the corridor was broadcast. The day of that news report was the day I'd gone on a diet that lasted throughout my teenage years and broke my mother's heart. When I shot up from five foot four to five foot ten over the following years, my weight became something I didn't need to monitor as closely any more, but I never forgot the humiliation that report had put me through – and I vowed never to go on TV again, for any reason whatsoever.

The story came up in conversation one night with Alvin. He didn't quite get my concerns when I mentioned how much I'd hate ever to go on TV again.

"But you were eleven! Everyone looked crap when they were that age. And you're gorgeous now."

"I know I'd still see that fat girl if I saw myself on TV though. Anyway, it doesn't matter. It's not as if I'll ever need to go on TV."

Women could say all they liked about men never listening, but I could never complain about Alvin in that respect. He had perfect recall when it came to conversations we had and when we sat down to write the pre-parental plan, it wasn't long before the TV thing came up.

"Remember what you said about never wanting to go on TV? Well, maybe we should do something that involves TV."

"Oh yeah. That makes total sense, Alvin."

"Hear me out. How about we apply to be extras on a TV show? It'd be a quirky day out, the type of thing we'll never take the time out to do when we have children, and it would mean the spotlight won't be on you and yet you'll get to be on TV."

"Except that I don't want to be on TV."

"Ah, get off the stage, Tammy. If you're an extra on a TV show, nobody is even going to notice you're there unless you tell them. Come on – it'll be a laugh! And, you know, it won't be good for our kids to see you being afraid of our camcorder as they'll only grow up to be self-conscious too."

"You say 'our camcorder' like there's a remote possibility that we might have one someday."

"I'll order one tomorrow and follow you around the

house filming everything you do if you don't get over yourself."

I wasn't overly gone on the idea, but we had to pick five items each and chances were that Alvin could come up with something I'd be a lot more scared of – so I hesitantly agreed. Besides, he was probably right. Most people didn't pay any attention to the extras in the background of scenes in shows. Did they?

Now, we pulled up outside *Iarthair*'s TV set forty minutes after we drove through Galway city.

"We're a bit early, but let's go inside and see what's going on," Alvin said.

I could feel enthusiasm for what lay ahead oozing from him. He bounded up to a man who had a Gaeilge TV swipe-card dangling from his jeans pocket and asked him where we needed to go. The man directed us to a prefab where all of the extras for the day would wait until filming was ready to commence. A beautiful twenty-something girl with pierced eyebrows ticked our names off a list as we entered the draughty prefab, then prepared two hot whiskeys for us. We sipped our drinks as I surreptitiously checked out the rest of the extras and wondered what our role would be. Hopefully we wouldn't be the token couple in love, hugging and kissing as we walked down the street or something. How awkward . . .

"Are you okay?" Alvin said. "You've gone bright red . . ."

"I'm grand! Maybe it's a bit early for this whiskey."

"Never stopped you before. Remember that weekend in Limerick when we went to a pub on the Dock Road for breakfast and ended up drinking from seven in the morning until the pubs closed that night?"

"I sometimes think I still have the hangover from that

pub crawl. We must have gone to every single pub in the city!"

There it was, that shared smile again. Then suddenly – dramatically, actually – Alvin's smile fell. His look changed to one of consternation as he stared at the top of my head. My hand moved involuntarily to my hair. I'd only had my roots done three weeks ago! Was it dandruff? I ran my hands through my hair and flicked my fingers out at the bottom in a bid to shift whatever it might be.

"*Ow!*" I said as someone directly behind me went "*Aaagh!*" I turned around to apologise to the person I'd just accidentally hit.

"I'm . . ." The apology died on my lips. "Adrienne!"

"What are you doing here?" Alvin said.

"Going on the show, of course. Why, what are *you* doing here?" Adrienne pulled up a chair and sat between Alvin and me. "Grab a chair and sit opposite me," she said to Clarissa.

Yes, Clarissa. She was there too.

I looked at Alvin and raised my eyebrows, waiting for an explanation, but he seemed to be as confused about this as I was.

"When I told you my plans for today, Adrienne, I wasn't inviting you along," Alvin said, ostensibly to Adrienne but looking at me as he spoke, as if he was pleading his innocence. He told her his plans? Sure that was practically the same thing as inviting her along! Why was Alvin so blind to how badly his sister wanted to keep us apart? In my more diplomatic moments, I could see why she would want to – after all, she didn't know why we'd broken up, just that I'd ended things and turned her brother into a mess – but we were never going to work things out with people like Adrienne interfering.

199

"I thought you might like a bit of *decent* company." She looked at Clarissa as she stressed the word 'decent'. "I told you I was going down the country this weekend for that friend of mine's party last night, remember? It was in Galway city, so we were in the area."

"You never said 'down the country' was Galway. Technically it's *not* 'down the country' – it's due west!"

"They needed loads of extras for today's filming so there was no problem getting a pass. We're all going to be guests at a wedding, apparently," Clarissa said.

Next thing we'd hear that the bride and groom were going to be played by Alvin and Clarissa. Nothing would surprise me when it came to what Adrienne was capable of. I smiled insanely, determined not to let my frustration at the presence of our unwanted company show, and got up to see if I could get another hot whiskey. I didn't think there was any parenting book in the world that would advocate radically increasing your consumption of alcohol as part of your pre-parental plan, but that seemed to be exactly what was happening to me . . .

27

I was delighted when we were ushered off to prepare for filming. Clarissa's inside scoop had been correct, and we were taken to the costume department to find suitable attire for a wedding. It seemed like only seconds before a beautiful figure-hugging red cocktail dress was found for Clarissa. After ten minutes of looking, there was still nothing suitable for me to wear.

"You're very tall, aren't you?" the lady in charge of wardrobe said to me accusingly. She looked at me suspiciously, as if I'd been sent to mess up her day.

"I'm hardly the first tall person to ever walk in here," I snapped. I was five foot ten – it wasn't giraffe territory!

"Hormonal," Adrienne hissed at the wardrobe lady. "Don't pay any attention to her."

"Ah. Pregnant." The lady looked at my stomach and nodded.

"I am not pregnant!" I almost screamed.

"I meant that she's on the blob," Adrienne kindly clarified. It wasn't even true, of course – as if I'd share the details of my cycle with her!

"That explains the bloating so," my new best friend muttered. "Okay. Let me check the reserve supplies out the back to see what I have."

I glared at Adrienne, furious. She just ignored me.

Mrs Wardrobe came back with a fluorescent green monstrosity of a dress. "That's all I have that'll fit you length-wise," she said before turning her attention to Adrienne. I tutted at her rudeness like an auld wan before rifling through every rail in sight. Surely there had to be something I could wear . . .

Ten minutes later, I admitted defeat. Everything I tried on looked obscenely short on me, not to mention slightly hookerish for a wedding scene. I put on the dress, checked a few drawers to see if I could find a pair of sunglasses to protect my eyes from the fluorescent glare and tried to put on a brave face.

A tall man with a strong jaw-line walked into the middle of the room. "Hello, everyone. Can I have your attention for a few moments, please?" A hush gradually descended on the room. "I'm Pat, the producer," he said. "I know from your application forms that not all of you speak fluent Irish, so we'll stick to English for now – but you'll be hearing plenty of Irish before the day is out. We have an extra-special day ahead of us today, one that we hope you'll all enjoy and that some of you will be actively participating in."

Nerves slithered over me. What exactly did active participation mean?

"We'll be filming the wedding of two of our main characters," Pat continued. "Those of you who have been following the show will know that this couple's relationship has been beset by problems from the get-go, and unfortunately for them, we're not going to give them a break on their wedding day – because that would be rather boring, wouldn't it?"

Pat went on to explain that the wedding itself would be a tense affair, with the groom showing up so late that the bride believes she's about to be stood up. A litany of disasters would happen at the reception, many of which would involve some of the extras assembled and for which Pat would be looking for volunteers. The wedding scene would climax with the bride's sister getting up on stage at the wedding reception and taking a microphone off the band to announce that she was pregnant with the groom's child, a fact that he knew about prior to the wedding and he's then forced to admit to his new wife.

"Okay, first we need a man to bump into the mother of the bride at the bar and spill a pint of Guinness down her outfit," Pat said. "Any takers?"

Five minutes later, Pat had found not only a pint spiller, but a serial woman spinner (someone who would go from one woman to the next on the dance floor spinning them around) and a winder (someone who would hold the hand of a singing drunken man and wind it around and around over the course of the man's song – an old Connemara tradition).

"Aren't you going to offer your services for anything?" I said to Alvin. His arms were folded across his chest in the manner of someone who hadn't a notion of putting a hand up. I hoped he hadn't, but I felt like I had to say something to at least give him the option.

"And leave you alone with those two?" he whispered back. "I know you'll be too nervous now to volunteer for anything while they're here – you were nervous enough as it was before they came along."

"I'll be fine. Take part if you want – I don't mind," I fibbed.

"Nah. I'll probably need to keep an eye on Adrienne to make sure she doesn't get us all in trouble somehow with her big gob."

Adrienne and Clarissa hadn't volunteered for anything. They looked like moody pre-pubescents as they pouted and looked disdainfully at everyone. It was patently obvious that they had no interest in what was going on, which only confirmed my suspicions that they'd come to cause trouble. Although their presence was saving me from having actively to participate in this wedding and I should have been grateful for the unexpected reprieve, I wasn't. I was furious at them and felt sorry for Alvin, who'd gone to all this trouble to organise our activity and now felt that he couldn't even participate himself because of those two.

"Okay, nearly there," Pat said. "Last up, we need a man and a woman to be a couple who'll argue loudly throughout the wedding ceremony, the speeches and on the dance floor at the reception. The woman will need to pretend to be very drunk at the reception and will throw up on the bride's shoes just after the bride's sister announces the affair. So there's even a bit of acting involved in this one – who knows where it may lead you! The Irish is very basic and we'll provide you with the lines – there's only a handful. The only problem is that, as I'm looking around the room, I can see that most of the men here have volunteered for roles already. Can you just raise a hand if you're male and you've already volunteered?"

Every man from our group of extras raised their hand except Alvin. Every head in the room turned to Alvin.

"Fancy a spot of acting?" Pat said to Alvin hopefully. "How's your Irish?"

Alvin looked at me. Out of the corner of my eye, I saw Adrienne and Clarissa looking at each other. The cogs started turning. Alvin would end up being pressured into volunteering, and Clarissa would volunteer to be the puker. That meant I had to get to be the puker first. My worst nightmare.

"Go on," I said to Alvin. "I will too."

"But there's fake-vomiting involved for you if you do . . ."

"Always wanted to fake-vomit on TV." I smiled a fake smile to practise all things false.

"Okay, we'll be the couple. We both have good Irish," Alvin said to Pat.

I couldn't resist looking over at Adrienne and Clarissa to see their reactions. Adrienne sneered at me, and Clarissa refused to make eye contact at all. I had a momentary flash of satisfaction until I remembered the vomit issue again. Oh, and not forgetting the being-in-a-prominent-position-on-TV issue.

Alvin tapped my hand with his index finger. "This is going to be fine, okay?"

"It's not this bit that worries me . . . it's the watching of it . . ,"

"When it's televised, we'll watch it together and we'll have a laugh, I promise."

I nodded. Maybe he wouldn't still be in the country when it was televised, but he looked so comforting that I suddenly felt a lot better.

Pat took all of the volunteers to one side of the room to talk us through what our parts entailed.

"Now, the happy couple," Pat said to us when it was our turn for instructions. "When it comes to the scene in the church, you'll be arguing about the man leaving the house in a mess. You just have one line each." He passed us a sheet with our lines. I read them and wondered if this was some nasty person's idea of a candid camera prank.

My line in Irish was translated underneath in English as *'I'm sick to death of your clutter around the house!'* and Alvin's was *'Fine. Let's just not live together any more!'* Towards the end of our relationship, I used to complain constantly about Alvin's stuff lying all over the house. And we no longer lived together.

We practised our lines for Pat, and he was satisfied that we were comprehensible. "Right. Now, during the speeches, the woman will accuse the man of fancying another woman."

I could swear I felt Clarissa's eyes burning into the back of my head from the other side of the room as we rolled off the line of practice for this segment, which translated as me saying *'You've fancied her for years!'* and Alvin retorting with *'I don't fancy her and never have. You need help!'*

Thankfully, we could talk about whatever we wanted to in the dance-floor section as long as we did so with angry faces, because the sound of the band in the background would drown out any dialogue from the extras. As well as having to look angry, I would be tasked with swaying as drunkenly as possible. Then came the vomiting bit. My mind ran through several possibilities as to how it was going to be done. Each one was more scary than the last.

"We'll be giving you a drink that you hold in your mouth and then spew out over the bride's shoes," Pat said. "Sounds horrible, I know, but it's really not that bad and the drink actually tastes lovely."

"And here I was, hoping it'd taste of real vomit," I said with a half-smile. This was probably the least horrible option, but it was still too much for me even to contemplate. I would have to park it in my brain and deal with it when the time came. At least it was something I'd only do once in my life and then that'd be that.

"We'll probably have to get you to drink, hold and spew several times to make sure we get this right," Pat said cheerfully. "There's a bit of a knack to it, I'm told."

"Great." *Crap.* This was absolutely ridiculous and it was all Clarissa and Adrienne's fault. I should have let Clarissa be Alvin's partner in crime for this stupid thing, list item or no list item. But then an image of them laughing away together over their scenes entered my head, and I was glad that I'd managed to prevent that – not to mention the bonding fodder it would have given Clarissa over the next few days and weeks when it came to things to talk to Alvin about. I turned around and glanced at her. She looked bored stiff and pissed off as hell. *Good.* I cheered up slightly.

The day was a mixture of interminable periods of waiting around with our microphones turned off and bursts of action in which time dissolved into thin air. The church scene took two hours to film. Our two lines of dialogue were at the end of that scene. When Pat gave me the nod to tell Alvin I was sick of his clutter, I found it impossible to look him in the eye and focused on his nose instead. Thankfully, the witches had been stationed in a pew on the opposite side of the church. Adrienne would have picked up on even the slightest sniff of discontent straight away.

I wasn't quite so lucky when it came to accusing Alvin of fancying another woman. Adrienne and Clarissa were put at the same table as Alvin and me. Their eyes bored into me as I delivered my verbal assault. On the plus side, the speeches scene was filmed fast, and we quickly moved on to the reception. Although, was something that brought me closer to spewing really on the plus side?

Alvin went over to Pat just before the cameras started rolling to check what date this episode would be going out. Adrienne walked over as soon as I was alone.

"Are you looking forward to your *Exorcist*-style role? I know I am."

"Oh yes. I might even rotate my head in your direction."

"Alvin is going to find this all so attractive," she said as her parting shot before stomping back to Clarissa.

I ignored her. I had enough to do in trying to work out how to fake-vomit femininely rather than worry about her.

Once the bride and groom were on the dance floor, we were put into position and it was time to start looking angry. Adrienne and Clarissa were at the far end of the dance floor, paired off with two men. Adrienne looked like she'd rather be at her own funeral than here as she stared vacantly around the room over her dancing partner's shoulder. Clarissa was engaged in what looked to be a less-than-riveting conversation with her extremely tall dancing partner, and she looked in danger of suffering from a serious neck injury before the dance was out.

"How are you enjoying the day?" Alvin said with a frown that made him look like he had a monobrow.

"It's certainly different." I frowned too and swayed to one side a bit.

"It is that." He tutted and shook his head, then swayed too.

"I really enjoyed the scenery from Galway onwards." I gave Alvin a 'talk to the hand' gesture.

"I'm trying not to smile at what you just did."

"Me too."

We both smiled.

"Cut!" Pat walked over. "Guys, what's the smiling about? We need anger!"

"Sorry," we said simultaneously. It made me want to smile even more.

"You two are a couple, aren't you? Have a real argument over something," Pat said. "There's bound to be something you need to discuss that's on the backburner. Now would be a good time to dredge it up."

Shut up, Pat.

Pat walked away and the cameras started to roll again.

"Hmm. Pat could be on to something there." The monobrow was back. "We'll have to talk soon – it's overdue, Tam."

I stiffened. Not a good move when I was supposed to be swaying.

The time I'd spent with him since he came home flashed before me, each memory sweeter than the last. As soon as we started digging up the past, though, things could only go downhill. I knew I was living in a bubble, but I wasn't ready for it to be burst yet. I had to say something to get him off this topic.

"What's the point, Alvin? Unless you can tell me that you'll be moving back to Ireland for good, which I don't for one second expect you to, then what good would trawling through the past do?"

"Tammy, you should know that my going to Australia in the first place was just a knee-jerk reaction to us splitting up. The way that you totally refused to communicate with me was killing me, and I couldn't just sit around waiting for you to realise that how you'd reacted to our problems was a huge mistake. You were a few miles down the road and yet completely unreachable –"

"I'm not getting into this now! The point is that when your time comes to go back to Australia, all of this will have just been a bit of fun."

"You think I see you as a bit of fun?" He swayed dramatically.

I shrugged, wondering why he was swaying when that was my role.

"Why do you always think you mean so little to me? You're falling right into the very same trap you fell into before." He no longer needed to feign anger.

Neither did I. "That's not fair. I'm not talking about this any more." I pulled away from Alvin and remembered to sway. I was glad to have the opportunity to move away from him before this conversation got out of control.

He swayed forward. "Oh yeah, that's it. Pull the shutters down on the conversation. We need to talk about this, Tammy."

"And you think right here, right now is the place to do it? Are you mad?"

"If not here and now, where and when? I've been trying to broach this subject for ages and you've been shrugging it off. And we both know it. There's something else we need to talk about too and, in hindsight, I should never have asked you to do this plan with me before telling you . . ."

"*Cut*! Guys, well done," Pat said to the main actors in the show. He turned to us. "And well done to you two as well for the background work. That looked like a really authentic row. Now we move on to the most fun bit of all – the vomit!"

It seemed that for some people, no matter how old they got, vomit was still always funny.

"So, Alvin, here's the vomit drink. You were there when I explained to Tammy how we want this to be done, so you know the routine – drink, hold, spew and then probably re-take the scene, okay?" Alvin nodded and held his hand out for the drink.

What?

"I bet you're glad Alvin talked me into letting him be the drunken vomiter instead of you," Pat said. "I could see you were horrified at the prospect."

I nodded slowly. *Getting the episode's date of airing, he said* . . . oh Lord. Why was he always so bloody good to me?

Five retakes later, it was all over and it was time for us to go home.

"Listen, thanks so much for doing that . . ."

"Yeah." He barely looked at me as he spoke. "It was a bit of fun."

Eek. "Al . . ."

"Let's go." He located our coats and hastily handed me mine.

When we walked outside, Adrienne and Clarissa were just outside the door. Adrienne, as usual, was smoking a cigarette in one long drag.

"Right, where's the car?" Adrienne said as she walked up to us in a haze of smoke.

"Do you not have your own way back?" I practically snarled.

"We got the bus out here this morning and now it's midnight. How do you suggest we get back other than in *my mother's car?*"

"What would you have done if we hadn't been here?" Of course, they wouldn't have been here if we hadn't, but Adrienne was never going to admit to that. Neither of them had made any effort to enjoy the day.

"Anyone who's coming better get moving because I'm leaving right now with or without you lot," Alvin snapped as he strode away from us to the car. It was so uncharacteristic of him ever to lose his cool that all three of

211

us got into the car warily after we followed him. Whether or not the four of us would make it back to Dublin without killing each other was another thing.

Alvin rebuffed Adrienne and Clarissa's attempts to talk on the way home, blasting his indie music to high heaven. I didn't dare open my mouth. He was right – there was so much we needed to talk about. I just wished I could find the courage to open the floodgates.

For the first time that day, I was glad of the witches' company.

28

"What are you doing on New Year's Eve in three years' time?" I asked Alvin.

"I have a feeling you're about to tell me . . ."

"I've worked out that it'll take us three years to save up enough money for the wedding I want – I mean, the wedding we want."

Alvin grinned, but didn't pull me up on it.

"Now, I've taken into account that we'll have a lot of set-up costs if we have a baby, so that's delaying things somewhat – but it'll be worth it to be able to pay for our wedding outright. And you know I hate New Year's Eve – strange things just always seem to happen to me on that day of the year, for some reason – so this would give me a reason to always enjoy it from now on, if you're okay with that date?"

"Fine by me. And you know what, we should get that pre-parental plan underway as soon as possible – we might not have much time left for it if you get pregnant straight away!" He smiled. "I'm glad we're doing things this way so that our kids will be a part of our wedding."

"*As I pointed out before, I didn't sign up for plurals!*"

"*A lot can happen in three years, Tam.*"

"*True. I can't wait to see where we are in three years' time . . .*"

29

It was the night after my trip to Galway and I was bending Simone's ear about everything that had happened there.

"That man is so good to you," Simone pointed out.

"I know. He's acting like the perfect partner except that he's not really my partner."

"Alvin's far from perfect. He's one of the most untidy people I've ever met."

"Oh, leave him alone. You're not very tidy yourself."

"He's very disorganised too. I don't know how he's survived this long without you, actually – you were forever finding his keys or his wallet. If he was a woman he'd be called scatty, but because he's a guy then that's okay."

"That's only because he doesn't worry about the rubbish that everyone else worries about! And he's not untidy – he's just a bit of a hoarder and all of his clutter makes the place look messy when it isn't."

"Christ, you have it bad. The ultimate tidy freak is defending the slob . . . point of no return."

I was glad when I heard Jess coming in the front door. This conversation was getting a bit close to the bone.

"How was work today?" I said when she joined Simone and me in the sitting room. She looked a bit shaky.

"Eventful."

"Oh?"

"Audrey popped by for tea and a chat."

"*What*? She's found out?"

She sat down on the couch and tapped her gel fingernails against her teeth. "She certainly has."

"Well, I suppose it was about time for her to work out who her husband has been shagging, really," Simone said. "What did she have to say?"

"She asked me if I wanted to join her local sailing club so that we could compare performance notes. What do you *think* she said?"

"She called you some variation of whore, I'd imagine. Slut? Trollop? Flea-ridden prostitute?"

"Simone, do you actually think this is helping?" I said.

"I'm just speculating – it's what's expected in a situation like this. Part of the human condition. We can't escape from what we are."

"Drop it, okay?" I turned to Jess. "So did she just turn up at the office and ask for you or what?"

"Yes, she called to the reception in our building and asked for me. She didn't leave a name with them. I recognised her straight away sitting in reception from pictures Ciarán had shown me."

"What did she say when you walked into reception?"

"She didn't get time to say anything. I told her we were going to the café next door, walked out the front door and waited for her to follow me. If there was going to be a scene, I wasn't having it happen in front of the security guard – he's the biggest gossip in Dublin and it'd be back to my workmates in no time. She made sure she got a good look at me as I walked towards her, though. She managed to look me up and down about six times in a few seconds."

I was sorry for Audrey as I thought about how she must have felt as she gave Jess the once-over. Jess took her wardrobe for her job as a marketing manager very seriously – whether or not she took her *job* seriously was another question – and was wearing a tight, high-waisted pencil skirt today, a crisp white blouse and a black-and-white beaded necklace, matched with funky patterned tights and skyscraper black heels. She must have had time to straighten her hair this morning after the gym because it hung in glossy waves down her back with not a single hair out of place, even after a busy day's work. Her make-up was straight out of a magazine advertisement. By anyone's standards, she looked intimidatingly glamorous. To the wife of the man Jess was having an affair with, she must have been the last thing she wanted to see coming through the reception door.

"Of course, I was terrified, but I had to try to put up a good front until we got outside."

"So did she cause a scene in front of everyone in the café instead?" Simone asked hopefully.

"She made a bit of a show of herself all right. I sat down at a table, ordered coffee and asked if she wanted one, and she lost the plot. 'Are you going to sit there and order coffee as if nothing has happened?' she roared at me. I said 'Yes' – and that's when she really went demented. 'You're nothing but a place for him to park his dick every now and again!' she said. If she hadn't lost the plot with me, I would have explained to her that my answer was based on the fact that the best way we could have this conversation was to stay calm and keep things as normal as possible and, up to that point, I had every intention of apologising profusely to her for sleeping with her husband, but also to get it through to her how much I love him. But you know what I'm like when someone starts up with me, girls . . ." Jess trailed off, her face growing redder by the minute.

I sighed. "Go on. What did you say?"

She winced. "That it wasn't my fault if he hadn't had much opportunity to practise his parking over the past few years and was trying to improve his skills, and I could assure her that it wasn't only every now and again."

"Jesus, Jess." I shook my head.

"I know, I know. But she came looking for a fight, so I gave her one."

"Was giving her husband one not bad enough?" Simone drawled.

"What happened then?" I said quickly before I had to step in as a referee again.

"She ranted and raved for a while about me only being a bit part in Ciarán's mid-life crisis – and how I was just the first person stupid enough or easy enough to drop my knickers for him. He'd come back to his champagne lifestyle when he got sick of the cheap taste of lemonade."

"*Ooooh* . . ." Simone hissed. She almost sounded pleased at the insult to Jess.

"I know. Pathetic line, wasn't it? You'd think she could have come up with something more original." Jess moved swiftly along. "I let her vent for a while – I think she deserved that, to be fair."

"Never let it be said that you're not a reasonable person," Simone said.

Jess ignored her. "When she eventually stopped, I said that from her perspective and that of her children, I was sorry for sleeping with her husband and that I know he isn't mine to be sleeping with but, from my own perspective, I could never be sorry for what I'm doing because I love him so much, and I was sorry to tell her this but he loved me too. You should have seen the sneer on her face when I said that, girls. Then she just outright laughed at me. Said that I was even more stupid than I looked if I believed that he loved me."

This was not going to end well.

"So . . . I kind of flipped again. Told her that her whole marriage was just one big power trip and that she'd engineered their relationship so that Ciarán was completely dependent on her."

"I hope your coffee hadn't arrived by then," Simone said. "That would have been a perfect juncture for her to throw it all over you."

"It hadn't, but she might well have because the truth definitely hurt. Her face went completely red and she looked like she wanted to explode. She said I had no idea what I was talking about. I told her to go home and ask her husband if I was wrong – and, for the first time in their marriage, she should actually listen to what he had to say. She called me every name under the sun at that point – all of the ones you mentioned were in there, Simone, you'll be glad to hear. Then the coffee arrived, so I drank it back, left a few euro on the table for it and got up to walk out before this got even uglier. 'Where do you think you're going? This isn't over!' she screamed at me. At this stage, everyone in the café was staring over at us. I had to shut her up fast in case she followed me back to the office and spread my business all around my workplace – and yes, I know I'm the one in the wrong, but I knew I had to get tough for damage-limitation purposes. 'Women like you always blame the other woman instead of taking a good look at your marriage to see where it went wrong,' I said to her. 'Now, if you ever come near my workplace again, I'll be calling the police on you for harassment. I'll let you away with it this once as payback for me screwing your husband, but it ends here.' Then I walked out, hoping I looked more confident than I felt. She didn't follow me." She paused. "In hindsight, it really didn't go as well as it could have."

"Oh, you reckon?"

"Simone, I swear to you that I genuinely wanted to convey to her just how bad I feel about all of this mess –"

"To make yourself feel better."

"– but it just didn't happen."

"Because you couldn't resist the opportunity to mouth off."

Jess narrowed her eyes. "This is your fault, you know." She traced an imaginary line in the air from Simone across to me with a fingertip. "It's both of your faults."

"What? It's our fault you can't keep your knickers on with someone else's man? Now I've heard it all!" Simone was indignant.

"When I was young, you two drilled it into me always to stand up for myself, even if I was in the wrong. You said it was the only way I'd survive in our crazy family, remember? And now it's just a force of habit. It's like a reflex and I really can't help it."

Simone huffed and puffed a significant amount of air out of her downturned mouth.

"And you, Simone, were way worse for that than Tammy ever was. I remember when I was ten and you were seventeen, and you sat me down and made me repeat over and over for about half an hour that I'd never let anyone make shit of me. Do you remember that?"

Simone's eyes glinted. "Don't you dare use me as an

excuse for your dreadful behaviour. You need to grow up and take responsibility for your actions." She stood up. "I don't want to hear another word about this," she said, and walked out.

"Sorry about that," Jess said to me when Simone had left the room. "I shouldn't have said you and Simone are to blame for this – of course you're not. I'm all over the place these days. I'm sure you're sick of listening to Simone and me fighting too."

I shrugged. "Adrienne and I have come up with a lot worse in terms of rows over the years. How did Audrey find out, anyway?"

"One of her friends saw us together and Audrey has been spying on Ciarán ever since. He had no idea she knew until I rang him when I went back into the office after our confrontation. He went straight home from work and found her sitting in the living room with her mascara down her cheeks, a bottle of gin on the table – she had every victim cliché in the book going on. The minute he opened his mouth to explain how he feels about me, she got up and whacked him full force across the head, karate chop-style, then kicked him in the balls and buried a fist in his stomach. She disappeared out the door after that, and he hasn't seen her since. That was four hours ago."

"So what's Ciarán doing now?"

"Sitting at home waiting for her to come back."

Jess's face betrayed just how worried she was about this fact.

"Jess . . . what exactly is he going to say to her when she does? That he wants to be with you? That their marriage is over?" I paused, hating to have to say the words but knowing they needed to be said. "Or that your relationship was a mistake?"

221

The silence that followed answered my question – although it was only telling me what I already knew.

"I don't know yet," she eventually said. "I couldn't get a straight answer out of him. He's so confused."

I got up from my seat and sat beside Jess. "Honey, you know you're better than this . . ."

"He doesn't love her – he loves *me*," Jess proclaimed, although whether to me or to herself, I really didn't know.

"So why isn't he here right now with you?"

She buried her head in her hands. Wrong as I knew she was in everything she was doing, I couldn't but feel sorry for her. She'd fallen for the oldest trick in the book. She suddenly seemed so much younger to me again, like the little girl who'd followed Simone and me around for years. I put my arm around her.

"Jess . . . I'm only going to say this because I care so much about you, okay? I know you won't want to hear it, but just listen."

Immediately her back stiffened. I took a deep breath.

"Ciarán's not going to leave Audrey. Having an affair is a fantasy for lots of people until they get caught and they realise what they're about to lose. Then they get desperate, and will do anything to save what they have – including dropping their lovers like a burning piece of coal. I'm so sorry to be so blunt, Jess, but you have to realise that pining for a happy ending to this is not going to do you any favours."

Jess threw my arm off and got up, crossing the room and standing by the piano with her back to me.

"I'm not judging you, Jess. I know you're a good person and you're only doing this from a misplaced sense of love – but I just know that this isn't going to end well for you."

Jess whirled herself around so fast that if we'd had a wooden floor instead of a deep shag-pile carpet, she'd still be spinning to this minute. "You know what, Tammy? You have plenty of your own relationship shit to worry about. Don't suddenly start acting like you're the expert around here when you've made as much of a mess in the past as I'm making now."

She brushed past me before I could say another word and stormed out of the room.

I sank onto the sofa, realising that things with Jess were even worse than we'd thought. And God knows, she was right – this house had enough relationship crap to be getting on with as it was.

30

"Al, I got my period this morning. That's three months in a row now that I haven't got pregnant. I wonder is everything okay?"

"I'm sure it is. We'd have been very lucky for this to happen for us straight away just because we decided we want a baby."

I nodded, but I wasn't sure if I agreed or not. If everything was okay, there should be no reason why I wouldn't have fallen pregnant unless there was something up. I knew I'd done my ovulation maths right.

"Hmm. Well, hopefully we won't have to wait a full year. Maybe I'm ovulating earlier than expected or something."

"Looks like we're going to have to double our efforts this coming month. What a hardship."

"Terrible. I'm dreading it already."

"We should start doing the things in our plan before you get pregnant," Alvin said.

We'd done nothing about it since he last mentioned it because I'd been too consumed with reading every book *conceivable, pardon the pun, on getting pregnant even to think about the plan, and Alvin usually relied on me to get things underway.*

"When's your next free weekend?"

I shrugged. "Well, I have to pick a Saturday to have a work dinner party here sometime before the end of this month, and then we have my friend's baby's christening the weekend after next, so we should probably leave it until next month."

"Okay, next month it is." Alvin went to the wine rack and pulled out a bottle of red. "Let's drink while you still can." He opened the bottle, poured two glasses and handed one to me.

"Here's to your last period for quite a while," he said, lifting up his glass and clinking it against mine.

31

Pre-parental plan activity 6: Learn how to bake a cake

Alvin, I don't know much about kids right now, but I do know that they like cake. And when the time comes to bake and ice cakes for birthdays, christenings and whatever other excuse the kids come up with to sting us for a cake, I'll be the fool in the kitchen covered in flour and icing while you watch Sky Sports. Now, maybe I wouldn't want you getting in my way in the kitchen when the time comes, but I reserve the right to train you to be a slave even if the slavery is never called upon – it's only right!

"We're the only people here under seventy, Tammy. Just an observation."

"More of an exaggeration." The majority of the people around us were more in their sixties than seventies, to be fair. What else could we expect at a cake-decorating course?

Although Alvin was up for most things in life, the

concept of this activity was one that just seemed to perplex him – why would anyone bake a cake and then decorate it when you could buy a cooked and decorated one in any given supermarket? – but, in true Alvin form, he'd gone along with it anyway. He was still being somewhat distant with me since Galway though. He hadn't even answered the phone the first few times the previous day when I'd rung to arrange this. When we had eventually spoken, he'd been clipped and anxious to get off the phone. It was worrying, but now that we were face-to-face again he seemed to be thawing a little.

A rotund man standing at the top of the class clapped his hands. "Okay, let's get started! Welcome to my class, everyone!" Bucking the stereotype of a fifty-something woman obsessed with cooking, Gerry was – well – a fifty-something man obsessed with cooking. He was the home-baking expert for Ireland's biggest flour-milling and packing business, and was running these courses on the side. They were hugely popular too because Gerry had a highly prominent profile, always showing up on TV shows to talk about wedding and Communion cake-decorating and suchlike. Our course was a one-day introduction to cake decorating and didn't promise to be too hardcore, although my original plan had been to do a course that spanned ten weeks. From Alvin's point of view, that alone was probably a good reason for us to break up.

I looked around the class one last time to make sure Adrienne and Clarissa hadn't slipped in. After them showing up in Galway, nothing would surprise me. But no, we were still the youngest people in the room.

"Okay, ladies . . . oh, and gentleman. It's not often I get to say that! Welcome to the class, everyone. We've a lot to fit into today – you're going to learn about icing recipes for decorating cakes and the range of different icing on the market, how to perfectly ice a cake using a spatula . . ."

"A what?" Alvin whispered. I shushed him.

". . . and how to colour icing and use fondant to decorate cakes . . ."

Alvin looked at me and mouthed 'fondant' as he flipped his hand in a 'What the fuck is that?' manner.

". . . and we'll run through various cake decorating techniques, finishing with a lesson on how to decorate a cake board . . ."

"You are a cruel woman," Alvin hissed.

". . . so everyone sit down and make themselves comfortable and we'll spend a few minutes talking about all the different types of icing that are out there in the world." Gerry beamed with delight as he launched into a description of buttercream icing.

He didn't get far past his launch. The women in the class seemed to be more interested in having a bit of banter with Gerry than learning about icing, and the few minutes turned into a good twenty minutes of dialogue. To be honest, I had a feeling they knew all this stuff already and were just here for the *craic*. Alvin, however, wasn't experiencing any such *craic* and looked pained after the first twenty seconds.

"So now, it's time to get hands on." One of the women reached over and touched Alvin's arm, to a chorus of '*Woo!*' from all the others.

"I want everyone to choose a partner and work in pairs to produce all the different types of icing. Then this afternoon we'll ice our cakes according to a theme of your choosing and I'll declare one of the pairs to be the winner of a special prize."

"I'm cancelling my cheque for this course if you don't pair me up with him," a woman with short, straight ash-blonde hair said immediately as she pointed at Alvin. "Hasn't he a gorgeous head of hair?"

"He does," said one of the others. "He's like a grown-up male Shirley Temple."

Yet another of them leaned across me and touched Alvin's hair. "And by God, it's as soft as silk!"

"Is it a wig?" someone at the end of the row said.

"Alright, ladies, come back to me here," Gerry said with a frown. He probably wasn't used to competition in this class.

From the nonplussed look on Alvin's face, it seemed that Gerry was welcome to keep the attention all for himself. Alvin might be used to twenty and thirty-something women throwing themselves at him, but this was unfamiliar territory.

The cheque-cancelling woman, Bessie, got her way and was paired up with Alvin – money talks – and he was too respectful to question the decision. I wasn't though and made plenty of noise about wanting to stay in a pair with Alvin, but everyone just looked at me as if I was getting in the way. Good thing I was getting used to that since Clarissa came back on the scene or I might have felt bad. She had her uses.

I was paired up with a woman called Theresa, who didn't seem any happier about the arrangement than I was. All through the mixing of the various types of icing she barked orders at me, forcing me to assert my authority and challenge her on every single thing she said. By the time everyone else was finished all their icing, we hadn't even finished the first one. Alvin and Bessie seemed to be getting on famously though. He kept bending down low to talk into her ear and was being rewarded with hearty cackles. I'd often thought when we were together that if charm was somehow in the genes, I hoped our children would get his. I often resented how he seemed to glide through situations in life on his looks and his easy personality while people like me were always the fall guys. I always had to work at getting people interested in me and seeing that I was worthwhile. Alvin just had an innate attractiveness that extended to males and females, young and old, even bloody animals. That was how the world worked and I had to accept it, but sometimes I got sick of having to try so hard.

"What are you daydreaming about?" Theresa followed my eyes. "Ah. Keep those thoughts for the bedroom, lady. We've work to do here."

I forced my eyes back to my mixing bowl. "So what made you decide to do this course?" I said to keep my mind from wandering again.

"I'm trying to knock off one of my neighbours – had a row with her about her extension. She knows I'm a terrible cook and wouldn't eat anything I made when we were on good terms, so I'm hoping to upskill on the cake front, slip a bit of poison into the cake, make friends with her again and then catch her off the hop with my wonderful creations."

"Oh. That's nice."

"That's nice? That's murder! I've just told you I'm trying to bump off my neighbour and you don't react at all? That's what's wrong with this country these days – young people have no initiative! You should be threatening to report me! For the record, in case you get a pang of the guilts later, I'm here because I'm sixty-three and never see anyone but my postman. My daughter gave me a guilt voucher for this because she spends too much time at work and not enough calling around to see me."

"Oh." I was going to add 'Lovely' but who knows what kind of trouble that might have got me in. I decided to shut up. Alvin was right when he'd said I'd never been good at small talk.

Not content with your common or garden buttercream or royal icing, we concocted mixtures for rolled fondant, fudge icing, foam icing, glazes, ganaches . . . we'd all be wearing dentures from the ensuing tooth decay after this, not just the pensioners. Several hours of sniping between Theresa and me later, we broke for a quick lunch of sandwiches with a full set of icing under our belts ready for our return, when we'd inflict our efforts on some unsuspecting cakes. Bessie monopolised Alvin over lunch, guffawing loudly as if to make a statement to the other women that she was the one who'd bagged the prize. He seemed happy enough though, so I decided not to rescue him. I had an inkling that Theresa would clock me if I was seen to be consorting with the enemy anyway.

"Now, here comes the fun bit!" Gerry said with a flourish as he produced a spatula. I looked over at Alvin to see if there was any recognition in his eyes as to what a spatula was now that he'd seen one, but no, there didn't seem to be any 'Aha!' moments going on. "Keeping crumbs out of the icing is one of the biggest challenges you'll ever face," Gerry said, momentarily forgetting things like the economic crisis and high mortgage payments. He got us to gather around him and showed us how to glide the spatula over the icing correctly. When he'd done this to perfection, he used a combination of the different types of icing to decorate the cake and the cake board. The result was intimidatingly good. Theresa gave me a dig in the ribs with her elbow. "Are you taking that in? That's what we need to do, only better!"

Bessie heard her. "You haven't a hope," she said with a smile at Alvin. He looked confident too.

"Come on, Theresa," I said, my competitive edge rising. "Let's ice them out of the water."

An afternoon of intense concentration ensued. Every spread of the buttercream on top of the cake made by Theresa was monitored closely by me. Every move I made to smooth the buttercream into the side of the cake while spinning the cake stand on the turntable we'd been provided with was analysed by Theresa. Every now and again, Theresa and I would look at each other, nod and simultaneously throw a covert glance over at Bessie and Alvin's efforts. Bessie had no such discretion though, and was brazen enough to walk right up to us and gawk directly at what we were doing – until some of Theresa's icing accidentally went flying off her spoon onto Bessie's cheek.

The afternoon passed with an air of guerrilla warfare about it. When the time came for us to unveil our cakes, I felt quietly confident. We'd chosen Easter as our theme, and our Easter basket cake was an eye-catching spectacle of yellow buttercream, fondant Easter eggs and honey-glazed icing. I'd found a pipe cleaner and a yellow ribbon in Gerry's decorative supplies and had wrapped the ribbon around the pipe cleaner to create a handle for the basket. We'd covered our cake board with foil and created a yellow basketweave design around the sides of the cake, then piped yellow swirls around the bottom of the basket. I could see only the side of Alvin and Bessie's cake, but it didn't look overly promising. It was plastered in bog-standard patternless white icing and looked a bit uninspired. The cakes of the other two pairs in the class didn't look up to much either.

Gerry seemed to agree. His face was impassive when he inspected cakes 1 and 2. I felt a flutter of anticipation and couldn't believe I was this excited about potentially winning a cake-decorating competition, but somehow I'd been drawn into it all. And from the concentration that seemed to be going on at Alvin's table, so had he.

"Tammy and Theresa, what have you two come up with? Ooh," Gerry said as he circled around our cake, bending down to examine the icing on the side, "yes, I like what you've done with this!"

I winked at Theresa. She mouthed back 'In the bag'. I nodded.

"Okay Alvin and Bessie, let's look at your masterpiece."

I edged closer to get a proper look at the cake. If you were feeling generous, you'd describe it as a colourful iced hedgehog. There were lumps and bumps and sticky-out bits of buttercream everywhere you looked. I couldn't even make out what they'd written on it with icing.

Gerry peered down and inspected the cake more closely. "Well, would you look at that!" He then seemed to be lost for words because he left it at that.

"We chose to do a birthday cake," Bessie said, winking at Alvin. "Go on," she said, burying an arm in his back as she tried to push him forward.

Alvin lifted up the cake and walked towards me. "Happy birthday, Tammy," he said almost shyly. I looked at the top of the cake and realised that the gloopy icing writing said 'Happy 35th Birthday, Tammy' and the lumps of colour on top were meant to be balloons. It would be my birthday in two days' time.

"You remembered," I said. I really hadn't expected him, or anyone, to acknowledge the day. I always downplayed my birthdays.

"Did you ever think I wouldn't?"

All of the post-Galway animosity suddenly seemed to disintegrate.

"Aw! Aren't they the cutest pair!" Bessie said.

"I didn't think so at the start," Theresa said, "because your one here seemed a bit too hardnosed for him – he's a lovely fella, the kind you'd love your daughter to bring home." The deaf or invisible kind, apparently. "But, you know, I think she loves him as much as he loves her."

"She does. Did you see the looks that were passing between them earlier?"

"Yes. That's why I let him ice the cake."

"Erm, we're still here," Alvin said.

Everyone laughed except me. If I'd said that, I would have been hardnosed. Luckily, I was too busy buzzing internally just then to get introspective about that particular issue. It was a bit hypocritical of me to be so happy about a birthday acknowledgement when I actively told everyone to ignore my birthday, but let the world call me a hypocrite if it wanted to. All I knew was that Alvin remembering my birthday had filled me with the type of joy that made the world seem like a lovely, lovely place.

"Well, after that I don't think I've any choice but to deem Alvin and Bessie the winners!" Gerry said.

Everyone cheered. Gerry picked up two bags and handed them to Alvin and Bessie. They both looked into their bags.

"Flour," Alvin said. "Just what I need."

"Don't forget me for getting your wedding cake made when the time comes, will you?" Gerry said as we were leaving.

We made the appropriate non-committal noises before saying goodbye.

"Do you want to do something for your birthday?" Alvin said as we left laden down with cake and flour.

"Ah no. I'd prefer to just forget it's happening."

"But it's your 35th!"

"All the more reason to ignore it!"

I slipped my arm through his to take the sting out of my words. The gesture Alvin had made with the cake was all I needed for my birthday really. And, as an added bonus, we'd managed to have a Clarissa-and-Adrienne free date. By anyone's standards, that was a good day's work.

32

The first anniversary of the miscarriage was a strange affair. It would be Mum's birthday that day too, of course, and she was determined not to celebrate it in case she offended Alvin and me.

"But Mum, I'd kind of prefer if we were kept busy with something," I said when Mum called around the week before to announce that there would be no birthday celebrations this year. "The last thing I need is to have nothing to do but to sit around thinking about last year."

Particularly as I'm still not pregnant. *Taking the pill was a distant memory and we'd been trying for a baby for five months now. I'd already mentioned it to the doctor, but he'd repeated over and over that five months wasn't all that long to be trying after coming off the pill and, the miscarriage notwithstanding, we shouldn't be concerned just yet. I wasn't concerned. I was sick with worry. I didn't know how to be any other way. Alvin was handling it much better than I was and kept reassuring me that it would all happen when the time was right, but I wasn't so sure. I knew exactly when I was ovulating now due to a myriad of ovulation aids – between a basal thermometer, an ovulation kit, cycle beads, a monitor that detected ovulation using saliva and a whole section of a library's worth of books relating to ovulation, I was pretty sure I had it covered. Alvin was called upon to perform as soon as the signs of ovulation became evident, but the truth of the matter was that there was pretty much no downtime in our sex life anyway – so even on the very slim off-chance that I had somehow got the time of ovulation wrong, I really should have got pregnant anyway. So why hadn't I?*

My body probably needs time to regulate itself after coming off the pill. That's all. *I'd been repeating the words over and over to myself for the past few months, but I wasn't sure if I believed them.*

"Well, you don't need me to provide the entertainment for you, surely? Haven't you a fine man to keep you occupied that night, if you know what I mean?"

"Muuuum!"

The fine man in question was sitting right beside me on the couch while Mum sat across from us.

"Ah, will you whist and stop pretending to be a prude." *She pouted her lips at Alvin.* "If I'd had a man like you in my day instead of Tammy's father, by Jaysis, I wouldn't be stuck for things to do of an evening."

Alvin laughed off Mum's statement politely while I prayed for an immediate natural disaster to obliterate this moment (but that it'd only target me and my house – it would be that kind of selective natural disaster – I didn't want to drag anyone else into my troubles). Mum was great in millions of ways, but this was exactly why I always brought my problems to Simone and Jess's doors instead of hers and why I hadn't told her we were trying for a baby. Not only was I always unsure what was going to come out of her mouth, but her solution to every problem in life was to joke your way through it. I knew she meant no disrespect to us about the miscarriage with her words, and the fact that she'd cancelled her birthday celebrations when she was a hardcore party woman was a testament to her support, but I couldn't help but cringe all the same. A sense of humour got you through hard times, Mum said, and maybe she was right – but for someone who took life as seriously as I did, it wasn't much of a solution. And right then it was downright embarrassing, although Alvin managed to pass it off with his usual ease and had somehow got Mum on the replacement subject of why none of the milk companies had restarted the scheme of collecting milk tokens and exchanging them for kettles and the like.

"Don't you think it'd be a great help for people in these recessionary times?" he asked, not even red in the face from Mum's nudge towards the sexual-harassment route.

"You couldn't be more right, Alvin. I'm hearing that people are going mad for all things vintage these days, and that's as old-style an idea as it gets. You've an old head on young shoulders – a very good-looking head on very broad, fit shoulders, mind." She winked.

I swallowed a bit of vomit. From sexual harassment to flirting. Things hadn't moved on much after all. Thankfully, Mum had arranged to meet her sisters after her visit to us, so the suffering came to an end not long after that. She left amid assurances that she would be thinking of us on her birthday and that we should remember that we had an angel in heaven watching over us. I softened towards her considerably and almost forgave her the harassment transgressions – until she *pushed a tenner into Alvin's hand and told him to buy a packet of condoms and show her daughter a good time next week to take her mind off her problems. And then off she went, leaving me dumbfounded and Alvin wondering if I had been adopted.*

As it happened, we did spend the day of the anniversary doing as Mum had suggested – minus the condoms, of course. I happened to be ovulating, so of course we would be having sex. Afterwards, though, I worried myself sick that the baby we'd miscarried would know what we'd done and would see the way we'd chosen to spend the day as a lack of respect for him or her – but the reality was that if we hadn't been doing that, we wouldn't have known what else to be doing with ourselves either. It was one of those grey area days where, no matter what you did, it didn't seem like the right thing. I was glad when the day was over but consumed with guilt for feeling that way. I could only hope that out of the anniversary would come the happy outcome of a pregnancy.

But it wasn't to be. And so we embarked on another month of trying, both of us spouting clichés about how this month could be the month while I asked myself "What's wrong with me?"

Four months later

"Tammy, maybe we should go away this weekend," Alvin said when I walked into the sitting room after my shower. "We could do the first thing on the plan, the Road Trip to Anywhere, remember? We still haven't done anything from it!"

"Mmm, maybe. Let's talk about it later, sweetie. I'm heading up to bed now – care to join me?"

Alvin glanced at the clock. "Nah, nine is a bit too early for me. You go ahead."

239

"Erm, no. My plans for the evening can't be done on my own."

He frowned at me as if he had absolutely no idea what I was talking about.

"Alvin, I told you this morning that I'm ovulating, remember?"

"Oh, right, yeah." His eyes flickered towards the TV. "Look, I'll join you in a while – I want to catch Prime Time tonight."

"But that won't be over until about half ten!"

He shrugged. "That's hardly three o'clock in the morning! You'll still be awake at half ten!"

"OK, well, if Prime Time is so important to you, watch it by all means." I rolled my eyes. "But it doesn't start for another half an hour, so that's plenty of time to get things done . . ."

"'Get things done?' You make it sound so appealing."

"Ah, you know what I mean. So, you in?" I walked out of the room.

"No, I'm going to stay put for a while." His voice drifted towards me as I took my first step up the stairs.

"What?" I thundered back into the sitting room. "But Alvin, we have to take advantage of the timing!"

"Look, I'm not in the mood right now. I've had a long day and I want to relax and watch a bit of TV."

"You're not in the mood for sex? Am I hearing this right?"

"Maybe later, honey. Right now, I –"

"Maybe?" I ran over to the couch and crouched down beside him. "We can't do maybes! After nine months of trying for a baby, we have enough maybes in our lives! Maybe I'll get pregnant this month, maybe I won't. Maybe there's something wrong, and that's why I'm not *pregnant yet. Maybe we'll never have children, or even one child. And maybe we'll never find out what's wrong because you don't want to get tests done!"*

Alvin reached for the remote and zapped off the TV. "Here's a maybe for you, Tammy. Maybe you're ruining our sex life by making it all just about having a baby. Did you think of that one?"

I said nothing.

"No, I didn't think so."

"Al, don't be like that . . . ."

"I'm just telling you the truth. It feels like you're only thinking about whether this time is going to be the one that works."

"And is that such a bad thing? Me wondering if we've just made our baby? Aren't you wondering exactly the same thing afterwards?"

Alvin's exhale was so deep that it sounded like the air coming out of a tractor tyre. "It just feels like you're going through the motions with me now. It used to be so different."

"Well, excuse me for not being more of a sex kitten, but may I remind you that the fundamental purpose of sex is for the procreation of the species and not to make you or any other man feel good about yourself!"

Alvin face was filled with sadness when he looked at me. "It's not about how sex makes me feel. It's about us. I miss the old us."

This time, I was wise enough to hold my tongue and let him say his piece.

"While we've been trying to get one thing, we've lost something else. I miss that connection we used to have. I miss the fact that you used to want to jump me because of how you felt about me. It feels like nothing else matters

241

now except that I impregnate you. You never want to go anywhere or do anything . . . I'm not complaining about that, it's just that I'm worried about you . . ."

"This was your idea in the first place, remember?"

"Yes, but if we let nature take its course things will happen in time. I'll be up later, okay?" He turned the TV on again, the discussion over as far as he was concerned.

I stomped up the stairs, furious. An hour and a half's time could be too late. I wondered if I could get away with cutting the cable for the TV connection without him noticing . . .

33

Aunt Patty wasn't one to give up easily. When Simone relayed the details of her disastrous date with Derek to her mother, we'd all hoped Patty would leave well enough alone from now on – but Patty wasn't going to be easily deterred from any mission she might have. The evening after my birthday, she landed at our house slap bang in the middle of a programme about German literature that Simone had been looking forward to all week. Jess was visibly delighted at the distraction, but I felt sorry for Simone. Patty had that look about her – the look of a woman who meant business.

"What are you doing sitting there when you have a date to get ready for tonight?" Patty yelled at Simone without so much as a hello after I let her in.

"But I don't!"

Patty smiled knowingly. "That's what you think," she said with as much drama as she could muster. She sat down and explained that she'd set up an online dating account for Simone and had arranged a date for her in two hours' time with a man called Ivor. She looked inordinately pleased with herself.

"And it's so much fun too," she cackled. "You should have seen some of the things I said to those young lads to check their mettle. Have to sort out the men from the boys, you know."

"Oh Christ. I don't know what's more upsetting – that you're flirting with men that are three decades younger than you or that it's being done under my name. There's no way that I'm going on this date."

"You most certainly are. I've spent hours upon hours staring at pictures of young men, some of them who didn't even have a proper shirt on them, just a bare chest, sorting out the wheat from the chaff for your benefit. Do you think I actually enjoyed doing all of that?"

"Yes!" all three of us said concurrently.

"You're going," Patty said sternly. "Get up them stairs and get your glad rags on."

"Come on, I'll help you," I said. This conversation could go on for another twenty minutes otherwise, and we all knew Patty would be the victor in the end anyway.

It looked like Simone would have to wear the silver outfit again. It didn't augur well after how the date with Derek had ended up, but she had nothing else.

"Ivor!" Simone said in disgust as she stood in front of the mirror inspecting herself. "His name reminds me of Bovril – I mean, can you think of another word that spells the name Ivor if you jiggle a few letters around and lose a few others?"

"He might be lovely," I said. "Just go meet him and see how you get on."

So off she went to meet him in a pub called The Mercantile with a printout supplied by Patty of Ivor's online account profile picture in her hand. An hour and a half later she was back in the sitting room with a gloomy expression. There were no tears this time, but her despair was all too evident. Jess shuffled uneasily in her seat, knowing that she was likely to be eaten by Simone if she said anything at all.

I pulled my feet up and patted the couch. "Come on, spill it," I said. "Was he hideous?"

"No! He – was – *gorgeous*. His picture had made him look like Shrek compared to the reality."

"Oh! That's good. Isn't it?"

"It might have been if I hadn't made it so obvious that I fancied him. He walked over to me, said 'Simone?' and I was all 'Yes! Hello!' and sounding far too enthusiastic. I mean, Tammy, it's me we're talking about here – I don't do enthusiasm from one end of the year to the next, but the one time I really should be keeping it cool, out it comes."

"But if he's all that gorgeous, he might be used to getting that kind of a reaction . . ."

"Maybe. He wasn't waxwork-perfect-looking like Derek – he had a few kinks, like his teeth were a bit crooked but he still had a wicked smile, that kind of thing. Oh, and he was six foot five at least. The funny thing was that I was sure I knew him from somewhere. Anyway, there was a bit of an awkward silence when we sat down so I asked him how the online dating world had been treating him so far, just to say something. 'Not great,' he said. 'That's probably obvious considering I'm still on the lookout.' I said that wasn't necessarily the case and that some people like to have several people on the go, and he gave me the strangest look. 'Not you!' I had to say, realising what that had sounded like. 'But I've heard

245

about guys organising a different date every night of the week, or even two in one night. My friend's brother does online dating, and he arranges to meet different women for breakfast, lunch and dinner every Saturday. He says it's like shooting fish in a barrel. Chances are he'll get laid by at least one of the three of them at some stage.' He just blinked, girls. He stared at me and blinked. Of course, I went beetroot then. That story had sounded funny in my head – why had it just sounded vulgar when I'd said it out loud?"

"Em . . . because it was? You're a disgrace to the family, Simone."

"I'd usually argue with you, Jess, but I have to agree when it comes to that comment. Anyway, he recovered himself a bit and said, 'That wouldn't be my style. I'm finding it strange enough even being out in the dating world now. I was going out with my ex, Siobhán, for eight years, so all of this is new to me.'"

Great work, Patty. Setting Simone up with someone on the rebound is really going to get you the big day out.

"Something clicked into place as soon as he said the name Siobhán," Simone continued. "Ivor and Siobhán . . . I remembered reading about them in one of those magazines you leave lying around the place."

"You mean he's Ivor Coleman? The guy who was seeing Siobhán Lynch?" Jess shrieked.

Siobhán Lynch was a well-known Irish model who'd moved to London several months ago. She'd been something of a darling in the Irish media and there'd been much bemoaning of her loss on the back page of a Sunday newspaper when the news broke of her abandoning ship. Crikey, so this was the standard poor Simone had to live up to? A bloody model?

Simone nodded. "'Ah, that's right. I have you placed now – I knew I knew you from somewhere!' I said to him. 'Ivor Coleman of Ivor and Siobhán! Did you and Siobhán break up because she wanted to go to London for her career, or did she go to London to get away from Dublin after things ended between you?' He looked momentarily stunned. 'Okay, you know some of my backstory then. I don't really want to get into the ins and outs of what happened though if you don't mind,' he said. 'Just making conversation!' I screeched frantically. I really hadn't been fishing, but I could see why he thought I had. The conversation was well and truly going off the rails by then so I had to get it back onto normal, everyday stuff."

"Minimalism in Beckett's plays, then?" Jess nudged me. I stayed on my fence.

"I asked him where he was from. 'Out the Foxrock way,' he said. 'Oh, really? What part? I'm very familiar with the area,' I said. Simon had been from Foxrock, as you know. Still is, of course. Always will be. 'Foxrock Road,' he says. I swallowed. Hard. 'Oh right, yeah. Know it well. What part of Foxrock Road?' He was frowning slightly by now. 'The upper Foxrock Road.' And I'm there going 'No, no way!' He could not possibly be from the same bloody road as Simon!"

Oh no. Anything that brought Simon back into our lives in any way wasn't good.

"So I launch into this prattle along the lines of 'Oh, yes, a great road, lovely houses there . . . what part of it are you from? I mean, are you from the upper part of the upper Foxrock Road or the lower part, if you get me? The upper part being the bit that's closer to Cabinteely?' Simon is from the other end of it, the bit that was closer to Leopardstown. It's a long road, but there was every chance he and Ivor had gone to school together or something. And I'm sitting there thinking what if this went somewhere with Ivor and he brought me home to meet his parents some Sunday, and there was Simon visiting his in the house right beside Ivor's? Now at this stage, Ivor's frown was a full-on, no-Botox-could-ever-do-anything-for-you-mate one. 'Does it really matter?' he said. I go 'No, no . . . it's just that I'm . . . a bit obsessive about the layout of areas. It goes back to a geography project I had to do in Transition Year, you see.' He didn't. And I didn't blame him."

"Oh, Simone . . ." I covered my face with my hands.

"I know. Moving swiftly along was the only way to deal with this, I said to myself. 'So! What school did you go to?' 'St Brendan's,' he told me. The very same secondary school that Simon had gone to, girls. I thought they mightn't have been in the same year, though . . . Ivor looked younger than Simon. 'And primary?' I asked him. If they'd gone to the same primary school, they'd *definitely* know each other in secondary. 'St Luke's,' he said. 'Why?' I'm there going 'Oh, no why. And what age are you, Ivor? You never said on your online profile . . .' 'Thirty-one,' he answered. My heart sank even further. Simon would be thirty-two now."

I'd thought he was closer to forty even when Simone was with him. I guess all that misery had to take its toll somewhere.

"'A great age,' I said. 'And tell me, Ivor, do you go home to Foxrock much these days?' 'Em . . . now and again . . .' he muttered. I could see he was waiting for me to explain where I was going with this, but I was hardly going to say that I was trying to suss out how likely it was that he'd meet my ex in the local shop on a Sunday afternoon. So I just said, 'You probably go home for Sunday lunch every week, do you?' His face crunched up. '*Woah*, steady on. I'm getting exhausted here. You ask a lot of questions, you know.' I said I was just nervous and his face softened a bit. 'Fair enough. So where are you from yourself?' 'Em . . . the country,' I answered to protect my anonymity. Then his hard-man look returned. 'You have a Dublin accent,' he pointed out. 'My parents are both from Dublin, so they must have passed it on to me,' I improvised. 'I'm from . . . Kildare. And sure, Kildare, Dublin, they're practically all the one these days, right?' He comes back with 'I don't think you'd find many people from either county agreeing with you on that one. There's lots of inter-county rivalry between Dublin and Kildare.' 'Ah, that's all sports-related nonsense,' I said. 'You're not into the GAA?' he goes. I shook my head. 'No. You?' 'Love it,' he says. 'Oh,' says I. I wished with all my heart that the glass in front of me was full again, girls. By then I was thinking that the Sunday lunch scenario probably wasn't going to be an issue, but what if he turned out to be a friend of Simon's and ended up telling him about this weird girl he went on a date with? I'd die. So when he said, 'Another drink, Simone?', I went in there for some damage limitation. 'My name's not Simone. That's just the name I used for my online account. It's . . . em . . . Juno.'"

"Oh, Simone, you didn't?" I was trying really hard not to laugh now.

"'Juno? That's . . . unusual. Is that a nickname?' And I went 'Yes! Yes, my name is actually June. Everyone's just been calling me Juno since that movie came out a few years ago.' 'And you're calling yourself by that name now too?' he asks me. I nodded and smiled at him. 'Gas, isn't it?' He didn't look too amused. Then he goes 'You know, Ivor isn't really my real name either.'

"'I knew it!' I said. I'd had my suspicions all along. What parent would be awful enough to give a name like that to a poor defenceless child? 'Wow, you really picked a mad one, didn't you?' 'Mad?' he said. 'Well, it's not as if anyone would actually *want* to be called Ivor,' I replied. He goes, 'You don't like it, huh?' I said it was dreadful and laughed, expecting him to join in. 'My full name is Gulliver,' he says then. 'It just mutated into Ivor over the years.' 'Ah,' was all I could come back with. So his name pretty much *was* Ivor."

I burst out laughing. I just couldn't help it.

"Then he stood up, nonchalant as you like, and said 'You know, I think I'll hit the road.' Now, I didn't think it had been going well or anything, but we'd only been there about fifteen minutes! When I said as much, he replied, 'I don't think either of us could do another fifteen, though, do you?' He smiled what must have been his letting-them-down-gently smile and said, 'Look, you seem great . . . very unique . . . but I think we both know there's no spark there, so I won't waste any more of your time.' And then he just walked straight out. Not even a backwards glance. And to think earlier on I'd been there planning out how we'd get around the Simon thing if it went somewhere. It would be funny if it wasn't so tragic and hopeless."

"Newsflash, it is funny," Jess said. "It's also tragic and hopeless, but funny too. You have to laugh through all of this crap, Simone. What else is there to do?"

Coming from Jess, that was quite deep and quite up Simone's street of thought, too. I thought Simone would appreciate it, but she just groaned.

"Well, that's it now. I'm not putting myself through something like that again. Maybe I just have to mentally prepare myself for the fact that I might never meet anybody. We all seem to think it's going to be our lot in life eventually, as if we're somehow entitled to it, but that's not how life works. I know I wasted a few years pining over Simon, but I thought in the back of my head that someone else would eventually come along. But people don't just come along when you hit our age, do they?"

"Whatever happened to Positive Simone?" Jess asked.

"Oh, she's gone back to whatever figment of my imagination she came out of. It was temporary insanity for me to think I could be anything other than what I am." She sighed. "Nobody knows better than I do that we're put on this earth to endure misery and battle our way through the daily nothingness, but seriously, is this all there is when it comes to dating? Why does it all have to be so difficult?"

I sighed. "I wish I knew," I said sorrowfully.

"Oh, shut up, you! Don't think you can join me in this. You're not on my level at all. You have a man who adores the ground you walk on whether you can see that or not, and you're sitting here laughing at me and then trying to steal my thunder. No way!"

And with that, she got up and walked out.

"That's you well and truly told," Jess said before she did exactly the same thing.

34

As soon as I heard Alvin's key in the door, I was filled with dread. This was the tenth time I would dash his hopes.

"Hi, darling. How was your day?" Alvin took one look at my face and instantly knew.

The tear-stained look gave me away, granted.

"Oh, sweetheart. Come here."

I folded myself into his arms, biting on my lip to stop myself from crying.

"When did you get it?"

"An hour ago." My voice was muffled as I spoke into his chest, but it didn't matter whether Alvin had heard me or not. It made no difference what exact time my period had arrived. What mattered was that yet again, I wasn't pregnant.

"Any couple that has to try for this long usually finds out that there's something wrong." I rubbed my empty stomach. "Something just isn't right, Alvin. My periods are always regular . . ."

"That doesn't mean there's something wrong. You've

been working so hard recently, and you've said yourself that you've been stressed out of your mind with that big project you have on. Stress could well be the cause of all of this."

I pulled away from him. *"So if I just calm down everything will be fine, is that it? It's my own fault I'm not pregnant?"*

Alvin gave me a lopsided smile. *"Are you sure you're not? You sound a bit hormonal . . ."*

"Oh, for God's sake! That was low, Alvin!"

Alvin shook his head. *"I'm sorry. My sense of comic timing has always been up my ass. I was just trying to lighten things up . . . I know how upset you are . . ."*

"How upset I am? There are two of us in this! Aren't you upset? Is this just my problem all of a sudden?"

"Oh Tammy, come on." He threw his eyes up to heaven as he wriggled out of his jacket. *"You know this is what I want. I've talked about nothing else for the last ten months."*

"Well, as soon as this period has gone, we have to stop talking and start doing."

Alvin cocked an eyebrow. *"We've been doing nothing but doing. I've never had so much sex in my life. I'm not complaining, mind, but I don't think this is down to a lack of trying . . ."*

"You see! You see! You've just admitted we have a problem! We need to take action on this, Alvin. We need to go and get ourselves checked out . . ."

"The last time we mentioned it to the doctor, he said it could take over a year for this to happen. At this stage, we might just be putting ourselves through a load of poking and prodding for nothing . . ."

"I don't believe I'm hearing this." I tried to inject a

note of calm in my voice, realising I was on the cusp of losing it a bit – a lot – but failed miserably. "You've just called getting our baby sooner 'nothing'! Are you just playing along with this so you'll get loads of sex every night?" My voice went through the roof, but it was too late to stop it now. "That's it, isn't it? Poking and prodding doesn't seem to put you out one bit when it's you that's doing it!"

Alvin shook his head, then gave me a wry smile. "Thank you. Now everyone within a three-mile radius of where we live thinks that I'm a sex addict. That should earn me some interesting looks next time I pop to the shop."

I stomped into the sitting room and flopped on the couch. "For more tampons," I muttered. Yes, Alvin was that rare kind of guy who would happily go to our local newsagent's for me and buy the one thing most men would rather set up a factory and produce themselves than buy in front of someone they knew (Alvin, of course, was on first name and how's-the-family-doing terms with everyone who worked in the newsagent's). I wasn't someone who let my supplies of anything dwindle, so he hadn't had to do it often – only once, actually, when Jess had robbed my entire box during a visit – but I knew he'd do it every single month if I asked him to. And here I was, yelling my head off at him. Every word I'd just said replayed in my head in the space of a few seconds, and suddenly, I felt sickeningly embarrassed.

"I'm sorry, Al. I shouldn't be taking my frustration at all this out on you. I don't know what's wrong with me . . ."

"There most probably isn't anything wrong with you. We just need some more time . . ."

"I meant my temper, but thanks anyway."

"Oh, that. Well yes, there's something wrong there, but that's your personality and we can't change that. I like you anyway, so that's okay." He grinned, then leaned over and kissed me very softly on my left cheek. "We just haven't got lucky yet . . . in the sense of getting pregnant, I mean, not the other thing, obviously. We're very lucky in that respect." He put an arm around my shoulder and kissed the top of my head. "We have each other, and that's the main thing."

I nuzzled into his chest, then looked up at him. "Alvin . . . this is going to work out for us, isn't it?"

"Sure it is." He nodded, and pulled me closer. "Sure."

I'd never heard him sound so unsure of anything in all the time we'd been together.

Two months passed, bringing two more periods with them.

"We're going to have to take this to the doctor again, Alvin, and it's been a full year now so he can't fob us off this time. Positive thinking is all well and good, but it's a positive pregnancy test we're looking for here and we can't get me up the duff on hope alone. We need my Humpty Dumpties and your baby Kermits to be in good shape too and it's looking like I'm falling off the wall somewhere along the way, or you're losing your ability to sing, or both."

"Sorry? What language was that?"

"Well, what the hell else does Kermit do only sing? You know what I'm getting at here! There's either something wrong with me, something wrong with you, or something wrong with us. And we can't do anything about it if we're not even aware of it in the first place."

Alvin exhaled slowly. "Okay, you're right. Let's go to

255

the doctor. Just please don't ever refer to Humpty Dumpty and Kermit like that again. When all of this works out, I don't want to be thinking about my sperm and your eggs whenever we read the Humpty Dumpty nursery rhyme to the kids or see the Muppets on some retro TV channel. Some things are sacred."

If I'd known that was what was going to work, I've have said those words a long time ago. I was out of the room and on the phone to the doctor before Alvin had even closed his mouth.

35

Pre-parental plan activity 7: Hijack someone
else's kids for a night

Tammy, let's go back to how the idea of this list came about. You were worried about us seeing each other at our worst when we have kids and we're stressed to the hilt from all the screaming and the sleeplessness and the poo-covered clothes, and that's just us. But we really have no idea what we'll be like with kids, have we? We've never really had much to do with them in the practical sense. It's time for us to change that. I'll find the kids, you bring the headache tablets and the washing powder . . .

"Now whatever else you do, don't tickle Jamie's belly – it makes him projectile vomit every time," Alvin's cousin Faye said to us. "See those streaks on the wall? All vomit stains."

"Just out of curiosity, why did you keep tickling him past the first few times if you knew it made him hurl?" Alvin asked.

"He'd swallowed a few dodgy things like coins and Scrabble letters and it was easier than sticking fingers down his throat. Oh, he has reflux too – I probably should tell you that. So even if you don't tickle him, I'd watch out for the vomit either way."

I was already scared and Faye hadn't even started filling us in on baby Jamie's three-year-old sister Annie yet. Alvin said it hadn't been hard to convince Faye and Ray to go away overnight to a fancy country hotel while we baby-sat, mostly, I imagined, because Faye and Alvin had always been very close and she trusted him with her kids – we used to meet Faye and Ray at least once a week in the old days – but probably also because they badly needed a break. Ray's hair had receded halfway back his skull since I'd last seen him, and Faye had make-up on only one eye and was either oblivious to the fact or didn't care.

"It usually takes him about an hour to settle, so you might need to pop in and out of the room every two minutes or so to reassure him that he's not on his own," Faye instructed. "Best thing to do is to bring up a book, sit out on the landing and have a read for that hour between your visits."

"Would it not be easier to just stay in the room altogether until he's asleep?"

"No!" Faye and Ray said simultaneously in the same panicked tones as each other.

"That's the worst thing in the world you can do!" Faye said. "We've spent months – *months*, I'm telling you – trying to break that habit. If I come back and he won't go to sleep by himself because you've slept in the room with him, you'll have undone ninety evenings of the trauma I've put into sorting him out. Please don't make me send someone over to where you live."

"Alright, Faye, calm down a bit there," Ray said, looking embarrassed.

I was confused – if they had to pop into Jamie every two minutes until he fell asleep, surely that went against the idea that he should fall asleep by himself? But I said nothing. I knew the look of a woman about to blow when I saw one.

"As for Annie, here's a checklist of the things you'll need to do before she goes to sleep. You'll probably need to hold her down to brush her teeth. Try to pin her legs down with yours, otherwise you'll get a wicked kick in the back from her. Be careful when you're putting on her pyjamas too as she could get a sly knee lift into your stomach when she's facing you – she hates going to bed, the poor little divil."

I widened my eyes and smiled tightly. Was Faye ripping the mick out of me here? Surely she didn't just accept what sounded like temper tantrums and acts of violence from her three-year-old daughter – and, on that subject, surely she didn't expect me to accept them either?

Faye ran through a list of four books that I'd need to read to Annie – in a particular order, of course – then moved on to the precarious area of putting her down to sleep. "Now, it's slightly more difficult than it is with Jamie. Once she's asleep, she'll sleep for the night – but getting her to that point is the problem. She'll get out of the bed immediately, so just put her straight back in again, okay?"

"That's it?" I said. That didn't sound too bad. Comparatively.

"Yeah. You might be lucky – she might only do it about ten times because she doesn't know you and she might be afraid to push your boundaries too much. We usually get about twenty escape attempts."

Oh. I should have known. "Will there be any kicking involved in these ten attempts to put her to bed?"

"Oh jeepers, no. No, she's more into throwing herself on the ground than kicking while all of this is going on. She'll try to trip you up as you're carrying her in. But you'll be fine, you're big and strong and healthy and you'll be well able for her."

"I'd had no idea it would be such a minefield," I said, laughing slightly. It sounded like nervous laughter. It should have, because that was exactly what it was.

"Haven't you ever watched *Supernanny*?" She sounded annoyed, as if I had slighted her children.

"People who don't have children don't watch *Supernanny*, love," Ray reminded Faye. "If they did, the procreation of the species would stop completely. Don't ever watch it," he said to us. "They have the most badly behaved little fuckers in the world on that show."

I'd seen plenty of *Supernanny* and I wasn't sure about that. I was starting to think they might be in this house, God forgive me.

After Faye went through a checklist of things we needed to do for the kids in the morning – in *excruciating* detail – and assured us about twenty times that all we had to do was ring if anything went wrong and they'd come home, Faye and Ray eventually left at four, Faye reluctantly and Ray hurling himself through the front door and running to the car. I had a feeling he was going to throw both of their mobile phones straight into the nearest river so that we couldn't contact them.

"Now that's a pair in need of a pint," Alvin said when we eventually managed to shunt Faye out the door.

"We might need a few ourselves by the time we hit nine o'clock." I wouldn't have minded one right that very minute. Faye had made her children sound scarier than the shower scene in *Psycho*.

We went into the sitting room where Annie and Jamie were in repose, Annie on the couch and Jamie in his playpen. Ten-month-old Jamie was lying in a cocoon of teddies and blankets and looked like a little cherub. Annie's sleeping look was a little more sprawling, with a pink blanket bunched up in a heap at her legs and a cushion sliding out from under her head, but she radiated innocence and cuteness nonetheless. We sat down on the floor (actual seats were at a premium between the child-covered couch and an armchair that housed a pile of washing) and I breathed as quietly as I could while Alvin flicked through a newspaper and opened a Snickers.

Annie woke up first. She thrashed around on the couch a few times before opening her eyes, then sat up and looked around.

"You were here before," she said when her eyes landed on me. We'd called around the previous night for dinner so that the children could get used to us. "Where's my mummy and daddy?"

"Hi, Annie!" I got up slowly and sat on the edge of her couch. "Remember Mummy and Daddy told you that Alvin and me would be looking after you today?"

Annie pouted and frowned. "No, they didn't!" Then she looked at Alvin. "Is that chocolate?"

"Would you like an apple?" I said quickly. "Apples are the best –"

"I want *chocolate*!"

"No, darling, it's bad for you!"

"I want *chocccccccooooollllllaaaaaaaaaaaaaaaaaaaaate*!"

"Annie, stop crying . . ."

Annie did what she was told and stopped crying.

Instead, she screeched. I'd never heard anything so eardrum-penetrating in all my life. And judging by Jamie's reaction, neither had he. He woke up and joined in.

"You'd think he'd be used to hearing his sister screeching and could sleep through it!" I said as I ran to the playpen to pick him up.

"He just got a fright, that's all," Alvin said, stuffing the rest of the offending Snickers into his mouth. He looked as relaxed as someone at the cinema waiting for a movie to start.

"Alvin, do something!" I said when Annie was still screeching a good two minutes later. Jamie was up on my shoulder and still hadn't fully calmed down either, whimpering intermittently.

"Annie, can you show me how to use the remote to find the cartoon channels?" was what he came up with.

Annie's face remained hidden behind her hands. "*Mommy* finds the cartoon channels!" She took a deep, shuddering breath, then inhaled quickly and roared "*Aaaaaaaagggghhhhhhh!*" right into Alvin's face. Jamie startled on my shoulder and promptly recommenced bawling.

"She's too young to know how to use a remote – just get the kids' menu and choose something!" I shouted over the hullabaloo.

"Any idea where the remote actually is?" Alvin threw a few cushions on the couch aside.

I thought he was talking to Annie until he looked over at me with an enquiring expression. How was *I* supposed to know? "None," I said shortly.

Jamie stopped crying and started nuzzling at my neck instead. "I think this fella is hungry," I said, as if saying the words aloud would somehow feed him by magic.

When a bottle didn't miraculously materialise, I tentatively laid Jamie down on his activity mat and made my way to the kitchen. I read the instructions on the back of the formula tub, determining the amount of scoops and water that were appropriate to Jamie's age. The water had to be added first, so there was nothing I could do until the kettle boiled except listen to Annie's squalls. How many sets of lungs did that child have? And then Jamie decided to join the symphony again. I willed the whistle of the kettle to grow louder, not only to get Jamie his bottle faster but to drown out the noise.

The kettle finally clicked. I poured the requisite number of ounces of water into the bottle.

"Alvin, could you pick Jamie up and jiggle him or something until this bottle is ready?" I said as Jamie increased the volume of his efforts.

"I'm still trying to find the remote . . ."

"Fuck the remote! Forget about it!" It was going to take more than a cartoon to calm Annie down now that she was in full flow. I was thinking more on the lines of Xanax. Surely Faye had some somewhere, living with these two?

Annie suddenly stopped her wailing. I heard little footsteps making their way towards me in the kitchen as I scooped in the formula.

"Give me fifty cent for the swear jar," she said. She suddenly didn't look all that upset.

"Okay, pet, you're right. I shouldn't have said that bad word. Just go inside until I get the bottle ready . . ." I continued scooping.

"No! When Daddy says 'fuck', Mommy makes him put money in the swear jar right away."

Was that the fourth or the fifth scoop? "I'll give it to you as soon as –"

"*Now!*"

"That's enough, Annie." Alvin appeared at the kitchen door. He was remoteless. "Don't speak to Tammy like that."

"I don't like her! She's *ugly*!"

My face went on fire. The embarrassment. Even a three-year-old could tell I wasn't pretty enough for Alvin.

"Come inside with me. We'll find the remote and get those cartoons." He took her hand and I waited for her to resist, but to my surprise she walked along beside him when he gave her hand a gentle tug. I turned my attention back to the bottle and realised I'd totally lost count of the scoops. The instructions had said failure to make up bottles correctly could result in illness . . .

"Shit." I poured the contents of the bottle down the sink.

Jamie was still hollering.

"Any sign of that bottle?" Alvin yelled out from the sitting room.

"It's coming!" I poured in more water and counted the scoops, shook the bottle in the manner of a cocktail barman and turned on the cold water tap, propping the bottle up against a plastic bowl in the sink so that the water flow would hit the side of the bottle and cool down the milk. I went back into the sitting room and picked up Jamie to cuddle him. His cries seemed to grow louder when I picked him up, and he beat his arms against my shoulders as he sobbed into my chest. When I left him down again after five minutes to get his bottle, there was a snail's trail of dribble and snot all over my top. I dabbed at it with kitchen roll before turning off the tap and getting the bottle.

The bottle had slipped onto its side and the lid was

now full of water. What did that mean? Was the bottle contaminated now? Had the water seeped into the bottle through the little sucky hole-in-the-teat thingie?

Jamie was now screeching as if someone had chainsawed his arms off.

The raucous sound of the screeches seemed to be coming closer. Suddenly, they were right in my ear.

"How much longer will that bottle be?" Alvin had picked Jamie up and was rocking him over and back.

I explained my concerns.

"Yeah, I wouldn't risk giving him that. You're going to have to start over."

I emptied the bottle, filled another one and held it under the stream of running water. Jamie was already purple from crying and looked like he was veering dangerously towards turning blue from his exertions. When I looked at him, all I could think of was Violet from *Willy Wonka and the Chocolate Factory* when she turns into a giant blueberry.

After the longest five minutes of my life, the milk was finally at the right temperature. We returned to the sitting room where Annie was sitting on one of the couches with a sulky look on her face, staring at cartoons. Alvin sat on the couch with Jamie and fed him the all-important bottle. I sat beside them, feeling clueless and useless in equal measure.

"Do you want to feed him while I get his solids meal ready for later?" Alvin said. "We don't want to get caught on the hop like that again."

I nodded reluctantly. I wasn't too taken by the thought of feeding him, but solids was probably a whole new scary world too.

"Mommy always rubs Jamie's back until he gets a

windie," Annie said without tearing her eyes away from the television after Jamie had guzzled about half of the bottle.

"During the feed or after it?" I asked Annie.

"What are you doing?" Alvin hissed from the kitchen. "Don't let her know we don't have a clue what we're doing or she'll walk all over us for the rest of the day!"

"*During* the feed." Annie broke away from the TV for a few seconds to give us the benefit of a condescending post-toddler look.

"I'll wind him when he's finished the bottle, which should be in approximately one minute at the rate he's going," I said in my most authoritative tone.

"*During*!" Annie repeated, but I ignored her.

As soon as Jamie had finished the bottle, I tried to hand him to Alvin. "His bib is wet. I need to find him a new one before I wind him."

"Mommy uses a towel," Annie said. "A bib isn't big enough. He does a lot of sick sometimes."

"I'll get it." Alvin walked over to the pile of clothes on the armchair and burrowed his way through them. "No towel," he said. "I'll get one from the hot press upstairs."

Jamie started crying again. I tapped his back in a woodpecker fashion.

"Harder," Annie said.

This time, I clapped the palm of my hand against Jamie's back vigorously. He rewarded me with a ripper of a burp and a crying cessation.

"Well done, you!" I lifted him up to face me and smiled at him. He smiled back. "That was brilliant, wasn't it, little boy? You're the best little boy in the . . . oh, Jesus!"

Jamie had just vomited down my top. It had gone right

into my bra, and I could feel it settling in a sickening pool on my chest.

"He often gets sick right after he does a big burp," Annie said – smugly, to my ears.

"Watch your cartoon before I put on the news, Annie!" I said, then instantly regretted it. What was I doing, losing my temper like that with a three-year-old? I wasn't sure if she was trying to help or to annoy us as much as possible but, either way, I had to remember who the adults were around here. Incompetent, dense adults, but adults in name nonetheless.

Alvin returned and handed me the towel. "Looks like I'm a bit late," he said as he took in the vomity scene.

"Could you take him while I change my clothes?"

I thrust Jamie into Alvin's arms and ran upstairs. Was it this full-on with kids all of the time? And even more worryingly, would I have been a really useless mother if I'd had a baby when I now felt like crying about having a chest full of baby vomit?

36

"I want to poo!" Annie declared loud enough for everyone in the neighbourhood to hear. "Tammy, come on!"

"But I don't want to poo!"

"Come on and wipe my bum!" Annie ran to the bathroom. It seemed like I had no choice but to follow her.

"Lift me up onto the toilet!" she said with a huge scowl on her face. She was growing grumpier by the second.

I did as I was bid. As I lifted her, I was sure I felt something on her back. I moved her top up and saw a red lump, rather like a water blister, nestling in her lower back. Upon closer inspection, I noticed more of them higher up on her back and a few on her belly.

Once she was settled on the toilet, I ran out to Alvin. "I'm sure Annie has chickenpox," I said in a low voice. I described the lumps I'd seen on Annie's body.

"Have you had it?" Alvin asked me.

I nodded.

"So have I. It's no big deal so. We'll just have to keep an eye on Jamie to see if it looks like he's getting it. I think babies have immunity to those kinds of things from their mothers until they're six months, but he's well past that now so he's fair game . . . but I suppose he'll have to get it sometime . . ."

"What are we going to do?" I cut across Alvin's ramblings. "What am I saying – we'll have to ring the guys and tell them to come home straight away, of course."

"But there's not much they can do about chickenpox that we can't – we just need to put calamine lotion on her and make sure she doesn't scratch herself."

"Oh, yes. From what I've seen so far, I can tell she's really going to listen to us when we tell her that."

"We're the grown-ups. She does what we say."

"*Tammy*! Come in and wipe me *now*!"

"In a second, sweetheart . . ."

"*Noooooowwww*!"

"Yeah, we're really running the show here," I said as I traipsed back to the bathroom.

I could have sworn the water blister at the bottom of Annie's back had increased threefold in size in the time I'd been talking to Alvin. It didn't help that she looked completely miserable and was reaching back to scratch her back.

"Don't scratch that itch because it makes it worse, okay? Just ignore it. Pretend there's no itch at all. Wouldn't that be fun?"

"But there *is* an itch! That's stupid!"

"No, it's fun!"

"It's *not* fun! You're stupid!"

I was way out of my depth here. I cleaned Annie up and brought her out to the sitting room.

"Are you going to ring the guys?" I said quietly as soon as I'd settled Annie in front of the TV to divert her from listening to our conversation. The last thing I wanted was for her to realise she was sick and to get freaked out.

"I don't think we should. They've probably just landed at the hotel. I think we should hold off on contacting them until the morning."

"But surely they'll want to know if their child is sick? They'll probably go mad at us for not telling them!"

"It'd be nearly Annie's bedtime by the time they'd get back, so there's not much they could do tonight anyway."

"What if she's awake all night and wants her parents?"

"The guys said she always sleeps through the night."

"But she probably won't when she's sick!"

"It's just chickenpox, Tammy. I remember getting it when I was young and there was nothing wrong with me except a bit of itching. Every child has to get it."

Why was he being so calm about all of this? "I think the guys aren't going to be one bit happy if we don't tell them. You heard what Faye said."

"And you saw the state of her. She needs this night away. Let's just let them have their dinner, drinks and whatever else they want to have tonight and we can contact them first thing in the morning. If we need to, we can bring her to the emergency doctor – there's one down the road. We'll be fine. This is the kind of thing that happens with kids."

"What happens to kids?" Annie said.

"They get to stay up late when their Uncle Alvin and Aunt Tammy call around," Alvin said.

"Tammy's not my aunt." Annie looked at me as if I was the virus around here, and then tore into a back scratch that would probably leave her scarred for life.

I ran to the kitchen to check Faye and Ray's first aid box for calamine lotion. It was the width of a bale of briquettes and contained everything from a turkey-baster lookalike object that flushed out wounds to sympathy stickers, but no calamine lotion.

I filled Alvin in. "I'll go to a chemist to get some and you mind the kids, okay?" I said to Alvin.

I'd expected a fight for who got to escape the house, but Alvin just nodded. "Can you pick up a few of those glucose lollipops you always see in chemists while you're there?"

"Do you think that's a good idea? I know she's sick, but it's late and the glucose might send her wild just before she goes to bed . . ."

"No, I meant for me."

"Oh. Okay then." Random, but I was too busy making my escape to question it.

When I got back shortly after six, Annie was having a rant. "But I *always* have chocolate cake for my supper! If my mommy was here, she'd let me have chocolate cake."

"Chocolate cake makes you grow horns out of your forehead," Alvin said.

"I think she already has those," I said under my breath.

Annie was now stamping her feet like Rumpelstiltskin in fury as she looked at her dinner of bangers and mash on her little table. She also had a brand new crop of spots on her face since I'd left.

"She's been scratching herself to ribbons while you were away. I'll start putting the calamine lotion on her back before she turns her body into the surface of the moon with pox marks."

Alvin took the first of the three bottles of calamine lotion that I'd bought and a packet of cotton wool. He poured a generous amount on a wad of cotton wool, went up to Annie and splodged a spot that had come up on her arm.

"*Aaaaagghhh*!" Annie ran to the other side of the room, screeching like someone who'd just had boiling water poured over them.

I ran after her. "What is it, Annie? Did it sting?"

"It's *cooooooooooooooooooooold*!"

"You hold her and I'll put some more on her back."

"*Noooooooooooooooooooooooooooooo*! It's too wet!" Annie ran out into the hall.

I followed her and tried to reason with her, but she covered her ears and started to wail. I tried to console and cajole her for a good ten minutes, to no avail.

"Let's give her five minutes to cool down," I said when I returned to the sitting room. "I'm sure she'll run out of energy soon after all of that crying and we'll be able to get the lotion on her easily enough."

It turned out that I had no idea of a child's energy reserves, even a supposedly sick one. I tried holding her down to put on the lotion, but gave up on the grounds of health and safety after Annie flailed so violently against me that she kicked me in the ear. Alvin tried bribing her with a digestive biscuit and she actually laughed at him before bursting into a fresh round of roaring. It wasn't long before we were all out of ideas and Annie was tearing at her skin again as new pox popped up.

"I want to do *paaaaaaaaaaaiiiiiiiiiiiiiiiiinnnnnnnnnnnnn ttttttttttttttttttttttttttttinnnnnngg*!" Annie screamed. "Mommy always lets me paint!"

And then, I thought of something. "Do you do face painting with your mommy, princess?"

Annie nodded. "How about we do some face painting then?"

"But Uncle Alvin said I had to go to bed after dinner," she said, sobbing a bit along the way.

"Well, I think we can let Annie stay up for another little while, can't we, Uncle Alvin?"

I found Annie's face paints in her toybox and put them on the table, then poured the calamine lotion into a bowl when Annie wasn't looking and placed it on the table. "Okay then. What would you like me to paint you as?"

Ten minutes later, I'd turned Annie into what I told her was the rarest type of tiger in the world – a white calamine-lotion tiger, with a few black stripes thrown in for authenticity. I mightn't have known a lot about kids, but I knew they weren't stupid.

"It doesn't seem to matter that it's cold when it's on her face, it seems," Alvin said as Annie admired herself in a mirror.

"I think she just got a fright and then kicked up for the sake of it," I said.

"Well, all I can say is well done. Getting it on her body might be a bit harder, though."

"Leave it with me."

I went upstairs and ran a bath for Annie while Alvin kept an eye on both children. While Annie was in the bath, I sat on the toilet lid with a packet of sponges and a pair of scissors. Luckily, the chemist had only had packets of three sponges available to buy together.

"What are you doing?" Annie inevitably asked as I snipped away.

"I'm making animal shapes." I handed her the first sponge. "Do you know what this is?" I hoped my cutting skills were up to scratch as she pondered my question.

"A rabbit!"

Phew!

"Yes! And now I'm going to make two more animals and you have to guess what they are!"

A cat and a cow later, I was ready to attempt my game. "Annie, would you like to dip the sponges in the paint in this bowl and make shapes on my arms with them?" I said as I slyly lifted up the plug and let the bath water drain away.

"And on your face too?" she asked hopefully.

I sighed. "Yes, and on my face too if you want."

Then she said the golden words I'd been hoping for. "I want animal shapes on my arms too!"

Annie squealed with delight as I dipped the sponges and doused her arms and face with calamine lotion – after she'd plastered me with it, of course. As she got out of the bath, I patted her gently so that I wouldn't burst any of the many chickenpox that had come up all over her little body and then put animals all over her back, legs and tummy too. She laughed all the way through it.

Alvin came upstairs just as I was about to put Annie into bed. I was glad I'd cleaned my face when Annie's back was turned. "Okay, little missy, do you want me to read your bedtime stories?"

"No! I want Tammy! Look what she gave me." Annie rolled up one sleeve and showed off her animal shapes to Alvin.

Alvin grinned. "Well, isn't Tammy talented? Okay then, I'll put Jamie to bed in my room so that I can keep an eye on him tonight. I'll get some M-E-D-I-C-I-N-E for herself there as well to keep her temperature down. She seems to be doing fine, so let's definitely spare the guys their phone call until the morning."

I read Annie's surprisingly engaging stories to her while Alvin settled Jamie in his room. When all the stories were read I braced myself for the tantrum, but Annie seemed sleepy.

"Why are you looking after me while my mommy and daddy are away?" she asked as I tucked a blanket around her.

"Because your mommy and daddy asked your Uncle Alvin to look after you while they were away, and I'm helping." Or trying to help, at least.

"But why aren't you looking after your own children?"

"I don't have children, sweetheart."

"But why don't you and Uncle Alvin have children?"

Why indeed? What was it about children that they knew how to ask the most pertinent questions ever while sounding completely innocent?

"We just don't."

"Will you have children next year?"

"No. But we're very lucky to be able to spend time with other lovely children like you and your brother."

"I like you spending time with me. You're very nice and very pretty too."

Alvin walked in with Annie's medicine. She took it without complaint and closed her eyes almost immediately.

"I seem to have somehow won her over," I said as we crept out of the room.

"You're a natural."

Tears instantly sprang to my eyes. He always used to say I would be.

"Tam, I'm sorry," he said as soon as he noticed my watery eyes. "I should choose my words more carefully."

"No, it's fine – I'm just tired. I always get emotional over the least little thing when I'm tired."

275

"I remember."

A tear trickled down my cheek. Alvin reached out and gently wiped it away with his thumb, then retracted his hand suddenly.

Neither of us seemed to know what to do next. The awkward silence soon grew too much for me. "Right, well, we really should go to bed. I mean, I should go to my room and . . ."

His face hardened. "I should go to mine. Don't worry, I got it the first time."

This was turning into a total dog's dinner. "Right, well, I better let you get to bed then."

"Yeah. Goodnight." He met my eyes, then dropped his. He looked like he wanted to say something else but was holding himself back.

I probably should have left the conversation at that too, but I suddenly found words spilling out of my mouth. "Alvin . . . do you really think I would have been a good mother?"

He smiled, all traces of hardness gone. "The best, Tammy."

We stood in the corridor, just staring at each other, neither of us uttering another word. Eventually, I gave Alvin an attempt at a smile before turning my back on him and walking into my room. For the first time in a long time, I didn't feel angry about what had happened. I just felt sad for both of us.

37

"That was good news, wasn't it?" Alvin said as we left the hospital. "The bottom line is that there's no reason why you're not conceiving."

"Maybe it would be better if there was. At least with a specific condition, we could do something about it. Unexplained infertility is nearly worse." I started to cry as we reached the car.

Alvin grabbed my shoulders and leaned down to look at me. "Hey, none of that, okay? Let's take the positives from this. There's no reason why you can't get pregnant. The doctors said the miscarriage seems to be unrelated to this and we're just one of the unlucky one in four couples who have to go through that."

"Then why aren't I pregnant?"

"It just takes time for some couples, that's all." He zapped the car door open and gave me a kiss before opening my door for me.

Since our GP had recommended us to a fertility specialist – an event that had coincided with what would have been the first birthday of the baby I'd miscarried –

I'd had blood tests done in the first and third week of my cycle to test my hormone levels and both of us had blood test screenings for sexually transmitted diseases. According to my fertility monitor, I was ovulating each month as expected. On our last visit, Alvin had given a semen sample for analysis and I'd had an internal laparoscopic ultrasound and a radiology procedure to check if my fallopian tubes were open or blocked. Results for all of our tests had come back normal. Further tests had ruled out the possibility of me having endometriosis or polycystic ovary syndrome. I hadn't had a uterine infection after the miscarriage that could have potentially caused problems with me conceiving again.

"I feel like such a failure, Alvin," I said when he got into the car. "What if I can't give you a child?"

"What do you mean? If we don't have a baby then that'll be down to both of us, not just you! Don't take this on yourself, Tam."

I stared out the window and wouldn't meet his eye, even when he leaned over to hug me.

Alvin retreated and started the car. "Now that you've been prescribed a fertility drug, things could happen fast."

"I wish they'd given them to me when we first noticed that I wasn't getting pregnant. I could be screaming my head off in labour right now this very minute if we had."

"You'll have the wonderful experience of excruciating pain very soon, sweetheart. If we don't think too much about it, it'll probably all fall into place."

I closed my eyes and tried not to cry again. While I loved Alvin's positivity, things didn't always work out just because you wanted them to.

The sooner those drugs took effect, the better.

38

Pre-parental plan activity 8: Watch dusk fall and
then stay up to see the day break

*Alvin, you are the soundest sleeper I've ever met, which
probably means that I'll be the one doing the night feeds when
we have kids because you'll just sleep through the baby crying.
As you'll need to learn to survive on a lot less sleep than you
currently get, let's have a practice run at having a sleepless
night by watching dusk fall and then staying up overnight until
a new day breaks. If you source the matchsticks to keep our eyes
open, I'll organise a list of things for us to do in between (a
hardship, I know - see the things I do for this relationship?).*

Our eighth activity was another one of mine that had
romantic undertones – just what we needed in our
confused and confusing relationship. I turned up at
Alvin's for the activity in my favourite winter coat. It was
a classic camel coat, fitted and accompanied by a wide
black belt. I'd put on a knitted camel beret too, but the

fact that it was warm and woolly was just a bonus in my attempt to look as good as possible.

Adrienne answered the door. Just my luck, but then Alvin had warned me that she was at home a lot these days. She'd been laid off in her job as a graphic designer in a games company and was now working as a freelancer. She was currently between jobs and it looked like she was in mooch-around-the-house mode. Claire was away at a psychic convention (you couldn't make it up) and I'd been hoping Adrienne would make herself scarce, but knew in my heart that I was hoping for too much.

Adrienne didn't even say hello. She just stared at my beret and sniggered.

"I'm here to see Alvin," I said after about ten seconds of standing on the doorstep.

"Really? I thought you were here to see me. I'm gutted." She stood aside and grudgingly let me pass. "Maybe you can give me a loan of that hat to cheer me up."

Alvin galloped down the stairs. "Hey, Tam. You look great." He touched my arm briefly as he passed and walked to the kitchen, calling me in. I shot a triumphant look at Adrienne as I followed him there.

As soon as I'd taken my coat and the contentious beret off and stacked the perishables from the picnic basket I'd brought over into the fridge, he threw an orange at me. "Get peeling. We don't have long before it gets dark."

"What are you doing?" Adrienne walked into the kitchen and started nosing around.

"Christmas may be over, but it's still mulled wine weather." He pulled a bottle of Merlot out of Claire's well-stocked wine rack. "If you want to make yourself useful, get the cloves out."

Adrienne found an excuse to make herself scarce as

soon as it became apparent that there was work to do. I peeled and sliced the orange while Alvin located the cloves, sugar, cinnamon sticks, brandy and ginger. A half an hour later, we ladled the mulled wine into two huge black mugs and made our way out to the patio.

I'd always loved Claire's cedar pergola. It was fully covered and had a three-seat swing that was inviting in all weather conditions. In the summer honeysuckle vines would creep and loop through the trellis at the side of the pergola, their sweet fragrance drifting on the balmy air. I settled into the left side of the swing, with Alvin on the right. It was just after four and the evening was already drawing in.

"The mulled wine was a good idea," I said, wrapping my fingers around the mug and huddling over it so that the heat from the wine warmed my chin.

"Remember the time we had it for breakfast the morning after I moved in?"

"Yes. And you moved in on January 31st – not exactly mulled-wine time, but it was all the lovelier for that."

The memory deserved a smile. I'd mentioned during one of our first dates in January how much I loved mulled wine. It was a throwaway comment that had come up in a conversation about how our Christmases had gone, but one that Alvin had squirreled away and done something about. I'd loved it.

A long silence followed my words, so long that the sky had noticeably darkened by the time we resumed conversation. I stared at it without really taking the panorama of impending night in, too conscious of who was beside me to be truly interested in anything else. This just all felt so odd. The last time I was on this swing there was no space between us. I was sitting on Alvin's lap after a dinner party Claire had held for a group of friends and family, my arms around his neck, his hand surreptitiously sliding up my thigh.

"I suppose you're wondering how we're going to pass the time until dawn," I said when the silence grew too uncomfortable to sustain and dusk had well and truly fallen.

"Mmm. I have a few ideas, but you've probably come up with something different."

"It involves a beach, but that's all I'm saying. Can you call a taxi?"

I restocked the picnic basket in the kitchen while Alvin called the taxi. Thirty minutes and a grilling from Adrienne on where we were going later, we were standing on Seapoint beach in Dun Laoghaire.

"Okay, help me pick a quiet spot to sit on for several hours," I said. The beach was reasonably lit and visibility was decent.

"We're not here for the water sports then? You're such a tease." He reached for the picnic basket. "Here, let me carry that."

I scouted around for a suitable set of rocks for us to park on until I noticed Alvin peeking into the covered basket. "This picnic sounds very . . . liquidy."

"You can't drink on a beach without liquids," I pointed out.

"Em . . . sorry, did I just hear you say we're about to do something illegal?"

"I didn't explicitly say that we were, but just to clear things up – yes, we are. Or at least, I am. You can just watch if you like."

"At the risk of sounding ridiculously obvious – why are we doing this?"

"Never let it be said that I don't take my non-comfort zone seriously."

"Blimey. Didn't see this one coming."

"Here looks pretty good." I pointed to a set of rocks at the far end of the beach. It was reasonably secluded without being in a dangerous location. As we got ourselves settled on rocks that were the size of restaurant tables, I looked at the ocean and was glad I wasn't too close to it. The only reason I wanted to do this was because I'd always heard of couples meeting on the beach and sharing cans as they shared their hopes and dreams for the future. It was something I'd never done, and when we'd written the plan, this had been part of my agenda for this list item. I could have reneged on it – Alvin would never have known – but I didn't want to.

Alvin rooted through the picnic basket. "Two cans of beer?"

"Yeah. One each."

He said nothing, but couldn't stop himself from laughing a few seconds later. "The comfort zone breaching has reached new proportions."

"Oh, shut up! Do you know how irresponsible it is to drink near the sea?"

Alvin watched me as I pulled the ring of the can and took a slug. "I've never seen you drink beer before."

"Take a good look, because you'll never see it again." I grimaced. "It tastes like sheep's urine."

"It's just that brand. There are other ones that taste just like dogs' urine and that's much nicer. You've a lot to learn about this kind of thing, Tammy."

We ate the sandwiches that I'd brought, the official part of the beach picnic, after we finished the cans. "So where's good to go out in town now? Has anywhere new opened recently?"

I rattled off the names of all the places I'd been to recently, omitting to mention that I'd been there on disastrous dates with other men.

"Do you go out much these days?"

"Yeah, I suppose I do between work events and everything else," I said. I didn't want to say no and sound like a sad loser who never left the house.

"Everything else?" He took a sip from his can.

"That's four questions now. I wonder what the other sixteen will be?" I said because I couldn't think of a suitable answer for what everything else might be apart from the aforementioned disastrous dates.

He laughed. "What I'm trying to find out in a not-as-subtle-as-I'd-hoped way is if you've been serious about anyone else since I left. I know you're not seeing someone now, but . . . well, has there been anyone on the scene over the last few years apart from the pillow seller and the other also-rans, if that's not a vetoed question?"

My heart jumped. *Now to formulate an answer that would make me look cool and desirable but still on the market all in one.*

"Not really, no," I said.

And that wasn't it.

"Right." He seemed to be waiting for me to return the question, but I stayed silent. I prayed he would do the same.

It wasn't to be. "As for me, Tammy . . . there was someone, and I've wanted to tell you about her since I came home. It didn't last long, but it did happen and you need to know about it . . ."

"Was it Clarissa?" I interrupted.

He looked taken aback. "Of course not! Not this again, Tammy –"

"If it's not her, then I don't want to hear about it," I said immediately.

"So if I'd been with Clarissa, you would want to hear about it?"

"That's not what I mean, and you know it."

"But it's important that I tell you what's been happening in my life since we were together if we have any chance of making things work out between us!"

"If you'd been with Clarissa then yes, I think that's something I'd need to know about when she seems to be everywhere I look at the moment. But if it's anyone else, then what's the point? Why is it important that you tell me something that you know will hurt me?"

I think it was safe to assume that any chance of me looking cool was well and truly gone out the window.

"You know I don't want to hurt you – or, at least, you *should* know that."

"We didn't set out to hurt each other last time around either, but it still happened. Please, don't make it any worse by telling me things I really don't want to hear."

"We have to have this conversation eventually –"

"Not tonight. We won't be seeing in the dawn together if we do. Please, Alvin, let's leave it until after we've done the plan to talk about all of this. What happened last time around really knocked the stuffing out of me. If we think we can take this somewhere then we will have this conversation, but just not yet."

It took him a while to reply. "I'm enjoying this too and the last thing I want to do is anything that will ruin it. But I mean it when I say that there are things we absolutely will have to talk about. We're over two weeks into the plan now and we still haven't even touched on anything we need to discuss."

"I'm asking you to give me until the end, Alvin. I need time. Please don't make me say it over and over again."

The wind whipped around the silence that fell between us. I could see by the set of Alvin's face that he wasn't happy to acquiesce with my request. It was only a matter of time before he brought it all up again.

I gathered up the remains of the picnic. "Maybe we should go home," I said.

"Yes."

We walked back to the promenade in silence and got a taxi back. I didn't know what to think about our exchange. As if I'd want to hear about some conquest . . . and yet, I wasn't mad at him. He seemed to be suggesting that we talk about our exes so that if we started again, it would be with a clean slate. Like I wanted to know . . . the thought of him with someone else made me want to puke. I'd already obliterated cool, and desirable had been questionable to start with – publicly being sick was not going to help my cause.

When we got home, Clarissa was there. My heart thudded in my chest. A mixture of jealousy and adrenaline flooded me.

"Hey there," she said to Alvin without looking my way. She got up and kissed him on the cheek.

"Clarry called over to see you," Adrienne said pointedly to her brother. She also seemed in on the game to ignore my presence.

"You kids were out late," Clarissa said, continuing to blank me. "And is that drink I smell off you? Why wasn't I invited?"

"I'm sure you've seen enough of me over the years," Alvin said as he sat down on the couch opposite Clarissa and Adrienne.

I timidly pushed in beside him, suddenly feeling very unsure of myself.

"You can say that again. When you've lived with someone for as long as we've lived together, nothing is left to the imagination."

Alvin smiled. I wasn't sure if it was a dutiful smile born of politeness, or something more meaningful.

"Do you want to watch a DVD or something, Tammy?" Alvin interrupted my smile analysis.

I shrugged. I didn't want to spend another second in the company of the coven across from me, but I wouldn't give them the satisfaction of admitting that. "Up to you."

"We can listen to some music upstairs if you'd prefer."

"Oh. My. God. I just got transported back to the early nineties when Alvin used to smuggle a different girl into his room every week to 'listen to music'. He was a total slut," Adrienne said. "From what I saw in Australia, not much has changed either." She looked at Clarissa and they both burst out laughing.

"Let's go," Alvin said as he got up.

I followed.

"Why don't you pull her up over that kind of thing?" I hissed as we ascended. "Why are we the ones that have to go upstairs?"

"She's looking for a reaction. I wasn't with anyone when she was over in Australia – she's just trying to annoy you. You shouldn't give her the satisfaction of letting her know she's getting to you."

"You and Claire let her away with far too much," I hissed.

"She has her own problems." Alvin opened the door of his room. "Welcome back to The Cave."

Suddenly, I was the one with the problem.

39

The familiar smell of The Cave was excruciating to experience. I'd rarely been in this room without being naked within twenty seconds of stepping inside the door. My eyes strayed towards the bed as I wished to God that things weren't so stupidly complicated. I wished I had it within me to just throw caution to the wind and push him onto the bed. From everything he'd said so far, I didn't think he was going to knock me back, even if he was in a bit of a sulk with me since the beach. But where would that leave us? We had a lot of things to sort out before we could ever be together as a couple again. I needed to know we were solid enough to be more than casual shaggers for the duration of Alvin's holiday, because if we started this carry-on and he walked out of my life again I knew I just wouldn't survive it this time around.

I focused on the mess in the room to give myself something else to worry about. "If you fancy doing a spot of decluttering, I know someone who's brilliant at it."

"Hmm. I could do with a bit of help with this room alright – it's a disaster zone. Thing is, I know someone whose idea of decluttering is just to throw everything away. Do you think this someone could meet me halfway on this?"

"She'll try her very hardest."

"Okay then. I should have let you loose on this room years ago, but . . ."

But we always had something better to do in this room before. *Okay, okay. I get it.*

"Never too late," I said too cheerfully. "You go and get the black plastic sacks while I put on some music."

We started with his bulging wardrobe. Alvin had brilliant taste in clothes, but some of the things in his wardrobe had been around since the Britpop days. There was even a Féile '95 T-shirt in there. We pulled every last thing out and worked ruthlessly through the gigantic pile until we had three bags of clothes to be given to charity and one reasonably orderly wardrobe at the end of it.

We moved on to the fitness magazines, the sports memorabilia that spanned several decades, a box of DVDs that obviously were never watched when they weren't even downstairs where they would be watched, and a miscellaneous box of odds and ends.

"Em, retro much?" I pulled some VHS tapes out of the miscellaneous box. "Video players aren't even compatible with the TVs on the market now, are they?"

"Don't know. We don't have a video player any more."

"Alvin, Alvin, Alvin." I shook my head and hurled the VHS tapes into bags.

The rest of the room took so long that it was almost midnight by the time we finished up. Between his chest of drawers, his locker and under his bed, we ran out of bin bags. All that remained to sort through was a small grey metal storage box that was sitting on his locker with an alarm clock and an empty, crusty cup on top of it.

289

"How about this?" I put my hand on the box.

"No. We're not decluttering that."

"There must be something in it that you can get rid of."

"There isn't."

I was getting curious now. "Why, what's so great about it?"

"We don't all want to erase every memory we've ever had, Tammy."

"Is that what that is? A memory box?"

"I suppose you could call it that."

"Okay, if it's personal, forget it . . ."

"Maybe you should see it." He lifted up the clock and the cup and put them on the floor, and picked up the box.

I sat on the bed beside him as he took off the lid. He handed the open box to me. I saw cards that looked familiar. Notes with my handwriting on them. Ticket stubs for the cinema and the National Concert Hall. Passport headshots. Pictures of us – on a veranda of a luxurious holiday home we'd rented in West Cork one summer with the sea lapping in the background, at weddings and christenings, at the top of Croagh Patrick. An entire history of a time two people had once shared.

"Do you have any stuff like this?" he asked.

I didn't say anything. My voice would have broken if I had, and tears would have gone flying all over my face if I moved my head at all.

"*Alvin*!" Clarissa roared up the stairs. "I'm leaving!"

"*Bye!*" Alvin roared back.

It wasn't enough. The sound of Clarissa's dainty footsteps progressing up the stairs – rapidly – could be heard. I grabbed the lid and put it back on the box.

She knocked and walked straight in.

"Why did you bother?" I couldn't help saying.

"What?"

"Forget it." I put the box on the bed beside me and turned my back to her.

"Just wanted to say goodnight, Alv." She walked over and embraced him as if he'd just come back from fighting for his country in a world war.

I seethed until I could feel my innards begin to dissolve. *Push her off, will you!*

She eventually pulled herself off him with great reluctance, but then just stood there. God, this was ludicrous. We were like a pack of very mature-looking fifteen-year-olds.

"Let's walk Clarissa down to the front door," I said pointedly. I got up and swung the door open. I would lift her up and carry her down the stairs myself if I had to.

Adrienne came out of the sitting room to join the party in the hall as we bade Clarissa goodbye. Then she blanked us and went straight upstairs, leaving the two of us in the hall staring awkwardly at each other.

"Do you want something to eat?"

"Sure." I followed Alvin into the kitchen, glad of the fact that we had something to do in the immediate future other than skirt around issues.

As I helped Alvin chop vegetables for the chicken and vegetable stir fry we'd decided to make, I wondered if I should have tried to talk Alvin out of this list item. It was made for couples who would pass the time until dawn doing proper couple things, not two people who seemed to be always checking themselves around each other and second-guessing.

"Can we eat outside?" I said when the meal was

cooked. The house and my growing feelings for Alvin were starting to feel more claustrophobic by the second. "I know it's cold but I just need some air."

He didn't ask why. "Okay. We'll just turn on the patio heater."

We got ourselves set up and ate in silence. When we finished, I attempted to strike up some small talk. All I could manage was a comment on how much it was costing me to fill my car with petrol these days, brutal as ever at the small-talk game. Alvin stared off into space as he replied apathetically about a garage down the road reputedly having the cheapest petrol in the county. Seconds later, we heard a noise overhead.

"If you don't shut up and let me get to sleep, I'll stick petrol pumps up your *holes*!" Adrienne roared down at us. She banged the window shut again, but a few of the neighbours' windows opened to see what all of the racket was about. I could swear I could still hear Adrienne's voice echoing against the Dublin Mountains a minute later.

Alvin shook his head. "She's a classy girl for sure."

"Is she ever going to move out of home?" I said in a low voice. I knew it was bitchy, but Adrienne wasn't one to bring out the best in people.

Alvin shrugged. "She's been making noise about moving into town, but nothing concrete is happening. Between ourselves," he started to whisper, "she's seeing someone and they're thinking of moving in together, but she doesn't want Mum to know about it just yet because Mum won't be too happy at the prospect of living on her own."

"But it would be best to prepare Claire for the fact that it's going to happen, surely?"

"If it happens. She seems to be in a tumultuous relationship. Apparently, it's complicated."

"Do you think she's doing a Jess?" I'd shared my concerns about Jess with Alvin a few days previously.

"I don't think so, no – but when it comes to my sister, expect the unexpected."

We went back inside to the sitting room, where Adrienne would be less likely to hear us from her room at the back of the house – although she was so rude that a perverse part of me wanted to break into opera just to keep her awake all night. I couldn't sing for peanuts.

We watched mindless TV for a long while, then Alvin took down some board games that were stored on a series of shelves in the corner of the room and had been since the eighties – Scrabble, Monopoly, that kind of thing. Claire's house was like the Land That Time Forgot. Although it was clean and tidy, there'd been no decorating done here in a long time. I wondered if she was trying to preserve the house she'd shared with her husband.

After several very long games of Monopoly and many games of Scrabble, it was almost dawn and I could hardly keep my eyes open.

"Let's go outside so that the cold will keep us awake," I said to an equally droopy-eyed Alvin.

We went back to the swing and resumed the positions we'd had at dusk.

"How have you enjoyed this item so far?" Alvin asked once we were settled.

"It's been good. We seem to have picked up a few stragglers along the way, but what can you do about that? I'm getting used to that happening anyway."

Alvin smiled wryly.

"Alvin . . . why is Clarissa hanging around so much? I'm asking this for informational purposes only, not because I'm secretly jealous of her and want to have a voodoo doll of her under my bed or something." I already had one – not because I *wanted* to, but because Jess had bought a pincushion for me and christened it Clarissa to cheer me up. (Maybe we all needed to work on our maturity.)

"She's just looking for people to spend time with during her holidays. She's a good friend of mine and she gets on well with Adrienne, and all of her other friends are at work during the day."

"Are you sure that . . ."

Alvin looked at me expectantly.

"Well . . . I know you said earlier that you weren't with her, but that doesn't mean that's not what she wants."

"Of course it isn't! She didn't fancy me last time and she doesn't now!"

"Okay!" I put my hands up, palms facing Alvin. "Just a question. Just a thought. Just a possibility as to why she seems to be stalking us. That's all."

"Look, I don't care just as long as you and I get to spend some time together."

I sighed. "Okay. I suppose there were a lot of things we should have done together really, except we got diverted."

"Ah, come on. We did plenty when you think about it. I'd never have darkened the door of the National Concert Hall except you dragged me there. And remember that play you brought me to in The Gate that was just one big monologue that lasted for two hours with no interval? And we were the only people left in there by the end of it. Even the staff left, except for one poor article that had to close up the place."

"And we felt so sorry for the actress that you invited her to come for a drink with us afterwards," I said.

"She was much more fun in the pub than on stage."

"And oh God, I'll never forget that time when we went camping at that three-day concert in the country and it just rained non-stop for the whole three days!"

"Yes, I can still smell the mud."

And as we spoke, dawn started to break. The shadows of night that had played on Alvin's face lifted.

"There really is something beautiful about a breaking dawn," Alvin said dreamily. "It's full of hope and possibility."

"You're a soft git, Alvin Harrison."

"Yes, but you've always known that about me."

Of course I did. It was one of the millions of things I loved about him. And although he looked tired, he was as glorious as ever and I couldn't take my eyes off him.

He caught me staring and, instead of asking me why, he just stared back. Then he leaned forward, his body breaching the space between us. Unlike the time on New Year's Eve when this had happened, this time I *knew* he was going to kiss me. I also knew that once he kissed me, there was no going back. I was suddenly wide awake.

I wasn't the only one. The back door slammed and footsteps made their way towards us. Adrienne rounded the corner to the patio area with a face like a slapped arse.

"If you two insist on waking me up with your chatter, I might as well see what's so great about a breaking dawn." She plonked herself between us, where the kiss would have been if she hadn't interjected.

I sat on my hands so that I wouldn't use one of them to thump her. She was like those spirits Claire had told me about that wouldn't leave her alone.

But even her aggravating presence couldn't eradicate the fact that Alvin had tried to kiss me. He'd definitely, full on, one hundred per cent been about to move in for the kill when Adrienne and her sixth sense had muscled in and put a stop to it. I'd never fully allowed myself to believe that he wanted me as much as I wanted him, but he did. I'd seen it in his eyes. He may have been with other people in Australia and Clarissa may be trying everything in her power to get into his trousers, but he wanted *me*. That didn't for one second make things straightforward, of course, but it still made me glow inside.

"This reminds me a lot of when I was in Australia with you and Clarissa," Adrienne said to Alvin. "Is that how you got this idea – copying what we did over there?"

I leaned forward so that I could see past Adrienne. "You've done this already?" I said to Alvin.

"Well, yes . . . kind of . . . but not with you."

Evidently. With Clarissa.

Suddenly, the moment of our almost-kiss didn't seem so special any more.

"Right, well, that's the dawn done and dusted. I have to go." I felt sick, sick to the back teeth of pretending I was okay about things I wasn't okay about just because I didn't want to give Adrienne or Clarissa the satisfaction of knowing how I truly felt. I was sick to death of Adrienne and Clarissa, full stop. I was sick of being unsure about what to do. I was sicker than everyone in all the hospitals in Europe put together.

Alvin stood up.

"No, it's okay. I know where the door is," I said, leaving quickly before he followed me. And so ended another plan activity that had been shadowed by the family and friends police.

What a difference a couple of minutes could make.

40

When Alvin came home, I was sitting on the couch with a bottle of wine in my hand.

He turned on the light. "Well, this is all very . . ."

I took a slug of my wine. "What?"

"You won't like it. I'm just warning you."

"Say it!"

"Well, it's a bit . . . stereotypical, isn't it? The curtains pulled, the bottle of wine? C'mon, Tam. You can be a bit more inventive with your melancholy than this."

My period had come earlier that day, and Alvin had received a tearful call from me. I was so upset that I had to leave work early, an event that had never taken place before. Malcolm had been visibly shocked when he'd seen me packing up to go home at three o'clock, but his shocked look had quickly turned to one of disapproval. He reminded me that we had an important meeting scheduled at four o'clock, whereupon I burst into tears and told him that we'd just have to reschedule, wouldn't we? Uncharacteristically, I wasn't worried about the *ramifications of my cheeky emotional outburst. There were far too many other things to be troubled about.*

"I don't have time for original thinking between researching ways to boost my fertility and thinking about what a failure I am. I've been on the drugs for the last month and I still didn't get pregnant."

"You're a failure because you didn't get what you wanted straight away? This is how it works for the rest of the world, you know. A lot of things that are worth waiting for take time. This was only your first month on the drugs and it's highly possible that you will get pregnant very soon."

"But what if I don't? What if we try and try and nothing happens? When do we stop trying?"

"Let's just take it all a month at a time . . ."

I extended my hand. "Hi, Alvin. I'm not sure if we've met. I'm Tammy, and I'm completely incapable of taking life one day at a time, never mind your month."

"Well, maybe this is nature's way of telling you that you need to lay off the life planning for a while. And if nothing happens after a few years, there are other options – IVF, adoption . . ."

I nibbled my nails.

Alvin grabbed both of my hands and held them. "The nails have done nothing wrong. Leave them out of this."

"Alvin . . . if this doesn't work out, it could be the end of us, you know. We can make noise all we want about IVF and adopting and everything else, but just think of all the stress that'll cause us on top of the stress we're going through now. It'll be worth it if it all works out, of course, but what if it doesn't either?"

Alvin pulled me to him and spoke into my hair. "If it doesn't, then we'll deal with it the way we're dealing with what's going on now."

"Well, that's not very reassuring. I've been sitting in a foetal position on the couch for the last hour drinking wine straight from the bottle. Me, the woman who used to wear rubber gloves before even handling a bottle of wine." I had a thing about rats potentially peeing on bottles while they were in storage before they hit the supermarket shelves. I'd once seen a documentary about a woman who went blind from it. I was bad enough with my gammy ovaries without adding further health problems to the mix, but somehow I couldn't gather up the momentum to give a shit about it today.

"But you've drunk hardly any of it." Alvin took the bottle from me and held it up to the light. *"Less than a quarter. And your hair looks very shiny for someone who's at this caper."*

"Only because I had to go to work today," I mumbled.

"And I heard the washing machine going on my way in, and those clothes in the laundry basket over there were on the line when we left this morning."

"But I never usually leave the laundry basket in the sitting room," I argued. *"I usually tip the clothes out onto the rug immediately and sort them out into piles for ironing, then put away the laundry basket."*

"Ooh – for shame! Face it, darling – you are rubbish at wallowing."

"I'm rubbish at getting knocked up too. Maybe you should just end it with me now and start again with someone who isn't damaged goods." My tone was jaunty, but I'd secretly wondered more than once if that's what he should be doing. I didn't want him staying with me out of obligation.

"I told you before that I'm never going anywhere. Now, get up off that couch and tip the rest of that bottle

of wine into the sink. I'll get started on the dinner. Do we have any spuds?"

I couldn't but cheer up around Alvin. Maybe I just needed to give the drugs a chance. They'd kick in soon, surely. They had to.

The drugs kicked in, but not in the way I'd wanted them to. I knew I'd been moody in the past whenever my period arrived, but now I was moody non-stop and I couldn't attribute it to anything other than the medication. After taking it for three months, I was at the point where I was bursting into fits of uncontrollable crying or experiencing intense bouts of fury over absolutely nothing, and both were equally unbearable. The crying bordered on ludicrous and the rage was demonic. Even John McEnroe in his tantrums heyday would have quivered to see me coming when I was in angry mode, as I was making mincemeat out of everyone in my path. To add to the party, I became completely irrational. Alvin refused to speak to me for a full day after I chucked out a pair of his favourite (and most expensive) shoes just because I stubbed my toe on them in our bedroom. I couldn't understand why he couldn't see the injustice that had been done to my poor toe. When he challenged me on what the hell was wrong with me, I went into angry mode and when that started to dissipate, crying mode replaced it.

Three more months passed and I still didn't get pregnant. Of course, it was hard to get pregnant with a partner that had grown so nonplussed by my behaviour that he seemed to be avoiding me and sleeping downstairs a lot. He'd even given up asking me if I wanted to do stuff from our pre-parental plan. I felt bad for not having given his big idea a chance, but when the odds of us becoming parents were looking so bad, was there really any point anyway?

I didn't want to come off the drugs in case they needed more of a chance to take effect, but I also couldn't bear what they were turning me into. And even if I got pregnant, I knew the way the drugs had affected my behaviour had created a gulf between us. Even if I came off them, I couldn't help feeling that lasting damage had been done.

I'd never felt so hopeless. I just prayed there would at least be a baby at the end of all of this and, if there was, I would worry about repairing the damage in our relationship then.

41

"I think it's safe to say Alvin Harrison wants to ride you senseless," Simone said after I'd reported the box findings to her that evening after a day-long catch-up sleep. "You're already senseless though if you haven't worked that out by now."

"Hmm." I didn't want to jinx things by admitting she was right because I fervently hoped that he did.

After Adrienne had stuck her nose into our business yet again, Alvin had rung me after I'd arrived home that morning and sworn that the dusk-to-dawn incident in Australia had happened organically while Adrienne had been on holidays. They'd been at the beach that night and had decided to stay until the morning because Alvin wasn't working the next day and the girls had been having such a good time. Although I was still jealous, staying mad with him after seeing the memory box was not an option and I was already missing him by the time I got back to my house after leaving his.

I didn't get the opportunity to ask Jess for her opinion on it all because she'd gone into hiding since the

Audrey/Ciarán debacle. She left the house early each morning and came home after nine every evening and went straight up to bed. When we rang or emailed her at work, we got no reply. When we texted her when she was upstairs in her room over our heads to ask if she was alright, she never replied. I was furious with her by now for shutting us out, and although I was still worried about how she was doing, I'd accepted that she didn't want our support.

Later that evening, five days after she'd gone underground, Jess made her first tentative steps back into the world. She peeped a pale face around the door, said hi, then sat down in an armchair and stared at us as if she expected us to be happy or something. By this stage, we were too insulted at having been ignored for so long really to care. Besides, she'd chosen to emerge at the start of the first episode of the new series of *Curb Your Enthusiasm*, Simone's absolute favourite programme and one that was in my top five. I'd just scrubbed the kitchen for an hour, even scouring the sink, and the only drama I wanted in my sitting room right then was of the Larry David variety.

"So, it's over with Ciarán."

"Mmm," I muttered, feeling charitable. Although this was the best thing I could have hoped to hear her say, it bugged me that we were going to talk about this now just because she felt like it and sod it if we didn't want to.

Simone just reached for the remote and turned the volume up several notches.

Jess sat forward. "I thought you'd be happy about that, Simone."

"I thought you'd stopped talking to me days ago. Don't start again now. Not a good time."

"Oh, excuse me for interrupting your precious show just because my entire life is in bits . . ."

"Get real. Earthquake victims have lives that are in bits. Or the wives of men that have affairs."

"*What?*"

My God, would Simone ever learn? We could have tried to 'Mmm' our way through Jess droning on about Ciarán. Now, all we were going to hear was full-scale screeches.

I closed my eyes and took a deep breath. I'd watch the new episode on the Internet tomorrow. If someone didn't intervene soon – it was either going to be me or the goldfish, and it wasn't looking like he was going to make a move – we'd never get to watch TV again, as Jess was bound to shove Simone's head through it.

"Come on out to the kitchen and we'll have a cup of tea, Jess." I got up and jerked my head towards the door.

"No. Wine."

"A cup of wine, then."

"A bottle."

"The whole shagging wine rack if you like. Just come on."

She dragged herself off the couch and shuffled along behind me as I led the way to the kitchen, doing some mental calculations as to just how much money I'd have to give the bank every month in order to live on my own. I'd nearly pay it twice over at this stage.

I opened a bottle of red and poured two overly generous glasses, one to try to knock Jess out and one to keep me sane.

"So what happened?"

"What you all knew would happen. Gone back to the wife. End of story."

I nodded, and took a long gulp. Saying anything – anything at all – would be a huge mistake.

"Like you said, it was only when he thought he was

going to lose her for good that he realised just how much he loves her. A typical old line. Almost as old as him, the crochety old fuck for brains."

Another big gulp.

"Audrey held out for a full day. Wouldn't take his calls. Went off to live with her sister. Sister set the Alsatian on him whenever he called to the door. Didn't deter him. He bribed the Alsatian with a Meatball Marinara Sub and got into the house through the back door. Audrey had a fit. Threw a full saucepan of chip oil on him. It had cooled, luckily for him, but he reckons she would have thrown it even if hadn't. He slipped on the oil as she tried to wrestle him out the door again. Hit his head."

When Jess refused to form full sentences, things were bad. I gulped faster.

"Went to hospital. Together. Sister drove. Audrey held his hand all the way to the hospital, willing him not to die. Kept his eyes closed and pretended to be unconscious while listening to everything she said to the sister about him. Still loved him. Living away from him was just letting me win. Wouldn't be ousted by some slip of a thing with fake breasts. He didn't even speak up at that point and tell her they were real. Fucker."

This time, it was Jess who gulped. The entire glass.

"The next day, Thursday. He rings. He's outside. The wind is whipping into his mobile and I can barely hear him." She paused and refilled her glass with a sorry-looking hand. Two nails were bitten off. Two others were halfway there. The thumbnail just jutted out like an overgrown weed.

"Gist of what I caught is that although he still loves me, he knows he has to make a go of things again with Audrey for the sake of Aileen, the daughter he once called the Band-Aid baby. He won't be checking the phone he only uses to contact me any more – he's going to throw it in the river. He wishes me well, and thanks me for the good times. I tell him if he's going to dump me, he should have the decency to do it face to face. He says he can't hear me, and isn't it very windy today? Phone goes mysteriously dead."

She poured her drink down her throat and refilled her glass again.

"Friday. I ring his landline. His oldest daughter answers. She must guess who I am, because she hangs up immediately. I ring back immediately. Ciarán answers. 'Why the hell are you ringing this number?' he hisses. 'You didn't leave me much choice when your other phone is waterlogged,' I say. I hear him running up the stairs with the cordless phone. 'Lishen, don't ring this number again, chu understand? I'm telling you, Jess, just let this go. You're making it all more difficult than it should be.' He hangs up again. I ring back. It's off the hook."

She looked at her empty glass, then back at the bottle, and frowned.

"Did you drink all of that, you greedy git?" she said.

She went to the wine rack and pulled out another bottle of red. I wanted to stop her because she was already starting to slur her words, but I knew she'd just end up calling me a control freak and stomping off to The Whine Bar. At least here, I could keep an eye on her. I went to the fridge and pulled out a bottle of white for myself. I knew I wasn't going to get a look-in at the red.

"Friday evening. I ring the landline a few more times. It's engaged every time. Then I get a text from Ciarán's old number – the one that's supposedly at the bottom of the river. 'DO NOT contact me again. Tara told Audrey you rang and the shit has really hit the fan. It's over. Accept it and move on.' Did he actually think he'd get away with just dumping me that easily? I ring and ring non-stop for the resht of the evening. Eventually, bingo. It's back on the hook, and Audrey answers. I tell her to put my lover on the line. She hangs up. Phone'sh off the hook again."

I resisted the temptation to tell Jess how completely psychopathic she sounded. Ciarán was really under her skin.

"Saturday. Ciarán ringsh from a private number and says that not only am I a homewrecker, but I've turned into the pitiful other-woman type and to have a bit of self-reshpect. Oh, and he couldn't remember what he saw in me, and thank God he came to his sensesh. Then he hangs up before he can hear me calling him a spineless motherfucker. I ring his landline to tell him, but it's off the hook, surprishingly."

It was now Sunday. I thanked God that there had to be an end to all of this.

"Today." Jess poured another glass.

Enough was enough. I picked up the bottle and poured the rest of it down the sink. She didn't even register it.

"Best day yet. Oh yes. Thish time, he ringsuh me. Not to apologise. Not to explain. Uhno. To look after his dick again. He saysuh, 'Lookit, when the dust settles a bit, maybe we could meet up once a week and get back to what we're good at?' Bastard. *Bastard!*"

Jesus. "Jess, there's no way you're going there, do you hear me?"

"Shpare the pep talk. You'll be glad to hear that today, Shunday – is today Shunday?" I nodded. "Today, Shunday, is the day that I've come out of my coma. That yoke never loved me. I just thought he did for a while.

307

Worsh shtill, I thought I loved him. But, as of this morning, I know that's bollix. *Bollix!* Just like him. He only wanted me because I'm brilliant in the sack."

"So what happens now?"

Jess got up, closed her eyes and winced. "Now I puke."

And with that, she ran to the sink to reunite the contents of her stomach with the rest of the bottle of wine, and I resolved never to bother cleaning again.

42

"Do you want me to go on the pull for you?" I asked
Alvin as I traced patterns through the condensation on my
glass of Guinness with blackcurrant. "I'll make friends
with some women in the bathroom and ask them a few
questions about their fertility cycle. Or maybe we could
have a surrogate organised before the night is out – what
do you think?"

"I think we should have another round. We came out
tonight to forget about all of this stuff, remember?" Alvin
was smiling, but there was an edge to his tone.

I remembered. Remembering was the problem. No
matter where I was or what I did, my fertility problems
always seemed to be at the forefront of my thoughts. Since
we'd arrived at this pub, I'd checked out the belly of every
woman that passed and mentally assessed whether or not
that belly looked like one that had produced children. It
was madness and sheer masochism, but knowing what it
was didn't mean I could stop it. Next Thursday was going
to be the second anniversary of the miscarriage. Every day
that brought me closer to it saw me grow that little bit

crazier – or at least that's how I felt. The fertility drugs were turning me into someone I didn't recognise. I could only pray it was the drugs and this wasn't just who I was now – a moody, temperamental, irrational cow.

I forced myself back to sitting in the pub with Alvin. "Anything mad happening at work?" I asked for the sake of asking something.

"Well, Clarissa's leaving."

"Really?" Alvin had my full attention now. "Why?"

"She's decided to go travelling. She's starting off in South East Asia and then she'll see where she goes from there."

"Is she not a bit old to be taking a notion to do a gap year?" I said, and instantly regretted it. I sounded like Simone's mother.

"It's what she wants," Alvin said simply.

"So when's she going?"

"The weekend after next."

"Oh! And she's only just handed in her notice? That doesn't leave you guys much time to replace her . . ."

"No, she handed in her notice a few weeks ago."

"You never said."

"We haven't really been talking about anything other than babies recently."

There wasn't much I could come back with for that. I couldn't help feeling there was something odd about him not mentioning it though.

"Is she having a going-away party?"

"Yes, next Thursday."

Thursday. "And are you going?"

"Well, yes, I suppose so. It'd be pretty bad form not to, and I'm not doing anything else on Thursday anyway."

I tutted, almost completing my transformation into

Aunt Patty. "Alvin, Thursday will be the second anniversary of the miscarriage! How could you have forgotten that after everything we've been through over the last few months?"

"I haven't forgotten." He sighed. "Like you said, how could I have forgotten? We've spoken about nothing else recently but things relating to conception and reproduction."

"Then why in the world would you want to go to that one's leaving do?"

"I want to go to Clarissa's leaving do because she's been a good friend to me lately. I think it's best we keep ourselves busy on Thursday anyway. We'll only be thinking too much otherwise."

Lately? What did that mean? She'd been a good friend since I turned into such a pain in the ass? What kind of a good friend?

"And am I invited?"

"Well, I suppose, but you probably don't want to come, do you? You really don't like Clarissa . . ."

"So you think I should sit at home on my own reliving the miscarriage? Am I actually hearing this?"

"Everyone is hearing this." Alvin looked around. People were looking back at him – or, more accurately, at me. "If you've something to say, can't you just say it instead of shouting our business around the entire pub?"

I grabbed my coat and handbag and stood up. "If you think it's acceptable to go out drinking with your – good friend – instead of being at home with me on an important date, then there really is nothing else for me to say."

I got up and left. He didn't follow. I'd never stormed out on him before and hadn't known what kind of a reaction I'd get from him, but if I'd been a betting woman, I'd have expected him to follow me. Of course, I wanted him to follow me – I would have told him to get lost and all the rest if he had, but it was what I wanted all the same. But that wasn't what happened. And as I walked down the street on my own, the extent to which our foundations were crumbling truly hit me for the first time. This wasn't good. It wasn't good at all.

43

Our evenings were getting longer. The chats over the potatoes were getting shorter. Some nights we didn't even have potatoes.

We were becoming like strangers and I had no idea what to do about it. Talking wasn't helping. Talking was making things worse. Anything that came out of my mouth invariably sounded like a recrimination for something completely harmless. Anything Alvin said was pounced on and twisted. I thoroughly hated myself for it and yet was completely incapable of stopping it. How could I when I didn't even understand why it was happening?

Two nights before Clarissa's party, I woke alone in the bed. I could hear Alvin's voice through the ceiling, but I knew he'd gone to bed with me. I knew because I'd timed how long we would lie there wordlessly until he'd eventually fall asleep. Tonight, it was fifty-three minutes. A new record. He'd obviously woken up again. I looked at the clock beside the bed. It was ten past three.

I stepped lightly out of the bed and crept onto the

stairs. The sitting room door was open and I could clearly hear him. He was standing with his back to me, crying as he spoke to someone on the phone. I'd never seen or heard him crying before.

"I can't reach her," he said. "She's completely retreated inside herself."

There was silence for a few seconds, presumably while the other person on the call spoke.

Please, God, don't let him be speaking to Adrienne about us.

"There's no way she'll go to counselling, Mum. She won't even talk to me, never mind anyone else."

Claire. Thank God. It made sense – Alvin had mentioned that Claire had miscarried herself between having Alvin and Adrienne. Still, it was a jolt to realise that he was sharing our problems with anyone, even with Claire . . .

Silence again. "But we can't go on like this. I just don't know what to do . . ."

I couldn't listen any more.

I knew I should have gone into the sitting room after his call ended and talked to him, hugged him, kissed away his tears as he would mine – anything rather than creeping upstairs pretending I hadn't heard his conversation. But I was too ashamed. Ashamed, sickened, disgusted with myself and vaguely incredulous that we were at this point. The question was, where did we go to next?

I went to sleep in our cold bed with Alvin's words ringing in my ears. We can't go on like this.

The second anniversary had arrived. It landed with a thud on my consciousness that morning, somehow seeming more ominous than the first had. Thank God I not only had work that day, but a farcically full schedule. I had three hours of training in the morning, followed by three back-to-back meetings in the afternoon. It would be a crossed-legs day, the type where there wouldn't be so much as a free second to take a toilet break, and it was exactly what I needed. I picked out my favourite black skirt suit that morning, which probably looked like all of my other black skirt suits to everyone else but which gave me an extra boost of confidence. I put on that little bit more make-up than usual. I walked around the building with as much attitude as I could, hoping that if I could fake it well enough, it would somehow become real by osmosis. I was willing to try anything that would potentially make me feel better about being me on this day.

Alvin was still asleep when I left for work. We'd had a conversation the previous night about Clarissa's party. He'd said he still wanted to go, despite how I felt about it. We'd had another row about it, the kind that's left totally unresolved, and he'd fallen asleep on the couch. I hadn't heard him coming to bed, but I knew better than to wake him up in the morning to try to discuss things further. Coming between him and his sleep could only make matters worse.

He wasn't due into the adventure centre until twelve. I left my phone on Silent in training. I'd told him what was on my schedule the previous night, but I'd hoped he might text anyway. It would have helped. Just something to acknowledge the day that was in it. But no text arrived.

My afternoon meetings were fraught. Malcolm castigated everyone about the most inconsequential of matters in our weekly planning meeting, as if he was just looking for things to give out about. A negative mood seeped into the *second meeting, which unfortunately happened to be a brainstorming session about how to imbue positivity in employees. By the time we rang into a conference call with the States for our third meeting of the day, our enthusiasm levels had plummeted so far underground that we could have been mistaken for a bunch of miners.*

I returned to my desk and worked solidly for two hours on things that had built up throughout the day while I'd been away from my desk. At five past six, when Alvin was due to have finished his shift, I rang him.

"Hey," he said when he answered. His voice was a bit echoey, and it sounded like he was on his hands-free kit in the car.

"Hi. Are you driving?"

"Yeah, I'm bringing some of the gang into town."

There was no hope of having a row aftermath conversation so. "Okay. What pub are you guys going to?"

"Oh, you're definitely coming in so?"

"Yes. Is that a problem?"

"No, no. Just asking, that's all. We're starting off in Dandelion, but we're planning a bit of a crawl so we might not be there for long. Clarissa, where's up next after Dandelion?"

I couldn't believe it. He knew how I felt about Clarissa and yet there she was, sitting beside him in the car, today of all days.

"We're going to Major Tom's after Dandelion," Alvin said. "If you don't see us in Dandelion, that's where we'll be."

"I'm not going to go walking around Dandelion trying to find you! I'll ring you when I get into town to see if you're still in Dandelion and if not, I'll go straight to Major Tom."

"Okay, okay. I was just letting you know in case I didn't hear my phone or something."

I was sure I heard a giggle. "Who else are you dropping into town?"

"Oh, just Clarissa. The others were held up at work and they'll make their own way in."

So much for 'some of the gang'. It took everything I had not to say something. That would have been playing right into Clarissa's hands.

"Okay. Right. Well. I'll see you later then."

"Okay, see you then. Bye."

Clarissa's giggle rang in my ears long after Alvin had hung up. I had a horrible feeling, the kind you get when you know you're in danger but you don't know what you can do to save yourself. The kind that envelops you when you know that everything is about to slip through your fingers and it's too late to do anything to stop it.

I banged the lid of my laptop shut and ran to my car as fast as I could.

Dandelion was reasonably busy, but I nonetheless spotted Alvin and the gang straight away. All I had to do was follow Clarissa's loud voice. In a bar full of people who were chilling out with their drinks after a hard day's work, Clarissa was acting as if she was in a nightclub and shouting at the group instead of speaking, probably to make sure everybody knew she was there. Still, at least there were some other people at the table. They were all female and I didn't know any of them, but anything was preferable to seeing Alvin on his own with Clarissa – even if he was sitting in the middle of them, looking like the owner of a harem. He seemed to be engrossed in whatever tale Clarissa was telling as I walked over.

317

"Hi," I said loudly when Clarissa didn't stop speaking as I reached the table.

"Hey," Alvin said.

Clarissa looked up, said hi and continued with her story.

Alvin stood up and got out past her and the others.

He kissed me on the cheek. It annoyed me. Why on the cheek? Why not the lips?

"Guys, this is Tammy," he said, cutting across Clarissa and rattling off a list of names as he introduced me to Clarissa's non-work friends. Tammy. Why not 'my fiancée Tammy'?

"Let me get you a drink," Alvin said and walked towards the bar. I followed him, not only to attempt to sort things out but because the prospect of spending time with Clarissa was too horrible to contemplate.

"Just a sparkling water – it's a school night," I said pointedly when we reached the bar.

He ordered a glass of sparkling water for me and a pint of beer for himself. "You're drinking? What about the car?"

"I'll leave it in the 24-hour car park overnight."

"But what about getting to work tomorrow?"

"I'll get the bus into town early and collect the car. I'm not on until twelve again tomorrow."

"Alvin, are you sure it's a good idea to be drinking with all we have going on at the moment?"

"What do we have going on, Tammy? The two of us sniping at each other all of the time?"

"It's just a bad time for us, and I don't think involving drink will make things any better . . ."

"But they can't get much worse, can they? I don't see what harm a few pints can do to us now."

I tried to make eye contact with Alvin, but his eyes

were focused on something behind the bar. He was completely inaccessible, just like how he'd described me to Claire on the phone. "You don't want me here, do you?"

He dropped his gaze to the ground, then slowly, reluctantly, looked up at me. "It's not that, but we seem to be stuck in a moment or something. I really want us to resolve what's going on between us but we just don't seem to be able to. We try and we try but we go around in circles. It's so draining."

"So you'd prefer to be out with Clarissa right now? Well, that really shows me where I stand, doesn't it?"

"Tammy, don't say it like that. There's nothing going on with Clarissa. She's just a friend who happens to be female. I know you seem to have a thing about her, but . . ."

"No. You seem to have a thing about her. That's what I'm bothered about."

"All I'm bothered about is saving us. That's why I wanted to come out tonight. I thought it might relieve the tension in the house a bit."

"Oh yeah, that'll work. You going out drinking with another woman is really going to relieve the tension."

"Well, if you have a better idea, I'm all ears. I've tried and tried to pull you back from this obsessed place you're in, but I can't seem to get through to you any more. Nothing I do seems to be right, and I'm all out of theories on what we're going to do."

"So what are you saying? You're giving up on us?"

"Of course I'm not, Tammy. You're all I want. But I just wish we could get things back to where they used to be. And I also wish we'd started doing everything on that list we made before we got into trying for children."

"But what difference would it have made? We'd still be in this situation now. I'd still have problems conceiving."

"Yes, but you seem to be most worried about how I feel about all of this. Maybe the list and seeing me in new lights would have helped you to get to know me well enough to understand that whatever happens, you're the main thing for me. You seem to think you're – I dunno – not enough of a woman for me because you haven't conceived yet, and I hate even saying that but that's what I'm hearing from you, Tammy. And it's complete nonsense. I thought we knew each other well enough for you to realise that, but lately I'm wondering if we know each other at all."

"Don't say that," I said, trying not to cry.

"But I've told you the same thing over and over and it doesn't seem to be hitting home. Maybe the list wouldn't have either, I don't know, but if it helped enough to save us then it would have been worth it. Anything that would save us would be worth it."

I met Alvin's eye. "What are we going to do, Al?"

He shook his head. "I don't know. I just don't know."

His words chilled me to the bone. Whenever I'd turned to him for reassurance before, he'd always told me it was going to be okay, we'd work something out, all the usual platitudes. And now he was giving up on me.

"Well, look who it is." I felt an arm around my shoulder and suddenly found Elliott standing beside me bursting into a bout of cheek-kissing. "And aren't you looking . . . well, not as good as you usually do, actually! You're a bit peaky. You need this man to take you on a nice sun holiday with the other Ss involved as well." He put his other arm around Alvin and drew us all together, treating Alvin to his routine four kisses as he did so. Then he stood back, threw his arms down and sniffed the air. "I'm getting vibes. Bad vibes. Did I interrupt a row?"

320

"No. *This conversation is over*," I said.

"Ooh, *it's a nasty one too. Ah, you guys, can't we all just kiss and make up?*"

Any bloody excuse with Elliott. I would have laughed if my life wasn't just unravelling right in front of me.

"Have a good night, Elliott. You too, Alvin." It already felt like I was talking to the stranger Alvin would become if we split up. Or maybe it was a matter of when, not if.

He followed me as I walked away, but I could tell it was a perfunctory gesture. We met Les and Desmond as I reached the door.

"Ah, *don't tell us you two are heading off already! Can you not keep your hands off each other just for one evening?*" Les looked at Desmond and rolled his eyes. "*Young love, eh?*"

"I'm off home, Les, but Alvin's staying."

"But you *can't bail off home and leave this fella here! He's hopeless without you!*"

I wished Les's words were true. As I left, it seemed to me that the only thing that was hopeless was our future. We were falling apart, and I didn't think I could bear sitting around watching us slowly die.

44

Pre-parental plan activity 9: Surprise your partner
by doing something romantic that you'll tell your
kids about in years to come

*Alvin, I suppose parents have to be selective about telling their kids
about things they got up to 'back in the day', but there's one story
Mum told me about Dad's attempts to be romantic that always
stuck in my head. She'd been lined up by Granddad for a day of
work in the bog, something she'd told Dad she hated doing. When
she was eating breakfast that morning in advance of a hard day's
work, Dad arrived at the door and offered his services in her place.
Granddad was only too delighted to have Dad on board instead of
Mum as they'd get twice the work done and he didn't care who did
the work just as long as it was done. He did it because he didn't have
much money to buy things for Mum or to take her on romantic
trips, but years later when they did have a bit of cash to spend on
treats, he bought her plenty of nice things like jewellery that were
rarely mentioned. That bog story was brought out more times than
I can remember. I want us to have stories like that to tell our*

kids – not about bogs, just things that would fit the other person's definition of romance. This one is wide open, Alvin. Do your worst – I know I will!

It was two minutes past six in the morning. Alvin should have had the telephone wake-up call that I'd booked for him by now. I picked up my phone and texted him.

Your taxi will pick you up at seven.

He texted back almost immediately.

??

I sent a smiley face back. He wasn't getting any more info out of me for now.

The taxi collected me at quarter to seven and was at Alvin's house at seven, as promised.

"Will I just skip the pleasantries and go straight to 'I'm not telling you?'" I said when Alvin sat into the back of the car beside me.

He just laughed. When we'd written the list, we'd decided to put Alvin's final choice, which was to conquer one fear each, last. It just seemed to be the most logical sequence. I thought I wouldn't have a clue what to pick for Activity 9, but an idea presented itself when Alvin brought up the subject several times of wanting to celebrate my birthday and I decided I'd go with it.

"I'm guessing today might involve a ferry," Alvin said as we drove towards Dublin Port.

"Looks like you've busted me. I read online that Dublin Port has just opened a new exhibition centre with models of the roll-on-roll-off vessels and various cruise liners that pass through the port, and I thought it sounded like something you'd be interested in."

"Isn't it strange how exhibition centres only open from seven to eight in the morning?"

323

I laughed. "Okay. I've organised a trip to London as my part of our ninth activity."

"London?"

"See, you're surprised, which was exactly the point."

"I don't have any ID for travelling though."

"I do."

"It's not much use if only one of us has ID . . ."

"No, I have yours. I have mine too, of course. I kind of . . . stole your passport from your room the last time I was in your house so that we could do this."

"Well, congratulations on your sly kleptomania – I hadn't noticed my passport was missing." He passed his hand down my back lightly. "I love this, Tam. I thought when I went to bed last night that I'd still be asleep right now!"

"Don't get too excited," I said. "You know what going to London with someone who's afraid of flying will entail . . . the ferry, the long train trip down . . ."

"Who cares? We'll have a laugh along the way."

I smiled, secretly delighted with Alvin's reaction. Anyone else would have seen going to London this way as a pain in the rear, but he embraced the situation and was determined to get the most fun possible out of it – as I'd hoped he would.

Our ferry departed at half eight. The journey from Dublin to Holyhead took under two hours, although it felt like a lot less as we passed the time in the Games Zone area of the ferry. When we docked in Holyhead, we took a train from Holyhead to London – a journey that would take four hours.

"Where's the puzzle book?" Alvin said just after the train took off. Every time we'd ever gone anywhere together on a planned trip, I'd brought a puzzle book with me. It was just my thing.

"Do I look like a pensioner?" I feigned a shocked look.

"Tam, just take the book out. I know it's in there."

I sighed dramatically. "I only brought it for the sake of keeping up tradition."

Three crosswords, five Sudokus, two cryptograms, a few sandwiches and one snooze later, we arrived at London Euston station. To most other people my age and in my profession this probably wouldn't have been a big deal, but I could feel excitement bubbling in my chest. I'd only been to London twice before, once when I'd taken a bus from Dublin to London to visit my uncle's family when I was eighteen, and once a few years ago for a global work meeting that I just couldn't miss (an embarrassing affair from start to finish where I'd had to book a day's holiday just to accommodate the time it would take me to travel over, and another one to travel back). I produced a map as we left the station to bring us to our next destination. Alvin just smiled when he saw the map and asked no questions. I would have terrorised him with questions if I'd been the one in the dark.

We walked through the arches of King's Cross St Pancras train station ten minutes later. I looked around to locate where the Eurostar left from and where I could buy tickets.

"Paris?" Alvin said when I gave his Eurostar ticket to him five minutes later.

"That's what it says on the ticket," I said as nonchalantly as I could.

"But why?"

"You always said you wanted us to go there together someday," I said shyly. I could feel myself blushing. "I don't think I'll ever get over my fear of flying, so this seemed like the only solution. You kept saying you wanted to do something for my birthday and I thought I'd surprise you by making that happen even though I'm not all that interested in birthdays myself. And in keeping with the rules of the plan, this would have been something romantic to tell the kids about." I felt my face burning even more. That was about as loquacious as I'd ever been when it came to talking about the plan, and I didn't know where to look now.

"This is fantastic, Tam." He grabbed me and hugged me. It was quite a long hug and I wasn't sure it was just of the friendly kind. His face seemed to be lost in my hair. His arms were moving up and down my back a little too slowly. My hands wanted to stroke his neck. My body was starting to react to his proximity in a manner that was most unsuited to our environment.

I pulled myself away. "Let's go get that train," I said, my voice much too high. I didn't even look at Alvin as I walked. It was too tempting.

"So we're due in Paris at 6 pm," Alvin said. "Where are we staying, or is that a surprise too?"

"Somewhere Eiffel Tower-y. I've left it late enough in life to see it, so I thought I should book a place that has a good view of the blasted thing. It's probably very boring for you when you've been to Paris three times before, but I do have plans for us other than to gawk out the window at the Eiffel Tower."

Had that sounded suggestive? I started to blush again.

"Oh, I meant to tell you earlier that I brought the essentials for you – a new toothbrush, toothpaste, a spare set of clothes and all that – so don't worry about having to go shopping somewhere when we arrive at Paris Nord."

"I thought you didn't have any of my clothes left though . . ."

"I just picked up a few things yesterday." *Roughly translated as 'I spent hours yesterday picking out new threads for you.'*

"Are you sure it's not *my* birthday?"

We got a taxi from Paris Nord to the hotel. I had to bite my tongue to stop myself from squealing in a hugely undignified manner when I caught my first glimpse of the Eiffel Tower. When we got to the hotel, I was pleased to see that it looked just as luxurious in reality as it had done on its website. We walked into the hotel's expansive lobby and I went to the reception desk while Alvin looked around, taking the place in.

"How much do I owe you for staying here tonight?" Alvin asked as we walked down a plush corridor to our rooms after taking a lift to the eighth floor. He looked worried.

"Nothing, of course. Do you think I'd bring you on a trip you didn't ask to go on and then expect you to pay for half of it?"

"You have to let me give you something towards it. This place must be costing you a fortune."

"Nah. Got a good deal online – the recession has some advantages." I hadn't. The hotel was charging a bomb for tonight's rate, but it wasn't as if I'd ever spent money on overseas travel before.

I hovered my swipe over a keypad beside a door. The door clicked open.

"Em . . . am I sleeping in the corridor then?" Alvin seemed reluctant to follow me as I pushed the door open.

"We have a two-bedroom suite in here." I beckoned him to follow me.

"Oh wow!" While the living room of the suite was beyond impressive, I barely noticed it. Our curtains were pulled wide open and we were staring directly at the twinkling Eiffel Tower. Every cent of that bomb was worth it.

We stored our limited luggage in the suite and left the hotel to walk to the Eiffel Tower. At this time of year, it was possible to climb to the top until eleven at night. We chatted easily along the way over a packet of peanut M&Ms Alvin had pocketed from the minibar, both of us brimming over with enthusiasm at the night ahead. I still couldn't quite believe I was here. If it hadn't been for the list, I would never even have thought of doing this.

We crossed Pont de Bir Hakeim and walked up Quai Branly towards the tower. "Much as I'd like to do the authentic experience of climbing the stairs to the top of the tower, we have a lot to pack in tonight so let's get the lift to the top, okay?" So we did. At the top, we took in the panorama of the Champs Elysées, the Arc de Triomphe, Notre-Dame Cathedral and Sacré Coeur, the illumination of night making everything look even more beautiful than I imagined they would during the day. It felt surreal not only to see these landmarks but to have Alvin by my side as I saw them. Even if he went back to Australia and that was the end for us, I knew I'd never forget this experience.

When we descended from the tower, we followed my map along Quai Branly until we reached Pont de l'Alma, the bridge where open boat excursions down the River Seine left from.

"Bateaux Mouches time?" Alvin asked.

"It'd be rude not to."

Our tour lasted an hour and fifteen minutes and gave us another perspective of the landmarks we'd seen from the Eiffel Tower, encompassing many more monuments and historical areas too. As soon as it finished, we got a Metro to Sacré Coeur. While the church itself was of course closed at this late hour of the evening, our aim was to experience the district of Montmartre. We wandered lazily from one street to the next, stopping to look at artists' work and browsing the range of items on sale on the streets along the way.

"Are you hungry?" Alvin said as we passed a hot-dog stand.

"Yeah, I could eat," I said. In truth, though, food was the absolute last thing on my mind.

We scanned the street we were on to see which establishment took our fancy the most. At the end of the street was an art shop that doubled as a crêperie. "How about here?" I said, admiring the paintings in the window as we stood outside.

"Sure."

The shop was poky but well laid out, allowing customers enough room to walk around and browse the art adorning the walls. Alvin ordered our crêpes and espressos while I perused the paintings. They were amazing but pricey. I wondered if they sold many here or if the main business was done elsewhere and this shop was just a promotional tool. The artist's name and website was listed under each painting. I made a mental note to look her up when I went home – she really was amazing. A lot of the paintings used Paris as a backdrop, but I was transfixed by one particular oil painting depicting a couple walking by a canal at night, the streetlight illuminating their happy expressions. The setting could have been anywhere. Those people were happy regardless of where they were. It was a simple concept, but it touched something in me all the same.

I was still looking at the painting when Alvin returned with the crêpes. He came over and had a look too before we finally got down to the business of eating.

"Like it?"

"Love it."

"Let me buy it for you . . ."

"No, no, we don't want to have stuff to carry around. Let's eat and go home."

"Okay." His eyes were dark and remained on my face for a few seconds longer than usual before he sat down.

Tasty as the crêpes were, we ate them functionally. Having to eat felt like a nuisance that was slowing down the progress of our day. And although we would soon be heading back to the hotel, it felt like the day and night shouldn't end yet. I wasn't sure how it was going to pan out, and yet I had a delicious feeling of anticipation. Alvin hadn't even brushed off me since we'd left the hotel, and yet something was bubbling between us. I glanced up from my crêpe, caught him looking at me and knew he was feeling exactly the same thing.

We didn't even speak as we walked back to the hotel. No words passed between us until we walked into the suite.

"I'm going to bed," I said before the door had even swung shut behind us.

"Okay."

"Goodnight so."

"Yeah, goodnight. And thanks for this, Tam."

"No problem."

Technically I made the first move, but I didn't have to do much. I took a step towards him, arms outstretched to hug him. He propelled himself into my arms as if I was going to change my mind if he didn't get there fast. This hug took up where the King's Cross St Pancras one had left off. I immediately felt Alvin hardening. I pressed myself into his body, letting my arms fall downwards and pulling him towards me even more.

"Are you sure you –"

I stifled the rest of his sentence with my mouth on his. He responded instantly, hungrily. I moved my hands around and yielded an inch of precious proximity to open his belt, my body screaming out for him as I pulled him to the king-sized bed.

It still made no sense. There were still a million questions in my mind about our relationship or non-relationship or whatever the hell it was. But at that moment, all I knew was that *this had to happen*. I would never think clearly again if this didn't happen. Paris and all its charms no longer existed. Nothing existed except us and what was happening right now. And as he entered me, there was only one thing going through my head. *Thank fuck.*

When I woke up, Alvin was staring at me.

"I've missed you," he said simply, brushing my hair back off my face with his hand. "I've missed us."

"Me too," I said. My voice was husky, and not from sleep. I slid towards him.

Two hours later, we were still no closer to getting up to go to Paris Nord than we'd been when we'd woken up. After hours of frantic sexual tension-fuelled activity the previous night, we were now rediscovering the more tender groove we usually inhabited as a couple. The prospect of ever leaving this room again was unthinkable.

"We have so much to sort out though, Tam," Alvin said as we reluctantly got dressed. "I actually don't know where to start."

"I know. And I'm really not trying to fob you off this time, but right now isn't the time to even hint at going there. We are *so* late. I don't think I've ever been late in my life before!"

331

We just about made it in time for our return Channel Tunnel journey. Although I couldn't say the trip over hadn't been enjoyable, the return one was much more so. There wasn't a puzzle book in sight. And although Alvin was right and we needed to have a talk that probably wasn't going to be altogether comfortable, all thoughts of that were put aside as we resumed where we'd left off in the hotel insofar as the bounds of decency would allow us. There'd be plenty of time for talk later. After the last few days, I knew one thing for sure – I was never going to be stupid enough to let Alvin go ever again.

45

I was practically floating inside my car as I pulled up outside Alvin's house the next day. We hadn't arranged for me to call over, but I was looking for an excuse and activity ten was still on the plate to be discussed. If the texts he'd sent me that morning were any indication, I had a feeling he'd be pleased to see me. Every time I thought about us being back together, I smiled. In fact, I hadn't stopped smiling since Paris. I still had no concrete idea of where all of this was going and Alvin had only a few days of his holiday left before he was due to go back to Australia, but for the first time since he'd come back, I allowed myself to believe that we would somehow work this out. It wasn't going to be easy to dredge through the past, as I knew we would have to, but if we could get through that and come out the other side then the logistics part would surely be easier. Alvin could move home and we could take things from there.

As I got out of the car, I stopped smiling. Clarissa was walking up from the direction of the nearby LUAS stop.

I watched her as she approached. She wasn't even all

that outstanding looking really – she was confident good-looking more so than truly beautiful, in the sense that her self-assured manner lent great weight to her slightly above average looks. You'd swear she was a queen with the way she carried herself, though, as though nobody in the world was better than her. And it worked. It seemed that every man who came in contact with her either became infatuated with her or was in awe of her. Either way, it was a pretty powerful position and one you had to commend her on. Or you would have if you didn't dislike her enough to choke on the words, like I would have.

I reached the gate just as she did. "How much rent does Claire charge you?" I said as I opened the gate, making sure I walked in first. It was beyond childish, but Clarissa seemed to bring out every negative ion I had in me.

"Sorry?"

"Well, I take it you've moved in, have you? You're always here."

"Rather like yourself so." She breezed past me and marched up the driveway. Her long hair blew into my face as she passed by. I would have preferred to have someone whack my face with a haddock than have her horrible hair anywhere near me, and wished dearly that I had a scissors handy.

"I have a reason! What's yours?"

"Oh, Tammy, just go away. Let's just go inside and find different sides of the house to be on. I'm having a bad enough day without adding you and your moods into the mix."

"Me and my moods?" What was Clarissa on? I stopped walking and touched her arm. "Wait a second. I've been more than patient with you turning up on every date I've had with Alvin, Clarissa. If you want moods I can give you moods, because I've had enough of you following us around."

She pulled her arm free, but didn't walk away. "What makes you think you have the right to get in a strop with me for being friends with Alvin?"

Her smug expression made me want to explode with rage. "You know very well that Alvin and I have history, but all you ever do is interrupt any time we have together or try to cause trouble between us."

"Oh, be quiet like a good girl. I'm really not in the mood for this." She turned her back on me and walked towards Alvin's front door.

There's nothing quite like being patronised to turn an internal explosion of rage into a full-on tsunami. "*You get back here!*" I roared at Clarissa, now heedless of the fact that Alvin, Adrienne and Claire could probably hear every word I was saying. "I've kept quiet for long enough. I want to know what you're playing at!"

She shrugged. "I have no romantic interest in Alvin. If you and he aren't getting together, it's not because I'm with him."

"But you're always with him! Wherever he goes, you're always there!"

Clarissa sighed deeply. "This is all getting so tiresome." She rang the doorbell repeatedly.

Adrienne answered, giving me daggers as soon as she saw me.

"Tell her," Clarissa said immediately. "I'm bored to death of this whole thing."

Adrienne looked surprised, then anxious. "Just come inside," she said to Clarissa.

"No. I'm fed up of being your pawn in this." Clarissa cocked her head at me. "Tell her, or I will."

Adrienne exhaled loudly, but said nothing. Clarissa folded her arms across her chest.

"Are you going to force me to say 'Tell me what'? What's going on here?" I looked from Adrienne to Clarissa, and back to Adrienne. They both looked at me, then back at each other. And still nothing was said.

"Looks like it's down to me, then. As always." Clarissa gave Adrienne a dirty look before sending it my way. "I'm not interested in your ex or in being involved in your so-called love life in any way. I'm being used by Adrienne to make you think things won't work out between you and Alvin, and essentially to make you piss off out of his life just like you did last time. And no, you don't even need to ask me why, because I'm going to spare you the indignity of having to prise the information out of me. See, I'm much nicer than you give me credit for."

She turned her eyes back to Adrienne.

"This one and me are together, although you'd never know it from the way she treats me. I've been getting involved because anything that keeps her happy keeps me happy. It's just a pity it doesn't seem to work both ways, isn't it?"

What?

"Oh, for heaven's sake!" Adrienne ran her hands through her hair. "Get inside, Clarry. We need to talk. And as for you," she said, "Alvin knows about this. Don't think you can use this as an excuse to run to him with some gossip that will give you something to talk about. He's not here, by the way."

Clarissa walked inside and Adrienne slammed the door in my face. I could hear them shouting at each other seconds later, my presence already forgotten about.

The ramifications of what I'd just heard hit me as I

336

slowly made my way back down Alvin's driveway. If Adrienne was telling the truth, Alvin had known that I had no reason to be jealous of Clarissa but had said nothing. He'd seen it very clearly but had let it fester. He'd let me tie myself up in knots about something that was never an issue.

I got into the car, feeling like a different person from the one who'd got out of it five minutes earlier. I picked up my phone to ring Alvin. It went to voicemail. I left a message asking him to call over to my place as soon as he could.

There was a text on my phone from him by the time I got home.

Just leaving town now and will call to yours. Good timing – need to talk to you about something important anyway.

I threw my phone on the couch. *Oh, we'd be talking alright.*

46

When Alvin came in from work, I had all of his bags packed. I'd left them in the hall so that they'd tell as much of the story as possible for me.

I'd labelled each suitcase with great care. Alvin's outdoor and work clothes. His solitary suit, which I'd had dry-cleaned for him the day before and had packed between two of the ergonomic pillows he loved so much. His casual gear. A suitcase of footwear, mostly sports runners, all washed and air dried and a pair of buffed and polished shoes. A bulging suitcase of CDs that were individually covered in bubble wrap that I'd ordered online especially for the job. And a huge box full of editions of Hot Press *and old* Beano *annuals.*

I took a deep breath as I sat on the edge of the armchair when I heard Alvin's key in the hall door. I exhaled as slowly as I could when I heard his footsteps stop at the suitcases after he'd walked in.

Minutes passed in complete silence. I had no idea what Alvin was doing. The silence in the house threatened to suffocate me, and yet I knew that when Alvin walked into this room looking for answers, I would wish I could embrace the silence again.

I got up and walked out to the hall. Alvin was just standing there, staring at the suitcases. His face told me nothing. He didn't look up.

"This is the hardest thing I've ever had to do," I said.

Silence followed my words. Alvin's eyes never strayed from the suitcases.

"I would move out myself except that Dad would never forgive me."

The silence prevailed. The need to fill it became even more desperate.

"If I thought there was any way at all that we could fix this, believe me, I'd do it . . . I'd do anything . . . but we can't. We'll end up destroying each other."

Alvin shook his head.

I needed this to end. "We can't do this any more, Alvin. You need to go now. It's best for both of us."

His jaw tightened, but he still didn't say anything. My panic levels grew and tried to choke me.

"I can't offer you anything!" I said before I wasn't able to get words out any more. "I need you to go!"

Alvin walked to the front door and put his fist through the glass. I should have been horrified, both at Alvin for doing something so completely out of character and on a practical level – that glass had been expensive – but the sound of something shattering seemed appropriate. What was one door when two lives were going the same way?

Alvin and his bloodied hand turned around to face me. And still he said nothing.

"Please, if everything we once had meant anything to you, please go."

He shook his head again, but it was more of a defeated

shake than a defiant one this time. He finally walked towards me and picked up two of the suitcases, then dropped them again and put his good hand on my arm before lowering his head and trying to look directly into my eyes. I pulled away and walked backwards until I'd put several feet between us.

"You just can't let me love you, can you?" His voice was so low, so raw, that I barely caught the words.

I looked up slowly. I forced myself to look at the pain on his face, pain that I'd caused through trying to save him from further hurt. I forced myself to drink in every detail of his expression because this was probably the last time I'd ever see him.

He was the one who looked away first. A split second later, he'd turned around and walked out the door, leaving nothing but reminders of his presence behind him. His suitcases. Fragments of glass that had fallen inwards instead of out. Two trails of blood. His scent.

In the dead hours that would follow, I would remind myself that I'd done this for him. That he deserved better. That I had nothing left to offer him. But in that moment, as I watched his blood seep into the carpet without making any move to clean it up, all I could do was sink deeper and deeper into self-recrimination for how disposable I'd made him feel.

Maybe one day he'd understand. I could only hope.

47

Alvin's smile when I opened the door almost melted my heart – and my resolve to be cool with him until I got to the bottom of what Adrienne had said. I was instantly back in Paris in my mind which was not good before a potential confrontation. I thought of Clarissa and Adrienne's mocking faces and hardened up a bit.

Although he was smiling, Alvin didn't look quite like himself. I'd still recognise him in a police line-up, and maybe even a *Where's Wally* picture at a stretch, but there was something about his demeanour that wasn't quite right. Well, he'd be looking even more out of sorts by the time I was finished with him if what Adrienne had said was true.

"Come in." I opened the door to let him pass.

He walked into the hall and kissed me. I returned it as dispassionately as I could. Maybe he was innocent, but I had to keep a level head until I found out and him kissing me was *not* conducive to that.

"What is it?" he said, immediately picking up on my mood.

"Is it true that you know Clarissa's gay and is with Adrienne?" I said rapidly.

Alvin's eyes widened. It was a sure-fire indication of his guilt. I'd seen it so many times over innocuous things, like once when I had to work late and I asked him to pick up my dress from the dry cleaner's for a wedding we were going to the next day, and he'd clean forgotten. (I hadn't acted like it was innocuous at the time, mind.) I couldn't quite believe I was seeing it now.

He nodded slowly.

"You've known from the start?"

"Tammy –"

"Yes or no?"

"Yes, but –"

"You *knew* I thought she fancied you!"

"I told you over and over that you had nothing to worry about with Clarissa! Quite aside from the fact that she's with my sister, I knew she was never interested in me but you just wouldn't listen –"

"She was always all over you when you worked together, then she comes thundering back into your life after living with you in Australia, a fact you'd failed entirely to mention – of course I was going to think she fancied you! You could have put me straight, but you didn't!"

"It wasn't my business to. I gave Adrienne my word that I wouldn't tell anyone until she was ready to tell people herself –"

"I'm not just anyone! You should have told me, Alvin. And if not about them being together, you could have told me Clarissa is a lesbian – you surely knew that from living with her!"

"Yes, I've known that since Australia – but if I'd told you that, you could well have cottoned on to the fact that she's with Adrienne, and what if you had a row in front of Mum or something and blurted it out? Mum doesn't know about Adrienne's sexuality yet. Adrienne only came out recently and she's looking for the right moment to tell Mum –"

"You only had to tell me to keep my mouth shut about it and I would have!"

Alvin's expression grew dark. "Stop interrupting me and listen to what I have to say!"

"No! Not when you've put me through all this jealousy for nothing!"

"If there was jealousy, you put yourself through it! Maybe, for once in your life, you can think about things from my perspective! Adrienne's business is not mine to share around!"

"What do you mean, 'for once in your life'?"

"What do you think, Tammy?" His face reddened. The colour looked out of place on his sallow complexion. "As soon as things got tough, you bailed instead of fighting for us. After everything we went through, you eliminated me from your life and never once gave me the means to get in touch with you! Me, the person you were supposedly planning on spending the rest of your life with. I don't remember you thinking about things from my perspective then! And now, despite everything that happened in Paris, you're jumping down my throat about something that you should have enough sense to know I couldn't do anything about! You have some cheek to be blowing hot and cold on me like this, do you know that?"

Woah! When I thought about what was going to happen after our Paris-love-in, this was the last thing I would have expected. It sounded like Alvin was about to spill out a year and a half of anger at the worst possible time because I'd burst the dam of arguments.

"We both know that staying together would have destroyed us," I said weakly.

"No. *You* decided that staying together would have destroyed us. I had *no* input in our breakup. I hoped that us doing the plan would give you the opportunity to tell me if you regretted your decision – but here we are, weeks later, and you've given me no indication of any regret at all. And when we finally got it together in Paris, you never even told me you loved me. Was that just sex to you?"

"Of course it wasn't just sex! You didn't tell me you loved me either, you know!"

"I've tried to tell you that through every single thing I've done in the plan! Anyway, why do I have to make all of the moves? I've been holding back on telling you so much to see if *you'd* tell *me* how you felt! When are you going to meet me halfway, or are you ever?"

"I'm doing my best, Alvin . . ."

"This is your best?" He shook his head. "There's only so much of this I can take. I came over here today to tell you something important, something I've been trying to tell you for ages but you kept blocking me out, but now I'm wondering if there's any point. I thought we'd made progress in Paris, but here we are, back to you pushing me away again. This clearly isn't working, is it?"

A desperate chill enveloped me. Throughout all of the crap I'd been through with Alvin, he'd never once said it wasn't working. And now that he'd said those words, things had taken a dangerous turn.

"Maybe I should have accepted things were over first time around. I would have spared myself a lot of pain if I'd done that." He walked to the front door. "Looks like we won't be finishing that list."

I shook my head. "No! Wait, Alvin. Ending our

relationship was a dreadful mistake and I've paid for it every day since . . ."

He opened the door. "So why did you never mention that over the past few weeks? It shouldn't take us getting to this point to force you into telling me."

I walked to the front door and stood beside him, trying desperately to make eye contact.

"Please look at me! Alvin, I've never stopped loving you . . ."

"Then you should have told me. It should have been obvious to you all along that those were the words I wanted to hear. But not like this. This is not enough."

He opened the door and sped down the driveway with me calling after him uselessly. I knew he wouldn't come back. He got into Claire's car and skidded away from the kerb without even glancing my way as he left.

I realised with a sinking clarity that he was right about everything, and the Clarissa situation was suddenly meaningless. He'd given me another chance and I'd made the same mistakes all over again. I hadn't given him enough or believed in us enough, and now it was too late.

I walked slowly back into the house, feeling like I'd just lost everything in the world that had ever mattered.

48

"I can completely see his point," Jess said baldly through a mouthful of ciabbatta bread. She and Simone had met me in a café for an emergency post-row dissection lunch. "You've described every single one of your dates with him word for word, and he's given you a hint on pretty much every one that he wants to be with you. The poem, the hair tucking, the attempt to kiss you – he's all but telling you straight out that he's still nuts about you. What do you give him? Nothing but 'I don't want to talk about anything' and groundless accusations that he fancies another woman. Of course he couldn't tell you about Clarissa when Adrienne was involved."

"I'm starting to see that since our row. It's all such a mess."

"Well, you're going to have to clean it up because you two are bloody perfect for each other. Alvin's in his own little world and he needs someone practical around to keep his life on track. You're too serious and need someone fanciful and dreamy to pull you out of yourself. It'll work out – you just have to find a way over this."

"What about the fact that he's much better-looking than me?"

"I really am starting to wonder if you know Alvin at all." Jess was in her stride now and was determined to have her say. "If I was to sum him up in one word, it would be loyal. Look at what he's like with his family. His mother is as daft as a brush but he puts up with all her airy fairy ways and never says a bad word about them. His sister is nothing but a cow to him but he's always supportive of her. He is not the type of guy to be in love with one woman one week and another the next. He's not your typical good-looking guy – he doesn't even see it, Tammy. He just sees himself being lucky to have found someone like you. The poor devil thinks he's got the good end of the bargain." She snorted.

"We've been telling you for weeks that he's still crazy about you," Simone said. "You just won't allow yourself to believe it. There is *no* doubt about his feelings – except in your own head."

"You should know this." Jess was getting cross now. "He's been telling you, you know. You just weren't taking it in."

She was right. I only had to look back over the last few weeks to see a multitude of different little actions of his telling their own story. I couldn't admit she was right, though, or she'd crucify me altogether.

"And what about this thing he wanted to tell me about?"

"You'd know by now if you'd let him speak," Jess said curtly. "You hardly expect us to know about it, do you?"

Jess's phone rang. She cut the call off immediately and looked at Simone and me furtively.

"That was the tone you've set up for Ciarán's calls," Simone said immediately. "Do not tell me you're going back there . . ."

"Don't be daft." She put her phone in her bag, but she was blushing.

"Ah no, Jess! Are you seeing him again? Isn't it bad enough that one of us is messing everything up here?"

"No, I'm not seeing him!" She suddenly looked sheepish. "He is trying to get me to, though. He says he's sorry about how he treated me and wants us to have 'reconciliation talks'."

"He wants a ride," Simone clarified.

"You're probably right." Jess was actually nodding. "I was going to meet him, you know, but . . . well, I'm not so sure any more. Anyway, this isn't the time to be talking about my love life. So what are you going to do, Tammy?" She seemed pleased to have an excuse to turn things back to being about me.

I shrugged. "All I know is that I can't lose Al, girls. I just can't."

"Then you know what you have to do."

"I do, actually. I need to be honest with him about how I felt when I ended things. I told myself at the time that Alvin would know why, instead of giving him a proper explanation. It was a cop out – the easiest option for me – but he deserved so much more. Maybe it's finally time to explain myself."

Jess nodded. "I was actually going to suggest grovelling, Tammy, but honesty would be very good too. I'd never normally encourage anyone to grovel to a man but, by Jesus, you've made a balls and a half of this."

She was right. I just hoped that it wasn't too late to save things.

When I got to my car, I rang Alvin immediately before I lost my nerve.

My heart thumped in my chest as the phone rang. I held my breath until he picked it up. Eventually, I had to exhale. As soon as I did, the phone went to voicemail.

I was instantly worried. Alvin usually picked up his calls straight away. I rang again. Voicemail.

And so the cycle continued over the course of the next hour, with me driving home in between. Three calls, three voicemails. I felt a little bit sicker each time I rang.

On the sixth call, I decided to leave a message. "Alvin, I know you're mad but we can't leave things like this. I've been wrong about so many things and I want you to know how sorry I am. Please call me back when you can."

An hour later, I still hadn't heard from him and the walls were closing in on me. I'd deliberately dropped a few mismatched cups in the kitchen to give myself a clean-up job to do. The first one had refused to die, bouncing off the ground once before defiantly lying there in one piece. I had to throw it like I was serving a tennis ball to get it to go in the end.

Three cups later, the phone was still silent.

"But I'm all geared up for this conversation!" I yelled at the phone. "What if I go into chickenshit mode again? Ring, for God's sake!"

It didn't. I decided to try one more time.

"This is Alvin. Leave a message," his voicemail instructed me for the seventh time that day.

I hadn't intended to follow instructions this time around, but I found myself talking.

"Okay, Al, I will so. I know I don't deserve to be calling the shots after earlier, but please listen. I need to say this. You're right when you say I've been running away from talking about how everything ended last time around. It's because I'm so embarrassed about how I reacted." I sighed deeply and instantly regretted it. Heavy breathing down the phone wasn't the kind of message I'd been aiming to leave.

I closed my eyes and continued. "I finished our relationship because I thought I wasn't good enough for you, Al. If anyone was ever born to be a dad, it's you. If that was something I couldn't give you, how could I ever feel like I was enough for you? I was sure you'd wake up some day and realise you'd made a horrible mistake by staying with someone who couldn't have your children. The longer we were together, the harder it would be for me to accept it when you'd leave me. Besides, I thought you deserved better too and I loved you enough to let you go. But –"

A loud beep interrupted me. I realised I'd been cut off mid-voicemail. Alvin must have set up his voicemail for short messages only. I rang back and his phone went to voicemail again, as I'd known it would.

"Right, em, I'd hoped this would go a bit better, but as I was saying . . . yes, I didn't feel like such an emotional mess any more when I came off the fertility drugs after you'd gone and was able to see things more clearly, and I eventually realised that I'd done the worst thing imaginable in pushing you away. But by then, I was so disgusted at myself for how I'd treated you that I was afraid to let you back into my life in case I'd do it again. You tried so hard to sort things out, but I wouldn't let you. I had to control how to handle the situation, as per bloody always. I thought the best thing I could do for you was to just blank you out completely, and eventually, you'd move on from me to someone who deserved you more . . ."

There is was, the beep again.

"Oh, for God's *sake*!"

There was only one thing left to do. I ran to the keybox, retrieved my car keys and ran out the front door without so much as putting a coat on. I could only pray that this visit would be more successful than my last.

49

"Is Alvin here?"

Adrienne smiled. And now that she'd done it, I very much wished she hadn't. There was more warmth in Antarctica than in that horrible, mocking smile.

"Oh, he is. Come in, why don't you?"

I stepped tentatively inside. Any absence of the door routine had to mean something was up.

I heard Clarissa before I saw her. I should have known she'd have to have been involved. Her voice sounded weird, though – all high-pitched, and she was talking even more gibberish than usual. Things like "Aw, look at that!" and "Did you see that? How cute!" Cute was not a word I would have expected to come out of her mouth. Funnily enough, it sounded like she was talking about a . . .

"*Waaaaahhhh*!" An even more high-pitched voice, and one that was much younger than Clarissa's, travelled to every corner of the house.

"I didn't realise you had visitors. Sorry if this is a bad time, but . . ."

"It's perfect timing, actually. You should meet them. The baby is just the most adorable thing you'll ever see."

"No, honestly . . ." I felt the familiar baby panic rise in my throat.

"Look who's here!" Adrienne threw the kitchen door open.

Alvin was standing right in front of me. He wasn't alone. Beside him stood a woman I'd never seen before. And in his arms was the baby I'd heard. A baby girl.

Alvin's face seemed to drain of colour. He looked at me, then at the baby. Quickly, he passed the baby over to the woman. She kissed the baby's curly black hair protectively as she took her. Claire looked at me sympathetically. Clarissa's eyes flicked to Adrienne. Nobody seemed quite sure what to do.

"Isn't anyone going to do the introductions?" Adrienne said eventually. "Tammy, meet my beautiful four-month-old niece Emmeline . . ."

This couldn't be happening. No way. *This is not happening!*

Alvin walked towards me. I backed away.

"No." I turned and tried to run to the front door. "No!"

"Tammy, I've been trying to tell you for so long . . ."

"Leave me alone!" I somehow managed to open the front door and ran out to my car. I got in and locked it internally before Alvin tried to open the passenger door. I pulled away with Alvin thumping on my window, shouting in at me to please give him a chance to explain. I drove down Alvin's road with shaking hands, a dead heart and the realisation that my life had just been shattered all over again.

50

"There is no point in buying four packets of frozen garlic mushrooms just because they were half price if you're going to leave them in the freezer for two years!" Jess's voice greeted me as soon as I turned my key in the hall door.

"But garlic mushrooms aren't the kind of thing you can eat every night!" Simone retaliated. "You have to wait until the mood hits you for a garlic mushroom . . ."

I walked into the kitchen.

"Are you okay?" Simone said immediately. "Your face is green."

"You didn't rob a few out-of-date garlic mushrooms from Simone last night, did you?" Jess chimed in.

I opened my mouth and wailed.

Five minutes later, I'd somehow managed to explain the bones of the story amid bouts of breathlessness and hyperventilation, and Jess had opened a bottle of cooking brandy and poured generous amounts for us all. We knocked it back and Jess refilled our glasses. I was just about to take a good gulp of round two when the doorbell rang. All three of us looked at each other.

"Let me deal with this," Jess said, her face grim.

I would have pitied Alvin if he hadn't just spent the past few weeks making a fool out of me. I fiddled with my phone, which had six missed calls from Alvin, as I waited for everything to kick off.

All I heard was "You can piss right off home again, Alvin Harrison" before Simone closed the kitchen door and walked over to the CD player.

"My mother brought over a CD of positive affirmations the other day. I think it's rubbish, but it might be the kind of thing you'd like," she said in a voice that was much louder than usual. She pressed Play. The sound of splashing waves filled the room, followed by a woman's voice singing '*I rejoice in love! I deserve to be loved! I shall be loved!*'

I could hear the deep tones of Alvin's voice on the doorstep through the singing, but couldn't make out any of his words. Simone turned up the CD.

'*I prosper through love! The love I give out shall be returned to me tenfold!*'

The CD nearly shook the house, but I could still just about hear Jess over it. It sounded like she was screeching at Alvin. Alvin's voice was raised now as he retaliated to Jess's verbal attack. "Could you knock that off?" I said to Simone. I couldn't help it – I had to know what was being said.

Simone turned the CD up even louder.

'*I will allow love to find me!* the CD proclaimed to the room, and most likely to the entire road. It sounded like we had a street proselytiser with a megaphone in our kitchen.

"*Turn it off!*" I shouted at Simone while simultaneously bursting into tears again. The front door banged shut. Jess's footsteps came towards the kitchen.

"What the hell were you singing all that crap about love for?" Jess rounded on me as soon as she came in. "I should have known you wouldn't have been able to handle that brandy!"

"You are joking, aren't you? That wasn't me! That was Simone's affirmation CD!"

"My mother's affirmation CD," Simone clarified. "I just put it on so she wouldn't hear what was going on!"

"Really? It sounded just like you when you're drunk . . . still, it got rid of Alvin. He wasn't for moving until he heard that, then he realised you were at the point where you're too upset to make any sense at all and decided to give you a bit of space."

I wrung my hands. "I'm the one who'll be giving him space. I *never* want to see him again."

Jess stood up. "Come on – coat on. If ever there was a night when The Whine Bar is needed, this is it."

Jess drummed her nails on the table and stared at me with an anxious expression. "So what do you think the deal is with the baby's mother? Is she Irish and has been home since Christmas too, or Australian and has followed Alvin to Ireland?"

I picked up my drink and gulped it before answering. "You might as well ask anyone else in this bar as ask me. They could still even be together, for all I know!"

I banged the glass back down with such ferocity that the table shook.

"Take it easy," Jess said. "I think I just felt the earth move there."

I thought I'd felt the same thing in Paris.

A *baby*. No wonder Alvin had been so calm about

Annie's chickenpox. Something like that was bound to be par for the parenthood course when you'd been through the experience of looking after a newborn.

"Alvin can't still be with the baby's mother," Simone said, cutting across my thoughts. "There's no way he would have spent all of this time with you if he was with someone else."

"You can't blame me for wondering!" I clenched my fists. "He's just omitted the most fundamental piece of information you could imagine."

Jess nodded. "And what a bitch to get pregnant when you're not trying, to have so many problems when you do try and then to find out that Alvin knocked someone else up . . . You poor old cow." She gave me a big hug. "*Why* did he not tell you?"

"Let's think about this logically," Simone said. "If he'd told you at the start that he had a child, would you have even considered doing the pre-parental plan?"

I shook my head to the point of seeing double.

"Okay. My guess, based on my knowledge of Alvin's personality, is that he was trying to get his foot in the door with you first . . ."

"Is that what you're calling it these days?" Jess pursed her lips.

"Let me finish! You know very well that Alvin wasn't after Tammy for just sex. I'd imagine he said nothing at the start because he had to tread carefully with you or he'd never see you again. I'm just playing devil's advocate here – I'm not criticising you, okay? – but you broke things off and never gave him a chance to have any contact with you ever again. That's like a death in a way, Tammy. You went from planning to spend your lives together to going through a miscarriage to trying for a baby and then to nothing. Complete nothingness. I know what nothingness feels like, and it's not good."

"That's no excuse, Simone. He still should have told me."

"I'm sure he was looking for the right moment to tell you, but something must have gone wrong somewhere along the way. I find it very hard to believe he'd deliberately mess you around after everything you went through together."

"But what we went through is *exactly* why he should have told me straight away."

My thoughts flicked to Adrienne and Clarissa. They'd been looking for an excuse to get me off the scene . . . surely they both knew about Emmeline before she appeared in Claire's kitchen? They probably had, but what difference did it make now? They were getting what they wanted either way. The scene in Claire's kitchen flashed through my head again, and a jolt of hot anger burst inside me. How could Alvin have allowed me to be humiliated like that?

"What I don't get is this – if the child is living in Australia, how could this have ever worked out between you two?" Jess interjected. "He's obviously going to stay there if that's where his daughter is."

"Tammy, do you think it's possible that Alvin didn't know about Emmeline?" Simone said, completely forgetting that a minute ago she had been arguing that he'd been looking for a way to tell me for weeks. "Maybe her mother just landed on his doorstep!"

"You don't just land on someone's doorstep from Australia," Jess pointed out. "Alvin hasn't been home in the last year and a half, so the baby must have been born over there."

"Not necessarily. Maybe he slept with someone who

was Irish and on holidays, and she just managed to get in contact with him recently through the Internet. Maybe she found out he was coming home before she got to tell him about the baby, asked for his address to send a Christmas card and then turned up at Claire's house!"

"Maybe you watch too many crappy films and you're letting your imagination run away with you. And to think that you gave out to us about watching *Cougar Town*! I bet you've been watching chick flicks on the sly too as well as reading your new book collection!"

"Oh, shut up. Anything is possible, Jess – in fact, when you think about it, the possibilities are endless."

I wasn't sure that line of thought was helping. I drained my wine. That would help.

"Maybe he thought you could make it work somehow," Simone said. "That you could live with it, you know? If two people want to be together badly enough, they can find ways to climb over obstacles."

"I'm no philosopher, but I'm quite sure that is something Beckett would not say," Jess pointed out. "That's more Dr Phil than Beckett."

I stood up, handbag poised at the ready. "The whys and the wherefores don't really matter, do they? All that matters to me right now is getting to that bar, because no amount of second guessing will change the fact that I have no future with Alvin. Not after what he's hidden from me. Oh, and let's not forget he told me to get out of his life the last time we spoke!"

They both waved their arms dismissively and gave me a series of 'He didn't mean that' and 'You pushed him into it, you great big twat' type of statements, but I just shook my head and walked away.

I was sorry I'd come. The girls were being amazing and

were just trying to support me, but discussing the possibilities of Alvin's thought process aloud was leaving me feeling more bereft than ever. I would have been better off in bed drinking vodka from a naggin with a straw (it didn't stain as badly as wine in case of spillages). The hope that had blossomed since Alvin's return had been obliterated, and everything inside me was withering by the minute. No amount of verbalising and analysing and shitetalking was going to unbollix this bollixed situation.

I returned to our table with the all-important – *lifesaving* – drinks. Excessive wine consumption wasn't my usual style because of the out-of-control feeling it engendered, but alcoholic oblivion was a welcome prospect right then. It wasn't as if things could get any worse.

The girls wore matching expressions of concern. They both looked so earnest that I almost managed a smile.

"I'll be okay, girls," I said.

The sound of my weak voice made them look even more worried.

"Honestly. I don't want to speak about it any more though. Let's just get pissed and talk complete shite about other things."

They looked doubtful, but shrugged in unison anyway.

"Did you see how Simone's face brightened up when you said that?" Jess gave Simone a dig in the ribs with her elbow. "She wants to hit you with a bit of absurdism talk. She might even let you choose the ism, under the circumstances."

"Nihilism through the medium of wine sounds good right about now." I drained my glass and lurched out of my seat for another.

Two glasses of wine later, my tune had changed. The shock of what I'd seen had passed and now I was pissed in every sense – and I wanted Alvin to know about it. My anger had grown over the course of the night to the levels of Uma Thurman's character in *Kill Bill*, when she wakes up from her coma and realises that her baby is gone. Alvin was very lucky that I wasn't an assassin in a former life, but I could still tear shreds off him in another way.

"Going to the bashroom," I said to the girls.

Jess frowned. "Don't ring Alvin. In fact, give me your phone."

"Don't go all mobile polishe on me! As if I'd ring Alvin while I'm drunk. As if!"

"You better not, or you'll regret it. Believe me, I know from experience. Promise me you won't."

I stumbled out of my seat. "Yeah, yeah – I have better things to do than ring him. Like pish. Have to go – it's an emergency."

I reviewed my phone as I walked to the bathroom. Five missed calls from Alvin while the phone had been in silent mode. Three texts. All various permutations of him asking for a chance to explain.

Standing in the corridor outside the ladies' room, I tapped Alvin's name in my Favourites list on my iPhone. Naturally, he was at the top. I didn't have any other 'A' names in there, but I'd saved his name as Aalvin just in case I ever added another A-named person with a second letter that came before l.

Tammy, you sad bitch.

His phone rang.

"Hello?" a female voice answered.

"Adrienne? Why are you anshering Alvin's phone?"

"Why are you talking like you've just had an anaesthetic at the dentist's? Surely Miss Perfect isn't trying to deal with her problems through alcohol?"

"I'm not intereshted in talking rubbish to you. Just get Alvin and stop trying to cause even more trouble."

"Alvin is busy putting his daughter to bed."

I looked at my watch. "At eleven o'clock?" At least, I thought it was eleven – I couldn't see very clearly any more. In any sense, if I was going to get all Simone-style philosophical about it. "You're only saying that to get rid of me. Shouldn't a baby be in bed by this time?"

"She was in bed. She woke up again. Babies that age do that, Tammy."

She didn't say 'But you couldn't possibly know that, could you?' but she didn't need to. The message was there in every syllable of what she had said. Alvin had promised me, sworn to me, that he hadn't told Adrienne about how hard we'd tried for a baby, but I now had every reason to doubt everything he'd ever told me.

I decided to hedge my bets on whether she'd known. "I betchu were dying to tell me about the baby."

"I promised Alvin I wouldn't, but it would have saved me a lot of time trying to get rid of you if I could have."

"Dcha know what? You're nothing but a cow, and it's about time I told you that. A cow and a bitch. And a . . ." I couldn't think of anything else. God, I was useless at insults. If only I could have passed the phone over to Jess for this bit.

Adrienne laughed. "Well, well. You don't sound quite as refined and together now, do you? You get a few drinks into you and we see the real you. I always told Alvin you were all fur coat and no knickers but he wouldn't listen."

"That's enough!" came Claire's voice in the background. "Give me that. Tammy, love, are you alright?"

"I can't believe dishes happening, Claire."

362

There was silence for a few seconds. "Tammy, are you . . . drunk?"

"No! Whyez everyone going on about drink when a baby has suddenly materia-matialised – appeared out of nowhere? Let's talk about the baby!" My loud voice suddenly deserted me. "That's not really Alvin's baby, is it, Claire? Tell me it's not. Tell me Adrienne stuck a curly wig on some poor child's head because she really does hate me that much."

Claire sighed heavily. "I know this must have come as a big shock to you, Tammy. I told Alvin time and time again to tell you."

"Yeah? Well, he didn't lishen. I hate him. Can you tell him that? I deshpishe him."

"No, I won't, because you don't," Claire said softly.

"I flipping well do, Claire! I ruined his life and I hated myself for it, but I was just beginning to move on from being such a stupid cow when he made me fall in love with him all over again, then I find out that he's given Dark Shirley Temple to someone else. How could I not hate him?"

"He's still in love with you, Tammy. I know it's difficult, but just give him a chance to explain."

"And what happens after that? He goesh off to his little family and I'm on my own forever? I wash doing okay, you know. I wash getting out there and meeting men. They were nothing compared to Alvin, but at least I wash moving on . . . hey! Do you know why I sound like Sean Connery?" And who was I talking to again?

"Tammy! You're one sly piece of work when you have a drink in you . . ."

I saw a few Jesses coming towards me. I tried to run

363

away so that I could be left in peace and quiet, but it suddenly seemed like the floor was trying to rise up to meet me, like some sort of old Irish blessing. And then, there was glorious peace and quiet in my chattering head for the first time in a year and a half. Not being sensible was the business.

51

The following morning, being sensible had its charms back. I raced to the bathroom and vomited repeatedly as the wine caught up with me. Mother of God . . . they didn't make hangovers like they used to. It felt like there was a jack-in-the-box on speed in my stomach pushing out everything I'd ever eaten for the past month. How had all this food got inside me? I was sure I hadn't eaten at all . . .

After five minutes of solid vomiting, I was finally able to flush the toilet and slam down the lid. I lay my clammy head on it, panting and wishing I could be run over by something. I realised that I was lying on the lid of a toilet that I wouldn't even contemplate cleaning without wearing three pairs of Marigolds and a SARS-style mask on a run-of-the-mill day, but it's amazing how little anything matters when you're sick. I tried to block out the events of the previous evening, but it was no good. Memories and thoughts and speculation started to invade my brain until my stomach churned anew and I had to lift the lid of the toilet again.

Eventually, I managed to crawl back to bed, noticing

three business cards on my duvet. Where had they come from? I reached out slowly for them and lay back on my pillows to read them. I'd never heard of the people whose names were on the cards, and although I recognised the name of the company they worked for I didn't know anyone there. I looked around for my phone and couldn't see it anywhere. I'd probably lost it. I knew I would care about this as soon as my hangover passed because that phone had been damn expensive. I was just drifting off into a merciful sleep when there was a knock on my door. Or was it a gunshot?

"Yeah?" I croaked. If it was the latter, maybe whoever it was would be doing me a favour.

Jess threw the door open. A woeful smell of chip oil wafted in the door with her, and then I remembered why my stomach had been so full this morning. I had a vague memory of cooking sausages, chips and beans when I'd come in last night and eating them with mustard – Jess had used up all our ketchup. It was a miracle I hadn't set the house on fire.

"It's twelve o'clock!" she announced.

"So?"

"Wow. You really are in a bad way." She sat down at the end of my bed. Even the slight impact of her tiny frame made me want to vomit again. "I thought you were dead when I didn't hear you pottering around downstairs at eight."

"I'm not sure that I'm not." This felt as close to death as anything I'd ever experienced. How was alcohol even legal? My head was thumping, and not just in the hangover sense – it felt like I'd been hit with a baseball bat. I'd never been hit with one before to know exactly what that felt like, but surely it would have been in and around the same awful feeling I had at that moment. I put my hand up to the main source of the throbbing.

"Why is there a gigantic fecking lump on my forehead?" I said to Jess, the panic in my voice scaring me even more. I would have dived out of bed to look in a mirror except that moving my hand to my head had nearly been the death of me.

Jess grinned. "You don't remember the great belly-flop then. Just as well, just as well."

Oh no. No no no. "Remind me," I said through gritted teeth.

It turned out that I was lucky to have teeth left to grit. The last thing I could vaguely remember was running away from Jess so that she couldn't take my phone, but she informed me (while trying not to explode into laughter) that I somehow managed to trip over my own feet and fall face down at the feet of a group of six businessmen. I was apparently out cold for a few minutes, but came to and wanted to carry on drinking as if nothing had happened. Meanwhile, Claire was still on the line when Jess retrieved the phone from the floor. While Jess was explaining what had happened, I'd gone over to the businessmen "for a chat" and had left with all of their phone numbers. I would have thought Jess was making the whole thing up if I wasn't currently picking the other three business cards out of my hair.

Jess delved into her pocket and pulled out my phone. "Hutch has been ringing and texting you all morning. I bet you anything he's on his way over here right now when he's not getting any joy with the phone. You really should take a shower just in case he gets past me at the front door and bursts into the room or something. You smell really bad, and even if you tell him you never want to see him again – and after seeing you in action last night, I have absolutely no idea what you'll do any more – you don't want his last image of you to be the way you are right now."

Anger bubbled from somewhere within me and erupted. "He had his last image of me yesterday! I looked pretty good then, apart from my *expression*!"

"Tammy . . . you're practically growling. You never growl, even when I use your Crème de la Mer. Try to stay calm."

"Even when you *what*?"

"Didn't you know? Oh. That might explain the lack of growling so . . . can we forget I said that? We have a crisis on our hands here, after all – we don't need two."

"To be resumed, Jess. For fuck's sake, that shit is expensive."

Jess lifted up the bottom of my duvet.

"What are you *doing*?"

"Taking cover," came Jess's muffled voice. "Two expletives in one sentence from you means things are very, very bad around here. You get a right potty mouth on you when you're angry, do you know that?"

I leaned forward and yanked the duvet off her. Things were very, very bad enough without having draughts on my feet to contend with.

"How the hell else could things be? This is exactly what I was worried about when Alvin appeared on my doorstep – that I'd get hurt, and that all the moving on I'd done would be blown to bits. Well, score one for the worriers of this world – because I was bloody well right. If only I hadn't agreed to do the plan with him. Can you delete those new texts from him on my phone, please?"

"Do I look like I was born to wait on you? I'll delete

them if you make dinner for me tonight when you're making some for yourself. Deal?"

"It'll be about a week before I can eat again, but I'll buy you a takeaway if you just delete the fecking texts."

"I should have set up a curse box coming in here and I'd have been able to live on takeaways all week. Now, before I do this, are you absolutely sure you don't want to read them first?"

"I don't! Just *delete them*!"

"Okay, okay!" She fiddled with the phone.

The doorbell rang mid-fiddle. I froze.

Jess ran to the window, opened it a smidgen and looked down before quietly closing it again.

"It's him. Didn't I tell you he was on the way? I always thought I had psychic abilities . . . maybe I should hook up with Claire and start a new business."

"So what if he's here? I'm not answering the door and neither are you."

"Not even to tell him you think he's a lying piece of shit? Go on, let me do it."

"No. He's getting nothing from us – no communication whatsoever. That's what will hurt him most now."

"Spoilsport. But okay, you know him best."

"It seems that I don't know him at all, Jess. I just know that nothing he can say will make me forgive him for not telling me about Emmeline."

"Maybe you should give him a chance to explain when things cool down, though –"

"No, Jess! There's nothing to explain!"

"Okay! I was just saying! I'm just trying to help –"

"Well, please don't. Throwing my phone over would help – I want to turn it off before he starts the calls again."

Jess obliged. Then the doorbell rang again, for longer this time.

"He'll have to give up eventually," Jess said chirpily. "He'll be gone in a minute or two, you wait and s–"

"*Tammyyyyyyyyy*! Open the door!" Alvin yelled.

"Wow. I never knew you could hear so much upstairs at the front of the house," Jess said. "Do you want to plait my hair there while we're waiting for him to go? Remember we always used to do that when we were ki–"

The doorbell rang again. Jess threw her eyes up to heaven while she waited for it to stop. She hated being interrupted. But stop it didn't.

"He must have his finger pressed down on it, the big child! Can I *please* poke my head out and tell him to fuck right off? He's begging for a bollixing."

"*Tammyyyyyyyyy*! Come on, just let me explain! One chance, that's all I want!"

Jess tutted. "I wouldn't be surprised if he gets a ghetto blaster out next, like Lloyd Dobler in *Say Anything*."

I closed my eyes, willing the entire situation to go away. And immediately, the doorbell rang again.

"That's it!" I got out of bed and stomped downstairs, going straight to the kitchen and retrieving my bread knife.

Jess's face blanched. "Tammy, that's a bit excessive! I know he's being a pain, but come on!"

I marched into the hall, right up beside the door, and cut the cord of the doorbell. I handed Jess the knife instead of putting it back in the kitchen. "Have to go upstairs and puke," I explained. "Plug out the landline for me too, there's a dear."

Jess came up a few minutes later with a cup of tea and a digestive biscuit.

"Thanks, Jess. Is he gone?"

"Em, no. But he can't camp out there all day."

Jess's phone rang.

"It says 'Private'. Do you think it's Alvin? I'm expecting a call and I really should take this . . ."

"Go ahead," I said. "Just hang up again if it's him."

"Hello, Jess spea–"

I could clearly hear Alvin on the other side of the phone. "Jess, please, can one of you let me in? Tell Tammy I just want five minutes!"

"It's him," Jess mouthed, her eyes wide.

"No shit," I mouthed back.

Jess jumped off the bed. "Will you ever just *piss off*? You need to go on a course that teaches people how to handle situations, because you, Alvin Harrison, are absolutely useless at it!"

"I said 'No communication'!" I hissed at Jess, but it was too late. She was off on one.

I got up and went into the en suite to get a basin and fill it with water. When I came out, Jess had moved into the hall. She was still giving out to Alvin.

I opened the window quietly and peeped down to locate Alvin precisely before tipping the basin's contents over his head. I banged the window shut without saying a single word to him.

"I was just getting going when his phone went dead," Jess said as she walked back into the room.

"He won't be ringing anyone else for a while on that phone," I said before running to the bathroom to puke again.

52

The girls had called the cavalry in.

"Eat this now before I stick your head in it," Mum said.

Aunt Patty flanked her on one side, Aunt Gobby on the other. Without Mum giving them a word of instruction, they moved forward in a perfectly synchronised movement to form a semi-circle around my armchair. If I was to get past them, I'd have to knock them down – and like most people on my mother's side of my family, they were built like tanks. Not good opponents to be up against when you hadn't eaten in days.

"Porridge," I said in disgust. "I thought you said you wanted me to eat?"

"It was good enough for you years ago," Mum said before picking a spoonful and pushing it into my mouth.

I swallowed the lumpy gloop that had been deposited in my gob. "Okay, okay. I'll eat it, but at the kitchen table, all right? I don't ever eat in the armchairs. Imagine if a lump of goo fell on the material – it'd leave the kind of stain that would remind you of a slug's trail, only thicker. Ugh, I can't even think about it."

"She's getting better," I heard Jess say to Mum as I walked to the kitchen.

I wished. My anger had dissipated and I was sorry about that. Its replacement, despondency, was a poor substitute. I'd taken to the bed (without a naggin of vodka with a straw, but I wasn't ruling it out in the future) after pouring the basin of water over Alvin's head and hadn't left it properly until this morning, two days later, bar a few bathroom visits. Between my hangover and the effect of misery, my appetite had vanished completely. All I'd had was a few cups of tea and bites of toast here and there.

Alvin had called to the house another four times. Jess, who was working from home this week, had opened the downstairs window and gone through the rigmarole of telling him to go away on the first three occasions. The fourth time, she said she felt too sorry for him to say anything and just shook her head instead before closing the window again. "I know I'm supposed to treat him like public enemy number one, but he looks wretched, Tammy – really broken. And he refuses to leave for about an hour after I tell him to jog off. He just sits there with his back to the front door, like some poor urchin huddled into a street door for warmth. He sat through fifteen minutes of hailstones yesterday."

"It's a pity it wasn't thirty," I said before diving under the duvet again.

I left my phone off unless I needed to contact someone (usually to ring downstairs to ask the girls if they'd bring up some tea). Whenever I turned it on, there would be notifications of more missed calls and several texts from Alvin. I deleted them and went about my business of moping. I hadn't checked my email or social media accounts in case he'd tried those avenues too.

Mum dragged me to the bathroom after I somehow put away the porridge and shoved me into the shower. When I came out of the en suite, she was laying make-up out on my bed.

"Here. Put this on after the rest of your eye make-up." She handed me an Urban Decay Heavy Metal Metallic Eyeliner. It was very glittery and very green.

"Where did you get this?"

"I bought it for you in Clerys."

"Erm . . . thanks, but can I ask why?"

"Ah, when Jess and Simone told me what happened, I thought you could do with a bit of sparkle."

I attempted a smile. That was Mum – the world could fall apart all it wanted to, but you should still put your face on in the morning.

"Please tell me this isn't because you've arranged for Alvin to call over and you're trying to get me to look halfway decent."

She shook her head. "No, love. I'm not getting involved other than trying to keep you alive and clean. Only you know the best way to handle this." She patted my hand. "Now, come downstairs as soon as you're ready – there's important work ahead."

I had no idea what she was talking about, but anything that involved distracting myself from my tormented thoughts sounded good. I threw on my clothes and make-up, added a healthy dose of green glitter to both eyelids and went downstairs.

"It's like twenty years ago, only without *A Country Practice*," Simone pointed out as she peeled an onion.

The mothers had decided that we needed to cook. Some good wholesome food would sort out any problem under the sun, apparently, so down to work we got. They'd brought ingredients to make shepherd's pie, lasagne, beef stew and chicken curry, along with containers to store them in before freezing them. When they were finished with us, they proudly boasted that we'd have about a week's worth of dinners for three – which would give me a chance to come out of whatever fog I was in without fading away. I was quite sure that it was going to take more than a week, but I didn't want to sound ungrateful so I kept that knowledge to myself.

The next few hours flew by. I decided to project manage the six of us, something that didn't go down too well with Patty, but under the circumstances she let it go. I assigned the cooking of the meat to myself. I was taking no risks after my hangover vomiting extravaganza. Jess was on rice and pasta sheets, and setting the table while they boiled. Patty was on potatoes and side dishes for today's dinner. Simone was in charge of the food processor and general food chopping duties. As we had to rotate the pots and pans a lot, Gobby had the responsibility of cleaning them between courses and also keeping the work surfaces clean and the dishwasher stocked. Mum would assemble the dishes when all of the ingredients were fully cooked, put them in the oven and time how long they needed to be cooked for.

We all got in each other's way, fought over saucepans and argued over everything – basil or oregano in the lasagne, or both? Low fat or full fat cheese on top of the pie, or none at all? It was tremendous *craic* and despite myself, I somehow managed to forget about Alvin for a few seconds here and there. It wasn't until we were sitting down to lash into plates of steaming shepherd's pie and I saw the pile of potatoes in the middle of the table that my lip started to quiver a bit. Gobby noticed it and grabbed the remote.

"You know, *Neighbours* is on around this time," she said. "Who needs *A Country Practice*?" And sure enough, she found it on one of the channels. Everyone turned their attention to it while I took a minute to compose myself.

When we finished dinner and cleaned up the kitchen, Gobby produced a packet of cards. I don't even know how long we sat at the kitchen table playing various games – 25, 45, even good old Snap – but it didn't matter. Nobody seemed to be in a hurry.

It was almost bedtime when they started talking about making a move. I saw them to the front door, thanking them profusely. Patty and Gobby made no reference to the Alvin situation, but Gobby gave me a quick hug that somehow mutated into slaps on the back and Patty told me that soup-making was also good for keeping the mind occupied. When it was Mum's turn to say or do something, she looked at the ground. I was surprised – although times like these were awkward for everyone, Mum usually wasn't someone who'd be stuck for something to say. But then she bent down, put a hand behind my foot and picked something up. Something envelope-shaped, with familiar handwriting on it.

"You've got mail," Mum said quietly. She held the envelope out for me to take.

"I don't want it. Throw it in the bin for me, would you?"

She shook her head. "If you want to throw it away, you'll have to do it yourself. Make sure that's what you really want to do before you get rid of it, though."

I ran my hands over my face. The day had been going so well. Was there no escape?

"You know something, Tammy pet? It's hard to make

a decision unless you have all of the facts. That's all I'll say on the matter."

She pushed the letter into my hand. I didn't know whether to let it fall or not, but then my fingers crept around it as if someone else had made the decision for me.

'Tammy' was written in large letters on the envelope, with two lines drawn underneath. All I could think of when I saw it was the list, and how it had brought us back together. The envelope was bulging, but I wasn't surprised. The birthday and Valentine's cards I'd received from Alvin over the years had always been more like essays than greetings, and the couple of letters he'd sent from Australia – ones I'd never opened – had looked meaty too. But of course, it would be long when he had so much explaining to do, wouldn't it?

Simone sauntered into the hall. I knew she was checking up on me but trying to look like she'd just wandered out there.

"Oh, there you are. Why don't you come into the sitting room and watch some TV with us?"

I shoved the envelope into Simone's hands. "Can you bin that for me?"

"From Alvin? When did it arrive?"

"Sometime when we were all making enough noise not to hear the letterbox ping, it seems."

"Ah, Tammy. Would you not open it? You've been here before –"

"That was different. This is worse – so much worse."

Jess came to join the party. "So where are we at? Hatching plans to murder Hutch?"

"Not quite," Simone said just as I answered "Yes."

Simone filled Jess in on the letter, and how I didn't want to open it.

377

"Why would I want to read this after how he's deceived me?"

Simone eyeballed me. She looked nervous. She glanced at Jess, who nodded in what I interpreted as support.

"I'm sorry, Tammy, but I don't think he had any other choice but to do what he did. You went into complete shutdown on him last time, don't forget."

"And don't faint when I say this, but I completely agree with Simone's theory," Jess said. "We completely understand how hurt you must be and we'll stand by you no matter what, but we wouldn't be up to much as your best friends if we didn't tell you what we've been saying behind your back."

Simone gave Jess a sharp look. "She means that we think the best thing we can do to help you is to be honest about how we see this. And I don't know much about kids, but I'd say it's pretty hard to spend several weeks away from a four-month-old baby. He must really want you back if he's willing to make that sacrifice."

I stared at the wall. Eventually, Jess shook me gently on the arm.

"I'm no great philosopher, but to my mind, all of this is less about you being angry with Alvin for not telling you and more about whether you can live with him having a child with someone else. That's what it's going to boil down to."

I met Jess's eye, then looked at Simone.

"All I know at the moment is that I have another long night of thinking ahead of me, girls."

"Think about opening this while you're at it." Simone pressed the letter back into my hands.

53

I just hate that moment when you know you might not have been as right as you thought you were. Take, for example, when you realise that your convictions were based on anger and hurt and might not be entirely rational or fair, or the moment when you see the part you've played in creating a horrible situation when you were hitherto convincing yourself that you were the victim. Even though a part of you knew that you weren't entirely blameless either. I was having a gala moment where all of the examples that were running through my head met in a riot.

There was no denying it. Alvin *had* been looking for the right moment to tell me since his arrival on my doorstep on New Year's Eve. How many times had he said we had to talk about what had happened in our lives since we'd last been together, only to be cut off at the pass by me? He'd been walking on eggshells around me, afraid to insist on saying stuff that I didn't want to hear in case I ran away again. It didn't mean I wasn't still pissed off as hell at him, but he wasn't entirely alone in making this situation a complete mess. And now, I was doing exactly what I'd done the last time – refusing all contact with Alvin – and look at how that had worked out. Regardless of who was to blame this time around, hadn't I learned anything?

I wasn't sure if I decided to grow up a bit in that moment, or if the slight sense of normality I'd experienced that day had made the fog lift enough for me to see another avenue of thought. It could also have been the fact that Simone and Jess had vocalised something that I'd thought myself but had put to the back of my mind. Maybe it was a combination of all three factors. But whatever it was, right there and then, I decided to do what I hadn't done last time around. I opened the damn letter and started to read.

Tammy,

I know I have a lot of explaining to do. I don't know if this letter will make any difference, but I have to try. I wish I could tell you everything face to face.

First of all, I want to say I'm sorry – both about how you found out about Emmeline and how we left things the last time we met. That argument probably doesn't rate highly on your radar now after what you've discovered, but I want you to know that I didn't mean it when I said I wanted you out of my life. How could I ever want that? I was furious after our row and said things that I regret.

I'm sure you have a million questions about Emmeline. Let me start by telling you about what happened with Emmeline's mother, Jane. I met Jane, who's from Cork, through some Irish friends I made in Australia. We weren't in a relationship. It was all very casual, Tammy – friends with benefits, if you want to put it that way. Jane was just out of a relationship too and didn't want anything too serious. You were still shutting me out at the time and it was killing me. You have no idea how lonely I was without you, and you seemed to be telling me that you had no intention of ever having anything to do with me again. I thought being with someone else might help . . . don't get me wrong, I didn't set out to use Jane - but whenever she instigated something with me, I found it hard to say no. She knew about you, and that I wasn't over you. She also knew that what she and I were doing was just physical and would never go anywhere else, and she was fine with it. That's all it was to her too.

We stopped sleeping together after a few months because it all just felt a bit empty, and I started making plans to return home and fight for you again. I hoped that by then you'd have had the breathing space you seemed to need. But then Jane announced that she was pregnant and suddenly going home wasn't an option any more. It was a huge shock to both of us. Pretty ironic too when you consider what you and me went through. (Clarissa was really supportive when this happened, by the way. She's been a very good friend to me - but, as you know now for sure, just a friend.)

There was never any question of us becoming a couple just because she was pregnant. I told Jane I'd fully support her, of course, but we weren't going to make it as a couple just because something had forced us together. We had to get on for the sake of the baby, so staying as friends and not complicating things was the best option. A lot of people in that situation do try to make it work out

381

between them, but maybe there was more between them in the first place.

I couldn't tell you then, Tammy. It was still so soon after what we'd gone through and I knew it would break your heart. I closed my social networking accounts and stopped contacting mutual friends from home so that you wouldn't find out second-hand.

As time went on, I hoped I would be able to forget you, or at least move on from you – but it just wouldn't happen. When Emmeline was born, I realised that her birth was the first thing to have made me happy since I lost you. It really hit me hard then that you were gone, that we'd lost our relationship for no good reason. I kept wondering if I would be asking myself for the rest of my life if I should have tried harder, and if it would be a mistake to not at least try one more time . . . and then, as I was looking through my documentation for something, I found the list. That made my mind up for me. Obviously I didn't want to mess you up by coming back, and I didn't even know if you would be seeing someone else by now, but I had to try.

My plan was to tell you about Emmeline sometime over the course of our first activity, but you refused to hear it. The same thing happened on every other attempt to tell you too. It was either just say it out at the worst possible time or wait for a better one. And then you called over.

You're probably wondering where Emmeline has been for all of this time. She only arrived in Dublin the day you saw her. She and Jane had been at home for Christmas for the last few weeks, staying in Cork. Jane called in here on their way to the airport so that Mum and Adrienne could see the baby before they went back to Australia. Adrienne met Emmeline when she came over to visit, but Mum only met her for the first time on St Stephen's Day in Cork. They were there from Stephen's Day to New Year's Eve, right up until a few hours before I called to your house.

Where do we go from here? Well, I know where I'm going, Tammy. Or rather, coming. Home. Jane stayed in Australia when she got pregnant because she was set to get good benefits for her maternity leave, but now she's planning on moving back. She wants Emmeline to grow up with her family around her, so her parents have given her a site on their land and she's going to build a house on it over the next few years. She knows, of course, that I never planned to stay in Australia long term and that I will be happy to move home too. I couldn't tell you that at the start without getting into the whole story there and then.

There is one problem, though. It could be a while yet before we move back. Jane has a very well-paid job in Australia, and she needs to continue to work to have money to build the house. She hasn't a hope of finding a job with the same wages here, and without wages, that house won't be built. Her dad is going to project-manage the build when Jane goes back to work, and she's staying on in Australia until the house is done. It could take a year, it could take two, depending on how much it costs. That means I can't move back home until Jane is ready. I would regret it for the rest of my life if I missed a year or two of my baby's life, and I know from spending the last few weeks away from her that I couldn't and wouldn't do it.

So why did I ask you to do the plan when this is

the case? Because I didn't want to live another day of my life without you, Tammy. I thought that if you were willing to start again, we could find a way to make things work. I know you won't fly to Australia so moving over to me isn't an option, but people do long-distance relationships all of the time. It would only be for a year or two compared to the rest of our lives. Emmeline aside, nothing means a thing to me without you. I live in Australia, yet the sky is greyer there than it is at home. Even potatoes don't taste as good. As the great philosopher-cum-activities instructor Les once said, I'm hopeless without you.

I asked myself so many times if it would be cruel to ask you to do the plan in light of how we couldn't have a baby together, but I think it was exactly the opposite. One of the points of the plan was for us to get out of our comfort zones and get over the fear factor in life, and if we'd stayed together and still didn't have a child, it would have been something we would have had to accept anyway. If the plan could help us overcome fear, it could only be a good thing.

If you still feel anything for me, Tammy, please get in touch straight away. I'm leaving soon and we're running out of time. I'll be at home for the rest of today. Adrienne is at Clarissa's, still trying to sort things out, and Mum will give us all the space we need. If I don't hear from you, I'll finally get the message. I won't contact you again.

Alvin

PS I've put the list in the envelope. You know, I think I've covered activity 10: conquer one huge fear *each. Mine was that you could reject me again if I came back into your life. Maybe you will, maybe this is it for us, but I'm glad I tried – because as I said to you a few years ago, anything that could save us would be worth trying.*

It's up to you now . . .

All I could do when I finished the letter was stare at the list. It was in tatters by now, with some of the words partially worn away by the folds. I scanned the ten activity titles that we'd written in red pen again, even though I knew them off by heart by now, then went back and read the descriptions of each item. I read it over and over, remembering and deciding.

Eventually, I went downstairs. I met Simone in the hall with her hot-water bottle as I threw my coat on.

"Are you going where I think you might be going?"

"Yep. I'm going to finish that goddamn list."

Simone's face brightened.

"Are you going to be okay about Emmeline?"

I thought about her question for a while before answering, even though I'd been doing nothing else since I'd read the letter but think about this very issue.

"Truthfully? I don't know. I can't say I'm okay about things now, but maybe I can learn to live with them. It'll take time and it's going to hurt at the start, but she's Alvin's child and I could never begrudge him something that he's always wanted."

Simone smiled. "You better go and tell him that so."

I smiled back quickly before grabbing my keys and running out the door. I only hoped I'd still be smiling in an hour's time.

385

54

As always, Adrienne answered the door and not Claire. She instantly tried to close it in my face.

"Hey!" I launched my body against the door and pushed against it with rage-fuelled oomph. Even by Adrienne's standards of rudeness, this was something else. "I need to talk to Alvin!"

"You're wasting your time . . ."

"For once in your life, stay out of our business!" I pushed past her and ran into the house. I burst into the kitchen, the most likely place I imagined Alvin would be, but there was no sign of him.

Claire walked out of the utility room. She looked apprehensive.

"Tammy. How are you doing?"

I shrugged. "Put it this way, Claire – if you know of any spirits looking for someone to fuss over right now, I wouldn't mind a bit of help."

She walked over and hugged me. "I can imagine how tough all of this is to take in. I'm sorry I couldn't tell you about Emmeline. Alvin made me promise I wouldn't and it had to come from him –"

"It's fine. I understand your position in all of this." I returned the hug, then pulled back so that I could look at her. "Claire, do you know where Alvin is? I really need to talk to him . . ."

Adrienne burst into the room after me. "Tell her nothing, Mum!"

I felt like I was in a scene of a bad detective movie.

"You, pipe down! Anyone who's meddled in a relationship as much as you have in theirs has no right to open their gob at all. When I think of all the money I spent on putting you through college . . . all the negative auras I had to put up with reading over the years to fund a degree you never ended up using anyway . . . and you wouldn't think you'd even gone to the small school with the way you carry on. You'd be better off focusing your energy on getting a job instead of interfering in your brother's life, not to mention spending all of my money . . . the first thing to go in a recession is aura cleansing –"

"She wasn't good for him, Mum!"

"What is your problem with me?" I jumped in. "Why have you always thought I wasn't good enough for your brother?"

"I didn't say you weren't good enough. I said you weren't good *for him*. How can you not see that? You just walked away from him last time around without ever giving him a reason why, and then wouldn't have any contact with him afterwards when he tried to sort things out. Who does that after spending years with someone?"

Obviously, Alvin had honoured his word and hadn't told Adrienne about our baby issues. I couldn't refute

Adrienne's sentiments without getting into explanations, so I let her words go.

"All he's ever wanted from you was to be adored. Our parents gave him a few too many sensitive genes and it's been a burden to him all his life. He's a – a *hand-holder* of a boyfriend. He needs to be with someone that he can wax lyrical with about feelings and romantic bullshit. But who does he end up with? Someone like you, walking around with your big car . . ."

I let that one go too. Now wasn't the time to point out glaring speech inaccuracies.

". . . and your house in the nicest part of town and your long coats and your touched-up-twenty-times-a-day-expensive-makeup and your professional voice . . ."

"Adrienne, what is the point of this attack on me?"

"God, you just don't get it – and then Mum says *I'm* thick! You have your own list, and Alvin is the last thing on it. All you care about is creating the image of a thirty-something's perfect world. Most women would be wetting themselves over someone like my brother, but you act as if he's lucky you have anything to do with him."

"You have it so, so wrong. Alvin is all I've ever wanted. Everything else in my life that you've mentioned is just stuff that I've accumulated while I was waiting to meet someone like him, or things I bought after he left to distract myself from the horror of a life without him. I don't give a damn about stuff." I took a brand-new Chanel lipstick out of my handbag. "See this? I only bought it last week and it cost several hours of hard work." I ripped off the lid, twisted the lipstick until it was fully extended and snapped it from its base.

"So what? That means nothing when you can go out

and buy another twenty of those from your wages next week."

"What do you want me to do – take out my keys and scrape the side of my car or something?"

"Yes. And then torch your house. After that, I'll believe you're not materialistic."

"Claire, do you actually agree with this nonsense?"

"No."

"Thank you!" At least someone in Alvin's family had a bit of sense!

"How could I, when the spirits have told me that you're a good girl? Shortly after you and Alvin first started seeing each other, I saw an apparition right here in this kitchen. It was where you're standing right now, actually – isn't that uncanny? It told me that if you're a tad controlling and uptight and a terrible worrier and sometimes a bit aloof with us, it's because that's your way of making sense of the world – and wouldn't it be worse if you were off snorting cocaine off dirty toilet lids?"

"It'd have to be a clean toilet lid for her. Haven't you learned anything, Mum?"

"Oy! Zip it! And so, Tammy darling, I've always given you a chance, even when I really didn't want to. Like that time when you insisted on sharpening my kitchen knives because you said they wouldn't cut through foam. Or when you turned up with a new toilet brush for the downstairs toilet because you thought my one was a disease waiting to be discovered and could well be named after me. Or . . ."

"Okay, I get the message," I mumbled. "I'm a pain in the ass."

Adrienne nodded so hard that her chin practically bounced off the floor.

"Everyone has their own way of being a pain, my dear," Claire said. "And there are folk who'd argue you could do worse than having someone around who'll sharpen your knives and buy you useful household things. You've changed a lot over the years too – you were only like that at the start. You're a much calmer individual now. Besides, we all have things to deal with behind closed doors that others might know nothing about."

I nodded. She didn't know that I knew that Alvin had spoken to her about our problems, but I hoped that somehow that nod could convey that I was grateful that she'd been there for him when I hadn't, ashamed and all as I was about that. I hoped I could count on the spirits to have my back if my nodding skills weren't up to much.

"And as for you," she said to Adrienne, "your attitude towards your brother's happiness shows that you're no saint either. You also have no grounds to talk about anyone else's behaviour after the way you've denied your relationship with Clarry. You'd do well to be a bit more into what you call the romantic bullshit yourself. And you let me think Clarry was trying to snatch Alvin from Tammy all that time . . . if I hadn't walked in on the pair of you arguing just before Jane and Emmeline arrived, I still wouldn't know you were a couple – or that you even liked girls, for that matter, not that that bothers me in the slightest. Poor Clarry is mad about you –"

"We're not discussing Clarry and me now," Adrienne said quickly. "As for Alvin, I just wanted him to be with someone who'd appreciate him." She threw me a withering look.

Enough was enough. I had nothing left to lose any more. "Okay. You want to know what I'm all about? This is it. I never thought I was good enough for Alvin. If I've come across as a bit aloof and detached it's because I always worried that he'd realise some day that he could do so much better than me, then he'd leave me, so I tried really hard not to get too attached to him. I should have trusted him more when he told me how he felt about me, but I was insecure and fucked everything up. Are you happy now? Does knowing that make you feel better?"

She shrugged. "Yes, it does actually. Alvin was right after all – you really are messed up, aren't you? He's always said that."

"Girls, just stop it. This is all pointless when . . . Tammy, there's something you should know." Claire came over to me and took my hands in hers. "Alvin's gone back to Australia already. His flight left an hour ago."

My heart sank. "But he wasn't supposed to be going for another two days!" I squeezed her hands so hard I saw her wincing.

"He was so pissed off at you dumping him yet again that he changed his flight," Adrienne said. "He couldn't get out of this country fast enough and follow his daughter back home."

"I don't believe it! I came over to tell him I'd fly back to Australia with him!"

"What, for a free holiday?" Adrienne sniped.

"No! Forever! Well, the next year or two anyway, or as long as it takes for Jane's house to be built."

Adrienne gave me a sceptical look. "What about your job?"

"What about it? I'll leave it."

"What about a long-term visa?"

"I'll sort that out too." Hopefully.

"Your house? The car? I'll take the car if you're looking to offload it."

"I'm not dying, Adrienne! I'm just moving to

Australia. Or I was until I found out he'd already gone without me. Oh God, this is so screwed up."

"What's with the amateur dramatics? Just get an instant electronic travel-authority-tourist-visa online through a good travel company and follow him over there. You can get that sorted in no time."

Adrienne looked perplexed. I'd never let Alvin tell her about my fear of flying.

"It's not that simple." I could barely say the words without hyperventilating and feeling as if I was about to suffocate.

"Yes, it is. Everything you've just said about Alvin means jack shit if your first thought isn't to follow him. If you want to save what you had badly enough, you know what you need to do."

I stared at Claire's custom-made astrology-chart tiles. "I suppose I do."

Claire patted my back encouragingly. "Go home now and sort out a flight and a visa for yourself, like a good girl."

"Don't tell him I'm on the way over!" My voice was slightly hysterical again. What if I wasn't able to do it?

Claire removed her hand from my back. "O-kay. I'm sure he'll love the surprise."

Adrienne folded her arms across her chest. "A word of advice, Tammy – when you get there, drop the Ice Queen act. Alvin needs more from you. And if what you've just told us is true, then you'll want to give it to him." She frowned. "That sounded wrong, and now I have a really nasty picture in my head."

I could only nod. The horrible suffocating feeling was getting stronger.

55

Back in the Celtic Tiger days when people seemed to think it was their right to spend a year living abroad after they left college, practically everyone I knew took off to Australia. Most of them planned a stopover in Thailand on their way to Oz, spending anything from a few days to a few weeks there exploring before going on to their easy-to-land jobs in the pubs and clubs of the Aussie cities. It was a ritual for many before joining the real world. I watched my former college classmates go one by one, and was never once tempted to join them. The mere thought of what they had to do to get there turned me into a shivering wreck. My biggest fear had dominated my life, and it was hardly going to stop now.

I was seven when the crash happened. My parents and I were flying back from a visit to my uncle Pat in Chicago, Dad's brother. It had been his fortieth birthday and Dad had insisted on us going over together as a family. It was my first ever flight and I'd been so excited, squealing with happiness on the way over as our flights took off and touched down. I'd squealed for a very different reason on the way back. Our return flight crash-landed in Dublin airport while making an attempt to land in heavy fog. It flipped over on landing, caught fire and sixteen people at the front of the plane died. We escaped with some minor injuries through an emergency exit, but I never escaped the event in my head.

Apart from my parents and my cousins, Alvin was the only one who knew the real extent of how bad my fear of flying was. Malcolm knew about it but didn't understand it for one second. "Your odds of winning the lotto are higher than the possibility of that happening again," he'd say dismissively whenever he mentioned what a hindrance it was that I couldn't fly to the US office. "Can't you just take a Valium or something?" As if Valium would help me. I'd taken a pair of them before going to the dentist years before and had ended up losing my balance and slipping on the stairs, skinning my arse as it bounced from one step to the next. Having survived that, I somehow managed to wander out in front of a car while walking to the dentist's surgery even though I didn't need to cross the road to get there. Thankfully, the driver managed to stop the car, but there had been only a few centimetres in it. I told the driver he'd done great work and thanked him for sparing my arse from another hiding, momentarily heedless to the fact that I could well have killed the pair of us with my reckless behaviour. Then, because I was fifteen minutes early, some malign force within me convinced me to have a quick brandy in the nearby pub to steady my nerves. After downing it in one, I soon completely forgot where I was or what I was there for. I ended up in a beauty salon getting a full body spray tan done instead of going to the dentist, then sat down outside the local newsagents for a quick rest and woke up later to find that my handbag had been stolen. When the tablets wore off, I was horrified at how recklessly out of control my behaviour had been and resolved never to take the bastarding things again. The melting pot of feeling medically, physically and mentally out of control on a flight could only culminate in me being arrested upon arrival in London – or possibly, an emergency exit "accidentally" being opened and me being pushed out.

Alvin had tried to help – he'd been so desperate to help me conquer my fear so that we could open up new avenues of opportunities for ourselves. European weekend breaks now. Trips to Disneyland Paris when we had children. A trip on the Orient Express when we retired. First he bought me a voucher for four sessions with a hypnotherapist. They went so well that I truly believed I could fly the plane myself at the end of them. Alvin was thrilled, and promptly booked us two tickets on a flight to Cork. It would be a perfect fear-conquering quick flight, and we'd get a weekend away to boot – surely we were onto a winner.

I knew I was in trouble as soon as I saw an overhead plane as we reached the airport. It was as if I'd taken a step back in time and the progress I'd made in hypnotherapy had never happened – or rather, the progress I thought I'd made. I hid my panic from Alvin as best I could, hoping it would pass. Of course, not only did it not go away but it got progressively worse with every second. I fainted twenty-three seconds after we walked into the Departures area and woke up to find Alvin hovering over me as I lay on the ground with suitcases and trolleys grazing my feet. We went home. Despite several more attempts to fly to Belfast, Kerry and Knock (just for a bit of diversity), I never made it onto the plane. Alvin gave up booking these ghost flights when it became clear that they were doing more harm than good.

We said it was one of these things we'd try to tackle again someday, but in the meantime, there were plenty of places around Ireland we hadn't seen and we'd fulfil our couple's holiday needs that way. I knew in the back of my head when we wrote the plan that conquering my fear of flying would be the obvious option for me for activity ten. As time went on and our problems conceiving took over, it wasn't something I ever had to face. Now, it looked like my choices were to meet my worst fear head on or lose the only person who truly understood me and made me happy. Every miserable second that passed made me realise that I couldn't sit back and just let him go, which left me with no choice but to say hello to my fear again.

The only problem was that I hadn't a clue how to.

56

When I got home and checked my phone, I saw something unexpected – a missed call from Adrienne. The only reason I had her number in my phone at all was in case of extreme emergency. Nothing less than Alvin falling off a high building and breaking his legs – actually no, I'd need something even more serious than that – would ever prompt me to use it, and for Adrienne's part, I knew Alvin had given her my number but she'd never used it. I also had a text telling me I had a voicemail. This was all I needed . . . it was probably some new diatribe from Adrienne about some misdemeanour or other that I'd supposedly done to her brother.

"It's Adrienne. You probably saw it was me and didn't bother answering. That's what I'd do if you rang anyway." Dead air. *"Okay, this isn't going as I'd planned. Forget I said that. Hard to break the habit of a lifetime. I actually rang to . . ."* More dead air. *"Apologise."* Coughing. *"I always thought you were a cold fish. If I'd known you were just insecure, I would have gone easier on you. It's good to know that you're just a mess like everyone else at*

the end of the day. I was also ringing to see what you're going to do about the Alvin situation. Are you going to fly out to him? He's only done this bunk because he thinks you don't want him. Mum can give you his address and phone number, and . . . erm . . . you make sure to let me know if there's anything I can do to . . . erm, help." Another long pause. *"I'm not going to pretend we're going to be friends, but if you're what makes Alvin happy, I suppose I can put up with you."*

"What's with the shocked head on you?" Jess said when I walked into the sitting room. She handed me an emergency bar of chocolate. She'd insisted on going out to buy it when I told her Alvin had gone, but I was feeling too sick inside to eat anything and she'd have to put it away herself. Somehow, I couldn't see that as being a problem to her.

I answered her question as soon as the shock wore off and I recovered my voice. Simone listened in from her position on the couch.

"I would say that's a turn-up for the books, but what difference does it make when . . . well, you know."

"Yes, I know. When I'm too much of a wuss to get on a plane."

"Your words. But he said in the letter that he was willing to do a long-distance relationship until he moves home . . ."

"Well, I'm not! How can we wait another few years to get things sorted? It needs to be done now, but I just can't bloody well do it!"

"Hypothetically, if you *could* get on a plane and move to Australia, would you do it? Would you leave your job for him?" Simone asked.

I didn't even have to think about it. I gave her the same answer I'd given Adrienne.

"Your house?"

398

"You guys would mind it, wouldn't you? I'd let you live in it rent free if you'd just take care of it for me."

"Oh, of course," Simone said.

"You said that a little too quickly," Jess said to her. "You'd probably have squatter's rights on the place after a while."

"I wouldn't care," I said. "I'd give the house away if I could just have my old life with Alvin back."

"Then there's only one thing for it," Simone said. "You have to get on that plane. There's no way around this, Tammy."

"I can't . . ."

"Wait for him and hope it works out, so. The end. Now, stop talking about it." Jess turned her back on me and watched the telly, obviously taking a tough love approach.

I went out to the kitchen, sat at the table and buried my head in my hands. I felt wretchedly disappointed in myself. Why was I always so afraid? I thought back to every fear that had consumed me over the years – my awkwardness, potential failure, looking stupid – was there anything I wasn't afraid of? And how much of that could I overcome? Was it mind over matter? And was my fear of flying greater than my fear of losing him? He could talk about long-distance relationships all he wanted, but what if he met someone else in the meantime? For all of his good intentions, it could well happen.

After a very long time, I got up and went into the sitting room.

"I can't lose him, girls. I'll never get over it until the day I die if I do. I have to do whatever it takes to save things with him."

Jess raised an eyebrow. "Okay, it's a bit melodramatic but it's going in the right direction. Keep talking."

399

"I have to get over my fear of flying. I don't know how I'm going to do it, but I have to."

As I said the words, my entire body started to shake. Simone and Jess couldn't but notice it, and Jess softened a bit.

"You can do this, Tammy. You've always been able to do whatever you wanted to if you put your mind to it, you auld bitch."

"Thanks." I smiled unsteadily at her. "I'm going to make a few phone calls before I change my mind, and maybe you could continue your pep talk when I come back? Simone, feel free to join in with that too. I'm going to need all the encouragement I can get."

Simone nodded, but then a faraway look came over her face and I knew she'd started thinking about something. I left her to her undoubtedly profound thoughts and Jess to the chocolate and made my way back to the kitchen.

First, I rang Malcolm to discuss the possibility of taking a sabbatical from work, an option that was available to all full-time employees. Then I selected Adrienne's number.

"Hell . . . o."

"You don't need to sound so cagey. I'm not going to bite," I said. "Do you mean what you said in your voicemail?"

"What, no hello? Diva behaviour alert . . ."

"Do you?"

"Well, yeah."

"Good. I'm going to need your help . . ."

57

"You don't need to come with me," I said to Jess and Simone as we all piled into a taxi. "This isn't a three-person job . . ."

"Do you actually think we're going to let you chicken out of this?"

"As if I would," I scoffed, although it was hard to carry off a convincing jeering tone when my voice was all high-pitched and helium balloon-esque.

"You can't after paying so much for your flight," Simone said. "Imagine how much grocery shopping you could have done with that money."

Even the taxi driver sniggered at that. If I ever got through this Alvin situation, I really had to help Simone get a life sometime afterwards.

"We're coming with you, by the way," Simone said casually as we walked into the departures area at the airport.

"What? You can't come to Australia! Like you said, the flight costs a fortune!"

"No, we're flying to London," Simone clarified.

"Why?"

"We took a notion to go shopping on Oxford Street, of course," Jess said. "Why else?"

"The flight to London is only an hour," Simone interpreted. "If you can manage the London leg, it'll give you confidence to get on the next flight – and if me and Jess are on the London flight with you, it'll fly."

"Because it wouldn't have taken off at all without us? For someone who reads a lot of books, that wasn't a great turn of phrase . . ."

"Oh, shut up!" Simone's face brightened. "You see, Tammy? You'll be so busy arbitrating as usual that you won't even notice the flight time passing by."

They were wasting their time. As I looked around the airport, fear engulfed me until I thought I was going to pass out. I would have done anything else in the world not to lose Alvin, but I just couldn't do this. I'd told myself over and over that I could, but now that I was here, I knew otherwise. I felt bitterly disappointed in myself again, and devastated that Alvin was going to slip through my fingers, but this flight was something I just could not do.

The girls were going to freak.

"Jess, I thought you were meeting Ciarán in an hour's time for reconciliation talks? Not that I want you to do that, of course – but I don't want to waste your time here if . . ."

"If nothing. Anyway, I changed my mind. I can do better than a dick-dipping balding fatso. I shouldn't have been messing around with another woman's man anyway. It's not cool. I was a right bitch to Audrey and I'm not proud of it."

I could see that the effect of being dick-dipped by the balding fatso in question was still hurting her. "But why

402

now? We've been telling you for ages that you can do better!"

"It's because of you, if you must know – you and Hutch. It's because Ciarán won't get out of bed to get me chocolate even though the shop is right across the road from us because he's afraid that someone he knows will see him. That's more important to him than what I want. Hutch falls over himself to do things for you, and it just makes me think '*That's* what I want'."

"Really? I've fluffed things up with him over and over, he's living in another continent – oh, and he has a child he didn't feel he could tell me about!"

"Funnily enough, it was discovering that Hutch had a child that cemented my decision. He has a whole other life, but it still isn't complete without you. When he called around, I could see how heartbroken he was at the thought of losing you and as you've said yourself, he tried to tell you so many times but you didn't want to know. Yes, it's very complicated between you two, but he really does love you. I want someone who adores me that much."

"Me too," said Simone. "Being around you two has made me realise that maybe I shouldn't give up on trying to meet someone just as special to me as Alvin is to you. Like Jess said, things between you two are as complicated as it gets, and yet I have a feeling that you two are going to make it work if you can only get on that damn plane. And if you two can make it, there's hope for anyone – even someone like me. So no pressure, but you getting on that plane today could decide my entire future too."

"And I also want to be with someone who's willing to fly to the other side of the world for me even though they're terrified of flying," Jess added. "Not you, by the way. Just someone who would do that for me."

"That would all have been very touching except for one vital point. I can't do this, girls. I thought I could, but I'm just not strong enough . . ."

"Of course you can. Hey, it's just struck me that you've never experienced the joy of duty free! Let's get security over and done with and go shopping."

Jess and Simone printed out our boarding passes from a free-standing machine and led me over to the check-in area. I thought my histrionics would start at the check-in gate, but I found myself strangely numb there. It wasn't threatening because it didn't mean I'd actually get on the plane. I bought some moisturisers I didn't need in duty-free just to fill some time, choosing stuff I thought Simone would like so that I might be able to save her a few bob sometime in the future, and produced my boarding pass at the checkout as if I was a normal passenger who was about to go on a flight.

"Right. Down to the serious business." Simone and Jess took one arm each and led me to the airport bar.

"You guys sit down. I'll get this," Simone said. "I have a redundancy to spend, after all." She and Jess exchanged a look. Both of them looked like they were trying not to laugh.

"Ooh, look!" Jess nudged me and nodded to a guy in a suit. He looked unremarkable to me, but Jess ogled him until Simone returned. That was a lot of ogling, because Simone was – and I couldn't quite believe this – *allowing herself to be chatted up at the bar*. By a guy in red-check trousers. An incidental fact, but a fascinating one. This day was getting more surreal by the second.

Simone eventually came back to us with a tray of drinks, red-cheeked and smiling broadly.

"You wouldn't want to be dehydrated around here,"

Jess said, grabbing her vodka and 7 Up. "You, drink up," she said to me, handing me a big red cocktail from the tray.

Why didn't she just shout 'Heel!'? "Will you stop talking to me like I'm a dog?"

"I'll give you all the respect in the world if you get on that plane."

I picked up my cocktail and slurped it, thirsty as hell. I should have just asked for water. In fact, I didn't ask for this because I wasn't given the option of asking for anything. I couldn't wait to get out of this airport and go back to being a control freak.

But then I thought of Alvin and how special this thing we had between us was, regardless of what he hadn't told me. He made me feel like I was the only person in the world for him. I'd never find anyone like him again, nor would I want to. I had to get on this plane.

But I couldn't.

I drank up. "I'm going to die alone, or else with you two." Why did my voice sound so slurry after just half a drink?

Jess just nodded. "Come on, let's go for a walk," she said.

The girls abandoned the rest of their drinks after encouraging me to knock back the remainder of mine and flanked me on either side.

"Eyes to the ground," Jess commanded. "Don't look up."

I didn't need to ask why. It didn't matter because I was only humouring them anyway. If I refused to get on the plane just as it was about to take off, the argument to convince me to go would be shorter than it would be if I started up now. At intervals as they dragged me along,

Simone held a newspaper that she'd bought earlier up against the right-hand side of my face. No newspaper could block out the acoustics though – ominous, loud sounds that I didn't dare identify with words. I kept myself calm by continuing to tell myself that nobody was getting me on any plane that I didn't want to get on.

After about five minutes of walking, we seemed to be in something like a tunnel. The girls found seats in a crowded area on the left. Jess grabbed my body and turned it to the left.

"If you want to look at something, that wall is good." She pointed to the world's most unremarkable wall.

I took out my phone to check it for the first time since we'd left. I'd given up looking at it after Alvin had sent me a text yesterday telling me what I already knew – that he'd gone back to Australia early. It had been a clinical text, an information-purposes-only one. There was more warmth in one that I'd received from a homeware store an hour afterwards informing me of their in-store offers.

Multimedia message from: Alvin

I opened it with a shaking thumb. I had to look at it for a few seconds before I realised what it was.

"What's that ugly-looking thing?" Jess said, looking over my left shoulder.

"Oh, I like it," Simone said as her head hovered over my right.

"It's a painting that I fell in love with in Paris but wouldn't let Alvin buy for me," I said breathlessly. The image on my phone was of the painting as displayed on a PC screen, and had clearly been taken on a cameraphone.

I scrolled down to read the text underneath.

Bought it anyway on the Internet. My part of activity 9. Will be sent to your address. A. x

406

"There's even a kiss at the end of it," Jess said. I could have sworn there was a tear in her eye.

"*Ladies and gentlemen, we'd like to announce that Aer Ireland flight E1 TUC to London will now board from gate G34 . . .*" a voice from a Tannoy announced.

Jess and Simone didn't move. They didn't look at me. I'd swear they weren't even breathing.

I watched everyone's feet around me get up to join the queue. I threw brief intermittent glances at the queue as the walkway to the plane swallowed people up. I thought about Alvin again.

"I can do an hour," I said when everyone else had boarded the plane. "If I've had a breakdown by the time I get to London, I'll get the ferry home – but I owe Alvin this hour." I felt strangely calm, more in a slightly out-of-it way rather than a serene one, but I'd take whatever crumbs were on the table.

"Let's go," Jess said.

She and Simone hopped up from their seats and frogmarched me to the plane. I looked at the picture message on my phone as I allowed myself to be led, never looking up once and pretending with all my heart that I was anywhere but here.

58

"That was officially the most anticlimactic hour of my life," Jess said as we disembarked.

I couldn't believe it. I had just flown to London and I was still alive. I hadn't had the heart failure I'd been expecting as the girls had led me to my seat on the plane – I'd felt like I should be screaming by then, but my mouth stayed steadfastly shut. And all the while, a weird fog of displacement enveloped me. I couldn't even seem to remember all of the facts and figures I'd once known off by heart about fatal plane crashes. That must have been one strong drink Simone had given me.

Jess had sat by the window, with me beside her and Simone to my left in the aisle seat. We were buckling our seatbelts when Simone emitted a screechy noise.

"What?" I asked because I felt I had to, not because I was really interested. I was feeling a bit drowsy all of a sudden. "And could you buckle my belt for me? I feel a bit weak and my fingers don't seem to be working properly."

Simone wasn't one bit concerned about my non-functional fingers. "The guy who chatted me up at the bar is on this flight," she hissed as she fixed up my belt. "He's walking down the aisle now."

Jess craned her head up. "The guy with the spiky brown hair?" Simone nodded.

"He's not bad," Jess said.

He stopped when he reached Simone, oblivious or uncaring about those behind him. "We meet again," he said to Simone.

Then Jess saw the trousers. She guffawed loud enough for the entire plane to hear.

"Sorry," she said when he looked over at her. "I'm just laughing at your trousers."

"*Jess!* I'm so sorry about her." Simone's face turned an uncomfortable shade of violet.

"Ah, don't worry about it. This time tomorrow, we might all be dead anyway."

"Don't say that around her!" Jess screamed, pointing at me.

"She's a nervous flyer," Simone said in a little voice, as if that would make the difference in me not hearing it.

"Oh, I just meant that the world could end at any moment. Sure it's all pointless anyway, isn't it? You're born, you live, you die."

"You'll die sooner than you think if you don't move along now," a frazzled-looking woman behind him said.

"Nice to see you again," he said to Simone. "And nice to meet you, nervous flyer. You, not so much, but I admire your honesty," he said to Jess before he shuffled along reluctantly.

Just as the plane was about to take off, I started up.

"I have to get off!" *Here comes the heart failure.* My heart was pulsing in my ears and I could barely breathe. I fumbled at my seatbelt, but my hands were shaking too much to open it. Jess pulled my right arm towards her with both of her hands and Simone did the same with my left. Meanwhile, the plane was gaining speed on the runway. And then I felt my stomach go backwards.

"Now, there you go," Simone said. "Takeoff's over. We're in the air and there's no going back."

"Accept your fate and shut up, in other words," Jess said. "You can't go anywhere now except to London."

I leaned my head forward between my legs and gasped for air. I tried desperately to displace. *I've fallen asleep on the couch and this is just a bad dream. I need to make an appointment for an eyebrow wax soon. I think I'm out of frozen peas – I must check the freezer.* Nope – I was still on this fecking plane, about to meet my death. My gasps became less desperate though and my breathing started to regulate itself somewhat, despite my terror. I suddenly felt horribly tired. I closed my eyes and tried to breathe deeply.

When I woke up – not of my own accord, as I had to be shaken awake by the girls, who must have changed my position because I was now sitting back in my seat – Jess told me we were in London. She was smiling at me and thumping me on the back for reasons unrelated to getting me to wake up. Apparently, I'd been brilliant after takeoff – which had been easy as I'd seemed to be in an unconscious type of sleep.

And that's when I copped it.

"Simone, did you put something in my drink?"

Simone looked sheepish. "I stuck a straw in it . . ."

"Simone! What did you put in it?"

"Just a crushed Valium . . . or maybe two . . ."

"I should have known."

"We had to get you on that plane, Tammy . . ."

She rambled on for a few minutes about how life was all one big endurance test and if Alvin made coping with the futility of existence that little bit easier, then wasn't that great and loads of other stuff I'd heard a million times before.

"You know what? I only have one thing to say to you."

Simone put her hands up to the side of her face like a shield. "Okay, hit me with it."

"Do you have any more?"

"*Yay!* That's the spirit!" Jess threw her arms around me and squeezed me tightly. "Something tells me you're going to have no problem getting on the next flight. Especially when you'll have the best friends in the world flying there with you."

I thought she meant the Valium tablets at first, but then both of the girls broke out in excited smiles and giggles. *Giggles.* I don't think I'd ever heard Simone giggle in my entire life.

"You don't mean . . ."

"We do! Oh come on, we're hardly going to abandon you in London!"

"But the flights must have cost you guys a fortune!"

Jess pointed to Simone.

"What are redundancies for?" Simone said somewhat bravely.

"But that has to keep you going until God knows when . . ."

"Thanks to you, I have hardly any rent to pay because you undercharge me. I can live on a euro a day. I think I'll be okay."

"Don't forget that she was working for ten years before that and saved like a trooper," Jess pointed out.

"This is the first thing she's ever spent money on really. The second thing is going to be a whole new wardrobe in Australia, by the way."

"I'll have to reimburse you the cost of the flights, Si . . ."

"No way. You've been good to me over the years and now it's my turn. And the drugs are hidden down my bra, so don't argue back with me or they're staying there."

"I'm sure she really wants them now that she's heard that . . . although she probably wouldn't care if they had been stored suppository style as long as she got her mitts on them. Now, keep your eyes fixed on the floor for the rest of the time we're here, Tammy, okay?"

We made it from where we got off the first plane to where we were to get on the second one. In this journey, it really was as simple as that for me. I took in no details. Our flight to Sydney, leaving in ninety minutes' time, was going to take twenty-six hours. *Twenty. Six. Hours.* No pill could knock me out for that long. We had one technical stop in Singapore for a few hours, which would be of absolutely no help to me.

My moments of freedom expired and boarding time beckoned. "Right, it's sleeping pills time." Simone handed me two pills. As Jess correctly anticipated earlier, I didn't care where on Simone's person they'd come from. "Ever taken them before?"

I threw them in my mouth and swallowed them dry. "No."

"Water is for wimps, eh? Those should take effect in about an hour, all going well."

"An hour? Oh God . . ."

"I've taken those before and been out like a light ten minutes later," Jess said quickly. "Hurry up, let's get on the plane in case we end up having to carry you on. You'll probably sleep for a good twelve hours on those things."

When I stood up, my legs buckled under me. "Girls, no! We could die! Even if we live, the sleeping tablets might make me wee in my sleep . . ."

The girls grabbed one of my arms each, threw them over their shoulders and pulled me along like a drunk as I listed everything bad that could happen. They showed my boarding pass and passport to the relevant people, explaining that I wasn't drunk – just an insufferable pain who didn't like planes.

I was less calm this time, squealing as they led me to my seat. I moaned softly as I sat down, causing Jess to go all tough love on me again. "Zip it! You sound like an old woman keening at a wake! Nobody's died – yet, but I can't guarantee I won't put you out of your misery if you don't stop it. Corporate Whore Tammy would be morto at how Flying Tammy is conducting herself." She belted me up and ordered me to belt my mouth up too.

"Here's something that'll take your mind off the flight," Simone said, patting my hand repeatedly until she got my attention. "Check Trousers asked me for my phone number on the flight to London!"

"Great," I said between whimpers.

"Isn't it? He wants to meet up when I get back to Dublin! He's just over to London for a few days. Isn't that mad?"

"No, not really. He probably only has reason to be in London for a few days."

"Oh, good girl, Tammy. Keep talking there, that's the stuff." Jess patted my other hand encouragingly.

I sat back, closed my eyes and tried to block everything out. "Listen to some music," Simone said. "You'll have to turn off the MP3 player for takeoff, but there's a few minutes to go before that." I felt earphones being plugged into my ears.

When Simone took the earphones out, I didn't know if I was about to cry, get sick or black out.

The plane shot down the runway. Jess squeezed my arm. When I started to whimper again, she pinched it instead.

"*Ow!* What are you *doing*?"

"This is called a pinch. I thought I taught you all about those when I was a kid? And here's another one."

She pinched and pinched my arm like a woodpecker. "Stop it!" I roared at her, slapping at her hands, but it was no use. And Jess played dirty. These weren't baby pinches – they were full on, black-bruises types of pinches. And as she pinched and I slapped, the plane left the ground.

"And we're up!" She dropped her hands onto her lap. "You can thank me later for taking your mind off the takeoff. Well done – you're on this plane until the bitter end now and there's absolutely no way out!"

"Is that meant to make me feel better, you lunatic?" I sounded cross, but I smiled after I said it. I hadn't chickened out. I was going to Australia now and that was that. Even though I'd booked the flight and got the visa, I'd never fully believed that I'd be able to do it.

"Alvin's gaff, here we come! He'll surely have a party for us while we're over, won't he?"

I rubbed my arm as the girls speculated on what Alvin would recommend for us to do in Australia, babbling on as if there was absolutely no possibility that this wouldn't work out. I chose to believe they were right, and that it would. I had to.

I looked at my watch. We were only a few minutes into our twenty-six hour stretch. I closed my eyes and breathed deeply, and prayed for sleep to come. The last thing I heard before I fell into a comatose state was Jess telling

Simone to take my watch off so that they could lie to me about how much longer we had left on the flight when I woke up.

"Ladies and gentlemen, welcome to Sydney."

Every man, woman and child on the plane burst into applause that went on for far too long. "Thank the Lord for that," a man behind me said. "It sounded like someone was giving birth on this plane. Remind me to put in an airline deafness claim when I get home."

"Me too," Jess said wearily. She looked like she'd aged ten years over the course of the flight.

When I'd woken up after the sleeping tablets wore off, I realised where I was and screamed like a banshee. Ten seconds later every child on the plane joined my chorus, frightened out of their wits at their rude awakening. I had air hostesses on top of me straight away trying to calm me down and shut me up. I felt like a criminal, and yet I couldn't stop screaming for a good five minutes.

"Can we have something alcoholic for medicinal purposes?" Jess said to one of the air hostesses.

"I don't think it's a good idea to give her alcohol – it might make her worse . . ."

"No, it's for me. I can talk her down, but if you want me to do it then I need a drink."

The air hostess nodded and ran away to get Jess's drink. Simone rubbed my arm. "I know how you feel. When I think about how pointless it all is sometimes, it makes me want to scream too."

"*You* make me want to scream!" Jess shouted. "Go back to sleep and let me handle this!"

After downing her drink in one mouthful, Jess forced fed me a bar of chocolate to line my stomach and then crammed more sleeping pills into my mouth. When I woke up after the second sleep, I knew instinctively that we were nearly there. My eyes were only open for a few seconds when Jess clamped her hand on my mouth.

"Don't you dare!" she shouted.

I held up my hands in surrender. She slowly took her hands off my mouth.

"We'll be landing soon, so no hissy fits, right? This is the easy part! The landing means this nightmare ends for all of us!"

"Amen to that," the woman in front of us said.

I didn't want to fall at the last hurdle, but I was terrorised at the thought of the plane bouncing along the landing strip. I put my head between my knees and whimpered incessantly until the plane thudded onto the landing strip and it was all over. I'd barely noticed the landing and suddenly felt very stupid. But for once, I could live with that feeling. We were here!

59

Sydney was exactly as I had imagined.

I smiled as I took in the vista of the Sydney Harbour Bridge against the backdrop of a blue sky from the balcony of my hotel room near Sydney Opera House. The hub of activity on Circular Quay raised my adrenaline. I couldn't believe I was actually here. In a parallel world, I would have been living here with Alvin and life would have been so different. But maybe it wasn't too late to do that . . . and maybe it was, but at least now I was here to find out my fate.

I clutched my mobile for dear life as I said goodbye to Simone and Jess and left the hotel to walk towards the city centre, waiting for a text from Alvin's flatmate Robert to let me know he and Alvin had arrived at the Irish bar. I hadn't contacted Alvin directly. If I rang him and told him I was here, the element of surprise would be gone. I needed that to be there when we met so that I could read on his face whether or not I was too late. With Adrienne's help, I got Clarissa to contact Robert and tasked him with helping me to keep tabs on where Alvin would be when I arrived – and with keeping his mouth shut about me being in Australia, of course. I'd been hoping to just turn up where he lived that day, but Robert informed us that he, Alvin and a group of other lads met in an Irish bar in town every Saturday for lunch and to watch sports on TV, and there was no way of keeping Alvin at home without rousing suspicion.

I almost jumped out of my skin when my phone vibrated in my pocket. "In Hot Toddy's Bar now" Robert's text said.

I walked faster. It was time to do this.

Traffic and footfall in the direction of the city was increasing with every step I took, suggesting that something big was going on that day. And there were quite a few people very colourfully dressed, most noticeably a woman in her sixties who was tottering along the pavement just in front of me wearing a purple feather boa with matching purple heels, a pink ballet leotard with a tiny tutu and not a lot else. The faint sound of music wafted on the air. Then I turned a street corner to find an explosion of colour flooding my retinas in the form of a rainbow banner, and guessed that there must be a gay pride parade taking place. I smiled, enjoying the atmosphere of bonhomie that prevailed as I walked closer to the city even if I was starting to feel very dull in my plain white T-shirt and faded denim skirt.

My enthusiasm waned somewhat as the volume of people crushing their way en masse towards the city centre grew bigger and bigger. I'd had no idea of the scale of the event. Would I even be able to find the bar if the streets were thronged with bodies? The music's volume grew stronger as I approached Hyde Park in a horribly frustrating shuffling movement that was getting me nowhere fast except into the armpits of the flag-waving people all around me. Before long we were at a total standstill. A few panicked enquiries resulted in me finding out that this was where the Mardi Gras Parade would begin. Hyde Park was a prime viewing location . . . which meant that I was going nowhere.

I pulled out my phone, almost donating my elbow to someone's ribcage as I did so, and texted Robert. 'Can you leave the bar and ring me now please?!' Five minutes later, there was still no call. I re-sent the same message. Five more minutes passed with no contact from Robert. With great difficulty, I managed to manoeuvre my phone up to my ear and rang Robert's number. No answer.

The parade was about to start and the colourful crowd was going crazy. The first float was about to leave. It was decorated with four gigantic psychedelic pink love hearts surrounded by pink and purple flowers all around each side of the float, through which you could watch the mankini-clad performers. '*Love Shack*' was emblazoned on the front of the float below one of the hearts. The mankini gang were limbering up for what appeared to be a dance routine.

I couldn't move. The only thing that was going anywhere around here was that float.

There was nothing else for it. I thought I'd covered the whole going out of your comfort zone thing, but it looked like I'd have to give it one last go . . .

"Let me through!" I yelled. "I'm part of the team for that float!"

Hardly anyone heard me through the buzz of music and laughter that filled the night air. Those that did looked at my lightly made-up face and my plain white top and raised their eyebrows. But somehow, through a combination of convulsive wriggling and being propelled by some kind souls (or maybe they just wanted the shrieking Irish banshee out of their earspace), I made my way to the top of the rows of people that lined the street.

"Hey!" I waved my arms furiously at the flamboyantly costumed people on the float. They waved back. A few looked wary.

"I need to join your float," I yelled up at the person closest to me on the float.

He looked me up and down. "Lady, I think you're a little confused. This isn't the Stepford Wives convention . . ."

"No, you don't understand. I need to get to a man . . ."

"Stop right there. You do know what this parade is all about, yes?"

"Of course, but . . ."

"Then go figure." He started to walk away.

"No! Listen to me!" I jumped onto the float and climbed through a love heart. The smell of the flowers flooded my nostrils. I spotted two seats at the very corner of the float, grabbed the man by the arm and dragged him over.

"Hey! Security!" He looked out of the heart to get the attention of a security man, but the nearest one was otherwise occupied by someone who'd fainted.

"One minute. That's all I ask."

I caught him by the shoulders and pushed him backwards into his seat before he could say anything. He was as light as a jockey and hadn't a chance against me. I planted my butt on his lap to make sure he couldn't escape, then threw my arms around his neck to make the whole experience a little more like two old friends chatting. I ignored the fact that not only did none of my friends wear mankinis but I never sat on their bare flesh either – only a cursory detail that wasn't relevant, really.

I filled him in on my entire story as fast as I could. He seemed to be too flabbergasted by my cheek (in terms of behaviour) to move.

He shrugged when I finished recounting my tale. "Well, I guess this *is* the love float . . ."

I seized on his sniff of encouragement. "So you'll help me then?"

He smiled. "You've pinned me down on a good day. Although can you please unpin me now? This is bringing back very uncomfortable memories of my pseudo-straight teenage years. No offence."

I jumped up off his lap. He brushed himself down, took me by the hand and led me to the other side of the float.

"Emergency costume department," he said flatly as we stopped in front of a cardboard box full of clothes. He bent down and rifled through it, then whipped out a garish red creation trimmed with feathers in a medley of other colours.

"A showgirl outfit? I'm trying to win the love of my life back, and you expect me to wear something that has tassles hanging from the nipple area? Are you joking me?"

"But it's your colour!"

"No way am I –"

"If you want to stop him in his tracks, you'll wear this." He folded his arms across his chest. "It's non-negotiable. See that security guy?" He wiggled his fingers at a beefy man, who smiled back. "He's my boyfriend. Doesn't he look like he'd be good at picking you up, putting you over one shoulder and carrying you right off this float?" He smiled wickedly. "Trust me, he *is* good at it."

"And this is your idea of you on a good day?"

I walked behind the box of costumes and hunched

down. Thankfully, the gigantic outline of the heart at the front of the float completely obscured the crowd's possible vision of me. It was far from a vision I was going to be in this get up.

"Turn around!" I roared at my new friend before I pulled my trousers off.

"In case you haven't noticed, honey, I'm not on your boat. Just pretend I'm not here."

I sighed. He was right, I suppose. "I'm Tammy, by the way. What's your name?" I said as undressed and re-dressed as fast as I could. "I usually know the names of the people I give lapdances to."

"I bet you do! I had a feeling there was a fireball beneath those dreadfully sensible clothes! My name's Randy. And go on – take your best shot – I've heard it all before."

"And you love every minute of it, I'd say. Is it short for anything? Randolf?"

"There's nothing short about me, princess. No, I'm just Randy. Wow, look at you!"

Thankfully I couldn't as there was no mirror near the emergency box of costumes, but looking down at myself, I could just imagine the overall effect. What I couldn't imagine was Alvin's reaction when he saw me in this.

"Come on, Randy! We're about to start!"

"Okay, Tammy. Let's do this."

I froze. "What? I didn't hear them call for a Tammy!"

"Uh uh. There are no passengers on this float."

"But don't be daft . . . I don't know the routine . . ."

"No, but you do know how to shake a pom-pom." He dived into the emergency costume box. "Stand beside me, look pretty and shake your booty as well as these." He handed me two luminous green pom-poms and dragged me over to his group.

422

Music began to blare out of the float's sound system. The team of dancers began what looked like a samba routine. I shook my pom-poms, trying to hide as much of myself as possible as I did so.

"You look like an old lady in a nursing home stirring her tea! *Shake it!*"

So I shook it, fearing that Randy might accidentally bump into me and send me flying into the crowd if I didn't. He seemed like someone who would be a dangerous enemy. I tried to ignore the people in the crowd who pointed at me, and even though I could lip-read them asking each other what the hell I was doing, I just smiled back at them. After a while, it was quite liberating. I was making a total eejet of myself and yet my world wasn't falling apart because of it.

"Where exactly do you want to go?" Randy yelled at me.

"Hot Toddy's Bar!"

"Then you're about to be reunited with your man, because Hot Toddy's is just up here!"

I gulped. It really was time now.

60

I looked to my left and saw the sign for Hot Toddy's Bar, the name bookended by big green harps. It was about as stereotypical an Irish pub as you could find, with a gigantic shamrock emblazoned on the window and Irish flags hanging over the harps.

"How am I going to stop the float to get off?"

"You jump, of course."

"Crowdsurfing wasn't on the list!"

Randy laughed. "Your face! You've gotta work on being less gullible. Gimme a sec. And don't take offence at anything I say, 'cos I'm gonna ham it up to make sure the crowd get behind you." Randy walked up to the float's singer and grabbed the mic from her. "Okay, everyone, listen up! First of all – driver, stop the float! We have an emergency!"

A hum went up in the crowd. Randy walked to the front of the float, clearly relishing his role. Given the scale of the crowd, it took a lot of shushing to quieten them down and get their attention, but when they realised that the parade was going nowhere until they gave this guy their attention, they eventually piped down.

"See this woman? I've stopped the float because of her."

There was the distinctive sound of boos. Loud ones. The kind that would deafen you.

"You see, she's made a big mistake. A huge, life-changing one that'd make you glad you're not her."

I hung my head. Cheers, Randy. The crowd were giving me the looks you'd give someone you suspected of burning down a maternity hospital.

"There's hamming it up and hamming it up in it!" I hissed at him.

He looked genuinely confused. "What language are you speaking? Shut up and leave this to me!"

I shook my head. If that was his idea of getting them behind me, I was glad he wasn't trying to turn them off me. I'd be stoned before the night was out.

"But now she's about to make up for it. The love of her life is right behind you all in that bar." Several people turned their heads towards Hot Toddy's Bar. Randy's voice through the microphone was so loud that the whole street could surely hear it – which meant that no matter how loud it was inside the pub, surely Alvin would too? Oh God. I was hoping the element of shock might help me to get him to at least speak to me. All it would take would be for Alvin to look out the window through the leaves of the shamrock to see it was me.

"She's come a long, long way to win him back, and we all want to help her, right?" Randy continued.

Silence.

"I *said*, we all want to help her, *right*? This is the love float, people! The start of our parade!"

"Yeah – our *gay pride* parade! She's after a guy!" someone in the crowd pointed out.

"You're missing the whole point of what we're doing here! We want acceptance of our choices, right? Doesn't that mean we accept others' choices too? It doesn't matter if it's boy and girl love! Today is a celebration of the whole freaking shooting gallery of love! Right? *Right?*"

"Yeah, give her a break!" someone else shouted.

I smiled gratefully in that direction.

"So here's what I want you to do, people! Tammy here is going to get down from this float and walk into that pub to claim her man with all of you guys chanting her name all the way. Let's get this thing going!"

"No! Don't tell them my name! I want to surprise Alvin!" I yelled, but Randy waved my words away as if swatting a fly. He started to clap and chant my name, then pumped his arms up and down to encourage the crowd to do the same. Both the clap and the chanting of my name was uncertain and intermittent at first, limited to the section of the crowd that was directly in front and behind us, but soon spread along the crowd further down the street like a Mexican wave until it reached thunderous levels.

Randy walked behind me and pushed me to the front of the float. "Make way, guys – she's coming through!" he shouted into the microphone. I threw the pom-poms behind me. "Good luck, doll! Here's my business card if you want to invite me to the wedding!" Randy pulled a card out of an arse pocket of his mankini (who knew mankinis would even have arse pockets?). I tried not to recoil at how hot it felt – this man had gone out of his way to help me, after all. "Thanks, Randy," I said as he shoved me off the stage. Thanks indeed, I thought as everyone moved to one side to let me crash onto the pavement on my knees. Crowdsurfing suddenly seemed like it would have been fun.

I picked myself up. The crowd moved backwards to let

me through in a fashion that was reminiscent of the parting of the waters in the Bible, still chanting my name. I felt a timely rush of adrenaline as I reached the door of Hot Toddy's Bar. Then I looked up and saw several faces at the bar's window, all of them staring at me. Thankfully, Alvin's face wasn't among the assembly. Turning around and waving goodbye to Randy, who was performing an energetic hip-thrusting routine which may or may not have been related to my situation, I saw the float move on. There was nothing left for it now except for me to walk inside.

So I did.

The bar was as still as if there was nobody in it, even though there were people at every table. The only sound as I walked through the door was that of the background music. Every set of eyes in the bar were now on me.

I walked through the pub, trying to look as if nothing had happened and I wasn't even aware of anyone looking at me. I glanced at every table and every set of bar-propping guys as I passed through. Robert must have brought Alvin to sit on the barrels out the back by the looks of it. I had reached the back of the pub and was just about to turn around and walk back up again – which would be a walk of shame in itself, as doubtless everyone would think that I'd been stood up – when I spotted him at a table to my right with some guys who must have been Robert and the other drinking buddies. He was staring right at me but I couldn't read his expression. Shock? Disbelief? Fear? Fight wrestling with flight? Put it this way: he looked as though he'd seen a ghost. Not a good reaction, on the whole.

I couldn't move. I willed Alvin to get up and come to me, but he didn't. The hush in the pub seemed to amplify until the near silence pounded in my ears. Even the background music had stopped.

I jumped several feet off the ground when someone behind the bar put the music on again and turned the volume up dramatically. At least one person in here had something to do other than gawk at me gawking at someone and being gawked back at. I didn't think I was capable of registering any thought at that moment that wasn't an Alvin-related one, but I realised that the song was 'One Way Or Another' by Blondie.

And suddenly, a pattern formed in my head. A pattern that led me to do something without me even realising I was about to do it. *Coyote Ugly* . . . our conversation on the night of the hen party . . .

"Can you turn that up louder, please?" I roared at the barman, who was leaning against the bar with his arms folded. He shrugged, then pushed himself lazily up into a fully standing position and walked over to the bar's sound system. While he was walking away, I hopped up on the bar and started to sing along with the words.

"*Join in, everyone!*" I screamed to the most sedate crowd of daytime drinkers I'd ever come across in my life. When nobody took me up on the offer, I sang louder. I danced, gyrated and made a total show of myself for the next two minutes in a way I'd never done before in my life. I didn't look once in Alvin's direction.

When the song finished, I got down to an explosion of applause. Well, either applause, jeers or hoots of laughter – probably all three. I stood beside the bar, panting from my exertions and wondering if I should walk over to Alvin or run out of the pub. I was still in making-my-mind-up mode when Alvin hove into view. His eyes were fixed on my face, his expression severe.

I was almost breathless with nerves. "Say something," I managed to croak out.

"You have tassles hanging from your nipples," he said.

"I thought you might notice."

"And your singing has got even worse over the years."

"Yep. I haven't a note in my head and I've never been so embarrassed in my life. Anything else?"

He smiled. "What took you so long?"

He scooped me up and pulled me to him, kissing me gently at first but then urgently until I could no longer breathe.

"*Yes! Tammy got her guy!*" Randy burst through the door of the pub, followed by an entourage of people from the float.

"Haven't you got a city full of people to shake your tush at?" I laughed as he came over and hugged us as if he'd known us all his life, looking Alvin up and down and mouthing 'Hot' to me after I introduced them.

"There are plenty of other limelight-hoggers on that float to continue my good work. Flirtinis all round! You're paying, by the way."

"Do we have to name our first child Randy now because of this?" Alvin said to me as he bought the drinks.

"Maybe one day, if we're lucky. We have a few things to work through first."

"Such as your awful taste in clothes?" Alvin pulled one of my tassles, his eyes lingering too long on where he'd pulled it from.

I smiled. "Amongst other things. But we'll get there this time, I promise you."

"I know we will."

Randy popped up between us. "And if you don't want him, I'll have him," he said.

"Sorry, Randy. I have plans for the rest of this guy's life and they start right now."

"Where would we be if it wasn't for plans?" said Alvin. "Speaking of which, it looks like we've both covered Activity 10 now. And I suggest we now frame and hang the list in a place of honour. You'll probably want to choose the frame. I wouldn't dare."

I laughed. "Well, you'll have to direct me to the right shop until I get my bearings in my new country of residence," I said. "But in the meantime, there's only one place I want you to take me. Home."

And we left the pub to start the rest of our lives.

Pre-parental plan activity 10: Conquer one huge fear each

By now we'll have done plenty of things that were outside of our comfort zones, Tam, but let's go out with a bang. Think of the thing that scares you most in the world and then do something about it. If we can get through the others, we can do this too.

We should now be at the point where we've bombed our comfort zones into oblivion, discovered new things about each other and are feeling ready to show our children how the whole life thing is done when the time comes. But even if we're still a little afraid, that's okay. Everyone is. We just need to remember that as long as we're together, we're invincible in our own way.

And even if that's the only thing that comes from this plan, then I think it will have been worth every second.

61

Two years later

Emmeline gathered fistfuls of apple-blossom petals and released them into a wicker basket that she'd dragged outside from my kitchen. A light breeze carried some of them away on their journey from her outstretched hands to the basket, but she didn't mind. Methodically, she bent down and resumed her self-inflicted task, steadfastly ignoring the range of play equipment around her.

"If only she knew just how much time, effort and money we've put into ordering and installing all of that stuff." Alvin pointed at the swing, slide, playhouse, trampoline, treehouse and climbing frame that were right beside Emmeline. The top half of our garden was now an outdoor play centre, but we didn't mind. We were delighted with it even if Emmeline wasn't bothered. This was Emmeline's first weekend alone with us since she, Jane, Alvin and I had all moved home three months ago, and although we may have gone overboard on making sure she had enough things to entertain her, we hoped they'd all get plenty of use over time.

"Don't worry. I have a feeling Jess will be up on that

trampoline approximately two seconds after she arrives," I said.

"Daddy, come here!" Emmeline commanded. "Messy! Help!"

"I'm surrounded by neat-freak women," Alvin said, rolling his eyes as he walked along the grass to Emmeline.

"Hey! You can't include me in that category any more," I said. I'd relaxed the tidiness rules a lot since Emmeline had come into my life. Toddlers and tidiness were a contradiction in terms.

"I suppose you've calmed down a bit. If you can go to bed tonight without loading the dishwasher after this party, I'll declare you officially cured of your Tammyness."

The bottom half of our garden was our designated garden party area for the night. It was Alvin's birthday and we were having a barbeque, more for the purposes of catching up with everyone than to mark the occasion. We'd already celebrated that by taking a trip to the States and Canada, one we'd always wanted to do but had been unable to until I'd conquered my fear of flying – something I'd worked on incessantly in my time in Australia through more hypnotherapy. Although it hadn't worked for me before, I seemed to have broken the back of my fear from my Dublin to London to Australia flights. Alvin's constant support and encouragement hadn't hurt either.

Jess arrived first, ten minutes before the invite time. "Am I seeing things? What's going on with this Jess-Arriving-Early-For-Something Shocker?" I said as I hugged her on the doorstep.

"If you stopped gallivanting across the world, I might actually get to see you once in a while and wouldn't have to resort to this kind of thing. It's not good for my rep." She held me at arm's length and looked me up and down.

"You look great! I missed you, you auld bitch. You better be sticking around for a while now. The Whine Bar has never been the same since you got the travelling bug."

I'd no sooner closed the door than Simone landed in.

"You've a great colour," Simone said. "You're glowing."

Jess didn't miss a beat. "Are you?"

I laughed. "Don't be daft!"

Simone frowned. "Jess, maybe Tammy doesn't want to go there with that kind of talk . . ."

"No, it's fine," I said, and I meant it. "The time when I'd be in bits from speculation on me being pregnant or not is in the past."

"I knew it would be, Tammy. See, Simone?" Jess stuck her tongue out at Simone, like she used to do when we were kids. Simone stuck hers out in return. Then all three of us burst out laughing.

"Alright girls, I know you're only looking for an excuse for a barney as you don't live together any more and it's probably been a while, but how about we move things out to the garden? Alvin is looking forward to seeing you both."

Simone and Jess stayed in my house while I was in Australia, until something very unexpected happened. Simone and Habitual Misery parted company. She admitted that during her attempts to be Positive Simone, she hadn't quite let go of the comfort blanket of her old friend, self-indulged sadness – but after she saw Alvin and me getting back together despite the mess we'd been in, she decided that happiness was possible after all and she was going to make a concerted effort to get out there and live her life. Check Trousers rang her when she returned from Australia, but she refused to be anything but a friend to him at first because she wanted to get her head together

433

before she got involved with anyone. Then, while booking a trip to see Beckett's grave in Paris (not everything had changed, of course) despite her dislike of the place, she rang him to see if he'd be interested in going grave-spotting to test out his stripes. He jumped at the chance. They were now living together and Simone had never been less miserable in her life. Not only that, she was now my colleague of sorts! She'd secured a job as an auditor in Branda while I was in Australia (the picture from the swingers club had never surfaced), something that everyone who knew her was not only happy but extremely grateful about as her moaning about money had decreased dramatically after that. And in an even more unexpected turn of developments, the book on money-saving strategies that she'd written just for her own purposes had been published! Jess had sent it off to a publishing company and they'd snapped it up, deeming it topical enough to sell well but tongue-in-cheek enough for them to have plenty of talking points relating to it from a marketing perspective. What they didn't know was that it hadn't been written in a tongue-in-cheek fashion at all and that Simone had been deadly serious in everything she'd written, but she was willing to turn a blind eye to misperceptions if it meant that she'd make money out of the book. She'd already written a follow-up for her own purposes before she'd got the book deal, about how to teach your children to save as they grow up in preparation for the recession that will inevitably happen in their lifetime. The remarkable thing from her family's point of view was the indication that she was now thinking about having children.

As for Jess, her life was a lot quieter now. She'd moved into a shared house with a man and a woman she didn't know less than a mile away from my place, and firmly established them as her new Whine Bar buddies. I wouldn't have expected her to have the less eventful life out of her and Simone, but as I'd discovered over the last few years, life moved in mysterious ways.

My parents were next to arrive, closely followed by my aunts and their long-suffering husbands. Claire, Adrienne and Clarissa were the last to get here.

"Where is she? *Where* is the most beautiful granddaughter in the world?" Claire roared dramatically as she thundered into the house.

"Erm . . . sunny evening, big garden . . . that's not a hard one, Mum," Adrienne drawled.

Claire was too busy making her way out the back to find Emmeline to acknowledge Adrienne's words. Alvin had asked Claire to be Emmeline's official minder for the night while he cooked the barbeque food, and she was evidently relishing her role already.

"Here's some grub – I would say I cooked it myself, but the packaging might just give me away." Clarissa handed me three huge quiches.

"She thought about taking the packaging off and passing it off as her own, you know, but I told her you'd sniff shop-bought food out a mile off. And you'd probably say it too."

I would have taken offence a few years ago, but now I knew that was just something Adrienne would say. I laughed as I laid the quiches on a kitchen worktop and ushered Adrienne and Clarissa out into the garden to join the others. There was nothing going on but people moving in with each other since Alvin and I had gone to Australia. Adrienne had come out publicly and she and Clarissa had resolved their issues, resulting in Clarissa moving back to Ireland permanently. They were now renting a city-centre apartment together and Alvin said he'd never seen Adrienne happier. I'd never even seen her *happy* before her relationship with Clarissa, and she was definitely easier to be around now.

I'd also finally got to the bottom of why Alvin always treated Adrienne with kid gloves. He said she'd never really got over her father's death when she was twelve and had a nervous breakdown as a teenager as a result of school bullying, something she didn't want me to know before but didn't mind me knowing now that she'd established that I was – and I quote – "as fucked up in her own way" as she was. And while we'd never be bosom buddies, things were definitely a lot better between us now.

It wasn't long before the garden came alive. The buzz of conversation mingled with Emmeline's intermittent squeals of delight as she pulled the head off a marigold or found a squirming woodlouse to pick up in the flower beds. The smell of charcoaled apple-cider marinated steak wafted in the air, with Alvin cooking up a storm at the barbeque helm. I drifted from person to person and tried to catch up with all the news. A good half an hour was taken up on talk of how Patty's husband had done a garden overhaul (project managed by Patty, naturally) that wouldn't look out of place on one of those garden makeover TV shows. The fact that they both had the numbers of divorce lawyers on speed dial after the whole experience (according to Simone) wasn't mentioned. Claire had expanded into rune readings and numerology, ostensibly because she'd had the calling but really because she'd set up a college fund for Emmeline. I, in turn, told the people I hadn't seen since I'd come back about how much I'd loved experiencing a whole new lifestyle in

Australia, and how lucky I'd been to get a transfer to Branda's office in Sydney while I'd been there – and even luckier to be transferred back into my old job again upon my return home.

We waited until everyone was fed and watered and Claire had put Emmeline to bed before drawing everyone together.

"We have good news that we'd like to share with all of you," Alvin said when he had everyone's attention.

I instantly saw Jess poking Simone in the side.

"As you all know, we're just back from a trip around the US and Canada . . ."

"It'll be called Springfield or Albuquerque," Jess said confidently – and loudly.

Alvin was undeterred by the interruption. ". . . where something very special happened. Tammy and I got married at Niagara Falls."

A collective whoop erupted in the garden. My mother and my aunts threw themselves at us, enveloping us in suffocating hugs and almost breaking my hand to check out the ring that I'd slipped on my finger just before we'd made our announcement. Everyone else took their turn to congratulate us too, throwing in the odd dig about not giving them a day out but generally being thrilled to bits for us when all the joking was done.

Simone and Jess, as always, were by my side when the fuss died down. "I'm so, so happy for you," Simone said, her face beaming. She was like a completely different person, and it suited her.

"Me too," Jess said, also smiling. "But I'm a bit disappointed that you're not up the duff."

"Does a wedding not cut it these days? We have a hard audience in tonight by the looks of it."

"Well, I've never seen you so happy," Simone said.

"And I've never heard you say the word 'happy' so often. I don't know what to make of it."

"You'd think she'd be a bit more contented now that she's finally seeing someone decent, wouldn't you?"

"What? Who?" You turned your back for one second . . .

"My housemate." She blushed like I'd never seen her blush before.

"Oh my God. You really like him, don't you?"

I expected her to give me some guff to the contrary, but to my surprise, she nodded. "Yeah. It's early days, but I think there's something really good there."

"So don't fuck it up, okay?" Simone said, but she was smiling.

"I won't if you won't. God, what's happened to us? It looks like all three of us are finally getting our lives together."

"It only took thirty-seven years," I pointed out.

"Oy! Some of us are younger than others. And faster learners."

"Are you slagging my wife again, Jess?" Alvin slipped his arms around my waist and joined our group. "I hope so. She did nothing but complain about how much she missed it while she was away. And apparently my philosophical insights are nothing compared to yours, Simone."

"We can move back in again if you really want us to," Simone threatened.

And so the night continued, full of laughter and stories and an eventual singsong by the uncles-in-law that Emmeline miraculously slept through. I was sorry to see everyone go, but at the same time, I couldn't get them out of the house fast enough.

"You go and check Emmeline before we go to bed," I

said as soon as the front door closed behind the final guests to leave.

"I was only joking about the dishwasher earlier," Alvin said. "You do what you have to do."

"I have to give you your birthday present yet, remember? Upstairs. Now."

"Oh, okay. I can't argue with that . . ."

We walked upstairs hand-in-hand, only breaking off when we reached the turn-off for Emmeline's room. I undressed, got into bed and waited.

I watched him as he walked to his side of the bed and pulled the duvet back. He stared at the pregnancy test on his pillow for several seconds before picking it up.

"It's early days yet," I whispered. "But it's there."

Alvin stared at the test for a long time before I saw him cry for the second time in our lives together.

And this time, I was there to kiss his tears away.

If you enjoyed

Can We Start Again? by Shirley Benton

why not try

Looking for Leon also published by Poolbeg?

Here's a sneak preview of Chapter One

Looking

for
Leon

SHIRLEY
BENTON

POOLBEG

Chapter One

The *shame*.

There I was on the front page, flashing my knickers.

It all made sense now. Why my normally laid-back mother had suddenly developed chest pains and had to hang up when I rang home from Las Vegas and innocently asked, "Any news?". Why my brother had laughed hysterically when I rang back, worried sick, to ask if Mum was still alive. As for Dad, he'd just hung up immediately when it was his turn to pick up the phone, but he was known to do that kind of thing so I hadn't been worried.

I should have been.

A drunken flashback that I'd been trying to evict from my brain suddenly came flooding back. Oh God, oh God. I tore open the red-top newspaper that my brother had kept for me while I was in Las Vegas and seen fit to slip under my door that morning, so I would see it just before my return to work – his idea of a joke. Please don't let them have pictures of . . .

I squeezed my eyes shut and pulled my jumper over my

head. Then I fumbled for the beanie hat that I'd abandoned on the table only seconds before, and yanked that over my bejumpered skull too – but it only reminded me of exactly what I was hiding from, so I flung it across the room instead.

I wanted to launch into a self-indulgent rant about soulless photographers and ruthless journalists, but being one myself – a journo, that is, not ruthless or a photographer, soulless or otherwise – I knew how the game worked. Besides, there was nobody in the room to listen to the rant, and God knows I was enough of a freak now without talking to myself as well.

The knickers-flashing front-pager had been taken in the wee hours of the night before I went on holidays, when I'd stumbled – okay, crashed – onto the pavement as I'd attempted to hail a taxi. Where the camera had come from, I have no idea – although, with the state I was in, I'd probably thought the flashbulbs were people flashing their car-lights at me to say hello as they drove past. Sorry if that sounds vain – it's just that it happens a lot to me. But how the pictures inside the club had been taken, I just don't know. When I'd spotted the ladder in my tights while out dancing with the gang, it had seemed like the most sensible thing in the world to rip them off right there and then. As we just happened to be dancing beside a pole, it would have been rude not to do a little dance around it while I was ripping the aforementioned tights off. And everyone knows that a pair of tights make the world's funniest balaclava, so it had made perfect sense to pull the tights over my head and demand free drink at the bar . . .

I was absolutely ruined in this town.

I pulled my jumper back down so that I could breathe

again and ran to my laptop for salvation. My online bank account was the only thing that could save me. The only logical thing to do was to fly back to Vegas as soon as possible, a place where people had a sense of humour about those kinds of things – you did something like that in Vegas, and you ended up with your own show. Over here, you just made a show of yourself. I swallowed hard. My credit-card transactions had stacked up . . . how could a bit of shopping possibly have come to that amount?

I slammed the laptop shut. The only way I'd be flying was by the seat of my pants when it came to talking my way out of this.

But God, the Devil, or whoever else was pulling the cosmic strings, wasn't finished with me yet. As I ripped the incriminating pages out of the paper to tear them to shreds, I spotted a picture on the next page. Well, I didn't so much spot it as it jumped out at me, really. My heart thumped. Johnny, the guy I'd broken up with shortly before I went on holidays, was staring down the top of some sequined scrap of a woman, with the obligatory perma-tan and tattooed lips – her, not him – although I wouldn't be surprised if he had them too. The caption under the picture flashed across my eyes, but I had to read it a second time to take it in. What the hell . . . ?

> Johnny Meagher, Éire TV news anchor, enjoying the company of a luscious lady after breaking up with Andie Appleton recently.

After breaking up with *me*? I broke it off with *him*! Our relationship had been a disaster from day one, and I couldn't wait to get the hell out of it. How could anyone think that *he'd* done the breaking up? The man had followed me around like a chewing-gum stuck to the sole of my shoe for months!

I was so busy stamping on the paper while shouting obscenities that I didn't hear Mum come into the room.

"You'd want to stop jumping on the paper, or you'll be late for work," she said, as if I was just drinking a cup of coffee or something. "Oh, and I'll be driving you in today."

I stood still, all the fight gone out of me. "Look, Mum, it's nice of you to try to cheer me up, but it's going to take more than a lift to work for me to get over this!"

"Oh, that's not why I'm doing it. You just can't drive yourself to work."

"What, you think I was out last night and I'm still drunk? Just because I got caught once acting a little tipsy doesn't mean I'm an alcoholic!"

"Oh, don't be daft. Now, come on before the traffic gets too bad."

I looked at my shaking hands, and realised that driving in my state of shock might not be such a good idea.

I allowed myself to be shooed into Mum's car, thinking that when I got home from work that night I'd definitely take my own one out of the garage for a spin. I did love cars, and my Merc was my pride and joy. I'd spent an absolute fortune on it and I hadn't even driven it to the airport when I went to Vegas in case someone reversed into it in the airport car park. It was much safer in Mum and Dad's cosy garage.

I settled down into the passenger seat, and tried not to cringe anytime we drove past a woman wearing tights. This too would pass; I, of all people, should know that. As the gossip columnist for a newspaper, I knew how fast big news was replaced by the next drama on the so-called celebrity circuit.

Mum hadn't reprimanded me for my nightclub antics, and I was grateful for that. Still, that was Mum. Some would call her accepting. Some would call her just plain away with the fairies. No matter what happened, she would glide serenely through it all, leaving you to wonder if she was really taking it all in. Her other-worldliness had its moments, and this was one of them.

"Now, dear," she said as she pulled up in front of the offices of my newspaper, "here we are."

"Thanks, Mum. It was nice to get a lift today. I'll drive myself in tomorrow though, so don't worry – it'll be back to normal for you."

"No, Andrea, dear, that won't be possible." She never normally called me by my full name. My full name meant big trouble. "You see, your car . . . met another car, shall we say, and now it's more of an accordion than a car." She smiled, looking rather pleased with her pretty description of what sounded suspiciously like a written-off car.

"But, Mum," I said in a low voice, "how could my car meet another car when it was in the garage all the time I was away?"

"Well, it wouldn't have if it was in the garage, of course. But when your brother took it out . . . well, there was every chance it would encounter other cars on the road, as cars do. And you know Adam – he was never even any good at that Operation game years ago, so a steady hand on the steering wheel is slightly beyond his capabilities." She looked out the window thoughtfully. "Or maybe it was the speeding. One or the other."

"What? How did Adam get the keys of my car?" I yelled when I finally recovered the power of speech.

"Good Lord, there's no need to shout! He took them from the key-box, of course. What do you expect when you left them in such an obvious place? What if we'd had a burglar? You might as well leave the keys in the ignition as in the key-box. You'll have to take this up with your brother. He'll be back from his holiday in Spain in about two weeks, he said. Got some last-minute deal for a song and flew out this morning." She looked at her watch. "Speaking of flying, I must fly myself. Go on, get out!"

Mum shoved me out of the car, and then drove back to whatever planet she was on today (I was now firmly in the 'away with the fairies' camp).

I physically shook myself. If only I'd stayed asleep that morning . . . a few hours ago I was dreaming about being reunited with that impossibly charismatic man that I'd met in Vegas. A few hours ago, I was happy and had some hope. And now look at the mess that constituted my life . . . everyone in the office had better have the sense to leave me alone today.

I somehow managed to drag myself to the front door of my office's building, where I met Jason, my least favourite colleague.

"Hey, Andie, was that you I saw on *Crimecall* last night with the balaclava? *Ahahahahaha*!"

And so it began.

If only things had worked out in Vegas, it could all have been so different . . .